LOUIS HAMELIN

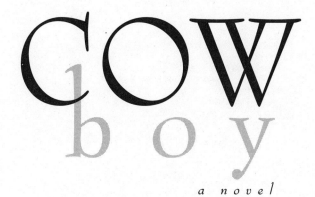

a novel

THE DUNDURN GROUP
A SIMON & PIERRE BOOK
TORONTO · OXFORD

Editor: Marc Côté
Design: Scott Reid
Printer: Friesens Corporation

Canadian Cataloguing in Publication Data
Hamelin, Louis, 1959–
[Cowboy. English]
Cowboy
Translation of: Cowboy.
ISBN 0-88924-288-7
I. Murray, Jean-Paul, 1960–   . II. Title. III. Title: Cowboy. English.

PS8565.A487C6813 2000   C843'.54   C99-930507-7
PQ3919.2.H315C6813 2000

I   2   3   4   5   04   03   02   01   00

Canada

THE CANADA COUNCIL | LE CONSEIL DES ARTS
FOR THE ARTS | DU CANADA
SINCE 1957 | DEPUIS 1957

We acknowledge the support of the **Canada Council for the Arts**, the **Ontario Arts Council,** and the
Book Publishing Industry Development Program (BPIDP) for our publishing program.

Care has been taken to trace the ownership of copyright material used in this book. The author and the
publisher welcome any information enabling them to rectify any references or credit in subsequent editions.
J. Kirk Howard, President

Printed and bound in Canada.
✿
Printed on recycled paper.

Dundurn Press
8 Market Street
Suite 200
Toronto, Ontario, Canada
M5E 1M6

Dundurn Press
73 Lime Walk
Headington, Oxford,
England
OX3 7AD

Dundurn Press
2250 Military Road
Tonawanda NY
U.S.A. 141

To Maurice Poteet

1

VICTORIA day

HE WAS AN AMERICAN INDIAN KNOWN to his friends as Cowboy. He'd picked up the nickname one night when spotted tramping along the railroad, his lanky body silhouetted by the setting sun, wrapped in a long duster whose folds brushed against his leather boots. His friends were called Karate Kid, Donald Big-Arms, and Judith, who had a pale complexion, a generous pout, and a spry knee. They were the muskeg musketeers and Cowboy was their superman. They were a united clan, though I never fully understood their relationship. They all were at least cousins I think. Those from the encampment, and those from the cabin on the road to the reservoir. They were a progeny in full expansion, already carrying the next revenge of the cradles on its shoulders.

I had been parachuted into the region as a clerk, and was now holed up in my quarters, feet drawn back on the bedspread, stroking the cover of a book oozing wisdom. I was willingly adjusting to their image of me as a young academic who'd come north; a portrait they used to place me conveniently in their gallery of human types.

After a few days, when I said I was going for a stroll, Benoît and the Old Man exchanged knowing looks. This derogation of their iron rule was seen as a snub, a giving of the finger to the venerable building's vocation as an impregnable fortress. It was an implicit breech of contract which meant I immediately ceased being one of them.

Benoît gravely walked me down the aisle. The Outfitters' general store was impenetrable, incorruptible, obsessed with security. In a region where fractures and break-ins often replaced polite phrases, a simple lock didn't cut it. Benoît and the Old Man had explained this early on and seemed proud of their system. Sliding the heavy metal bar across the double flap, Benoît pushed the door open for me. The old trading post closed in on itself with a grating sound as the bar immediately resumed its position. The surrounding night stretched out beneath my feet.

The generator's rumbling filled the darkness like a sustained groan. Above me, blending its scattered notes with the myriad stars mottling the black velvet, a fugitive constellation of birds, back from its migration, was setting the stage for my meeting with Cowboy.

I was completely still. Head tilted skywards, back arched to the breaking point, shoulders nearly parallel to the ground, I scanned the heavens, focusing only on the fantastic pulsing mass of things. Suddenly, a tired and bitter call, both hoarse and aggressive, pierced the dark sky. I turned towards the lamppost which stood near the gas pumps, holding the chaos beyond its milky halo. Four low-flying geese skirted along the fringe of the vast aureola. They banked, obeying their leader's shrill entreaties, tracing a perfect circle above me, as I stood immobile, feet planted at the points of a compass. Having completed the figure, their instinct drew them farther away in tight formation, large and powerful in the distance.

I came back to earth. Before me stood the restaurant, already closed at this hour, and the deserted train station, a survivor of the golden age of Canadian railways. It was covered with grey paint, and had gummy white lintels. The scent of tar wafted over the area. I walked down the embankment that had stood between the station and me, and sat on the platform, stirring ballasts with my foot. A sheet-metal warehouse shimmered across the tracks, intercepting and echoing the generator's drone. I stood there for a while, looking around as though awaiting someone.

Three of them were walking along the rails, just like in a Leone film. At first, I only managed to see their long shadows gliding towards me on the ground. A lantern stood watch on the station's pediment, splashing my back with its creeping glimmer. They soon spotted me and came to sit nearby, hardly looking at me sideways.

The first one was tall, thin, and nimble, with an expression that was cunning and distressed. He wore a tracksuit, a sort of kimono that made him look like a comical judoka, a poor impersonation of Bruce Lee coming out of a B-movie brawl.

The second was strongly built, though a little portly. His features tensed and relaxed at every moment and his massive fists swung before him like pendulums. Donald Big-Arms was naive and rather simple, something those around him acknowledged without too much contempt. He'd sporadically burst out with heartfelt and astonished laughter.

The face of the third was perfectly round. His lofty cheekbones and Buddha eyes stood out amid impeccable features able to change any ill-timed feeling into a harmless wrinkle. I was amazed by his stiffness, but immediately understood the reason when he turned around: a tape-covered handle jutted from his sweatshirt collar, behind his head, like an artificial extension of his spine, or as though a Damoclean sword had split his head.

A smile eclipsed the rest of his face, detaching itself like a quarter moon. His eyes caught mine and, slowly raising his right hand to the back of his neck, he pulled out a gleaming machete and held it up. His contemplation reminded me of those Mexican peasants who wander through coconut plantations on the Pacific coast, and who, with a ritual sense refined by centuries of suffering and subservience, leave their dear machete on the bus's running board with apparent regret before taking their seat.

Cowboy silently handed me his weapon. Grasping it carefully, I performed a few clumsy manoeuvres under his approving gaze. At times, the three Indians traded short sentences, as unintelligible to my ear as the hoarse honking of the geese. We exchanged succinct thoughts, without words, while the generator's angry roar highlighted the piercing silence.

Hovering over the platform of this isolated station, like the whisper of an implicit pact between us, was a secret agreement which the machete would've secured. We heard ominous rumbling in the distance, and I shivered as I caressed the machete.

Mr. Administrator was talking. He was talking and stepping on the accelerator, as though his monologue was fuelling the van's engine. The machinery roared along the deserted road, his words trying to fill the desolate silence between us, between the trees and everywhere. The sandy trail was furrowed and potholed, meandering along the boreal forest, tearing through the endless web of black spruce, its lonely stretches clinging to the lakeheads, spiralling down into valleys, infinitely disappearing into the back country, while an inert storm closed in around us. At times, a dusty flag alerted the driver to a deep crevice in the middle of the road.

"To make a long story short...."

Lakes paraded by, lapping the roadside like frozen gems set in the peat, while the approaching twilight brushed them with amethyst. The forest was a lacy bower all round, its profile growing more pronounced. My new boss chattered away, spraying saliva on the windshield smeared with insects. He went on endlessly, in a high-pitched voice, eyes wavering between me and the road, readjusting the vehicle's course before looking at me again, forever concerned about my receptiveness, his head oscillating like a metronome lingering between indefinite collimations. He'd sometimes look for a word, sifting through his brain, poring over his paradigms; he'd catch his breath somewhat, getting lost in a contemplation of the unevenly gravelled network of ruts, then finally collar it, brandishing it triumphantly on the tip of his tongue, ready to spew it. The gleaming four-by-four, poised on its heavy-duty shocks, seemed to glide over this pathetic patchwork of potholes.

"To cut a long story short...."

Side roads ploughed through the dense foliage bordering the main highway. More often than not, the exposed forest appeared as a drapery hung in *trompe-l'oeil*, a double hedge denying travellers an infinite view of the territory. A few rows of spruce, carefully spared by loggers, camouflaged a huge wasteland of clear-cuts. Fierce winds would soon break the remaining trees like toothpicks. The endless row of conifers undulated like dark lace against the reddening sky. Might as well, I mused, comfort the tourist in his favourable impression of wilderness.

"In short...."

The Company had cut as much as it could, then cleared out. It had moved farther west, since operating out of Grande-Ourse was no longer profitable. Boy, had it felled and cut trees and columns of wood fibre, pulverizing countless tons of ligneous material; they laid out a main road, then secondary ones perpendicular to it and, finally, tertiary roads perpendicular to the secondary ones. Then they cut and mowed everything down far and wide. Clearing all this, ladies and gentlemen, is their business.

"Anyhow...."

Mr. Administrator's words faded into the engine's continual rumble and the air whistling against the windshield. Occasionally, between bumps, I'd respond with a vague gesture, eyes lowered on the boastful leaflet I tried to wedge between my rattling knees.

GRANDE-OURSE OUTFITTERS
A HUNTING AND FISHING PARADISE
CITY COMFORT IN THE MIDDLE OF NATURE

Pleasantly impressed by my knowledge of hunting and fishing, which I'd avoided saying was mostly theoretical, Mr. Administrator had hired me following a conversation at Place Bonaventure, during the Camping, Hunting, and Fishing Trade Show, where the preseason bustle had required his promotional zeal. He belonged to a group of businessmen who'd purchased over half the village of Grande-Ourse when the Company had pulled out a few years earlier, expecting to convert the private town into a tourist facility.

"In any event.... To make a long story short...."

I'd once heard about this village, which was unique in Quebec, as it was created by the industry exclusively to house forestry workers. Grande-Ourse's economy had peaked in the seventies when high-voltage lines had been run through the region, linking James Bay to the south of the province. Line builders had worked

like bees to erect the imposing pylons, which had become an
integral part of northern lore.

At night, in accordance with natural laws, something else
erected in their pants. The Grande-Ourse Hotel was always full;
dancing girls from Mont-Laurier and elsewhere willingly providing
additional services. At first, the dancing girls were driven away by
protests from the local worthies, though they were a small
minority. Then prosperity itself vanished, the blow being given by
the holy Company's departure. Grande-Ourse residents, however,
had kept the habit of drinking, eating, screwing, doing their
laundry, and living way beyond their means.

A fierce wind tore the brochure from my hands, and Mr.
Administrator hawkishly watched the document fly away. He
parked his car on the edge of the road and excused himself. He had
to check a welding joint on the trailer that, so far, had followed us
obediently. The road didn't like motor vehicles, shaking them like a
bronco trying to throw his rider into the landscape.

Our sudden immobility wrapped us in the north's palpable
silence. We heard faint bird songs, including the evening note of
the white-throated sparrow and other muffled and scattered strains.
Spring still had to dig in and invent itself. We were right at the
interval, at the vulnerable point of any awakening.

My driver, looking appropriately fastidious, leaned his white
head under the trailer, while I began looking around, crunching the
gravel with my clodhoppers. I spotted an idle grass snake on the
roadside, desperately trying to draw a little heat from the last rays
of the setting sun. It let me pick it up without resisting.

With childish delight, I showed my catch to the man, whose
immaculate hair was now smeared with grease. I waved the
creature under his nose, as he lifted his head, frowned, and
affected an expression that was disdainful, suspicious, and slightly
disgusted, "Alive?"

I nodded. "Only a little numb.... They crawl onto the road
to get some sun this time of year. They're cold blooded, you
see...."

As though to punctuate that brief account, the reptile
compressed a gland near its tail and squirted my wrist with foul-
smelling musk. Mr. Administrator grimaced and turned away.

Standing up unsteadily, he shook himself. "Chuck that thing! It reeks like hell! ... I checked everything out, we can move on...."

He turned his back to me as I slowly walked away from the road, moving my lips like a praying ophite, handling the snake as it tried to twist around my forearm.

❧

They seem to fear silence, fear that words will lodge like fish bones in their throats. Turning to others with all their energy, their words are entirely centrifugal, their conversation a feat of strength, a high-wire act. Sometimes it begins to waver at the edge of their internal abyss, so they look around for a pole, precariously clinging to hollow-sounding words; it always starts up again, hangs together as best it can, moves on, resonates in a vacuum, and so they invent their little web of fine-sounding truths. It finally creates a background noise as persistent as the generator's groan. Their language is all they have against the omnipresent threat of dilution into space. Words, propositions, perpetually fractured sentences, hold them together like the road ties them to the world.

Brevity is impossible in a diluted village.

When you keep your mouth shut in their presence, they imagine a kind of internal emptiness exists, and dutifully fill it with sounds, musing that keeping quiet is already a form of listening. They don't understand that you can make do with hearing, that they can be looked at without being adhered to, without your going so far as showing interest. They imagine that everything, even contempt, can be complacently uttered. I felt like one of those creatures Gulliver meets on the flying island of Laputa. I tilted my head forward, seeing lip movements. My ears had to be boxed before I realized someone was speaking to me.

Mr. Administrator was trumpeting his speech like a politician who, lost on the outer reaches of civilization, decides a handful of votes is better than nothing, after all, and who would harangue fish, firs, and spruce, if need be, just for the pleasure of convincing, and for the principle. When, having to correct himself, he realized he was deviating from the improvised plan he tried to impose on his prolixity, he abruptly stopped and looked around, watching for signs of weariness in his counterparts, leaving his start-up formula dangling in the still air, like a form of apathy. "To cut a long story short...."

The kitchen, like the bedrooms, was designed as a simple outbuilding attached to the general store. From the table, through the bay window, you could keep an eye on the stoic gas pumps, which looked more like worn landmarks, headstones or cairns than the outcrops of an underground reservoir. Beyond the restaurant, you could see the level crossing and the Grande-Ourse highway which, on the other side, continued to wind towards the lake, the hotel and northward. Another window, through the storage room containing the safe and the manager's office, looked out on the only aisle that was lined with shelves, at the end of which stood the heavily bolted main door. This casement allowed Benoît, the Old Man, and Mr. Administrator to exercise constant vigilance, even during meals. Apparently, no one had thought of organizing alternating shifts behind the store's counter. It seemed evident that meals were to be shared, and normal to allow the convivial unity to be broken repeatedly to trot to the other end of the building and tend to customer whims. Whoever bumped into a closed door only had to plunk his face in the wire-meshed side window to be quickly spotted by one of the diners. The greatly dreaded words would then ring out amid the gurgling of boiling soup or the ardent mastication of a hamburger, "Giiiiiilles! A customer!"

Gilles, that's yours truly, to help you. Gilles Deschênes. I'd become the humble servant in this village of fools, quickly learning that no feast could compromise the well-being of commercial exchanges. The simple intimacy of a vital function such as nourishment seemed taboo in this place. The grace Mr. Administrator muttered before sinking into his chair went hand in hand with the cash register's clear ringing.

Benoît, the group's youngest member, was conscientious, self-taught, and good at figures. Promoted as the Outfitters' manager at twenty-two, he rarely showed signs of being the least bit happy with life. People acknowledged that he had a certain sense of responsibility. That responsibility, and his birth a few parallels north of the national average, had been enough to earn him this thankless job the previous year, following a tavern conversation with nepotistic overtones. Ti-Kid Benoît saw no difference between recreation and work. He did everything diligently, at an intense pace, with carefully cultivated stress.

The Old Man, for his part, had no head for figures, but I swear he had no equal in scrounging a little fast profit. Whenever money was discussed, wherever it was located, even as far as Fort Knox, he'd clearly make it his business. The Outfitters didn't even have to pay him, couldn't afford it anyway. He had a pension, and was satisfied with little. He was still hanging around Grande-Ourse, working for the establishment locals despised, because he was driven by a competitive spirit where his welfare meant little. He now worked exclusively from devotion to the gods of mercantilism. The simple pleasure of shady deals and the deadly need to toil away always roused him.

For the last two years, however, Mr. Administrator had been doing his best to ease the Old Man towards the exit. But his attempts had been fruitless, and the patience of shareholders had reached its limit. A proper dismissal, therefore, was on the agenda for this visit. Contrary to his two assistants, Mr. Administrator lived in big city suburbs, travelling here only on inspection tours of variable length, during which he liked giving outward signs of sustained activity.

Every night he'd withdraw, greatly preoccupied with the mandate given by his associates, to sleep over in the large white house perched on a nearby hill that had once belonged to the Company's supervisors. The mere sight of this debonair decision-maker coming down the steep path, at daybreak, was like a cold shower to the Old Man, who was forever flinching. He smelled of hot soup, and knew he'd become a nuisance by setting the whole village against the business, by coaxing with flattery only to disparage afterwards, and by amusing with anecdotes before hurling retrospective curses. This imperishable little village continued to revolve around him; he always had his nose in everybody's business. He was on the lookout, constantly well-up on everything, as renowned as Barabbas in the Passion, and unanimously hated. When it was his turn to speak, he'd spring to his feet, his chair having grown too hot. He couldn't express himself while seated, and had to put all his weight in the balance, wobbling between each word, swinging his arms all round and swaggering like an old rooster with a flaming crest. He spoke like people fart, delivering each term by pushing it out, while Mr. Administrator encouraged him with gestures.

"The national sport around here is tongue-lashing the Outfitters! And it's open season all year, besides! Everyone's been on our back from the start, and now they want to challenge the price of electricity! Heartless wretches! Then there are those who boycott the store, who order supplies from Sans-Terre by railway, in conspiracy with the train guys! What do they want, for God's sake? All they do is whine, they're never happy, we always have to run after them to get paid, they quarrel all year, the only way they spend their time around here, neighbour pitted against neighbour, and everyone united against the Outfitters! Rotten, lazy, no-good, profiteering welfare cases!"

He was out of breath and stopped talking, wiping a rough tongue across the soup drenching his chin. For a short time, Mr. Administrator had been trying to interrupt him with a gesture that was both sweeping and composed. He got up and began to pace about the kitchen, highlighting some of his words with an imaginary wand.

"The problem around here," he said, sententiously, "is the absence of law, which is to say of any representative able to enforce it. In our society, the right to property is the foundation of all law. The only property that matters in this place is the one you can protect with a gun...."

Benoît nodded. The Old Man's only reaction was to burp haughtily.

"In short, we have to show them we're tough.... We're not here to do charity, are we? Let them buy their groceries in Sans-Terre if they want! It'll mean we won't have to play the public authorities! And Grande-Ourse will finally become a model outfitting camp. You see, friends, luxury tourism is incompatible with a local population.... But we're too kind, what can I say!"

"Too kind!" confirmed the Old Man.

The conversation then shifted to the upcoming visit of American fishermen. In fact, the long weekend in the third week of May, which coincided with the beginning of fishing season, ushered in the summer invasion. When mentioning the anticipated event, the Old Man's voice was but a gentle murmur. He wiped tears from his eyes. They were finally speaking his language.

"Real gentlemen, they are," he said. "Real gentlemen, yes sir!"

There'd be a real rush on Victoria Day, the Old Man assured me, people would line up at the gas pumps and at the counter.

❧

The general store remained the Outfitters' milch cow; for the moment, the only relatively profitable part of the economic unit created by the purchase of Grande-Ourse. Mr. Administrator was intensely optimistic. Due to the rather understandable lack of precedent — a private corporation purchasing a village was a first in Quebec's municipal records — he had ample leisure to delude himself with comfortable predictions, believing the opportunities offered to his administrative mind were infinite. Yet the transition to cushy tourism was turning out to be difficult.

The dead season dragged on, and quiet evenings were typical.

One morning in mid-May, fall made an unexpected visit: a snow-filled sky greeted me when I awoke. A frigid atmosphere permeated the store. For the first time, I was encountering a nomadic group that returned each spring with the break-up of ice on lakes. We were still only dealing with scouts from the dreaded horde: the tough ones, those familiar with the region, returning to open some rudimentary cabin secluded deep in a valley, and appraise the damage caused as much by the rigours of the season as the recklessness of snowmobilers. They were distinguished by their tans, which winter hadn't changed, and a good-natured savageness in their gaze. Among them were a few greenhorns who could be recognized by their blue colour. They invaded the store in a mad rush, accompanied by an angry wind, twirling around a little, somewhat agitated, rubbing their hands. They asked for warm gloves, pacing on the spot, then purchased the first boots they'd get their hands on. They'd left summer behind, and had just caught up with winter. Large snow flakes, chased between buildings by gusting winds, landed and lingered on the ground like lazy butterflies.

The sky cleared in the afternoon, and a pale sun broke through thick layers of grey. That's when I saw Cowboy and Karate Kid, the latter still wearing a kimono, apparently oblivious to bad weather. Cowboy was draped in a long maroon coat resembling a pea jacket as much as a bounty hunter's greatcoat, and wore a wide-brimmed hat. The two Indians were near the storefront, leaning over a plastic container. Armed with matches and twigs, they were tormenting an unfortunate grass snake imprisoned in a jar. The small reptile was now only a confused knot stirred by limp contortions. Mr. Administrator, standing on the doorstep, hands on his hips, looked down on them with full disapproval. Turning to me, he cleared his voice before hurling out, "Look at them! They seem to think it's funny!... They treated missionaries basically the same way...."

"With the weather we're having, it must be completely numbed," I replied, shrugging. "They're cold-blooded, remember ...?"

He looked at me severely, prompting me to add, "Just like fish: I read somewhere they suffer very little when hooked in the mouth. They have a rather primitive nervous system...."

"Primitive ...," repeated Mr. Administrator, dreamily.

He stared coldly at the two characters. Shivering, he finally went back in, where Benoît and the Old Man were going around in circles. "Any problems with the Indians lately?" the boss inquired.

Benoît momentarily dropped the pout that made him look like he was chewing his lips and mumbled, shaking his head, "It's been calm...."

"Calm," he repeated.

The boy, whose face appeared set with trepidation, also displayed a spectacular tranquillity. As though ashamed of debasing any words, Benoît felt the need to bury each phrase into his downy mustache. He ruminated a few seconds, then added, "Last week, for example, things got a little stirred up...."

That's all the Old Man needed to wade in with both feet. The brave fellow would gloat at the thought; he liked nothing better than griping about Aboriginals, Siwashes, and their depredations! He ambled towards us, choking and shuddering, eager to regurgitate the bitter fruit of his ruminations, and reiterate his petty apology about the legitimate use of force! He raised his arms, knowing his pantomime by heart.

"We're all snivellers, god dammit! That's the truth! We let them push us around like kids!"

The week preceding my arrival, Big Alexandre and his small gang of hoodlums and troublemakers, notorious in the region's reformatories, had turned Grande-Ourse into a wild-west town. The police finally sent a helicopter to clean up the place. Flying over Lac Légaré, which adjoins the village, the aircraft had managed to tip the canoe carrying Big Alexandre and his two cronies. As soon as they'd been fished out, the troublemakers were sent back to the porous halfway house, which had been like a second home during their adolescence. But tempers in Grande-Ourse remained a little overheated.

"You'll see next time! The police chief himself gave me free hand on the phone! They're fed up with being bothered by a handful of people who aren't even able to settle their own problems! You think they'll send a squad at taxpayer expense each time? For two or three savages who can't even stand up most of the time they're so drunk? *Let them in, and shoot! We'll come in and pick up the pieces.* The district police chief said so: BANG!"

He was cradling an imaginary rifle, shooting at everything in sight, no longer holding back.

"Take a guy in Pennsylvania who shoots at a robber, eh? Well, he doesn't get into any trouble! He's asked to fill out a form or two, then goes back to his living room! That's how Americans do things, in Pennsylvania, yes sir!"

He was hopping like a boxer when the bell rings.

"Bang!" he again rumbled. "That's how they do things over there.... Real gentlemen...."

He calmed down somewhat, imploring with every sinew a mad scramble for walleye, bears, and moose: all that Klondike of animal flesh which hailed passing seasons with sacred regularity.

❧

The road map didn't tell the whole story. Here, the Outfitters and its general store built by the old Company; farther on, the small uniform houses of its employees. Over there, the people, those who'd sponged off the large paper mill and ended up having to be drip-fed by the state after the milch cow had gone. Most now rented from the Outfitters, while others owned land at the edge of the woods. Some squatted discreetly on Crown land, on the fringes of the zone controlled by the new owners. At one time pampered by the Company (which, the Old Man had told me, even mowed the grass of employees, and picked up their garbage), the great majority had taken the change of regime very poorly. The railroad was a genuine boundary.

To the north: the hotel, owned by a certain Jacques Boisvert, and Lac Légaré where the same Boisvert moored his flotilla of hydroplanes, consisting of two Beavers and one Twin Otter. A practical detail: the dispensary stood near the hotel, but the nurse had to cover a large territory and rarely came around.

North of the rails, as well, lived the Indians.

To the south: the restaurant managed by a certain Moreau; the Grande-Ourse train station; and the tiny agglutination that orbited the Outfitters, facing the expanse.

Three times a week, at daybreak, the train smokily plunged into the area's apparent tranquillity, like a whistling blade cutting through a lump of butter. I'd then be awakened with little respect and a jolt. No sooner was I thrust into the bracing air, when we were already parking the pickup on the station's platform. Most of the perishable foods were shipped to Grande-Ourse by rail. Only blueberries grew amid the sand heaps and layers of peat. There was a day for fruits and vegetables, another for meat, milk, etc. The train would grind to a stop and we'd transfer merchandise with a semblance of enthusiasm: flaccid, dirt-covered potatoes, onions with shaggy tufts, wilted vegetables and bruised fruit destined to rot, poured into the back of the truck. Northern inhabitants are proud carnivores who harbour a secular suspicion of any vegetation. The more omnivorous ones had been prescient and had already reserved their ration of this weekly heap of pulp, fibre, and scraps, with the assurance of securing the best pieces. The remainder would moulder on shelves, giving off the usual smells.

A little farther on, boastful and cynical Grande-Ourse residents secretly slipped their grocery lists to some shifty attendant. The train's staff, however, were concerned about relations with local authorities. An employee always managed to toss us an issue of the *Journal de Montréal*, tightly wrapped around a high content of shock value and sleaze, and no fresher than the alleged scoops it had travelled with. It would lie imposingly on the table several days, before collecting potato peels or shrouding a fish.

The Indians used the train as much as they could to get around, since their socio-political status provided them economical access to it. They'd often be seen looking for an *authorization*, a permission written by a nurse or bureaucrat which they used as a free pass. They travelled a little everywhere that way, stopping along the line, visiting relatives scattered between Sans-Terre and Tocqueville, where many had modest apartments. They were railway nomads, suddenly disappearing, returning after three days, then leaving straightaway in the opposite direction.

Following the train's departure, a small crowd inevitably gathered in front of the store. The establishment's location in the middle of the woods made it the only dispenser of bare essentials, of which speech wasn't the least. In this backwater the need to communicate created genuine emergencies. People had to show they still existed despite everything; it was particularly meaningful to show it here, right in the face of Grande-Ourse's new masters. They had to talk, because to talk was to endure. Moreover, where else could they slake a northerner's honest thirst for a good price when, having risen early, they'd just thrown up their breakfast?

The Muppet was Grande-Ourse's most punctual boozer. I'd labelled him as such due to his habit of wriggling about and dusting the air with his pointed tuft of hair planted on a conical head placed directly on his shoulders. He was retired and lived alone in a small house, receiving a generous pension for services rendered to the administration, devoting it exclusively to savouring pints. That pastime had spared him the anguish of dealing with the gaping void which usually follows an active life. Each morning, with the reliability of an old cuckoo, he'd turn up smiling on his motorized tricycle, like a kid on his toy. We'd greet him with resigned sighs and the lethargy which overcame us so easily after breakfast. He came to renew his supply of brown bottles, especially hoping to escape the tyrannical silence of the night and the suffocating cage of his old bones. Benoît and I, dedicated to the higher interests of trade, lent an ear to this pathetic babble reeking of hops.

The Muppet had devised a clever scheme to get around the restrictions of the store's alcohol permit. Since the state strictly forbade him from slaking his thirst within our walls, the old blockhead had got into the habit of leaving an opened bottle in the cold room facing the counter. At any moment, mired in mid-sentence, he'd shake himself and casually head to the tiny refrigerated room, disappearing to have a gulp or two. He seemed to think nobody would notice his ridiculous puppet's game, nor realize that he looked more stupefied when he emerged from his glacial alcove. He eventually gave the impression of going in there to can himself in small doses.

Furthermore, everyone in the region was a pothead. When it wasn't alcohol, it was juice from fruit, vegetables, concentrates, pigments and chemicals, and soft drinks, mineral water, large-size Perrier avidly raised to the lips, Pepsi, which ruled over the area, while Coke conspired in the shadows, and milk, the healthful milk of families. Eyes closed, they'd fervently bring their lips to whatever contained liquid. Pegged to their bodies, the people of Grande-Ourse had a collective desire to wrap their lips around a bottleneck; they couldn't help it.

One morning, when I'd just finished reading for five hours through the fissures of my swollen eyelids, a small native family got off the train. The man was wizened and could've been either thirty or sixty years old; he was followed by a short woman who was withered and drunk, trailing her large posterior in a flowery dress, and a ravishing young girl no older than fourteen, throwing fire everywhere she lay eyes. They headed towards the store while, already inside, I was placing milk cartons in the fridge, carefully turning containers so prospective buyers couldn't see the expiry date: a trick the Old Man had taught me. He was eager to make a real shopkeeper out of me, showing me how to place fresher products out of reach behind the others, to get rid of dubious cases first.

The region's natives knew and feared the Old Man. He was cut from the same cloth as the trade artists who'd been our first settlers, and who were peerless in their ability to swap a pile of beaver pelts for a little firewater and a handful of trinkets. He was at his best with the Indians, finally able to give the full measure of his business acumen: funny as anything, sly as a coyote, quick to take advantage of the least hesitation, ruthless with gullibility, always ready to shoot you in the back.

I couldn't take my eyes off the shy young girl flanked by the strange couple. Meanwhile, the old woman was striving to mumble something in an exotic French moistened with several sputters. Beneath a madder shawl, her face was ravaged by age and pox, and marked by great sincerity. Old coloured rags dangled with some elegance from her twisted bust. Her husband was stoic and seemed to judge her outgoing mood with severity, quietly giving her meaningful looks of reproach. The Old Man turned towards me. Half his face was an amused grimace, "These are good people, Gilles! César Flamand and his charming wife Fernande!"

The Old Man was always able to muster the precise quantity of warmth for necessary effusions. He could appear totally affable when the game was worth it. But when the Indian woman proffered an expectant mouth, gaping and horribly humid, he couldn't help from jumping back and muttering excuses. He would've had the same reaction had someone shot him between the legs.

Cowboy had just slipped through the door and was observing the scene, a sphinx smile sheltering his moods. I saluted him with my fingertips before returning my attention to the young Indian girl. I was taking notes:

perfectly round cheekbones impeccably curved mouth eyelids in the grips of a crisis of sensual awakening a brand new little body filled with so much freshly discovered fragility

The trio soon left the premises, armed, on the Old Man's advice, with an entire selection of dubious acquisitions. In passing, they saluted Cowboy, who was blocking the entrance, stiff as a post. I approached him to observe the teenaged girl disappear.

"Who's she?"

Cowboy was smiling.

"Gisèle's daughter. Salomé."

"Where'd she come from?"

He shrugged.

"Social services. Her mother didn't take proper care of her."

The Old Man was already rushing towards us.

"Come with me, Ti-Kid Gilles, I've got a contract for you! Did you see old man Flamand? He's a good Indian, a hard worker!

Not a drop of alcohol in twelve years! We need more like him!
His old lady, however.... Misery me.... Did you see the little girl?
She'll do a lot of damage!... Hmmm.... Hey, Ti-Kid Cowboy!...
Wanna work?"

Totally wound up, he was thrashing about and poking at us, a
tangle of nerves and knots. Cowboy and I had our minds on
something else.

That morning, I was dispatched to help repair a shingled roof.
Unprotected from aerial attacks, I quickly fell prey to a cloud of
black flies. Although the insects launched the most vicious and
massively heinous attacks, I only noticed the extent of their havoc
when the party was over. Seeing me return covered with bites, the
Old Man cried out and rushed to the medicine cabinet at full tilt. I
was given intensive care.

It happened one Sunday. An itinerant clergyman had detoured
through Grande-Ourse, which hadn't been able to afford a
permanent pastor in a long time. Now and again, a priest who was
passing through would stay a while. This time, his services were
needed to administer first communion to a pair of converts already
tangled in a protocol that was supposed to be flexible. Mr.
Administrator suggested I accompany him to the service, to sound
out the population like in the good old days, when pipe-chewing
parishioners stood on the square, reaching into pig-bladder tobacco
pouches. But the steps to this chapel weren't very wide and, with
the flies biting, people tended to take them at a clip.

All the right-thinking residents of Grande-Ourse were there.
I'd put on a spotless cotton T-shirt with large draping folds, a kind
of mini-cassock, which must've made me look like a runtish White
Father who'd escaped from cannibals. Streaks of ointment on my
skin identified the most injured areas. The inquisitive gazes of
attendants converged on us while I took a seat in the back, beside
my boss. Heads turned towards us like filings drawn to the poles of
a magnet. People came here to pry as much as to pray. Mr.
Administrator smiled at everyone indiscriminately, as though to say
everything's fine, nothing to complain about.

I got a shock right from the introit. Two cherubs accompanied the celebrant: a chubby young white boy who seemed carved from soft marble; a young girl, Salomé, draped in the vestal robe of choir children. Her brown face contrasted with the garment and was exceedingly beautiful.

She piously lowered her almond-shaped eyes, while I gaped in admiration. Her modesty was the picture of passion. I didn't take a very active part in the ceremony. People moved their lips, emitting breaths and sounds, while Mr. Administrator mimicked them as best he could. Amid the murmurs, people would lean to their neighbour, inhaling the waxy redolence of their ears. Lukewarm chants alternated with hot gossip. The on-duty preacher, energetic and ruddy, was visibly relying on his instinct to find words able to move this potbellied and unrefined crowd. He spread the word of Christ without affectation, in his own gut-felt language, perverting Christianity's founding metaphors if needed.

"And so," he bellowed powerfully to the two converts nestled in the first pew, "what is the Eucharist, eh? What does it mean precisely? Well, my children, I feel like asking who you are exactly. Eh? Answer and you'll receive communion! Your host, my children, is a nice big stew with a really fat brown sauce dripping between your fingers! And later, when you're old enough to handle the bottle, the caribou your parents drink will warm your blood during ordeals! That, my lambs, is the nature of your Eucharist in this land of Cain, this land of Canadians!"

He was rampantly bawling the sermon, his exuberance soon managing to elicit reactions in the stomachs of attendants. And the rumblings that typified the end of services soon began rising in the incense-filled air. The priest punctuated his sermon with heavy taps on the curve of his stomach, which jutted towards his audience like a promontory. He sniffed ostentatiously, contracting the capillaries in his large nose, which were visible from that distance. He must've been rather familiar with the chapter about caribou.

When we got around to the grand apportionment, the first-time communicants accepted the miserable unleavened chip, just transformed into meatball stew by the magic of the Word. Veterans followed, enticed by all this juicy solemnity. Mr. Administrator decisively got up, turning onto the short aisle, hands joined over his mid-section, brimming with contrition. He had no choice: he had to continue polishing his image and playing the enlightened-leadership card. It was really funny seeing him mix with these characters, to whom he generally had to concede an impressive girth and more than a foot in height and muscle. The communion's elbow rubbing swept him along in its muffled swirl and, cupping his hands, leading the procession and leaning before the celebrant, he seemed to be begging for public understanding, indulgence, and approval.

I was overcome with hesitation as I was about to claim my share. I wouldn't normally have wanted to be in this sad comedy for anything in the world, nor to participate in its supremely facile gregariousness, returning with a host stuck to my palate, thin and bland as the taste of faith itself. As I approached the distribution point, screened from it by the large backs of attendants, Salomé's white dress dazzled me all the more. Her dark face seemed made of obscurity as she stood in the priest's shadow.

Head lowered, eager to get it over, I suddenly noticed the bright red stains on the nice T-shirt I'd worn specifically for the occasion. Mr. Administrator had just completed the formality and was returning towards the back, chin resolutely plastered to his chest. My heart beat faster as I made a rapid inventory of the mess. Tiny spatters stretched out like scars across my chest. Beginning to panic, I raised my hand to my neck, pulling it away smeared with blood. I then understood: my morning wounds had reopened, accompanied by new exactions from the bit braces that had found me on the way to the chapel. The result: I was dripping like a tap.

Following a second of terror, I stretched out my palms, placing the smeared one underneath. My stomach emitted something like a nervous giggle. The priest lowered his dismal eyes, while Salomé gazed straight ahead. I could no longer see anyone and, eyes overturned, was looking for flies on the ceiling. I was growing faint, and their little barter was taking forever. He finally plunked the host in my palm; I fell forward as though it weighed a ton, with Salomé's image swaying and waltzing in the air with total absurdity. Throwing her arms around my neck, she stirred the shoulder blades lying beneath her wings, and began avidly licking the host in the palm of my hand. My head crashed into the

ciborium and snow flew beneath the nave, as I registered the
brushing of a robe against my cheek. I think that was all.

❧

Our guard dog was giving a recital as the moon rose. The poor
devil of a bastard spent his whole existence chained to a
rudimentary kennel near the store. When needed, he could give the
alarm with conviction, not much else being required of him. But
when the moon was full, he yielded to heredity with breathless
vigour, singing the praise of the big orange ball, tilting his litany of
barks and whimpers at the firmament; it was enough to freeze
blood in your veins and urine in your bladder.

I was sleeping fitfully one night when he began to howl. Yet I
could've sworn his favourite satellite was in its new phase. I tore
myself from a stranglehold as humid as it was purely dreamlike. A
train whistled in the distance, while the mutt had started a genuine
concert. His chain scraped heavily against the ground, providing
backup harmonies while he ran to and fro. Beats worthy of a large
drum echoed from the main door, providing percussion. I went
down the hall leading to the kitchen, leaning forward in my briefs,
staggering as though a cement bag had been loaded onto my back
without warning. The Old Man was up, hair on end, wearing
shorts and an undershirt, spreading his stench. He'd always turned
down the privilege of having his own room, where he could have
had some privacy during the brief intervals when sleep came to his
proud and decrepit body. Exposed on the front lines, he slept in
the living room, always turning in last, curled up on a tired couch
whose springs ejected him for the least reason.

Benoît also appeared, eyes puffy with sleep, stifling a yawn as
well as a gesture of rebellion.

"Sleeping around here isn't easy ...," he said, gritting his teeth.

Blows continued to rattle the door panel, as the rumbling of
muffled anger invaded the obscure building. The Old Man made a
few steps, repeating to himself, in the neutral tone of a litany,
"Pack of dogs! They respect nothing! Pack of dogs! There's no
way.... Pack of dogs!"

Benoît had considered the situation, and taken time to put on
his pants. Being well-kept meant everything to this boy.... Well-kept

numbers, well-kept premises, well-kept appearance: everything had
to be well-kept and, as much as possible, kept quiet.

The Old Man and Benoît, standing abreast, peered down the
dusty aisle bordering the shadow-flooded shelves. The blows
gathered strength behind the door. Neither a word nor a shout
punctuated this patient display of impatience. A fist beating the
wood door, the crude rhythm of this pounding. Blows striking the
door, that's all.

Lending a music-lover's ear to this rolling of kettledrums they
knew very well, Benoît and the Old Man exchanged knowing looks.
The latter said with all the authority required, "It's okay, boys, we
can go back to bed!... They'll get fed up!... They must've been on
the train.... The train always brings Indians.... They'll get fed up,
guaranteed! Bastards.... "

While Benoît returned to his quarters, yawning to the point of
breaking his jawbone, the Old Man, finger raised, gave another of
those special lectures he really liked to hit me with at the drop of a
hat, "Never open!... N-e-v-e-r, d'you hear? Once their foot's in the
door, it's over! O-v-e-r!... Only thing left is the gun!... Baaaang!...
Oh, the bastards will get fed up.... They'll get fed up, guaranteed!"

As soon as we'd gone back to bed, they knocked with increased
obstinacy. The insistent and stubborn rhythm of the pounding, in
the midst of my half-awakened delirium, insidiously replaced the
throbbing of my blood. It was like the sound of a tom-tom in the
night, powerful and primitive, unrelenting and impenetrable. And I
clenched my fists in despair, absolutely wanting to sink into sleep
but continually caught, awakened by the controlled madness of the
drumming. I wanted to hit something as well, anything, just to
release pressure and somehow respond to the primary impulse
filling the night. But I remained there, proffering death threats
muffled by my pillow.

I finally got up and returned into the hallway. The Old Man,
expelled by the springs of his berth, passed in front of me in a
whirlwind, charging through the store, lifting a genuine dust cloud
in the finest tradition of cavalry regiments, bellowing like the devil
the whole time. He rushed to the door, tossing the bar like a mere
toothpick, then leapt onto the steps, continuously railing against
the undesirables, calling them all the names in the Bible, taking

stock of and trotting out all the church dishes and other liturgical hardware in an impromptu sermon whose main theme went something like, "Go to bed! You pack of dogs! Go to bed, go to bed! Pack of dogs!"

The vision of the hoary old man floating like a ghost in his underwear must've made a strong impression on the Indians, who retreated in disorder without even trying to parley. I glimpsed Donald Big-Arms' barrel-shaped figure through the doorway; he seemed to be hesitating, wavering on the spot. He split the darkness with a yellow smile and, blind drunk, proudly struggled to stand up before thinking of running off. Behind him, Cowboy was slipping away at a moderate pace, taking his time, calmly looking over his shoulder, as though underlining that such a strategic retreat implied no fundamental concession.

After scattering the riff-raff and addressing the one who'd lingered with elementary rhetoric, the Old Man returned to the back of the building, juggling prize inanities. The half-naked old fool went back to the unstable comfort of his springs, waving his arms as though to brush an entire battalion of demons out of his way. He'd acted in a semi-sleepwalking state, and was now busy realizing how rash his bravery had been. As he was about to pass by me, he snatched a can from a shelf and, waving it as though it were a projectile, turned towards the door, howling furiously,

"Next time, it'll be with a 30-30!... BAAANG! With a rifle, I tell you!... BAAANG!"

The old scarecrow's backside had been guarded anyhow. Benoît had surreptitiously worked his way into the manager's narrow office, which he often had to relinquish during the day to Mr. Administrator's inquisitive pen. A large unglazed window in the wall of that room allowed you to slip into the hallway. Benoît was seated on the edge of a pivoting chair, eyes opened with great difficulty, rifle on his knees. He was stiff as a rail. The Old Man murmured, with a hint of tenderness in his voice, "It's over, Ti-Kid.... You can go to back to bed, young fella.... It's over."

Outside, the dog was still howling. Benoît returned to his room, leaning the rifle against the wall between stacked boxes of bullets and a dictionary he consulted regularly in the line of duty, since he sometimes needed words to defend himself. And I fell back into the bay-coloured arms of my dreams, as though they were a parenthesis in the long insomnia that was beginning.

❧

A double streak of grease squirted from the hamburger fried the Old Man's way, and Mr. Administrator suddenly announced wearily, "I'm leaving today.... For Montreal."

He'd said this while massaging his jaw. Through the sharp sputtering of the fat, the Old Man's distinct sigh of relief could be heard as he leaned over a cast-iron pan spitting grease. He could keep his position by default. Once again, Mr. Administrator hadn't dared give him final notice, and he could see this as another reprieve.

"Another one? Hungry enough for another one?" he bellowed, artistically tossing the beef patty swelling on his spatula. "You'll never eat better ones, not even at McDonald's!" he added triumphantly.

Mr. Administrator looked at him furiously. Heartburn was curling his lips.

A little earlier, the previous night's raid had been discussed, a raid scuttled by our very own Old Man's courageous stand. Breaking his usual silence, Benoît then launched into an epic description of the Old Man's outburst, giving a detailed vignette of the terror that had stricken the intruders at the sight of this fury. The zeal of his panegyric plastered a delighted smile on the Old Man's mug, who probably saw this as an opportunity to boost his image in the eyes of the boss. He cleaved the air with his skillet, elated. "Baaang! Nothing but dogs!"

Mr. Administrator, sullen looking, concealed his face behind the golden back of a large hamburger. He repeated, in a quieter voice, "I'm leaving this afternoon."

A prolonged stay would've inflamed his ulcer. The previous day, he'd wanted to shake hands with parishioners outside the chapel, following the principle that he'd have nothing to gain by setting everyone against him. But his flaccid paw was left dangling in the breeze, bent like a fish hook. All he got were wary looks. Finally, the Muppet himself, tossing like a Cartesian diver, came over to grab his outstretched hand, only too happy to clutch some protrusion. But Mr. Administrator would've preferred to speak with some notable specimen of that crowd which, in recent years, had specialized in being indebted to his business. He looked around, diffident, giving me a worried expression mixed with resentment.

I'd attracted attention to us, though perhaps not exactly the way he'd have liked. They'd quickly carried me out, while the kneeling priest, with Salomé's help, busily picked up his supply of hosts, swearing. Slumped on the square's lowest step, I'd regained consciousness amid a circus of concerned faces more astonished than moved by genuine charity. Every tragedy has its good side, however, and a decent blonde girl, possessed of more initiative than the local average, had, with quiet assurance and self-confidence, wiped my pale face with a dampened altar cloth. I was conscious enough to hear her explain to the others, who were already anticipating my emergency evacuation, "It's only an allergic reaction, that's all.... He'll recover. There's venom in those tiny creatures, you know...."

"Who? Him?" an astonished voice cried out.

"The flies, stupid!" she answered him, smiling at me. "I saw a guy rushed to hospital after being bitten like that...."

I couldn't stop looking at her.

"A city guy, obviously!" decreed someone else, whom I couldn't see.

I'd managed to sit halfway up, "You're the nurse, I guess?"

She burst out laughing.

"The nurse, here, went to school with Armand Frappier. I hope I look a little younger.... No, I work at the hotel.... "

With those words, my boss dragged me off while, in our wake, the Muppet pedalled in the dust.

He left the following afternoon, other business requiring his attention farther south. He was made for managing from a distance, not for waging battle on the front. He needed a safety margin, a few hundred kilometres between himself and the source of his problems. Deep down, Mr. Administrator was a dreamer. Unlike the two others, he wasn't continually tormented by an energy that was pitifully down to earth. He needed that distance to maintain his illusions. From the top of an office tower in downtown Montreal, or from a patio lined with uniform flagstones and equipped with a volcanic barbecue, Grande-Ourse could still seem like the reflection of that resuscitated village, that playground for the rich he'd dreamt about one night, covered in his eiderdown.

CITY COMFORT IN THE MIDDLE OF NATURE

In fact, Mr. Administrator asked only to be reassured, and was never happier than when his alleviated concerns finally joined the other certainties in his personal collection. When his van disappeared over a nearby hill, the Old Man was beaming, feet firmly rooted to the ground.

"Sooooo ... long! Sooooo ... long!" he bellowed at the top of his lungs, making useless wide gestures.

As soon as the vehicle disappeared around the first bend, he breathed more easily, becoming more effusive, settling in more firmly. When his opinion wasn't asked, he'd crop up behind you, turning the screws in your back. He was everywhere at once, had five hands, bustled about like four monkeys! You'd feel like scratching whenever he wandered nearby. A capuchin, a marmoset, a ringtail monkey, a squirrel monkey! He smelled of suint. Often, while continuously talking to the walls behind which he'd grown proficient at finding us, he'd move slowly, imperceptibly, gently drifting towards the shower stall, his own stench having finally got to him. He took two or three steps backwards, turned around, procrastinated. The idea of leaving the conversation in our pathetic care offended him in the highest degree. He'd cling to his verbosity, it was his wall of protection against the insignificance of the inanimate world, against the outside night.

"Don't tell me he's gonna take a shower?"

"Course not ...," replied Benoît.

And he came back towards us, went off again, dithered about, shifting his weight from one foot to the other, then jumped on the spot, then backward and forward, following the steps of a complex choreography understood by him alone, moving from the passacaglia to the paso doble without transition and, in the end, as though to yield to a carefully prepared effect, slapping his forehead, totally excited, "Oooh! I forgot to tell you!..."

The following second, he again gesticulated, throat trembling like a bell, chattering abrasively, spring fully wound, a ridiculous hybrid produced by a deaconess and a leprechaun. He'd stand before us, spewing threats in all directions, choking on his moans, vilifying the thoughtlessness of some, pillorying others. The flow of his words greatly exceeded that of the shower head. He, at least, had no problems with flies, being so well coated with his own sebaceous layer.

I listened very carefully. In their eyes, I was a kind of likeable lost cause, a young thinker out of his element who spent most of his time daydreaming, opening his mouth, like a fish, only to breathe. I didn't miss any of the Old Man's words, that prolific gossip where each sentence, like a roof tile, partially covered another. I took advantage of the peace and quiet they allowed me to spy with impunity. I secretly scribbled notes, feeling the rest of the story would throw me into a role for which I had to prepare immediately. I soaked up all those ceaselessly repeated words, discharged with heavy throat clearings. I'd become a sensory sieve, a selective strainer. When the lump I imagined to be necessary would crop up amid all this mash, my prospector's ear would go off like a valve. I'd then be able to grasp that dark nugget hidden in the passage of time, and extricate it from the sand, exposing it to the light, making it the jewel which, one day, would redeem all.

❦

Folks in Grande-Ourse always returned to the same story, the famous one nobody said much about, but which was deeply repressed in everyone's psyche. The Affair ate at Grande-Ourse's social fabric, and Salomé somehow sprang from the tragedy which tormented the village like a burning thorn in its paw. The hotel's threshold had been the cradle of the curse which poisoned exchanges. It was a delicate topic, a build-up of explosive forces that had been swallowed by the darkness. The embers still glowed, watching over like a scar; even the Old Man, when broaching the subject, displayed a temperance that contrasted surprisingly with his customary frenzy.

❦

An Indian man and woman drive up to the front of the hotel in an old pickup. It's night and they're drunk. The man heads to the door, unsuccessfully trying to open it. He knocks. No one answers. He insists with heavy blows. His companion stayed behind. He wants one more beer, despite the late hour. Behind the door, a voice urges them to leave. The discussion is animated. The Indian man finally heads back to the pickup, shouting imprecations. He threatens with his fist. He's lost sight of his girlfriend. He fiddles around the vehicle for a moment, and heads back towards the hotel wielding a heavy axe whose sharp head shines in the darkness. Swinging the tool, he deals a terrible blow to the door. The crash of broken wood echoes in the night. And he repeats the manoeuvre, enraged. Blows thunder in cadence, slow and heavy. Soon, he opens a breach. Then the door topples over, torn off its hinges. The only sound from the interior is an oppressed silence. The Indian now utters incoherent words. Someone hands him a beer through the demolished entrance. He grabs it and drinks without asking questions, still belching a string of hazy words. He turns back, walking unsteadily, beer in one hand, axe in the other. He walks with difficulty, shouting his head off, bellowing wild chants. As he's about to reach the door of his vehicle, the first shot rings out. The Indian doesn't fall right away, only staggers a little more. Several gunshots will be needed to bring him down and stretch him out properly. The salvo then rattles the night, shaking his back with heavy shivers. He finally tumbles forward, spreading out full length, trying to hang on to the opened door.

Grande-Ourse hasn't finished hearing those gunshots. The door is summarily put back into place. Not a trace is left of him. Nothing. His silhouette can be seen lying on the ground, legs stretched out as though making a final broad stride and trying to enter the earth itself.

The Old Man was informed and came over. He picks up the body. A dead man is heavy, he thinks, slipping his hands into the armpits. Destination: the cold room, beneath the Outfitters storehouse.

That's what happened.

That's what would've happened, if a long story could be cut short....

❧

They could be seen approaching at a snail's pace across the railway, the entire band piled into an old verdigris pickup specked with rust. The scrap heap's contrasting candy-pink hood was touching to behold. The head of the clan, César Flamand, was holding the steering wheel. He was fascinating to observe up close: totally wizened, ugly as three sins, taciturn as a grave. His features were

always twisted by elaborate twitches and scowls, as though he'd
wanted to keep flies away from his face without using his hands. His
shoulders had portaged numerous summers and he was easily twice
as old as the age anyone might've given him. Roméo, the young man
who'd fallen under the bullets twelve years earlier, was his son.
Salomé was the daughter of this Roméo, and, therefore, César's
granddaughter. He'd stopped drinking in the wake of the famous
incident, and now dragged his sadness everywhere, as though it were
tethered to his forehead. Fernande was his second wife, with the
exception of a few casual cohabitations. Mature and deeply
wrinkled, yet just recovering from childbirth, she snuggled up to
him on the seat, beer squeezed between her thighs in the mild
evening. They looked like a pair of teenagers heading to the drive-
in. A raft of colourful children dangled over the side in the back as
the tires rolled over the gravel. Many of the kids belonged to César,
who still wasn't thinking of abstaining from the pleasures of
procreation. The others, snatched from bad mothers whose breasts
spurted more alcohol than milk, had been placed in the couple's
good care. Flamand's reputation for abstinence, and paternal
kindness taken to the point of self-denial, reassured social workers.

Salomé appeared calm and introverted amid the noisy fray.
Dressed all in red, she was shy and anxious, averting her eyes. Her
sisters, half-sisters, brothers, and half-brothers, a howling swarm,
swept through the entire store. The smallest ones, unsure and
incredibly cute, jolted along the aisle in short, hasty, and
conquering strides. Flamand and his wife wandered amid this
brood with indulgent smiles. All they wanted was to linger
tenderly. They had all the time in the world while the Old Man
taunted them amicably, "Hail! Hail César! Hail Fernande!"

They were the only Indians that Benoît and the Old Man saw
as not covered in war paint. This laudable effort at tolerance was
mainly due to the austere Aboriginal's tacit vow of sobriety. As
well, Flamand was fond of Benoît, perhaps because of his morbid
dolorism, and respected the Old Man, since that pale morning
when, suspenders dangling, the latter had gone to pick up his son,
back riddled with .303 bullets, in front of the hotel. Without ever
recognizing it openly, Flamand was deeply grateful to the Old Man
for having spontaneously performed the gruesome task.

Though he'd forsaken the bottle, you could see at first glance that César Flamand had drunk a great deal, to the point of saturating his yellowish flesh, and that before stopping completely, he'd had to go to the bottom of things, to where truth and horror lie. Whenever Flamand spoke, you always took a few seconds, at first, unsure whether that chain of imperceptible chin movements corresponded to a living tongue.

As soon as the mercury climbed a few degrees, the sale of Mister Freezes increased by leaps and bounds. It's crazy how much I'd sell of this *frozen pasteurized water* (as specified on the product label). I expected the parent company to send me a bonus at any moment. The craving for something cold spread among the young people, each wanting a small column of ice wrapped in cellophane. And Flamand, following the customary protests, would take grumpy pleasure in organizing the distribution. Salomé deliberately leaned on the fridge, where she remained still, literally seated on the supply of Mister Freezes. With a glimmer of defiance in her eyes, she waited for me to feign pushing her to tumble down gracefully. My fingers became several stems running aground. She again hoisted herself to the same spot, staring at me unexpectedly, pensively sucking her colour crystals, oblivious to the awful insolence of the purple stick liquefying in her mouth. Flamand coughed up the cash.

Rounds of Mister Freezes wouldn't have been complete without Admiral Nelson. He'd burst into the premises, inquisitive, as though he'd been able to sniff the chemical colourings from a distance. Little girls made fun of him, but he paid no attention and made do with claiming his share. Dealing with other humans was painful to him.

Admiral Nelson was a solitary boy, already accustomed to the minimal compassion the world offered him. He was a young Indian, about 10 years old, cheerful as the devil but able to be serious. Afflicted with a harelip, he chattered like a magpie and looked like a squirrel: he was prescient and nervous. Since he was called Nelson, his surname had followed quite naturally. His infirmity made speaking difficult, and you had to go up to him and lean over somewhat to make sure you got everything. Contrary to a majority of brothers, sisters, and cousins, Nelson had plans for the future and, each winter, on hills covered in grey pine, he trapped martens to be able to afford his dreams. He wanted to become an engineer, get his pilot's licence, and buy a hydroplane. Sometimes the Old Man would vaguely encourage his aspirations. This kind of acceptance of the rules pleased him.

Young girls from the band got into the habit of surrounding the store each night, a venue more respectable than the hotel after all. The Old Man, filled with impartial clairvoyance, suggested that they came to check out some new guy, evaluate the merchandise, as it were. They'd set out from Flamand's cabin beside the lake after supper, moving as a group along the railway, leaving it near the overpass, landing on the Outfitters like a volley of birds. Their arrival terrified Benoît, who wasn't the most sociable individual in such circumstances. His policy dictated that he conceal the pleasure he felt at this feminine invasion. No guilty inclination could get in the way of his business vocation. As soon as the first skirt was spotted in the area, he quickly took refuge behind the counter, stuck to the cash register, as though he feared the lasses would make off with the day's proceeds.

This impervious reserve undermined his popularity. Girls would finally get fed up with his grim expression and impassiveness, and I became the new focal point without trying too hard. When, from the confines of my room, I heard the shouts, laughter, and other warbling signalling their visit, I'd spring out of my lair, approaching with studied casualness, calmly going over to lean on a shelf. Their banter, interrupted by brief chases and democratically distributed blows, was quite simply dizzying. Nothing embittered the Old Man so much as this habit of cluttering the premises without the slightest intention of buying anything, of filling all useful space with the wind of frivolous prattle, often chanted in a foreign language, taking out their coin purses only when threatened with expulsion, something never really enforced since the general store couldn't disregard its status as a public place.

Salomé's shyness set her apart from the group. Her integration into the rest of the band, besides, was very relative: remaining stubbornly aloof from the teeming swarm, she looked at the ground, radiating a kind of heavenliness that was the antithesis of the surrounding merriment. She realized I was observing her and took refuge atop the refrigerator whose mass provided soothing warmth.

The provocative ingenuousness of the gaze the graceful shape of the cheeks the eternal anticipation on the mouth with curled lips the ebony hair the bronzed skin the indecent perfection of the face.

A precocious tendency for procreating, and the likely influence of genetic programming, determine that most Indian women mature early. Salomé was already approaching the crumbly ridge where she'd stand around the age of sixteen, and the burgeoning was breathtaking. During the peaceful nights that preceded fishing season, she opened the first breech in my vow to practice a little abstinence that summer. She gave me a taste for simply being there, after the meal, when the small troop that scattered through the store was trying to taunt Benoît. Simply being there to look at her, and forgetting she'd someday be twenty, thirty, forty, likely fat and wrinkled, perhaps a boozer, doomed to suffer the fleeting desire of empty-handed fishermen getting loaded at the hotel.

These young girls, barely emancipated from parental attention, were quickly promoted as baby-sitters, dragging along the most recent offspring of those prolific lineages. And then, carelessly displayed by their elders, the most beautiful tots in the world made their inaugural walks into the world, at my feet. They frolicked like ducklings on the old planks, rolling on the ground, wretched bundles of innocence that the social services had taken from decrepit mothers, relocating them to more stable homes. Their beauty seemed to reach all the way back to the origin, to the hardness of the egg, and I felt that if I'd been able to contemplate an Indian zygote for only a moment, I'd have experienced ecstasy, discovered the crux of everything and swallowed the core of the world.

❧

Benoît was trying to raise a brimming spoon to his mouth.

"They'll burn him, they'll burn him!" the Old Man repeated, walking back and forth.

We were seated at the table before bowls of steaming soup. Spoons swirled in the broth and the kitchen echoed with the sounds of our palates. The Old Man, with no request besides silence from warmed throats, was telling his stories. Sometimes it seemed as though only his voice held us in the present. Its music and false notes, distinct tempos, scores, signs and keys, its outbursts, sudden changes from low to high notes (when he'd strive to imitate Mr. Administrator's tirades) and the intangible structure of his rhythm affected Benoît like an irresistible lullaby. This was the hour when lack of sleep tried to catch up with the manager. The young fellow had the odd habit of drinking five or six instant coffees before turning in. Strange how he didn't realize the practice caused his insomnia; after all, it's only a temporary concession to unproductiveness. The Old Man never slept more than four hours a night, and took pompous delight in his ability to bounce to his feet each morning at dawn. At 4:00 a.m. sharp, all the pots and pans rattled at the same time, and the shrillness of the radio took on a chorus of crows getting agitated outside: the Old Man went into action, it was his hour of glory, he reigned on a sleeping world, he made himself useful. His favourite pastime during those moments was to wash the previous day's dishes and, since he was growing more hard of hearing, the transistor would bellow its stream of crackling at full volume, while the clanging of porcelain rose from the sink.

This infernal racket cruelly cut short our nights. I'd see Benoît nodding in front of me at the table, the amplitude growing more pronounced with the grating of the elderly human trumpet. He raised his utensil painfully, like the wand of a conductor lacking the strength to reach his crescendo. And then, oops, the spoon deviated from its course, missed its target and Benoît burned his cheek, drenching his lap with wonderful smelling hot soup; he suddenly awoke, cried out, and came to.

The Old Man would then agree to interrupt the meandering course of his reminiscence.

"Go to bed, Ti-Kid! Go to bed! You'll burn yourself!"

But in the shelter of his pride, Benoît stood firm. And, as though to highlight the danger of any quietude, we immediately heard urgent knocking at the door. Prompted by that signal, he stood up like a robot, turning his head slightly to look at the individual who'd disturbed his lunch. Then, eager to fulfil the requirement of his vocation, he'd hurry to the entrance. Forgetting his own problems, the Old Man would then take pains to go over the flaws and misfortunes of this blasted hamlet, this unredeemable pandemonium whose case could only be settled with a good lock! Everyone got their due; whites and their cowardice, shareholders and their smug ignorance, Indians and their laziness. Indians, those parasites, flea-bitten dogs, thirsty-horned animals only interested in ruining the business of honest citizens and sullying all that Grande-Ourse still had of industriousness!

To lighten his burden, Benoît was determined to teach me, if not how to count, then at least how to use the machine designed for that purpose. I was a very bad student right from the beginning. It must be said that, amid all the uninhabited space around Grande-Ourse, numbers enjoyed a special status. Appropriate names are a luxury found only with civilization. Over there, people didn't say *at Lake Such and Such*, but rather *at the Three-Mile Point*. They didn't refer to the *bridge over a given river*, but to the *Twenty-Mile Point*. The land had not been cleared, and therefore had to be explained. The pickup's odometer took care of place names and, obsessed with distances, people exorcised their seclusion by tossing numbers onto the map. They felt remoteness to be less frightening with those particulars nailed into it. Emptiness faded into the reassuring linearity of a collective consciousness marked with imaginary milestones.

Patiently and imperturbably, Benoît showed me the cash register's secrets. He initiated me to the keyboard's coded language, acquainted me with the joyful rolling of the till that jingled as it slid on its hinges, taught me the best way to handle crisp banknotes forming wads in different compartments, encouraged me to carefully examine the tape rolling out like a streamer from the top of the machine and, finally, inducted me into the secrets of the safe by entrusting me with its three-number combination.

"The important thing is to balance!" he liked to repeat gravely, with a somewhat sinister complacency.

Our finances, as I understood them, were based on the same principle as the black box: it was enough to know what went in, what came out, and to always establish an equivalency between the two amounts.

But the machine's keys refused to line up in the right sequence beneath my fingers. I added up gaffs faster than the price of goods multiplied by their number. Each new blunder stared my supervisor in the face, breaking his heart, as he leaned over the distressing white ribbon which was an insult to all mathematical rigour. When Benoît was out of sight, I'd settle on noting any calculation that didn't add up on a piece of paper which I then concealed under the cash, without losing my cool, whispering to myself, like an incantation: *Benoît will manage. Benoît will balance.*

It was important to show unflappable confidence before the shrewd and paunchy humanity that regularly filed through our establishment. I couldn't afford to hint at the least blunder in the eyes of those large woodsmen on welfare, bearded poachers with piercing eyes, brawny and griping lumberjacks on unemployment, and other friendly barbarians inclined to stinginess whenever it wasn't a question of eating or drinking. They would've pulverized me for less. I'd sometimes see their eyes bulge after they'd glanced the price of an item. They'd cry robbery just to test my resolve. I tried to remain calm, taking their money, recording transactions. I was gradually learning to figure them out.

They all seemed more or less cut from a pattern that took up space and was draped in abundant flesh. Midriffs were rather rotund. Local custom flaunted a joyful disregard for public health standards regarding consumption, and no restraint mechanism could've prevented those flabby paunches from spreading out and dangling around waistlines. Around here, stomachs were the last refuge of wealth.

Mornings when the heat wasn't too intense, Big Ben, a Métis, would show up on the horizon above the tracks, his four limbs making short and comical rotations around his pudgy body, like a locomotive's connecting rods in slow motion. Not much of him had been seen during Mr. Administrator's stay: Big Ben belonged to that race of honest idlers, unable to feign efficiency only to dazzle. Though not among the heaviest of his counterparts, he did carry about an imposing and impeccably circular mass.

When the Old Man introduced me to him, the enormous factotum stretched out his hand uselessly, in an uncertain gesture halfway between a handshake and a simple vague sign, a result of his arm's limited reach and his obvious reluctance to move his feet without a compelling motive. Quiet and modest, he gazed at the ground, its immediate view being forever denied him due to his corpulence. This fat boy, who was the perfect audience for any compulsive chatterbox, had mastered the art of tolerating the flapping of lips in others. He seemed intoxicated by the infinite variations in voice tones.

"What's happening with you, Big Ben?"

"Um Well Uh Well."

Perhaps to confront the contradiction inherent to his being Métis, Big Ben had created his own dialect which rested on purely iterative rhetoric. It always drew on the same monosyllabic repertoire reduced to a minimum, and borrowed from a level of evolution barely beyond the grunt. This lexical impoverishment seemed perfectly deliberate. Big Ben had everything of the friendly gorilla who'd accidentally discovered the principle of mantras.

"What's new, Big Ben, old buddy?"

"Well Um Well Uh."

He liked to examine shelf contents, walking along the aisle, hands on his stomach, getting excited over nothing, over the tiny breeze which, filtered by the half-open door, stroked his pathetic sweat-drenched carcass, or over a bag of potatoes delivered by the train that very morning and destined for the corner restaurant's foul-smelling fryer. Leaning with all his weight on the potato bag, he repeated, amazed, "Oh the nice potatoes! Oh Oh! Oh the nice potatoes!"

With his mouth in the shape of a heart, he'd catch his breath, lift his head, sponge his brow, "Oh the nice breeze! Oh! The nice little breeze...."

He'd come back down to earth, then, "Oh! The nice potatoes! Oh the nice potatoes...."

Big Ben nodded at everything the Old Man said, chanting his lone syllable, lovingly rocking it on his tongue. He was a fan of all-out approval, and could say yes sixteen times without changing pitch.

"Yes Yes Yes Yes Yes Yes Yes Yes Yes Yes Yes."

Big Ben was also the volunteer fire chief. One day, wonder of wonders, he showed me Grande-Ourse's fire truck. The antiquated vehicle, stored in a garage and forgotten by everyone, hadn't seen action in three or four centuries. Big Ben pampered it.

Raoul Legris was another notable character whose actions I'd carefully study. He was small, hard-hearted, sinuous, ageless. His greying mop, ruffled by an eternal night of partying, had two very stiff locks that gave him a pair of horns. Something bad and consciously crooked emanated from the grimace that was always on his lips. Legris was a rogue and didn't pretend to be anything else, which gave him an advantage over many of the people around him. He played his role as a villain with a fervour that could only make him sympathetic in the long run. He wasn't a Grande-Ourse native. His migration was the reverse of the tendency generally observed in rural regions: one day, he'd left his mediocre suburb in the Lower Laurentians, ending up in Grande-Ourse, at the end of the road and that of his resources. He worked for the Forestry Company at first, then for whatever required his dubious services here below. He had a good deal of pride for a bootlicker. This region had pleased him, having no law but the jungle's. He'd removed the licence plates from the vehicle he'd stolen in Saint-Thérèse-de-Blainville, disappearing into the landscape on the double. He quickly specialized, among other expedients, in establishing questionable friendships, especially with American tourists, who always wanted to buy lessons in local behaviour. Legris used his smile like others use a beggar's cup. Another pool of shady relations had been provided by the Indians. He went from one group to the next, acting as a contact point. There were Métis with brawn and Métis with brains. The mixed blood Legris had was in his brain. He was crafty as anything.

The first morning I saw him, he was in a rather sorry state and suffered from a crying need: a pair of ears, no matter whose, to be filled with the sound of his complaint. Posing as a victim with obvious satisfaction, he railed against a legion of nocturnal aggressors and, filled with meticulous self-pity, caressed the purple bruise adorning his forehead. Having merely got what he deserved, he rejoiced in having touched the Old Man with the moving tale of all his misfortunes. The latter was beside himself as he ran up to him.

"You, Legris! You! I knew it was you! You were behind the ruckus last night! I should've known! Legris is back!"

His counterpart awaited the rest, quiet and sarcastic.

"Same old story!" lamented the Old Man, calling on me as a witness. "The typical scenario: Legris gets the Indians to drink, buys beer all night, gets beat up in the morning and afterwards, has the gall to show up and complain!"

So much for the proceedings. The affair was understood.

"And now," the Old Man went on, "you'll ask me to call the Tocqueville police again? As if they weren't already on to your little number?"

Legris, who'd seemed distracted, straightened up completely, like an actor who's just been prompted.

"You think I'll let the shirt be taken off my back? They broke into my trailer and made off with a hundred pounds of meat! My freezer's totally demolished!"

The Old Man, secretly gratified by his role, was heading to the phone on the wall near the counter, fulminating. A determined Legris was on his heels, shouting, "Come on! Dial the number! I want the whole bunch locked up! Bastards!"

The Old Man dialled, affecting a solemn attitude. Receiver in hand, Legris interrupted the account of his misfortunes to collect himself for a moment. Something then clicked in his mind, and he abruptly hung up, burning with rage, "Don't need the pigs for that! I'll personally take care of the Siwashes! Without us, they'd still cover their asses with animal hides!"

Sharing his burden had been enough to wash away the offence. The Old Man wouldn't budge, but you could feel he'd calmed down considerably. The familiarity of this masquerade and the predictability of its outcome rewarded him each time. All Legris required was a little attention. Besides, seeking intimate conversations with the police really wasn't to his advantage. The Indians acted as foils to him; in fact, they allowed him to think he was superior, a kind of heretical Christ offering to suffer for their salvation.

But, to ensure everyone was happy, the Old Man still had to trot out his bugbear, infused with biblical wrath. "You son of a bitch! You wasted my time again! I've always told you: don't make them drink, don't make them drink! Never, do you hear?"

Fingers in his ears, Legris walked away sniggering, regaling in the commotion he discovered he was still able to cause. His bruises already began hurting less and he mused about other happenings.

"Never make them drink!" barked the Old Man, plunking himself before me, though I hadn't caused him any problems.

Passing near me, Legris repeated, fire deep in his eyes, "Without us, they'd still wear animal hides over their asses."

The Old Man often looked outside worriedly, vigorously scratching his groin.

"Still, fat Lili will have to show up, one of these days...."

When asked who Lili was, he shrugged compliantly. "You'll get to know her, don't worry...."

I believe I caught a knowing smile across Benoît's lips.

My progress with the cash register was hopelessly slow. My calculating knowledge was practically non-existent, and my preferred customers were Indians. With them, commercial relations were surrounded by a pleasant simplicity. Thrift had no hold on their imagination and they were completely oblivious to the most widely accepted notions of economy. One day, Cowboy came in to buy instant coffee along with Karate Kid. He went down the aisle, then returned with a tiny container he placed on the counter between us.

I nodded.

"You know, Cowboy, it's much cheaper when you buy a large container."

"Yeah, but a small one's easier to carry."

And he shoved it into the pocket of his jacket, while I stumbled on his logic. I heard him pronounce the ritual formula, "Put it on my tab."

I pulled a yellow card with overcrowded columns from a folder.

Cowboy and the Kid lingered for a while. We spoke about this and that, about the Incident, Salomé, Flamand, and the hotel. Salomé had dropped out of sight for some time, and they told me she was back on the reserve, participating in a family celebration. Cowboy frowned when I queried him.

"Don't know."

"Has she returned to her mother?"

Cowboy and the Kid exchanged glances.

"Gisèle must be in Sans-Terre...."

"In the bars...."

"Sleeps with the guys...."

"When she's able...."

"Lots of bars in Sans-Terre...."

"Bars filled with miners...."

"Miners?"

"Yeah, 'cause of the mines.... Gold, copper...."

"Lots of fights in Sans-Terre bars...."

"She sleeps with miners...."

They left. Barely had the door closed, when I gave a violent start: the Old Man's inquisitive head was perched over the cash register.

"That's how they are," he began in a spiteful tone. "They don't know the value of money! You could tell them a hundred times and it wouldn't change a thing.... Moreover, it means profit for us," he said, ending on an angelic note.

I understood he was referring to the tinned coffee.

He watched the two young people walk away.

"I overheard what you were saying.... Indians never forget an incident like that."

"What incident?"

He smacked his tongue, then continued, "The hotel incident! The young Boisvert fella's a dead man if he comes back here! A goner! He'll never set foot in Grande-Ourse again! Barred for life!"

He looked at me, speaking in a low voice.

"Eleven bullets! Eleven bullets in the back. I personally placed my fingers in the holes, young fella. I picked up the pieces...."

The Old Man said he'd been warned that night by the Muppet, who was taking a bath at his place to sober up, and who'd just picked up a whistling bullet in his water.

"A bath!" the Old Man exclaimed, staring at me. "At that hour, what a ridiculous idea!"

Night was about to fall over Grande-Ourse. In the congealing of the setting sun, through the fly specks, the low building could be seen, spanning its sinister mass of planks along the lake shore.

"Damned Boisvert!" whistled the Old Man between his teeth.

He scraped the dust with the tip of his shoe.

"What saved us the morning of the funeral is that everyone was there. Everyone! Whites and Indians! Spared us a civil war, that's for sure! Seeing everyone at the church impressed the Indians...."

"Even Boisvert?"

He shook his head, chin in the air.

"No sir! Naturally.... The police had already taken the son away.... As a principal witness. As for the father, no one saw him for a long time."

"Was he found guilty? The son, I mean...."

"Two years less a day in jail for the murder of a man, pal. It also didn't hurt that he was a minor, obviously...."

"What about the father?"

The Old Man shook his filthy mop of hair. A fine halo emanated from it, which a nearly horizontal sunray coloured purple. He remained quiet, but finally admitted reluctantly, "He was cleared. It seems he was away the night it happened ..."

I coughed slightly. "What happened to the young fella?"

Big Ben quietly crossed the room.

"Oh Ummm Don't know Uh Hmmm. No one around here knows, no one."

"And then," the Old Man went on, "everything started happening to Jacques Boisvert. His wife drowned on a fishing trip that very summer.... And he raised a lot of eyebrows, afterwards, when he started hanging around with Gisèle...."

"Where does this Jacques Boisvert live now?"

I got the feeling the Old Man was peering deep into my soul.

"Don't be in too great a hurry, son.... You'll see him soon enough, as well...."

❦

The general store could no longer count on a watch-dog worthy of the name. His decline accelerated as a result of his spending the whole night tangled in his chain tied to a creaking clothesline sliding over the small yard. He'd bark at anything, at the least stroller who was already at the other end of the village. The tiniest quarter moon was now enough to prompt his wailings. In the morning he'd be found totally crestfallen, twisted in the inextricable tangle of his tether. He became the principal disturbance of the nights he was supposed to guard. The Old Man referred to his rifle, the dump. Benoît suggested we wait.

The Old Man acquired a kitten from the gutter to thwart a tiny group of mice that had the nasty habit of using spoons as lavatories. The newcomer displayed a great aptitude and his progress was so rapid that he soon appeared to be aiming for nothing less than the position of guardian-in-chief. To sharpen his skills, the Old Man took charge of imparting him with the light paranoia he believed essential to the task. As soon as the entrance door opened, letting in a customer, the kitten would steal towards it, rivetted to the floor, hypnotized by the luminous horizon. But the Old man quickly ascertained the intractable element, tearing off after him, arms swinging and legs wobbling, with a resounding, "Get back in there, you little Hérode!"[1]

All the hair on his back was raised, as the feline escaped to the kitchen where he fully expected to beg for more accessible consolations. He got his name from these repeated scoldings: Hérode. More than anyone or anything, he'd run into the cruel paradox that underpinned the administration of his masters: being surrounded by infinite space all round, but settling for cultivating a siege mentality in the dark, like a precious endive. Despite the traumatizing aspects of the experience, Hérode forged himself a vigorous attitude and never completely succumbed to the culture of living inside a shell, prime examples of which were to be found in the Outfitters' general store: narrow-mindedness set up as a fortress; continence sublimated by a snarl at the whole world. Hérode was young and vigilant; he rapidly crossed, if not the entrance door, then the boundary between innocent games and real life, where wounds bleed, and suffering reigns. Endowed with a sandfly's ferocity, but incomparably better equipped, he knew how to dig into your back with one paw. He got into the habit of lurking under a shelf, near the counter, nestled defiantly between large bags of dog food. When a customer moved along the rows of canned food, Hérode would pounce on his legs with a tiny cry of enthusiastic resolve. He'd bite away, making no distinction between hairy pillars and varicosed columns. More than one tall character would fall flat, forehead against the ground, and more than one mushy skinned creature nearly fainted while our friend sharpened his claws on calves marbled like blue cheese. If a customer made the mistake of sticking a blind forearm into the shadows beneath the lower shelf, resolved to grab a bag of dog food, he'd immediately pull it out covered with a strange fur implant. He'd created a kind of de facto blockade around the central supply source for the village dogs.

The Old Man was beginning to worry. He clearly distinguished between protecting the Outfitters' assets and indiscriminately taking it out on all customers. But he also had to repress a smile when the people of Grande-Ourse started jigging in front of us, inspired by our cat's ground-level attacks. Moreover, how could you not get intense delight when the tiny cat diligently lacerated the crooked legs of the Muppet who was gradually anaesthetized by visits to the cold room and who chatted as though he didn't notice?

Admiral Nelson became the kitten's friend and official protector. When the Old Man chased the kitten, Nelson intervened and pleaded his cause. But the Old Man was unyielding on that point. He stretched out his arms like twisted branches, trying to grasp the immense reality of the outside world, offering himself as an example to mankind: youth and freedom were two calamities he'd been able to dispose of long ago.

"Poor Ti-Kid! A tiny cat! I don't give him an hour to live if he sets foot outside!"

One day, when Hérode had just taken an offensive position, rolled up in a ball amid cans of Dr. Ballard's, as I was daydreaming with book in hand, the door swung open violently and wind swept through it. The movement of air, combined with the surprise effect, nearly threw me off my stool. I put the book face-down on the counter to mark the page. A trembling mountain moved before me in all directions at once, swallowing space like a malignant growth. I had a vision of a goddess with a thousand purple nipples, able to crush your skull like that of a newborn, a twisted image of maternity, filled to the breaking point with its own matter. Rolls of fat rippled across her flesh like waves over the water while she spread over the surrounding floor with the same humid generosity as the ocean. I immediately understood with whom I was dealing, and felt like praying.

Instinctively, I turned to the back of the store, but no living creature dared betray itself. The aisle seemed longer than ever.

Lili looked at me with the eyes of a grouper about to gobble a piece of anything. After sizing me up, sorting me irrevocably among the nonentities, she quietly passed by, breathing heavily. Hérode made a slight hesitant jump, tried to look like a man-eater, then froze on the spot. He sifted through the limited web of his recollection, searching for something related to that humongous flesh heap. Lili swung her foot, ready to crush him, and he barely managed to dodge her, gaining considerable speed in his retreat.

"A cat?" grumbled Lili. "Must be vermin in the building.... Doesn't surprise me...."

She scoured the store, incessantly griping, sniffing the dust and pondering comments likely to be rather negative. She seemed quite determined to make me work for her money. Goods piled onto the counter at a distressing rate. Whenever I feigned to head towards the cash register, just to start reducing the heap quietly, she'd dryly tell me to stop.

"Not so fast, young fella! I'm not done.... You'll get confused if other customers come in...."

It was more than a word of advice. Clenching my teeth, I smiled at her.

I got the jitters as I was about to convert all this into numbers. Lili was staring at me. The least carelessness could be fatal. I immediately started blundering, getting hopelessly confused. She quickly lined up her purchases for the sole pleasure of seeing me get flustered. I mumbled confused apologies while she stood quietly and coughed, gloating in her victory. Only the euphoric jiggling of her flesh testified to the operation's complete success. She even added to the insult by pressing her glasses against the labels, giving me the prices in a loud and slow voice, filled with crushing superiority, as though she were dealing with a three year old. I had no doubt that following this demonstration she'd make it her duty to show everyone proof of my incompetence, as recorded in minute detail on the ribbon she angrily tore away as I cringed. Lili needed a scapegoat in life, and she thought I fit the bill. I felt this woman would get no rest from having reduced me to the level of an embryo only worthy of being expelled from this place with blows from a stick.

❧

Grande-Ourse struggled at the extremity of its road like a fish at the end of a line. The world sometimes let the line out, enticing with meagre prospects, and unfulfilled promises; the village would then go off in all directions, roughshod and half-cocked. The world gave it some line as though to help it drown.

Beyond a stretch of prowling dust strewn with sparse and shivering weeds, among the scattered houses that seemed to have been tossed there like dice on a green carpet, the Outfitters' warehouse raised its sheet-metal undulations, while the morning sun covered its sides with pools of light. The warehouse had served as a garage for the heavy machinery used back in the days of prosperity. Salvaged by the new owners, it now contained only a few dozen metal barrels filled with helicopter fuel. Hardly any of the air craft were now seen in the region, but people subconsciously watched for them; they were the roaring oracles of a recovery. Everyone knew that the Company's measurers were in the habit of cleaving through the air in one of those machines to cast their sharp glances at lines of future logs. Trees had started to regenerate north of Grande-Ourse and, in some places, you could see the kind of nearly mature plantings that make the calculators of surveyors quiver. As soon as a section of forest was thirty-or-so-feet high, regardless of trunk size, greed would kindle behind the expanding pupil of a planner holed up in his faraway lair. The most optimistic of the village's unrelenting dreamers discussed the possibility of attracting a sawmill, the last hope for this hamlet of seventy-five souls. Company measurers had in fact been seen flying over the surrounding area. People who mentioned the mill always did so with a respectful shudder. And sceptics, among whom the Old Man always held centre stage, would reply that people who only argued from morning till very late at night couldn't work towards a common goal.

Though many residents harboured a certain animosity towards

the Outfitters, I learned that Lili's dissatisfaction had a specific origin. A former cashier at the general store, as spiteful as she was irritable, she'd been ousted from her livelihood as part of the rejuvenation program, from which my being hired sprang, having bumped into a pocket of resistance in the Old Man. Lili was also rebellious. To get the better of her, Mr. Administrator had pushed thoughtfulness to the point of paying for her stay in a Montreal clinic where a team of doctors, studying the problem of her proportions, had finally recommended drastic measures. But the Lili type doesn't sweat it out very long at latitudes below the forty-eighth parallel. Designed to withstand intense cold, she'd return very quickly, between treatments, to nestle within her geographic navel. A well-known law of biology predicts that the size of a specimen within a variety will increase the nearer it gets to the pole. Lili illustrated that axiom. Her case was idiosyncratic. Specialists had lopped off thick slabs, but even rid of a hundred pounds she was still a nice whale calf.

She'd been hired in the days of the old Company and, over the years, her corpulence had become a measure of the town's prosperity for the locals. Lili had reached her record weight when high voltage wires had been installed, a time when ravenous males left their encampments at the edge of Grande-Ourse each night to eat and get concomitant attentions. As far as anyone remembered, no apron could've been tied around her waist, but Lili had a solid reputation as a gourmet cook. Her cuisine had been popular at the time, and the bed with a reinforced box spring awaiting nearby had also known heavy use. The hostess was able to make space for well-filled stomachs, since she slept sitting up, only in fits and starts, as it were.

Lili had kept her job in the store when the transfer of power occurred, and continued to impose the impeccable order that characterized her reign. She'd fiercely combatted rot and waste, mercilessly scrapping any suspicious product. The village's decline had made her lose a little weight, providing more space for wrinkles on her skin. Once easy men had departed, she began to moan. The villagers got used to it, but her attitude, in Mr. Administrator's view, was lamentable. Still, the dispensers of cash didn't come to Grande-Ourse to be terrorized. Lili awakened a primeval panic in men, an irrepressible fear of getting lost in a cavern of flesh, of disappearing beneath it with the sound of an avenging gurgle.

Fat Moreau's house was another symbol of the slump. The restaurant owner spent his time drinking at the hotel, devoting all his energy to spreading disorder. When told he was over-extended, he negotiated a credit margin with his fists. Besides, everyone knew where his money had gone. At the high point of the economic boom, when his restaurant's grills were red hot from dawn to dusk, he'd set out to give spatial dimension to his success. After jumbling the main lines of a plan on paper, he'd thrown himself into a housing adventure on his own. Everyone quickly agreed that it was immoderate. A hybrid construction, more Spanish castle than bungalow, was born on a neighbouring hill, as though to spurn the village. Moreau thought he was a handyman, working with the obtuse fervour and simplistic technique of a lumberjack building a log cabin. He'd chosen the only property available in the area, a lot in theory belonging to the British Crown, and counted on that conceited building to finally be able to scoff Grande-Ourse's new owners at leisure. Suddenly thinking he was a millionaire, he sank all his money into the project.

At first, the house had swelled up like a ball on the granite knoll, getting farther and farther from any reasonable proportion or notion of harmony. Meanwhile, he had to settle for a miserable hovel squeezed into a corner of the restaurant, surrounded by the smell of rank oil, arguing with his wife when returning from daily sessions at the hotel. His wife suffered from ringworm, and was as skinny and ugly as he was sturdy. She thought she was prodding her big bear's creative inclinations as best she could with her ceaseless recriminations, but the effort had hung fire. The sudden blossoming of materials, beams and boards, joists and slats, mouldings and piers, had languished. The residence really did dominate the village, but still had no glass in its windows, handrails on its stairs, doors on its hinges, shingles on its roof. Only bare wood, black paper, cement blocks, and plastic house wrap, while the project manager was immersed in prolonged contemplations, nose in his glass a little lower down the slope. Moreau and his wife continued to live in an atmosphere of cooled grease, sleeping and tearing each other to shreds, the image of a dream delivered prematurely between them.

"It's ridiculous," whined the Old Man, contemplating the mess. "Try to imagine what the Americans will think when they see that! After all, they know a thing or two about nice properties!"

He'd paced back and forth all night, scratching himself everywhere, very carefully turning away from the shower room each time he passed it in the hall.

"This is the big weekend, boys!" he constantly barked out. "The Big Weekend! You'll see, they're real gentlemen, mark my word! Real gentlemen! All the credit cards; you name it, they've got it!"

He was choking with anticipation, stroking his money purse, arching his back like a turkey, still chuckling, "The Big Weekend, boys! Victoria Day! Time for us to make a little profit, friends!"

And, indeed, came the morning of the opening. The Americans were there.

⁊

They'd arrived in the night, after going through the road decline inherent to such an expedition: luxuriously paved and panoramic freeways in the land of Uncle Sam; Ontario motorways that were still pleasant to drive on; flat and linear Quebec highways still very suited to vehicles; provincial roads that narrowed increasingly, broken up and worn down by pulpwood trucks in the upper stretches of the network; finally, the last leg, icing on the cake, the Grande-Ourse road: dust, bumps, stones, craters, potholes, and washboards. The Americans parked on the slightly angled ground, checked to see if they were still in one piece, then awaited day break. As the Old Man said so well, "Americans respect the sleep of others! A chap from Pennsylvania is allowed to shoot when someone bothers him at night!"

We found the Americans in our yard, early in the morning: three or four off-road vehicles, loaded like mules. The clock showed 5:00 a.m. The Old Man rushed to the door with Benoît on his heels. They hadn't been able to keep still since the previous day.

Still half asleep, the Yankees dragged themselves inside, putting their bones back into place. Those being initiated stared wide-eyed, asking all around, with timid smiles, "Are you open? Where are we now? Is this place open?"

Having driven through a steady procession of dark trees, they still didn't completely believe in the magic of this store surging out of the forest late at night. For a few hours, their civilized confidence had ebbed in the obscurity of the woods. Opening his arms wide, the Old Man thundered, "For you, pals, we're always open. Come in! Come in!"

They were marked by a slight stiffness, a subtle wariness of the gait. They walked as though in a conquered country, in enemy territory, guarding their rear, wearing wide-brimmed hats and sunglasses, chewing fine cigars and shivering in the morning; they were American. The Old Man offered rounds of fresh strong coffee, in real cups if you please, no *styrofoam* between us. Many knew him well and hailed him happily, comforted by this initial contact. Regulars who came up once or twice a season, saving all year to treat themselves to this trip in fish country. They weren't millionaires, but small investors who'd started with nothing, having grown relatively prosperous through hard work, and remaining sufficiently familiar with being hard up to not disown their origins. They shook the Old Man's hand, greeting him with heartfelt "How've you been, old sucker?" And he, the familiar face in this unknown territory, puffed out his chest, finally turning his back on this miserable village barely floating above the mud of its rancour.

As far as business was concerned, however, it was a completely different story. When these guys headed to the woods, they outfitted themselves as though the next war had been scheduled for their holidays. The previous day, the Old Man had made me fill a plexiglass window with an entire assortment of colourful baubles bristling with fish-hooks. Expensive for the most part, they rattled entrancingly when shaken. The Americans converged on the display, handling a few baubles, tossing a few of the most promising lures onto the counter to complement their tackle. But sales remained well below forecasts. They already had all the trinkets needed to confront the unfathomable.

America's large fortunes, the Old Man liked to repeat, were built on gasoline and the consumption deriving from it. The previous day, the Surgaz company's tank truck had generously irrigated the subsoil around the store, and the fuel pumps stood in the light like stelae ready to spit out smoke and gas. Benoît was the head pump attendant. While the Old Man made the Southerner's drool with stories of local abundance (shoals of walleye piled so high they came out of the water, hefty pike whose eyes you might poke out just by dipping the propeller, a huge bear who'd sharpened his claws on every healthy tree in the region), Benoît was on duty by the window. His protruding eyes suddenly widened. I edged up near him to peak over his shoulder.

A vehicle with Pennsylvania plates had pulled up in front of the lead-free gas pump. A chap wearing a long sportsman's cap emerged, and stood facing the pumps, a little stooped, holding a camera. He vaguely resembled a pilgrim praying before a row of menhirs. It was a while before I understood that the fellow was immortalizing with film the numbers on the pump's gauge. Of course, Grande-Ourse gas prices were astronomical because of the distance. But Benoît marked the occasion. He valued all of this a great deal.

"He'll at least have that to show his friends...." I said to console him.

The way he agreed told me this would be another long day for him.

"They even bring their own gas!"

The Old Man groaned, incredulous, gently knocking his head against the walls.

"How can an honest businessman make any profit? They even carry their own gas!"

The general tendency was for them to take precautions against the hazards of the local economy. The Americans let their host country take care of the wildlife, but preferred making provisions for everything touching their comfort. On this road which, past the village, kept winding northwards another fifty or so kilometres, vehicles crammed with gear hauled trailers where forty-five gallon drums rocked softly with the bumps. Hiccuping and belching blue smoke, the wheezing machine stormed up the overpass. The foothills of Kilimanjaro wouldn't have been more of a challenge.

That Saturday, there was a non-stop procession. The general store was only a stop along the road, and people often forgot to do the honours. Mr. Administrator's concept was shattered. Other hosts, located higher up along the shores of the large reservoir, attracted fishermen in a hurry to drop their lines. They preferred plywood camps to the ghost town cottages offering CITY COMFORT IN THE MIDDLE OF NATURE. Waters there were more bountiful. To be honest, Grande-Ourse's immediate surroundings had long ago been cleaned out of any legitimate aspirant to the record books.

Collapsed, head in hands, the Old Man understood, he certainly did, his American friends.

"They'll get their nice Evinrudes stolen in the village! You can't leave anything at the edge of a lake around here! An Apache will take off with it, then Legris will syphon your gas!"

The weight of years suddenly caught up with him, and he let out, in a voice that was the essence of disillusionment, "I'm through, young fellas.... Through! It's my last summer here, guaranteed! I'm through...."

Benoît had heard that speech hundreds of times, knowing it by heart right to the end. When the Old Man, to complete his act, began to juggle with the fantasy so dear to him, which he contemplated with affection like an old mistress, concerning the pontoon he'd buy one day. It would be a spacious platform he'd transform into a genuine aquatic lounge, with deck chairs and a built-in bar, ice-filled coolers for the fish those gentlemen would catch continuously, simply pivoting on their well-padded chairs as though they were still seated behind one of those desks where they run an entire conglomerate. Yes, the Old Man would build himself a clientele, a real one, this time, golden pensioners, people of private means and heads of empires who'd open the floodgates of their opulence for him, and the Old Man would then be far from Grande-Ourse, living much higher up, on the shores of the large reservoir, and limitless horizons would open before his pontoon covered in filthy-rich American fishermen.

He withdrew for a short nap. We could rest easy. When the Old Man said he was *through*, the emphasis of the assertion seemed to spin him around like a stripped screw inside a nut.

On Victoria Day Monday, Donald Big-Arms showed up at the store completely drunk. He'd just gotten off the train, helped by a slight nudge from the conductor. His right fist was bandaged. All hell had broken loose in Sans-Terre, he confided modestly. The Old Man had been alerted and rushed in. Spotting the Indian gesticulating, he looked at him from the depths of his despondency, solemn, seeming to say: one more nail in my cross. Go ahead. Bring them on. A guy from Pennsylvania would take out his gun. Bring on some Indians.

Donald Big-Arms informed me that a large American had laughed at him and said he was dirty. If this were hard to deny after three days of partying, it still wasn't something to tell him. I could see the violence going back up his arms, filling his huge fists.

"Next time, you'll see.... Next time."

With no transition, he struck a shelf with a heavy blow, sending three ketchup bottles tumbling down. Benoît rushed over to pick them up, furious. "Hey! That'll do!"

Donald Big-Arms looked at him, and Benoît appeared less anxious to make his intentions clear. The Old Man didn't even bat an eyelid. In the face of this new snub, he seemed ready for the worst. He gave into the laws of adversity with limp gratitude. But a shock suddenly brought him back to life. His face lit up and, while the Indian examined the deep gashes in his hands with detachment, he scurried towards the door. "Crazy Sam! Oh Boy! Crazy Sam! You old bastard!"

"He's one of the gang," Donald breathed into my face.

The newcomer looked rather old, with his triangular head covered in white curls, weather-beaten face, several-day-old beard, and eyes surrounded by diverse wrinkles. The whole array was shaded by the inevitable cowboy hat pulled down over his forehead. He lifted his hat with a flick of his finger and the men embraced ruggedly. At first blush, Crazy Sam suited his nickname: his gaze was a little crazed, livid and quirky; you never knew whether it was focused on you, fell a little short or if, on the contrary, it went over your head, losing itself in the distance.

"Certainly a little cracked," I said, affecting a polite cheerfulness.

The Old Man wrapped his arm around him and made the

introductions. The hand, strangely cold, rooted me on the spot for an instant, while the Old Man launched into an ode to his friend. "This is a good customer! A real good customer, boys! Crazy Sam has been coming here, to Grande-Ourse, for at least twelve years! Old Sam's never missed a season! Comes up in his Jeep, light as a feather, and has a trailer permanently parked at Lac du Fou. Buys everything at the store! Everything!"

Crazy Sam's conduct certainly deserved a certificate for good behaviour. The Old Man plunged his free hand straight into Crazy Sam's pocket and howled, at the height of euphoria, "Everything in his pockets, nothing in his hands! A real good customer, I tell you! Not the kind to drag a forty-five gallon drum from the United States.... Crazy Sam understands the economy!"

The Old Man had just been revived, and was wildly enthusiastic. Crazy Sam was his kind of tourist: once rich, and now just about ruined (no one knew it yet), but always extravagant. A former marine who'd been a magnate before going bonkers, he was now easing into early retirement by writing in-depth articles on hunting and fishing for specialized magazines. He and the Old Man were a nice couple, two complementary individuals: the naive rich man and the clever skinflint.

I stared at the newcomer intensely, while he glanced at us with his interior drift. His eyes floated above his gaze like two corks over the waves.

We heard a booming sound behind us. Donald Big-Arms, whom everyone had forgotten, had given another blow on the upright of a shelf, and more ketchup bottles came crashing down.

❧

After supper, weighed down by a pair of those hamburgers patented by the Old Man, I went down by the lake to stretch my legs. The weather was crisp, the lake rippled and sombre. A gaggle of alert geese glided along its surface behind the hotel. Every year, they lingered on the lake, prolonging their migratory pause; it was said they'd then place themselves under the protection of Jacques Boisvert, the pilot. More than once, he'd nearly beheaded some boater who'd gotten a little too close to his winged brood.

The generator saturated the low sky with its serpentine

vapours. As long as it burned diesel, it remained the symbol of the village's vitality, of its refusal of cartographical euthanasia. Farther on, the setting sun set fire to the hangar's sheet metal.

My legs, aching from inactivity, took me to the other end of the village. I picked up the pace when I passed by the hotel. My fascination with that den of depravity was equalled only by the terror I felt at the prospect of going in without invitation. I went down a sandy trail which opened onto the dryness of a spruce forest; that's how I accidentally stumbled on the cemetery.

It was disarmingly simple and poignantly small: a crude enclosure covering a hundred-or-so metres, with a roughly built cross at the centre, and graves lined up on both sides of the perimeter. A rather basic wire fence guarded the sleep of the dead. I opened the pitiful gate and walked into the enclosure.

The tombstones were scattered. Many graves were only marked with small rudimentary crosses, completely crooked and engraved with laconic epitaphs. I slowly walked around. The soft grass and dry scrub had been pulled out. The mineral soil was bare and the heavy sand seemingly wanted to hold back every step.

Cemeteries are usually fertile areas where rich lawns and flowerbeds thrive, thanks to the humus of decomposing bodies. But the soil here was sterile as the back of a dune, and the enclosure looked like an arena. I lingered over the inscriptions. Any soil filled with corpses seems attractive and studying societies through their final resting places is informative. In Grande-Ourse, industrialization still hadn't reached the market of the dead. It was a far cry from society life. A raven cawed in the distance, and I thought of those platforms where Indians once placed their stiffs, abandoning them to the vultures.

Closer to thee, my Lord.

Among the meagre monuments, a peculiar corner quickly caught my eye. A rectangle of yellowed grass covering the exact area of a grave. In short, it was imported grass: two or three rolls of greenery which, in suburbs, are spread like carpets over freshly tilled soil. Tufts of yellow weeds clung to this patch of dried and crackled grass. A faded pink floret tilted its soft corolla over the site. The cynical sand, the patient mineral, triumphed all around, matter's inert mask. This corpse was alone among his peers in not having been forgotten. With the help of vegetation, a semblance of life persisted beneath this final facade. He'd been honoured with a beautifully crafted grey headstone, decorated with a modest painting: a forest and water scene filled with fish and game. A canoe floated over the water's chalky course, and its occupant was armed.

You could say epitaphs are the most finished of literary forms. I was looking at something very succinct. For summaries of the hereafter, numbers speak best.

Two dates: 1956-1975. Life is a simple parenthesis, we are sandwich-souls. Roméo Flamand, dead before his twentieth birthday. *Roméo Flamand. Shot in the back.* That's what should've been written. He'd barely reached manhood when he was buried in this large sand patch. The stone, with its rounded top, looked like a milepost the road to Grande-Ourse had led to over the last twelve years.

I felt strange, standing there motionless. I knew the Indian still wielded his axe beneath this bed of sorrow and this wilted flower. You could've rolled up the grass and taken it away, blown on the flower to extinguish its waning bloom. But you couldn't have done the same with the past smouldering beneath the rebel grass, its roots sinking into blood.

❧

Trying to find my way back, I detoured over a hill to get a bearing and stumbled on another kind of cemetery: the village scrap yard. I decided to drift among the bodies for a while. Lacking a permanent police force, Grande-Ourse had acquired a reputation as an ideal hideaway for stolen vehicles. By limiting their travels to the immediate area, people could openly drive around without licence plates. But vehicles setting out on this Calvary rarely lasted long enough to hope to make the trip back. The car graveyard was densely populated.

I suddenly stopped before the remains of a hydroplane. The aircraft's tail, deprived of its stabilizers, stood vertically, supported by the crushed cabin that formed its plinth. The paint on the fuselage was peeling, having carried off part of the lettering and identification number. I couldn't help whistling in admiration. The plane seemed to have crashed right there. I was sure the pilot had survived; my only explanation being an impression: the structure standing above the cockpit exuded a defiance of death.

I headed back to the lake, but a densely thicketed embankment blocked my way. Lowering my head, I tried to weave through, but a root caught my foot and I nosedived, landing on my elbows, tumbling downwards while branches savagely whipped me in passing. I landed hard at the edge of a clearing, stunned and nearly out cold.

A purpling sky filled my eyes. The glistening blade of a large scythe swung over me like a monstrous wing. The setting sun sparkled blood-coloured reflections on it. I could see nothing else: a long curved blade filled my horizon. Dull and icy laughter greeted my astonishment. I rose to my knees; a man stood before me. His silvery hair betrayed his age, but his body was vigorous. He had a wizened and hard appearance, a sun-baked face, a very white smile beaming with sweat and sarcasm. He again burst out laughing. I became aware of my grotesque position, kneeling in front of him, and stood up. He held his scythe with both hands, with instinctive off-handedness. I couldn't help but move back when he swayed it slightly.

I'd surprised him while he was clearing what could be called a yard. Wild stems proliferated near a mobile home at the edge of the lake. Farther on, hydroplanes dangled between the sky and a reflection of the forest on the perfectly still water. The man looked around, breathed, and quietly said, "Damned underbrush, grows back every spring! Oh, well.... If it wasn't that, it'd be something else...."

He gracefully twisted his wrists, and a tiny section of greenery flew towards the tip of my feet. I held back a start, remaining calm. For a moment, he seemed only vaguely aware of my presence. Then he lowered his tool, observing me with interest.

"What are you doing here?"

The tone was sharp, but not excessively hostile.

I was about to explain that my sense of direction was defective when he cut me off.

"And who exactly are you?"

He again burst out laughing, as I opened my mouth. Then, no longer paying attention to me, he resumed his mowing, in large fluid movements, supple and relentless. It looked easy. At the end of one harmonious sweep, I had to break into a dance step to dodge the sharp point. He moved away, turning his back to me. A wooden sign on the house's pediment bore the inscription, BOISVERT AIR SERVICE.

Pared back by budgetary restraint, the train consisted of one locomotive and two cars. When I climbed aboard, the ticket inspector discreetly pointed me to the back. Later, during the Tocqueville stop, in the middle of the night, the same man directed the Indians to the other side. A barely enforced segregation, a mild apartheid which seemed completely natural to the train's staff. You didn't need first and second classes: everything was subtly suggested. Aboriginal families, the mother nearly always accompanied by a swarm of children, and the husband, more often than not cheered up by recent drinking, made rather touching groups. They'd likely disturb the rest of the few solitary and sleepy business travellers whose heads nodded gently over the benches, in the quiet car reserved for Whites.

Drawn out of my drowsiness by a stop, I sat up and looked out at Tocqueville, a mid-sized industrial town pressed against the Company mill, beneath a smelly and blazing fire. The Saint-Christophe Hotel's tired neon sign could be seen in front of the station across the street. Indians getting off the train often went over directly, placing themselves in the protection of the patron saint of travellers, only leaving the sordid bar to climb into one of the large cars, heading for new adventures. There as well, racial compartmentalization was the rule. Boozers from both camps shared parallel haunts and habits.

I'd had to go to Montreal to deal with a family obligation (a wedding on the eve of Pentecost). Afterwards, I'd wandered a little through the city, sad and unsettled. No sentimental ties held me back and I was relieved to again have to quit the avid and glowing metropolis. I was returning to the simplicity of Grande-Ourse, to the complexity of its desires.

Since my train was only leaving Monday, I continued to roam the next day, detouring to the *Café Central*. Musings on tradition wandered through my head, and I'd barely slept. A chap was seated at the bar to my right, flopped on his elbows, busying himself with familiar rantings. No doubt pushing thirty, the two deep ridges stamping bitterness on each side of his mouth made him look much older. He was drinking brandy, and an empty stool lay between us.

"This is my own bottle," he proudly explained. "Yeah, because around here, you see, they don't carry this brand, they order it just for me...."

I struggled to ignore him. He got animated when he learned I was from Grande-Ourse, and going back. He told me he was working on a plan for a book inspired, as though coincidentally, by a story from that region. He didn't have to explain, I knew what he meant.

"You know," he whispered, leaning towards me, "one thing's always bothered me about that...."

"One thing?"

"Yeah, the guy, you know, the young guy who took the rap...."

"Yeah?"

"Well, turns out he...."

I looked around for the barmaid. She was busy flirting at the other end of the bar. Pivoting a few more degrees, my badgerer continued, "I think eleven bullets is a whole lot for one single magazine...."

I shrugged with an attentive and detached expression.

"From what I could gather, you're not the only one who believes that...."

"Oh, really?"

"You want to write a detective novel?"

"Maybe...."

"How's it moving along?"

"One step forward.... One step back...."

He mused for a moment.

"I don't get it!"

"What's that?"

I hadn't been able to avoid showing annoyance. He was vexed, taking his time to answer.

"The subject ...," he said slowly. "Or rather, the predicate ... the one found guilty is only the predicate.... I already have a subject and a predicate, but still have to find a verb."

He was breathing hard, both excited and weary. His confusion bothered me and all I could do was wish him luck. He exhaled smoke from his cigarette with unusual strength.

I gestured impatiently at the waitress, who seemed to be ignoring me. My neighbour then hailed her in a language I didn't recognize and, before I was able to intervene, she brought over his personal bottle.

"You're going to taste some of this, pal...."

He poured the rich mahogany liquid and, as he tilted the bottle in front of me, I read the label that shone beneath the streaks of light: Christian Brothers.

Then felt fire on my tongue during the night.

The train finally got under way. As we were about to leave Tocqueville and plunge into the forest, I drifted into the stream of my thoughts. I remembered a story I'd read in the papers before leaving about this famous railway: a fight had broken out between an Indian and the train staff one winter night bristling with black spruce, many kilometres from any inhabited area. Beer bottles had been used, and the miscreant passenger had been finally subdued and tossed off the train unceremoniously. Besides, this little train stopped rather frequently in the middle of nowhere, to let off a group of sportsmen or take on a band of Aboriginals who'd lit a fire along the tracks as a signal.

As the train pulled out of the small northern town, Cowboy and Karate Kid walked up the aisle, stopping beside me. Interrupting my daydream, they dropped onto the bench facing me. With no preamble, Cowboy spoke quickly, in a low voice, "D'you have twenty bucks to lend us? For the train guy."

"The ...?"

"We each give him ten bucks and he leaves us alone."

I looked at them stupidly. Not fully understanding what this meant, I only shrugged. This refusal, whose expression was perhaps too vague, reassured them. Cowboy sank into his seat, Karate Kid as well, while I tried to fill the silence with a terse account of my urban problems. I noticed the Kid had a nice black eye.

"Things get rough in the bars?"

"They always want to fight."

I handed my ticket to the conductor when he came around. He then leaned over the two Indians, who looked at me with confidence, and waited. The railway employee, suspicious, glanced at me then focused on my counterparts.

"You don't have your tickets," he bellowed sullenly.

His tone made me react. I took out my wallet but, still hesitating, opted for a compromise, pulling out only ten dollars, telling Cowboy apologetically, "It's all I have, pal."

Don't know if he believed me, but the shame of this cowardice would follow me the rest of the trip. I felt that the trace of defiance I discovered in myself was ancient and well anchored, that I'd have a long way to go before shoving it aside and tearing it from my heart. Cowboy neglectfully stretched out his hand, snatched the bill and showed it to the conductor. An official admonition followed, after which the ticket puncher disappeared swearing to God he'd be pleased to toss out this vermin at the first opportunity. But his fingers, meanwhile, had clenched the ten-dollar bill. My friends were smiling again, seeming to feel that ten dollars was a more-than-adequate kickback in the circumstances.

Via Rail forgot the formalities and, to celebrate the success, the two fare-dodgers invited me to take part in a small ritual, well-known for its bonding virtues. We stepped outside to get better ventilation, forming a circle at the juncture of the two cars, amid the dizzying racket of the elastic anteroom, a nodal point where the colliding waves merged. Cowboy left the group for a moment, disappearing into the other car. He came back with a girlfriend who had a full bust, a beaming smile and jeans that stretched over well-rounded buttocks. She moved the whole lot like a professional tease. I'd often seen her with Cowboy and Karate Kid. Judith must've been nearly twenty-years old, and already had a girth likely to put any scale out of whack. Following a winter on the reserve, she was returning to live with her mother in a cabin located some distance from Grande-Ourse.

She immediately took a huge shining to me. With perverse complacency, I already could see myself squeezed by the fat girl in that infernal accordion.

Even before I first met Indians, I fully suspected that we'd inherited from their elders the custom of smoking in a circle. A childish habit, but always a good way to befriend your neighbour. The yellowish cylinder danced between our fingers and we passed it around, moving from side to side to keep our balance. Its quality was very average. Above a certain latitude, you smoke what you can. I looked at Judith through the joint smoke and, at that precise moment, she was extremely real, as it were.

Cowboy must've read my thoughts; he said, expelling the dope from his lungs, "Judith went to see her boyfriend."

I remained quiet and the Kid added without hesitation that the boyfriend was none other than Big Alexandre, staying in a halfway house at the moment. The list of his misdeeds, I was told, included having broken into the general store twice.

No one spoke for quite some time. I furtively observed Cowboy, this secret Cowboy, his round cheeks pumping our communal joint. The lucidity brought on by the drug allowed me to penetrate into the shadow of that face shaped like a full moon where the melancholy and folly of his race went hand in hand. He suddenly started coughing uncontrollably.

Karate Kid opened his mouth and eyes that were now frenzied and protruding, like a fish hooked in the mouth, death already taking hold of his body. He was getting emotional, and becoming comical.

"You're a friend, Gilles," he said gravely.

I pretended not to have heard and, now at a loss for words, turned around, leaning towards the window which sucked in the bracing air. I exhaled a plume of smoke into the cold air devoured by the metal, and what I saw took my breath away. A long stretch of countryside paraded by against the train's undulating side, and beyond the tight rows of spruce gathered like mourners beside the railway. And above, oh above, a flurry of frozen stars filled the ether with its milky light. The ink had receded everywhere, space had vanished, millions of light years had changed into confetti for my sole pleasure. I was becoming a puff of smoke. Head tilted back, as the sky filled with the satin stream of the aurora borealis, mouth open, throat burning, I was inhaling this astounding night, like Brel's sailors blow their nose in the stars and, intoxicated by the benevolent power of the locomotive, speeding along its iron furrow

like a prehistoric mole, I understood that the real night was here, at
the bottom of this large gold-bearing cauldron and in these earthly
smokes mixed with the amoebic masses of the galaxies, and that I
was already a part of everything that would happen under the
darkness from now on. The train howled as it swept me along
towards the north of the night.

2

SAINT-JEAN-BAPTISTE day

GILLES IS ON DUTY THAT NIGHT. *Hanging glasses upside-down above his head. Sometimes, a drop falls on his forehead, with an impact of lead. He fills other glasses. Full glass, empty glass. Full glass. The men are thirsty. Full glass, empty glass. Rinsed and suspended to that large light above his head. Another drop hits his forehead. An already high forehead, which he wipes. It's hot. To make yourself invisible. A glass barman.*

His mother has gone to his sister's in Montreal. Squabbling's in the air. She usually takes care of the hotel. The Americans are shooting pool at the back of the hall. Drinking since late afternoon and blind drunk. At the other end of the room, Roméo Flamand and his girlfriend quietly sip drinks. Flamand, his girlfriend. Flamand deflowered Gisèle when she was sixteen; she's already near the peak of her charms. Gilles looks at her and sponges his forehead. Flamand orders two more beers. His long hair is very dark and shiny, tied back in a pony tail. He breathes like the bellows of a forge. His chest seems made of copper. Gilles keeps a low profile, is flattened and transparent. A glass barman. He looks ahead. Raoul Legris, hairy and evil-eyed, is leaning on the bar. Straddling a stool, he crackles banknotes on the bar. American money. He pivots, turns towards Flamand and Gisèle, over there.

Another drop hits Gilles, sliding along the arch of his eyebrow, plunging over his orbit, going around a nostril, then following the curve of a dimple, softly moistening the corner of his closed lips. The men are drinking at the back of the hall. Full glass, empty glass. Full glass. Americans playing American billiards. Gilles is in charge of everything. His father, as well, went fishing this morning with a trollop from Montreal who has lots of money and an impotent husband. An old couple that's loaded. He's stingy and wasted; she's decent and generous. She's overflowing. Full glass, empty glass. A full stomach. Boisvert promised to return by nightfall. Gossips say that when he guides up there, it's because the woman has the requisite charms. It's July and Gilles is hot. These walls and that half-open door. Balls collide on the pool table, and the barman sponges his forehead.

❧

With Saint-Jean-Baptiste Day drawing near, the Old Man said he had to make a trip for supplies. He actually intended to get a decent load of beer. Rail transportation was too expensive for such imposing consignments. The Old Man would head to town and rent a truck, loading it with enough beer to set a Guinness record. He'd been talking about the deed for a good fortnight when, sometime in mid-June, he decided to go into action.

That morning, at the front of the store, we were a small and sleepy group. Benoît looked at us tirelessly with glazed eyes. The Muppet emerged by intervals from another station in the cold room. Big Ben was trying to hitch his perfect rotundity to some sufficiently solid support, repeating to whoever would listen, "Oh, the sun, the beautiful sun, Ooh."

Near the entrance, Legris showed off by fingering the perimeter of his most recent wound, sniggering up his sleeve. He wanted to tell everyone that, although he was as gregarious as the others down deep, also needing to hear a human voice in the morning, he'd never be fooled by the old swine's play-acting. The latter, at that very moment, was exerting himself among them, rebuking Legris, "You were seen hanging around Crazy Sam's trailer, you devil!"

Legris expectorated a gob of undefinable hue. The Old Man was walking towards him, hand raised, but the swipe got lost in swirls of luminescent particles created by the rising sun through the window pane. Legris didn't even bother protecting himself.

"Crazy Sam promised he'd hire me as a guide this year, yes sir!"

The Old Man sighed. Oh, he personally knew the solution to all their problems! Only thing needed was for his advice to be taken. Before these few captive souls in the grips of boredom, his words defied destiny, addressing Grande-Ourse's shaky posterity above all their heads. He was on the verge of dizziness as he spoke, like someone walking at the edge of a cliff. He spoke ceaselessly. Everyone knew he'd disappear like the simple iridescence on water drops at the first stop. He'd sometimes leave a phrase dangling almost as he'd started it, picking it up again, seeking what followed, soon looking for what he ought to have sought first, looking for himself all the while in the gaping void that swallows bankrupt memories. His entire world suddenly sank into a swirl of silence. He was already dying a little between his words.

The Muppet emerged from the cold room, shaking a head that could barely be distinguished from a neck as wrinkled as an old shoe. He said to the Old Man that he ought to hurry and bring his truck back, since the beavers were really busy around the small bridge at the Seven Mile Point, threatening to flood the road at any moment. The Muppet hadn't failed to notice changes in the water level, nor the distressingly low quantity of our beer supplies.

The Old Man gave neither a positive nor a negative reply. The only beaver he cared about was the one stamped on the nickels he could pocket. He disappeared and immediately returned, holding a 30-30, ashen-faced with rage, cursing the great boss of the confederal bestiary, that damned emblem of Canada, I won't stand for it, and that, henceforth, this meant war! He commandingly placed the weapon in my hands, pushed a khaki cap down over my eyes, and ordered me to follow him.

Legris sniggered and Big Ben said: "Oh, Oh," and an accordion's squeal could be heard coming from Mr. Muppet's neck.

The Old Man insisted on driving a precious-looking vehicle along these totally broken-down roads. A Dacia, made in Romania no doubt to travel over peaceful and rustic landscapes. It hadn't cost much, but its eccentric shape clashed with this hostile territory and its occupant was the laughing stock of the village.

I climbed aboard and, laboriously clutching in, the Old Man got us under way. A favourable incline immediately helped the

departure's success and the movement that followed. My driver
missed a shift on the large hill, the engine stalled and the vehicle
began to back up while the Old Man looked for the brakes.
Bystanders were slapping their thighs in front of the store.

"Damned beavers!" the Old Man grumbled.

After wrestling with the stick shift, he finally managed to get
us back on track, and we reached the scene of the showdown at a
snail's pace. The road narrowed abruptly there; two dull-surfaced
lakes swelled on either side, as though anxious to meet, their waters
marbled with foam. A brook, hidden by the small bridge, joined
them. The structure dated from the days of the Company, and
foresters were in theory responsible for its maintenance. It was now
on the road to decrepitude and wavelets had already started lapping
the narrow deck's belly. Looking worried, the Old Man leaned on a
pillar where crude notches registered changes in the water level. He
immediately concluded that the suspects were extremely active and
I awaited the launch of a visibly imminent punitive action, weapon
against my shoulder. For the moment, we settled on pacing up and
down the bridge's surroundings.

"Maybe we should look for their lodge," I suggested in a
low voice.

"Hmmmm...."

"We'd have to come back and lie in wait at night, at dusk...."

"Hmmm...."

The Old Man seemed reluctant to leave the road. He
shrugged, pretending to believe that our mere armed presence, at
the edge of their domain, would give the highway sappers a
beneficial fright. I was going to venture another tactical
consideration, but the Old Man stopped me with a gesture. He'd
spotted a can of Budweiser at the edge of the road, grabbed it, and
placed it at some distance in front of a sand knoll.

I was holding an electrifying object, a genuine legend of the
North-American arsenal: a 30-30 Winchester, the ancient rifle of
cowboys. Trying to control my breathing, I raised the weapon, a
gesture seemingly conscious and mechanical, as though controlled
from far away. Put one knee to the ground and the heavy killing
device seemed made of silence in my arms. I pulled the trigger and
the projectile raised a small plume of dust a good metre from the

can, which rapidly dissipated, while a frightful tearing froze the forest. On my second try, the bullet pierced the sand one inch below the target which went flying vertically through the air, intact. It was already an improvement. I could see the gash on the side of the dune. But the Old Man prodded me to be off. The peal of the discharge had been enough for him and he seemed to think it would be enough for the beavers as well. The small family must've been mocking us under its roof of branches, in the musty shadows filled with the flash of yellow incisors. With the rifle on my knees, I was pensive and vaguely dissatisfied, filled with a strange fascination for what had just happened, as though I'd stepped onto the threshold of an ancient and important discovery.

❦

Grande-Ourse lived under the sign of hope. The whole town played the lottery. These people, so quick to disagree about all possible subjects, would mysteriously stick together when the Old Man, an unparalleled leader wherever money was concerned, organized a collective participation in the 6/49 lottery. Everyone hurried to give him their contribution. Most, however, quickly learned to have their arms twisted. When time came to collect dues, Legris and Moreau invariably had gone fishing, the Old Man having just missed them. He railed against these evasions whose perpetrators, he claimed, didn't hesitate to sacrifice the common good to their immediate interest. He'd become the accredited publicist of fortune. It was a marvel to see him going through his newspaper to find the section with the winning numbers, clipping it feverishly, pinning it to the store's bulletin board. He'd spend long moments contemplating those naked numbers, musing about their power to create dreams. A simple and secret process, like setting a trap: people placed their future in the hands of a half-dozen sure numbers hurled through the emptiness of uncertain immensity, knocking wood while they awaited. It seemed that the 6/49 was the only thing that could still save the village.

Benoît had another image of the jackpot. A spirited and energetic woman would step off the train one day, and fall in love with him as she entered the store. She'd never leave Grande-Ourse. And he'd rebuild the crummy village with his bare hands, realizing an economic miracle for which he'd be acclaimed as a genuine hero. For Big Ben, the jackpot was the huge black bear he'd been doggedly tracking for over a week; listening to him, it must've been the Sasquatch's brother at the very least. He'd devote a good half of his days to him, borrowing the Outfitters' truck for the mission, driving off at the majestic speed of a knight straddling his mount. Benoît would protest, "He's going to hide in the woods, so he can twiddle his thumbs!"

But the Old Man emphasized the anticipated profits this amazing hide would represent when shown to the Americans on their arrival, with the innocent remark befitting the circumstances, "One of the smallest bagged this year, isn't that right Big Ben, pal?"

"Ooh Oh Oh Oh yes Oh Oh yes."

Every night, Big Ben returned empty-handed, flopping down in front of the store, oblivious to the swarms of blackflies bumping into the thickness of his fat hide. He sighed powerfully, looking for a comfortable position on the cement stairs. His exhaustion was supposed to convince us the chase was no picnic.

"So, Big Ben, pal? How'd the bear hunting go?"

The Old Man's attitude showed he was ready to believe any seamless yarn.

"Oh Oh the big Bear! Oh! Ooh! Followed the tracks! Oh the damned big Bear! Oh not far! Tomorrow! Oh tomorrow the damned big Bear!"

It was always impossible to learn more about the roving bedside rug. The beast existed where it had to, sheltered from imaginations. Everyone here had a plan, a fantasy, a mental edifice more or less in the process of collapsing.

Jacques Boisvert hovered above the fray. His wonderful arrogance made him elusive and he was unlike most of his peers. Their solid parochialism invariably brought them back, after a few wrong-way turns down one-ways, from the big-city streets to their tiny point of origin on the map, while Boisvert allowed himself outings into society. His Beaver gave him a perspective that necessarily relativized Grande-Ourse in his mind. Based on Lac Légaré with his hydroplanes, he'd take nature-sampling enthusiasts farther north than any of his immediate competitors. Boisvert spent winters down south, living the high life, chasing women and drumming up future customers among the powdered noses in Miami. High society is where he'd set his winter trap line. Since his wife's death, he'd brought more than one poor little thing back to Grande-Ourse who, quickly disillusioned, set sail after a few months.

The last one to date, his official chick, as the Old Man would've said, was Brigitte. He'd harpooned her one night when he'd gone on an epic drunk in a St. Denis Street bar, where his transient loathing of celibacy had taken him. Jacques Boisvert could look quite the gentleman when he wanted. Although well into his fifties, he looked dapper, and thought highly of himself. And he needed a woman to run the hotel, since he never set foot there. Haunted by bad memories, he preferred to concentrate on his sky. With shrewd brevity, he'd told the lady about his intense and untamed life over in his fiefdom, nestled amid pines, firs and spruces sprinkled with incidental fetuses of humanity.

Brigitte was thirty years old, had an iron grip, and a heart-shaped face. Even Moreau, it was said, behaved in front of her. Boisvert was still peerless in his ability to choose a woman. And, moreover, able to fly after drinking twenty-six ounces of scotch. No one had ever seen him drunk. It must be said that, up there, space for zigzagging was plentiful.... He always landed his Beaver like a water lily. He crashed only once (which explained the shell I'd seen in the scrap yard), getting out without a scratch, of course.

Every time the character's name was brought up, the Old Man had trouble containing himself. An old, carefully maintained rivalry existed between them, fuelled by the pranks of the one, and the swaggering of the other. It was a battle to the finish between the perennial braggart and the man of action, the big talker and the terrible doer.

That day, amid feverish preparations for leaving, Boisvert burst into the store. I was posted behind the counter and, with his dark stare lingering on me as though neglectfully, I thanked fate for placing me out of his way. Hérode narrowly escaped the pounding of the large work boots, taking refuge in the arms of Admiral Nelson who stood at attention nearby. Boisvert, supple and straight, headed for the Old Man, rolling his knotty shoulders. He stood in front of the grandfather, fists on his hips, and summed up what he really thought. "You can't cross the Seven Mile Bridge with a heavy truck...."

The tone was scathing and irrefutable. He'd already turned around and was heading away. The Old Man's reply caught up to him at the doorstep. "I know that road like the back of my hand!"

Boisvert turned around theatrically, and said jeeringly, "You probably do know the back of your hand well.... But we're talking about beavers here, not rats!"

He gave free rein to his mirth. The Old Man, who'd paled, pointed a spirited digit at him, "I know that road inside out. And I know what I'm talking about!"

Boisvert came back towards him, very calm, plunking his lean face two inches from the Old Man's mug. He was totally calm when he asked, "Do you know what cutting off the road means right in the middle of fishing season, you old fool?"

He leaned forward a little more. By closing his jaws sharply, he could've bitten off his counterpart's nose. "I fully realize you no longer have much to lose here.... But I'm waiting for customers! And they have to use that damned road!"

This time, he headed for the exit, the scent of a threat wafting in his wake. "You'll be answerable if you don't change your mind."

No longer bothering with the Old Man, who was on his heals hiccuping with indignation, he stopped beside me and quickly examined the visible part of me. He grabbed my arm without much tact, kneading my biceps. My right hand opened under pressure from his calloused fingers, and he examined my palm with disdain.

I was no longer breathing.

Boisvert blurted, for the benefit of a worried Benoît. "Will you please tell me where you dug up this one? Another salad eater, eh? Did flies fix you up like that, pal?"

With a sigh, he let my arm drop. "Well. We might still be able to do something with you."

He was already outside, pulling me along with a gesture. I protested feebly, but he wasn't listening. Benoît was alarmed, letting out mechanical yelps, "Hey there! Hey there! Hey there!"

Boisvert didn't let him get a word in. "Seems the beavers are doing some damage at the Seven Mile Bridge. Since you're already going to test the bridge, I hope you won't prevent me from giving them a little trouble on top of it!"

I followed him to his truck. The only resistance Benoît now offered was the comical puffing of his cheeks. Boisvert took out a hefty wood handle with a hook at the end from the rear compartment of his vehicle.

"Have you ever handled a gaff, son?"

"Oh, gaffs hold no secrets for me...."

His was huge, resembling a whaler's harpoon. Over there, the kitten had just rid himself of Admiral Nelson, and was sprinting towards the train station. The Old Man shot out of the store like a bombshell, hopping after him, waving his bony arms like plier jaws. The Admiral was hot on their heels in no time, while the Old Man skated on the crunching sand.

"Get in there, you little Hérode!"

Boisvert got behind the wheel and I sat beside him. He drove off, raising dust, skirting around the gas pumps, nearly flattening this fine crew, restoring his good mood in the process.

❧

The Company man had built a culvert between the two lakes to help drainage. By narrowing the discharge, but allowing the same outflow, the device created an irresistible temptation for beavers. They only had to stack a few branches before the pipe's upstream opening, and bind the whole kit with a little mud that becomes hard as cement. Building a dam here required very little effort. Blocking culverts along the road beside the railway was typical of beavers in the region.

It was cold and damp on the inside. Having to squat as I moved, I had water up to my chin. Thrusting my metal hook towards the channel, I looked like an amphibious rodent. I could hear Boisvert's taunting and muffled voice, "Careful, Big Ben's on the bridge! I can see the pillars bending from here."

Benoît, who'd finally rallied to the effort, had insisted we bring along Big Ben, more as a means of hanging on to an illusion of authority than from a concern to be really useful.

Plying the gaff with great effort, I was trying to break the resistance of the piled materials. Disentangled pieces drifted off like torpedoes, gathering momentum as the gap widened, the current pointing them straight at my head. A fair-sized piece of wood came crashing into my lower lip, which was awash with the water, and I swallowed a good mouthful.

"Harder than punching numbers on a cash register, eh?" exclaimed Boisvert, whose feet must've been somewhere over my head.

"Ooh ...," echoed Big Ben.

I tried to smile, though my jaw was numbed with effort. After being confined to the general store, I felt this swim to be quite refreshing. I definitely preferred the culvert to the cash register's keyboard, finally getting the impression I was taking on the Nordic world's real structure, its massive cohesion, its stubborn and intricate make-up. Hunched up inside this underground drainage pipe, crushed like an Atlas by the steel-toed boot which, above me, pounded the clear side of things, I was waving my Bayard's lance, chilled to the bone, holding my end, standing firm. Boisvert wouldn't have my hide. He'd soon see, up there, what I was made of. As the dam gave way and the gap widened, the imprisoned depths stirred around in the pipe and I hung on to a piece of wreckage like a castaway.

Later, in the afternoon heat, squeezed between the driver and a drowsy Big Ben on the truck's front seat, I gave a start. Boisvert had just said point-blank, "Indian women and their asses give us a lot of trouble around here, right Big Ben, old pal?"

"Well, Ooh."

Big Ben had sprung from the ass of one of those Indian women, but didn't really have an opinion.

The ripped seat scattered patches of stuffing like pollen in the wind. On either side, the forest crackled beneath the June sun.

I smiled naively.

"In grade school," Boisvert said to me, "they teach you that they're monsters, Christian eaters. Then, in your universities, they show you they're good guys, ancestors to the granolas, and that we're the bad guys. Say, in passing, there must be some nice young girls at university.... Oops."

He turned the wheel and the vehicle swerved abruptly. This wasn't enough to avoid the deep crevice winding across half the road like a broad sardonic smile. Boisvert was thrown to the roof, his head pushing in the sheet metal. Knocked off balance by the manoeuvre, Big Ben fell over with all his weight and, without awakening, nailed me to my seat. Boisvert swore and, barely slowing down, got the vehicle back on course just in time to spare us a dip into another lake that loomed out of the forest right then. I heard him grumble that an entire load of gravel would be needed to fill that crevice alone. He was again totally in his element. His swerves became routine along the Grande-Ourse road. I managed to free myself from the half-breed and the gravel road once again filled my view. Jacques Boisvert had just recovered his train of thought. "That's where I found mine! University! To her, I was heaven sent; a little adventure in the far north is precisely what she was dreaming about. Naturally, living up here requires character. She knew the score, as it were."

"Yeah," approved Big Ben, who was now fast asleep.

"Do you know what she was studying before I carried her off? Sexology! Oh! Oh! Needless to say, pal, I taught her to shelve her theories before hopping into bed!"

He was proud of himself.

"What's that?"

The indescribable Dacia had just left Grande-Ourse and was bouncing towards us. Boisvert headed straight for it, narrowly avoiding a frontal collision, and the small van went flying crookedly into the ditch, then jack-knifed back onto the middle of the road, having completely spun around. A turn left us with that image. Through a resounding laugh, Boisvert managed to articulate, "He can't hurt himself seriously at the speed he's going! But he's a public menace and shouldn't be allowed to drive. The pieces he scatters each time are worse than three-headed nails!"

From atop the hill, Grande-Ourse appeared miserable and grumpy beneath its porous roofs and crumbling shingles.

The Old Man's departure left a gaping void in our daily lives. Benoît's silence fell on the premises like a millstone. Generally, with the most taciturn people, you can feel an interior debate going on, an intimate notion under scrutiny. But Benoît's silence exuded a disagreeable impression of totality; it held dominion over all parts of his being. Benoît lacked imagination and imagination is the only excuse for silence.

We could still hear Big Ben's Ohs and Ahs, his Oh yeses and Oh yeahs, and the Yes Yeses that the burning soup, in the kitchen, had soon transformed into Ouch Ouches. But this automatic approval no longer responded to anything and perpetuated itself in a vacuum.

Even if his silence suited me, Benoît occasionally felt some kind of moral obligation to loosen his lips. He also felt the need to fight off the stranglehold of the space condensing within this boundless tranquillity.

"A strange one!" he'd belch as soon as an unidentified car appeared at the village entrance, his arched eyebrows betraying a nascent preoccupation. When two or three vehicles followed each other on the road, he'd rub his hands, feigning to be onto a good deal.

"It'll give us a little jolt...."

He yearned for these modest satisfactions with his entire soul, and you felt like patting him on the back. All Benoît knew was this constant commitment to a business whose destiny had become his own. The only time he'd dared venture into the hotel, overpowered by the insidious corrosion of winter isolation, in the middle of February, Big Alexandre and a crony had broken a window and left with a few provisions, a good part of them liquid. Since then, Benoît had let the Old Man's ferocious example win him over. He became the champion of unwavering vigilance, a loyal second fiddle to the iron rule.

Idleness soon wrought its havoc. We only opposed it in principle. All attempts at reconciliation soon foundered against an imposing yawn. To overcome the silence, Benoît found nothing better than the diagnostic theme which, repeated every possible way, now gave emphasis to all our actions. "Things are dead.... Things are dead...."

The unfailing Crazy Sam alone continued to patronize our establishment. Other Americans would have nothing to do with our services. Neither millionaire nor financial tycoon had shown their face. Only penny pinchers going fishing up north.

To kill time one morning, I honed in on a spider that had settled on the Muppet's shirt collar. Dangling from a translucent thread tied to the large horn-rimmed glasses of its host, the mischievous arachnid had landed on his shoulder as he chatted, naturally unaware of its acrobatics. I delighted in imagining the tiny creature knitting a whole web, neatly tying the poor man, wrapping him like a newborn, mummifying him, allowing us to store him in the basement, beneath pyramids of empty beer cases where he'd be quietly preserved, instead of rotting before us. We could've placed a cannula at the corner of his mouth to provide him a constant supply of alcohol. That coma would've differed very little from his regular life.

Besides, the whole village seemed to have been put on ice. People managed, waited for a spark, the kernel of an event that would shake up the grim routine. From the depths of my hideout, I confusedly felt Grande-Ourse would one day have to take revenge. And was eager to see Jacques Boisvert reappear with his gaffs and his grip. Days when I accompanied him, I'd return dead tired and count my blisters. I'd jot down observations, details and ideas in a notebook to figure and grasp what eluded me, like the coffering in a mine shaft surrounds the black collapsing centre. Sometimes, in late afternoon, my head would tilt back, and before sinking into sleep completely, I'd hear myself snoring. At night, I saw beaver families gnawing at the road like a large trunk, trees stripped of bark, dykes breaking up, lakes emptying like bathtubs, Boisvert toppling like an idol, the village suddenly revealing itself.

☙

Legris tears himself from his stool and returns to the pool table. Around it, four men calculate trajectories. Legris circles them as they circle the slate table. He repeats his litany: Nice shot, pal! Nice shot. That's why we like him. One player regularly pockets the balls. A regular guy. Lanky but muscular. When the coloured spheres scatter at the break, the beam from his blue eyes seems inclined to diffract and follow the course of each one. Blond curls protrude from the cowboy hat worn askew. He's well into his forties. He dispatches an expert combination and heads towards Legris (Nice shot, pal!) to whisper something.

Gilles wipes glasses. He doesn't drink. His glass of milk, at night. Chocolate-chip cookies. Another round! orders the one called Crazy Sam. The others drink from bottles. He pours himself a glass. Gilles wipes his forehead with the same rag he uses on the glasses. Don't look back, show nothing. A drop hits his temple. Soap mixes with his sweat. The salt of days. This overheated room. In the corner, Flamand and his girlfriend remain very quiet. At times a sweet word or two. Gisèle chuckles, says yes. Word for word. Tender. Temple to temple. The agony of that view, her face. A drop right on the forehead. See nothing, show nothing, glass barman. Clean, dirty. Full glass, empty glass. Full glass. Again wipes his face, getting a hard-on, opens a bottle. Just the once won't hurt. A wave of desire wells up inside him; he feels that rectal surge rolling and breaking. Fills a glass and drinks.

Boisvert son of Boisvert.

He likes it. The bitterness. Legris passes before him, heading for the Indian. Flamand and Gisèle. Legris glides along the ground, hands in his pockets. The rebellious look he keeps for auspicious evenings. The Americans are laughing. He turns around and gives them a knowing sign. Crazy Sam pockets another ball. Legris reaches the Indians' table. Gilles drinks his beer. It's too hot behind that bar. Over there, Legris gesticulates and sniggers. Gilles sponges his sweaty forehead. Twilight gradually creeps through the open door. Night fishing is about to end. Favourable hours. Suspend your flow. Our most beautiful days. Falling from a glass, another drop crashes into the corner of his eye. Sprinkling. A region of water just like there are water beds. No lilacs here. Only mosses and lichens. A symbiosis of algae and fungi. A complex connection. Boisvert and his Beaver. Gilles empties his glass in one gulp. Calms the nerves. Scratches a testicle, two testicles. Pours himself another.

●

The Indians discreetly saluted me when they entered the store, setting themselves in the background. After putting down a ghetto blaster belching heavy metal, they remained perfectly still. I was officiating behind the cash register. They carefully studied me.

"What's up, fellas?"

"Nothing."

They'd got up late and looked haggard. Sometimes, they'd interrupt the break to get a little food, eating it on the spot, without relinquishing a disinterest which might've seemed exaggerated to the uninitiated. Cowboy and his friends were especially fond of canned sliced mushrooms and the large Pacific shrimp that cost so much. Judith was wild about them. Seemed to subsist on that food alone. Her special diet. Cowboy was working the can opener, handing her the round container filled with white and pink crustaceans soaking in their juices. Judith devoured them, looking at me with bright eyes, drank the briny liquid and moved on to the mushrooms. Her black eyes, like a pair of small raptors, hovered around seeking a perch.

Benoît would blush to the roots of his hair whenever hazarding to look her way. He was really hot for her. An old story. When she was around he'd look at her like a lovesick puppy, eyes bulging, even forgetting to close his mouth. His saliva would spread like left-over ejaculate at the corner of his bloodless lips. And Judith strutted about, arousing him, talking only with thrusts of her entire body that made her clothes obsolete. It wouldn't have been surprising to see them simply fall off, like dead leaves or slough shed by a dragonfly. She was toying with him.

"Don't you have anything to do?" he grumbled, staring at the floor at the tip of his shoes.

"No," replied the natives in chorus.

They didn't seem to relish my association with Jacques Boisvert, and conspicuously kept away from me for some time. To entertain them, I'd devised a little number imitating the Old Man, sort of a mixture between Chuck Berry's duck walk, and the scampering of a crab. I'd refined it, adding a series of voltes that crowned the inevitable final charge. This variation was a resounding success.

Mister Freeze in his mouth, Admiral Nelson continued to haunt the premises. He'd come in like a whirlwind, immediately looking for the cat. Sneaking up behind him, Hérode would claw furrows into his calves, and the battle would begin. Nelson often inquired about the Old Man's return. In the latter's absence, he'd take Hérode out for short strolls. Over the last few days, Admiral Nelson's favourite pastime had been to pester me with a refrain that said basically this: Salomé has the hots for you. I chased him away with a gesture whose heedlessness was perfectly studied; he'd run off, cat on his heels, as though he'd fulfilled a mission. Immediately afterwards, whenever customers showed up, I'd make mistake after mistake, with the cash register getting worked up.

The Sunday following my brief stay in the city, Jacques Boisvert cut a path through the Indians blocking the entrance. He was coming to get some ice. He always needed a lot to supply customers on far-off wild shores. We had a makeshift method:

filling plastic bags with water, then piling them into the freezer. Boisvert asked me to help him carry many of the large ice blocks to the cooler in his truck, and I followed. Listening to heavy metal, the Indians looked at us carry armfuls of ice. Boisvert looked straight ahead. Cowboy grimaced, the sun right in his eyes.

"This one's for you, Boisvert!" he shouted.

I turned to the large illuminated head. His back to the door, Cowboy held a small cylindrical object between his thumb and index. Boisvert didn't stop. Strangely, a snow-white dove flew over us right then. I'd never seen that kind of bird here. I caught up to Jacques Boisvert, who was barely hurrying.

"A 30-30 bullet," he said quietly.

❧

Wresting a muffled snap from the bridge, he stopped his truck at the edge of the road. The water had risen since our last visit, reaching the top of the deck on the dyked side. Puddles seeped through disjointed boards. Farther on, the swollen lake hinted at flooding the shoulder of the road. Boisvert whistled knowingly. Setting his foot down, he observed, with a mixture of amusement and acrimony, "The old blackguard will surely have a bath! At least that much will be accomplished...."

He came and went continually while talking, multiplying simple and effective gestures, handing me the gaff with a sharp movement, giving Big Ben the oars, asking me to help launch the small aluminum rowboat that would allow us to pursue our inquiry. He'd harass me with the greatest ease, lashing me with a word, an intonation, a biting silence, secretly defying me. A morgue took the place of his mind, and he condemned in me the moron exiled from the metropolis.

"Oh Oh the beaverrrs Oh."

Big Ben was panting, thrashing about with his gaff like a rutting walrus. We were standing on a dam the width of a sidewalk, nearly 50 metres long, an imposing structure controlling the flow from a chain of small lakes encompassing our two bodies of water. From one side of the powerful construction, dark waves suddenly concealed the silty bottom. A crude channel provided drainage for the overflow. On the other side, a relatively strong current cut a path through the tangle of branches, and bubbled at the surface of the discharge. Balanced on the uneven dyke, Boisvert wielded the gaff, continuing to feel that handing out gibes was his duty.

"Students aren't good for much! What do they pay you at the store? Minimum salary, I hope!"

"Hey, Big Ben, try to choose your side if you fall in the water! If you do it on the lake side, the flood will carry us clear to the Saint-Lawrence!"

"The Archimedes principle," I grimaced, diverting a bead of sweat from my forehead that was crinkled with effort.

Boisvert briefly hushed up, looking me over. Then burst into frank laughter, deliberately plunging an elbow into my side.

I went into the brook, moving downstream, the yellowish mud sticking to my heals like suction cups. I didn't really mind getting wet. Saw it as one way to escape the swarming blackflies that our operations had disturbed. Boisvert had volunteered me for all the amphibious missions. Besides, the strength of these structures never ceased to impress me. You had to sweat blood and water to dislodge even one branch from the awesome mud casing that held it like a vice. Once a first gap was opened, a kind of chain reaction occurred, and the current began cooperating with the saboteurs. The disintegration spread to the edges of the wound, the debris breaking free at a faster rate, torn from its shackles of sludge, swirling into the foam. I heard Boisvert yelling at me from the dyke, trying to say something above the rumbling that increased with the seconds. "In the days of the Company, we could easily get dynamite! Boy, did we ever make those beavers jump!"

The grip of the sludge was already reaching my knees. I tore my legs from the suction one at a time. Struggling downstream from the break up, I perched on an intact segment to look at the swelling water swirl the brown mire into a cloud of mustiness. Boisvert approached, looking in the same direction.

"Yes sir, didn't take years with dynamite...."

Gaffs dangling, we'd completely stopped moving, awaiting the outcome. Boisvert lit a cigarette while Big Ben "Oh Ooh the beaverrrs" tried to catch his breath. Boisvert sighed with satisfaction.

"Well, Gilles?"

He pronounced my name with a strange emphasis, stressing the G before allowing the ticklish vibration of the *Ls* to run along. As though the name were a mitigating circumstance in his view, an encouragement to sympathy. But I stood up defiantly. "Well, what?"

Taking his time to answer, he was scanning the dark water.

"Gilles," he began, "I was just wondering.... What's someone like you doing in our wonderful big frog pond?"

"Well...."

He suddenly turned around, gazing at the lake now streaming powerfully through the gap. Didn't allow me to satisfy his curiosity.

"My wife lies somewhere in that direction," he continued severely. "Remember that, Big Ben?"

"Ooh...."

"The propeller got tangled in a net some Indians had set. She was wearing waders, and disappeared in a flash. I dove in after her, but my strength finally gave out. I felt as though my scull were being crushed."

I remained quiet as he puffed his cigarette. We could hear Big Ben breathing. Boisvert nodded and shook himself. "I had a damned beautiful tackle box.... Must still be there, at the bottom, Don't count on me to fish it out. Anyhow, I don't go fishing any more...."

He turned towards me.

"That's why, when it comes to going into the water, Gilles, old pal...."

I jumped when, like a cannon fired at close range, a resounding explosion shook the lake's outflow. My entry into the water was remarkable, both feet sinking into the movable substratum, hanging on like the paws of an anchor. I had a long second to realize water was filling my lungs. Unable to move my boots in their casing, I saw the end approaching, then felt something along my back. I grabbed the metal hook poking my shoulder blade. An overwhelming force pulled me from the mire. I came out of the brew so quickly I thought I was running across the water, and was soon out in the open, lying across the dyke, busily expelling a few litres of water. Above me, Boisvert and Big Ben hollered with laughter, the former still firmly holding the imposing gaff he'd used to overcome the stream.

Benoît seemed worried I'd show excessive indulgence towards my native friends. He now carefully laced his words with fine allusions to the presence of those deadbeats at our doors, covertly suggesting I should be more selective about my friends. The atavistic foe had his foot in the door. Though he appeared peaceful, you couldn't trust him, he wasn't pacified. Truth was, those pariahs were bad for business, hanging around the storefront like drifting folkloric debris. Business took place between serious people, between those who had, and those who wanted. Those who only hung around, surveying the instructive exchanges, threatened to irritate honest practitioners and interfere with the whole process!

For the moment, war with the beavers had achieved its goals. Water levels had begun to ebb. Benoît was looking for an excuse to get me away from the store. Thanks to Big Ben's account, people throughout the village vied with each other in mocking my swim at the foot of the beaver dam. Since then, I'd learned the tiny creatures are very sensitive; the least environmental disruption (an abrupt lowering of the water level, for instance) is enough to cause them a lot of stress. Only a short step lies between an impromptu reconnaissance of the abuse site, and disagreement displayed with a powerful swipe of the tail on the lake.

Everyone had a good laugh, but this was merely the goodwill of amateurs. I could only shudder about what the Old Man could've done with the anecdote, had it been placed in his good care.

Benoît finally took me aside. "A group of Americans is coming for Saint-Jean-Baptiste to go bear hunting, and we don't have a single house ready!" he explained all at once, sucking his moustache.

Later, I headed for the mission that had been given me for the first day. While climbing the hill, I spotted old Flamand working away gently and stoically atop a stepladder graciously provided by the Outfitters. The Old Man, who'd hired him with the lure of a lump sum, had a good nose: paying an Indian for piece work was a bargain. The idea was to exploit that slightly indifferent nature combined with an astounding gullibility about all money matters.

Whenever the Old Man swindled someone that way, we'd hear him gloat for a good while.

"Highway robbery! Oh oh oh! Couldn't do any better with a rifle!"

I entered the section of the village which offered the rest a dramatic glimpse of its future. Green cottages neatly lined up, their bright yellow shutters faded long ago. This had been the industrious arm of the small village, home to several lives entirely devoted to the all-powerful of the Company. Everything was now abandoned and decrepit. Mr. Administrator wanted to transform the giant mother Company's ex-fiefdom into a luxury haven offering CITY COMFORT IN THE MIDDLE OF NATURE to extravagant tourists. The prospectus even went so far as promising a movie theatre where tourists would get a small patch of Hollywood after dinner, like in the Company's heyday. But the parish hall, which had once housed the projector's magic, had stopped showing films long before anyone could remember. It was even slated for demolition by the promoters. The real picture was in Mr. Administrator's head. To this day, the reality of Grande-Ourse had refused to submit to its glossy paper forecast.

Old Flamand was scraping paint off the exterior of the lofty white residence that housed Mr. Administrator during tours of inspection. Its second storey and gables made it command the surroundings. His profile wrinkled, armed with only a scraper, Flamand had undertaken the metamorphosis of the large chrysalis with the chronic indifference of his race. And the majestic slowness which the Old Man, proud of the verbal contract between them, definitely counted on to pocket a few dollars.

He'd seen me approach but only turned towards me at the last moment. My dilettantish appearance seemed to awaken his suspicion.

"How are you?" I asked with enthusiasm.

He seemed to ponder his words before saying, "Takes a long time."

His mind elsewhere, foot askew on the rung, he was looking towards the top of the wall: a barn swallow had fastened its nest under the eaves. It would have time to raise its brood before the Indian reached the area. It was hot. Dust raised by the whirlwind

caught you in the throat. Summer seemed firmly settled in. Lower
down, Lac Légaré was rippling. Flamand knit his brow and, seeing
the tool I was holding, "You too?"

"Yeah, me too...."

He looked at me gravely before going back to work.

Cap firmly in place, I took off with long strides. But before
heading towards my workplace, I turned around one last time:
perched on a stepladder like a bird of ill omen on stilts, Flamand
was wearing away Mr. Administrator's house bit-by-bit.

❧

*An antique electric pool table lies at the back of the hotel. Every young pelvis in the
village had rubbed against its chrome. It's defective, and all games are free. People
take advantage of it. The repair man still hasn't found time to come over; Grande-
Ourse is quite a detour. In short, it's a pinball for the poor. Legris has returned to
his friends. Nice shot, pal! Nice. shot! Gisèle trades words with her boyfriend.
Seems like the start of a spat. She gets up and crosses the room, approaching the
electronic billiards. Presses the machine with her hands, tightens the little spring like
a small muscle, shooting the ball into the upper areas, timidly shaking the box,
aware of those four bodies behind her, five with Legris who's slicking his hair.
Gisèle is gradually taken over by the game. The current seems to pass through her
hands, moving to her skin, spreading through her body hair, polarising all of her
small body, opposing it to the surrounding heaviness. The glistening ball bounces
from one block to the next.*

*The Americans drop quarters into the metal slots. A heavy cascade of ivory
quakes the machine's entrails. The money mechanism repeats its jangling refrain.*

Nothing is free. Nothing is free.

❧

The kitten's growing popularity attracted lovely company. Female
customers especially used this unflagging pretext to remain in the
store. Salomé was his queen. She found him irresistible, and he
returned the compliment. Catching him by the legs, she'd lean over
him like a mother speaking in a tone of reproach and false
supplication. Hérode would then waddle on his hind legs and
dance for her.

Brigitte, the lovely blonde living with Jacques Boisvert who'd
helped me when I came out of limbo the day of the first

communion, visited the store with increasing frequency. She had to run errands for the hotel almost every day. She adored kittens and, while Hérode tried to tear off her finger, lying on his back, she'd make conversation with me. Benoît would speak to her with only the utmost respect. Besides being a rather sumptuous blonde, her skin as diaphanous as that of the Indian women was swarthy, she bubbled with intelligence. I found her very appealing. Setting eyes on her, I was immediately overcome by a rectal shiver which, for me, signals the urgency of desire. She'd slip me one or two sidelong glances whenever she dropped by the store. Nothing very consistent, only a simple warning. Not nearly enough, I admit, to start getting excited. But my celibacy was weighing me down. The beginning of summer isn't the best time to soft-pedal the urges. While I slaved away inside empty houses, the humid heat sparked a languor along my pelvis. And scraping old paint from walls was mediocre sublimation. Naturally, I could always masturbate in peace inside the dwellings deteriorated by passing years, but the monotony of the act reminded me far too much of the boringly repetitive nature of my tasks.

One sweltering afternoon, Benoît had to take medication to an old man with cancer who'd chosen to die in the middle of the woods in a shack north of Grande-Ourse. Ti-Kid Benoît took along his fishing rod. He'd check out one of the small nameless lakes scattered along the way. Benoît hadn't had a minute's leave in over a month (I mean a real vacation rather than the continuous idle waiting which was a greater strain on the nerves than the most backbreaking chore). A Cessna sent by the local community health centre delivered the medicine, and he asked that I relieve him at the cash register, staying long enough to feed me his line of invaluable advice flavoured with affected piety. Leaving me alone at the helm deeply worried him.

"No beer to the Indians!" he trolled with passion. "No credit to Legris! Legris gets no more credit!"

All he had to do, finally, was drive off in the pickup. I could already tell he'd have trouble relaxing. Without a customer in sight, alone with my thoughts, I had a pang of libido. I was pacing up and down before rows of seductive bodies, able to think of nothing else.

That's when the post office girl came in. She avoided boredom by coming to the store as often as she had items to buy. This spared her, among other troubles, that of drawing up a shopping list. Married to a crabby and despotic lout whose grip she'd flee at every opportunity, she didn't care whether people listened to her platitudes. Moving enormous legs striated with varicose veins, she paraded before me, perhaps somewhat turned on, but only revealing a grumbling friendliness. She talked and talked while I prayed for her to leave. Hérode had laced into her legs and the lady's stockings were soon only indecent shreds. She finally granted my wish, moving painfully towards the exterior, passing Brigitte as she entered the store.

I immediately understood unchristian things would happen. It was in the air. Brigitte was swinging her hips in a way nothing less than titillating. All space between us was steeped in the sweet perfume of hormones. Her smooth legs jutted from very tight, athletic-style shorts, and her slender chest was wrapped in a loose fabric leaving two large patches of white skin uncovered. Unbecoming glasses overshadowed her expression, but everything else was swathed in a pleasing display of charms.

She passed by me, turned her head and gave me a look that triggered the red alert. I blushed. The freezers, pumping Freon at full capacity, gave off incredible heat. She swayed towards the one with the cold meats, opening the lid and leaning inside. Her prominent little butt is all I saw through a curtain of musky sweat. And, lower down, pallid thighs barely contrasting with the appliance's chipped enamel. The whole array was roused by a light shiver. She called out to me with a voice from beyond the grave. "Frozen hams?"

"I'll look," I said, holding my breath.

I paused at the entrance, grabbing the metal bar with both hands, sliding it sharply across the double flap, like I'd seen the Old Man and Benoît do so often. The store was closed.

I turned around and the light twinkled in her glasses. She'd observed the entire manoeuvre. I was approaching, and she again leaned over and stuck her nose in the poor-quality meat way at the back. The mass of her buttocks quivered like gelatine under the motor's gentle vibration. I tiptoed over to stand behind her. She repeated, in an irritated tone, "I can't find it."

"Eureka!" I intoned, shifting from one foot to the other.

"What?"

"Nothing. It's Archimedes. Heh, heh."

I was wearing cutoff shorts that were full of holes, threadbare, totally frayed. Looking at them drop to my feet, then hers, I pressed against the ass surging from the glacial air. She didn't try to straighten up, preferring to risk getting a cold. And when the episode was under way, spasmodic jolts lifting her torso, I lost my head and pulled the lid down over the smooth back spilling out of that totally lopsided strip of cloth, then continued to busy myself very professionally on the remaining part of her body. A sincere moan soared from the freezer, a sigh urging me to continue while someone knocked at the door, like a distant echo of our orgasm.

❧

At the time, fat Lili escalated the rebellion that was brewing against me under the very holy banner of public health. She'd set out to show me how totally inept I was, nothing less. When she'd enter, with complete elephantine elegance, I'd squeeze into a corner, already looking for air. Lili knew how to make the pressure rise in a room. Once the scalpel-wielding miracle workers had removed layers of flesh, they hadn't known what to do with all the remaining folds of skin their patient now used to bloat up with anger, like a porcupine fish flushed by a diver. On narrow flat feet that pointed inwards and never totally left the ground, she'd set out to find incriminating imperfections, raising the dust covering merchandise along the shelves, sniffing before declaring in her most terrifying contralto, "Well, you won't wear out your broom, god dammit!"

She took it upon herself to noisily move cans which, in her humble opinion, had been improperly stacked, and the surly tone poorly concealed the jubilation the exercise breathed into her. "You wouldn't happen to have a damp cloth, boy?"

When Lili showed up before the cash register, I knew I was in for it. Customers who witnessed these training sessions exchanged amused, almost embarrassed, looks. The rumour was moving along briskly in this village always on the look-out for new incidents: Lili had taken a sudden dislike to the clerk. Poor guy wouldn't last two weeks. Bets were taken: he'd be gone by Saint-Jean-Baptiste. That young fellow didn't measure up.

All told, I still preferred the way Jacques Boisvert treated me; there was a certain, almost friendly, respect to his aggressiveness, as though he felt I were an equal. He was smitten with realism, always curious about testing the stranger, and courted rivalry from a purely atavistic reflex. I'd confound him somewhat with my imperfectly defined edges, and the inability he saw in me of limiting my views to the petty and prosaic truths people use to go through life. It exasperated and intrigued him.

He scorned the obstinate egotism of his fellow citizens, while his own individualism constantly pushed him to go it alone; this wasn't the least paradox of his character. He now sought my complicity with amazing drive. He'd detected a tension between my bosses and me and enjoyed posing as an impartial observer. I was his lifelong enemy's weak spot and he knew it. Perhaps he sought my friendship like someone looking for a chink in the armour, like placing tiny cross hairs behind the withers of big game.

He stepped into the store one day. Lili was showering me with a stream of abuse that was now common, and I was girding for battle on two fronts. But, when he understood what was happening, Boisvert moved on the matronly woman, quickly routing her with a few well-chosen words.

"Gilles is doing his job!" he concluded magnanimously. "And no one misses the time when you'd bark at us without even saying hello!"

Lili furiously grabbed the bag holding her purchases and rolled her flanks towards the exit (she was unable to roll her shoulders alone), eyes carefully staring at the ground. But, before disappearing, she turned towards the exterior, as though addressing the whole village, and again bellowed, "That's right! Stand up for him! Protect him! Maybe you think he'll replace the other one?"

The remainder eluded us while her silhouette dissolved into the hot air. Boisvert was distressed.

"What can I say," he mused out loud, "her best days are gone. Another one who hasn't adapted."

To avenge me, Boisvert related a story: the previous fall, without leaving her truck, Lili had killed a moose she'd surprised at dusk slaking its thirst near the road, with a single precise shot from her military .303. Killed instantly, the big creature had collapsed in the middle of the swamp. Night was falling, and a half-dozen sturdy men had been needed to pull Lili from the morass along with the king of the forest. She mustn't have conceded too many pounds to her victim, and had been found mired to the floaters, threatening to sink with all hands at any moment.

He got me to laugh.

"Are we going back to see what the beavers are up to?" I enquired, filled with hope.

"Don't worry, Gilles. They'll rebuild their dam. Won't take them weeks, either."

He was pacing up and down, drinking a Coke.

"Meanwhile, the bridge needs rebuilding! But you know as well as I do no one around here has the time. Everyone's way too busy being idle...."

Before disappearing the same way he'd arrived, he stood in front of me, his tough-guy mug well taut over the framework of his jaw, stating calmly, "The hotel's expenses have gone up considerably in the last little while.... I wonder what she comes over to buy all the time...."

Our discussion closed under his dark gaze.

❧

Brigitte had a talent for being out of an essential ingredient right when, from the hotel, she'd see Benoît's dented pickup dash by, as he headed out for a while. Moreover, these crying shortages always occurred when Jacques Boisvert had flown away on business. The nice innkeeper then decreed that all taps be closed and rushed over. Though she didn't necessarily come in for spice, our exchanges weren't lacking for zest. I'd brazenly have her, with few preparations, being careful to slip the metal bar across the door beforehand, ensuring the inviolability of our retreat for the duration of a screw. Perverting the Old Man's philosophy to this degree delighted me. We'd collapse over cans of dog food, with Hérode the cat joining his claws to ours, or do it standing up, using a technique I soon dubbed the *commissionaire's position*.

My room? Too far. We were in a hurry and, anyway, the very

notion of intimacy remained suspect in this lair of zeal addicts. We were hungry and preferred the cold room, climbing onto mountains of beer cases whose ridges had been worn by the summer's consumption. We drank one, two, illicitly, to the health of the house, before tumbling down among an avalanche of interwoven cardboard boxes.

She liked to take the initiative and be at the controls of our low-level gymnastics, riding me with furious movements, her pelvis rolling like a racing connecting rod. She'd lean back far as possible to increase the pressure of my genitals against the inside of hers, and let herself go, pushing until it came out, ejected by the vectorial tangent of the magnetic motion. I held her breasts in my cupped hands — they'd dangle for nothing otherwise — and thought she looked like an actress when she placed her arms behind her neck, her open elbows drawing a beautiful lozenge. I was looking at that supplementary chest grafted perpendicular to mine, completely enjoying herself, getting visceral fulfilment, not to be interrupted please. God it seemed good for her. Solicited as such, my penis rested at an angle that differed from the rising flow. I relaxed and admired her as she started up on a grand scale. I settled for holding her hips that were puffed like the jowls of the wind, prominent as a maple canker, holding them like the command column of a diving plane. Pleasure was her lift, and I was her runway.

Sometimes I'd manage to free myself from the hypnotic sequence, and the scene would stand out with all its comical truth. I'd try to see reason, repeating, to preserve the seriousness and usefulness of the exercise, that it was advisable to hang on, to remain pressed against the other. I tried to avoid picking myself up all alone too quickly, and the revulsion was always sweet against my open lips.

I had a lot to worry about, and couldn't help thinking, among other things, that Boisvert would soon take things in hand. He didn't seem the type to let a young city fellow cuckold him. Brigitte did nothing to reassure me. She'd only give the corresponding part of her thoughts, "He often talks about you, these days...."

"Oh yeah? What does he say?"

"That working for the Outfitters will make you a moron."

"Which means he doesn't think I'm one yet!"

"He's very intelligent, as well, but prefers to rely on his strength."

We were taking a breath of cool air. She smoked a cigarette, while I blew a little vapour.

"I'm going to ask you a question," I spoke gravely. "What's a young girl like you doing in our wonderful big frog swamp?"

She laughed.

"I get bored at times. So I spend a weekend in town now and again. I'm glad to come back. You get attached to people. And then, there's him."

"Yeah. Him."

"Yes."

"What about your painting?"

The blow hit home.

"Who told you about that?"

"The Old Man. He told me you did nice *frames*...."

"All they see in a painting is the frame.... Around here, painting is what you do to your walls and house, to the bottom of a boat or the wings of a plane. Everything else is a waste of time."

"So you paint?"

She closed her eyes, then reopened them. "An old childhood dream. I used to draw.... Maybe some day."

She sighed.

"The hotel keeps me rather busy."

"And sexology?"

"Well, an old adulthood dream."

"So Grande-Ourse, if I understand, would be your old dream of old age?"

"Why not?"

I kissed her, but she got rid of my tongue, smiled, then grew pensive.

"They're dreaming of a sawmill, dreaming of money, dreaming of what will plunge them deeper into life. Know what? They're dreaming about reality."

"You wouldn't have canvasses to show me, drawings, sketches, things like that?"

She wiggled around a little.

"In my room.... Last thing you'll see alive...."

She let herself be kissed.

"I'll go. We'll do a study of sexual mores in Grande-Ourse!"

"Well, there's no shortage of interesting cases...."

"I want examples."

"White man in his thirties performs a rather early deflowering of a twelve-year-old Indian girl. White man found sobering up along the tracks, both legs cut clean off above the knees. Young girl's brothers shrug, saying you can't be responsible for all these careless people, really...."

"That's true."

"Indians have their code of honour, they never forget an offense. They say they hand down the memory of it from generation to generation, right to the final redress."

"Other stories like that one?"

"Perhaps. Indian woman raped by six or seven guys (at that point, we lose count) on hotel pool table."

"Really?"

"Ask Jacques, he'll tell you the story."

The problem with Brigitte was she always brought the conversation back to him. And, when wanting to add injury to insult, she'd suavely assert, "You look like him, you know."

❧

Gilles can't keep his eyes off her. Her slanting eyes. One drop. Two drops. The Chinese torture. He opens a second beer, the first gulp making his head spin. A lack of habit. Gisèle in front of the pinball. Reddish flashes light up her face. Red Light District. Flamand remains seated and looks on as well. Legris approaches Gisèle.

Close up, Legris is rather repulsive. He sweats, stinks. He's used to sleeping outside, anywhere, in the mud, manhandled and beaten up by his drinking buddies. He feels safe with the Americans. Gisèle pretends to ignore him. So Legris buys her another beer, without asking her opinion. That's the only possible hold. Whoever keeps quiet consents. The Americans have closed ranks behind him. Something's happening. Legris has put on the menacing look and roguish smile he keeps for grand evenings. And Crazy Sam buys beers for Legris who buys beers for Gisèle.

Gilles observes the scene, doesn't take his eyes off it. He loves Gisèle. Gilles drinks beer and all hell's going to break loose. He drinks beer and his father has gone fishing with that Montreal woman and her rich paraplegic husband. Gilles is paralysed.

My sudden distraction worried Benoît, and he soon found another occupation for me. We had to get ready for the bear hunt, an art largely based on the use of bait. That's how I was given the reins of Operation Carrion. During a previous stay in civilization, the Old Man had made arrangements with a butcher he knew, and, one fine morning, the miraculous shipment was there, within range of our staggered nostrils. The high meat, mostly giblets and butchery by-products, was squeezed into vaguely rectangular cardboard boxes, forming solid blocks. I first had to carry the wonderful piles of entrails, grappling with them, while their content oozed profusely on my clothes. Then I had to drive throughout the neighbouring countryside with an entire load of really fetid carrion. My mission: to set up hunting areas in the heart of bear territory. The aroma would handle the rest.

Following the laws governing microbiological processes, the flesh was already rotten, and supposed to reek more than hunters lurking in a blind.

The citizens of Grande-Ourse soon learned to predict my coming with redoubtable infallibility. An unmistakable scent preceded me everywhere, drawing a procession of large bluebottle flies in my wake.

And to top it all off, the operation's launch coincided with the climax of a heatwave. The rot was literally going into fusion, with a syrupy black juice delicately flowing through the fissured cardboard, staining my Levi's. Nonetheless, I continued dumping my heaps of entrails over sites likely to be good lookouts, moving on to the next stage, pedal to the floor.

Returning from these expeditions, I had a compulsive inclination to consult the rear-view mirror, and wouldn't have been surprised to see an entire delegation of bears already on my tail.

At the store, people got out of my way with a sort of respect, asking no questions. Except for Benoît, who seemed not at all bothered by the odour. Had it only been up to him, I could've foregone the shower and immediately sat down at the table. The Old Man's emanations had progressively immunized his sense of smell, like people living downwind from a pigsty or paper mill. But all my efforts to shake the smell of rotten meat were in vain. Boiling water, eroding five soap bars and applying specialized products wasn't enough to dissolve the minute particles that had penetrated all my pores. I had my own personal atmosphere, saturated to the core by this omnipresent putrefaction. I'd become an olfactory and involuntary human metaphor of death and the corruption of all flesh, haunting Grande-Ourse like a corpse who'd climbed out of a coffin.

❧

As happened every summer, the Recreation Committee cashed in a subsidy supposedly allowing it to hire a few young Indians from the area to perform menial work for a salary neighbouring social assistance. An area around a bunch of decrepit boards had to be weeded and the dump the playground had become needed to be cleaned. Like every summer, people soon began complaining about the small group's flagging punctuality. They'd all shown up the first morning, with an expression that might still pass for enthusiasm. The next day, the workforce had already decreased by half. Two days later, only Cowboy and Judith had shown up. Finally, Cowboy himself had deserted, a pathetic example hastily followed by Judith.

"Same thing every year!" lamented the man responsible for the project. "We land a nice subsidy from the government, give them the opportunity to work instead of twiddling their thumbs and pocketing their cheques every month, and look what happens!"

Cowboy and his friends kept a low profile for a few days, avoiding the sway of these charitable recruiters. Anyhow, the habit in Grande-Ourse was to count souls in a vacuum. The small school's register displayed a remarkable extensibility every fall, at the beginning of the academic year, thanks to the omnipresence of a handful of little Indians who spent the winter trapping with their parents. The number of registrations corresponded to the aid provided, and the Ministry used a special math.

Brigitte visited less frequently. Perhaps she couldn't get over my odour. I'd gone back to the old houses, scraping their walls as though I were scratching a wound. I scraped like glaciers once clawed this ground, leaving profound streaks. A genuine cartography was born amid the layers of paint, with pointed continents, rounded islands, dark oceans and bordering seas, shredded shores, craters, crevices, plains, and folds. A rain of tiny flakes, scales, and plaster lumps surrounded my cap. Farther away, César Flamand was also at work, like a dried-up insect, plastered to the large white house's facade. His stepladder hadn't moved.

And desire smouldered everywhere beneath Grande-Ourse, universal, polymorphous, totally twisted. Brigitte's caution was understandable. She once came to join me in one of those dilapidated shacks amid sagging floors, concave ceilings, tartarous excretions oozing from walls, and chairs with uneven legs, fidgeting with impatience, anxious to eject hypothetical occupants; the furniture generally recalled the theatre of a riot after the squad had moved through. The pipes swallowed with difficulty; traces of urea and rust spots covered tiles and chrome. I gave her a dizzying tour of the place.

I wanted to take her in my arms, but she resisted, arguing it was dangerous. She feigned interest in a little picture I'd just taken down to clear the work surface. I managed to undo a button on her blouse, but she turned around as though hit by an electrical discharge and my heart jumped. Big Ben had silently slipped into the room, and was looking at us, cigarette butt fused to his fat lip.

"You scared me, Big Ben."

I almost added that polite people knock before entering. I was especially amazed that he could move that way, not even wresting a creak from these deteriorated boards.

"Aah don't be afraid Ah Ah no beavers here!"

"Very funny."

He sank into a dubious bed, whose moribund box spring sounded like a broken violin. A snoring hiccup made us jump, and was soon followed by the squealing of a circular saw broken by whistling noises. Brigitte hit me with her elbow. The half-breed was only looking for a good place to nap. I rolled the button with my fingers.

In short, Big Ben hadn't been snooping on us deliberately, but the alarm really gave concrete expression to Brigitte's fears. Problem was I could no longer stay still. One night, two days before Saint-Jean-Baptiste, I blurted half-heartedly, without looking at Benoît, "I'm going out."

He wanted to know my destination; I then heard myself say automatically, "The hotel."

His lower lip fell sharply. He swallowed: "Ah...."

I wasn't up to deliberating, already feeling I was a breath of wind in the dark night. Seeing my confident expression, he got up.

"I'll give you some money."

A protective hint in his mumbling had a bizarre effect on me. I felt my pockets. He was right. I'd done so well to this day, having board, lodging, and laundry, that I'd got into the habit of living with no money in my pockets, while my invisible salary piled up in Mr. Administrator's books. Unbeknownst to me, this climate would all but bring about the imperceptible metamorphosis. It was time to react.

Benoît spun the safe's dial, opening it in front of me. He crunched figures, getting other figures to crunch, always more figures, and to get what in the end? He solemnly handed me an advance on my wages. I was overcome by a real frenzy, a physical need to blow it all. Visibly abstaining from voicing his concerns, Benoît finally mumbled through his teeth, eyes lowered, "They'll fleece you. They'll fleece you."

He escorted me to the door, unbolted it, again telling me, "The Old Man's coming back early tomorrow morning. We'll need your help, Ti-Kid...."

I left without looking back.

❧

Two beers only, and his head is turning. In front of him: Flamand Legris. Legris Flamand. Legris has put his elbows on the bar. Flamand does the same. Side by side, kilometres apart. Centuries of solitude end up here. Legris. Flamand. Flamand. Legris, who's come over to get a beer for Gisèle. Flamand has come to get a beer, period.

Gilles serves them. Two beers to Legris, one to Flamand. He pops himself another. Green bills to one side, words to the other. Credit. Legris: with hard cash. The Indian: in the red. Legris changes his mind. He'll stand a beer for the Indian as well. Pay my friend. American money.

Gilles faces the door, leaning into the light cool air blowing across its threshold. A slight breeze caresses the locks on his forehead. He's still drinking, his head turns, a top, a teetotum, it'll unscrew, fall from his shoulders. A beheading.

Gisèle takes off. Her bottle-shaped shoulders. Her father's mockery. No head on her shoulders. So he says. The burden of responsibility. He's never been afraid. As a last resort, the rifle in the corner, under the counter.

Wind through the open door. Gilles looks at Flamand, then Legris. Gisèle and the Americans. One of them might still leave. They're bolted to the floor by the prospect of a little pleasure. They play their game. They, who give orders. The number of beers on the fingers of one hand. Peace. Legris gets back to his subject. He's going for a piss. Gilles avoids looking at him, shuns him, lifts his eyes. From the wall, the slaughter of a male smiles at him sadly.

❧

The building rose from the shadows, down at the edge of the lake. A long narrow structure, red leaning to burgundy, crawling on the grass-tufted sand. It was like a large creature lying down, dancing glimmers darting from its mouth.

For Benoît and the Old Man, the place was filled with all the evil forces in the region, an abyssal syphon where potential customers sank their scarce earnings and profits instead of investing them intelligently in transactions sponsored by them. Furthermore, they felt the hotel had always been guilty of an unforgivable vice: bad management. Boisvert had acquired it from a notoriously lax fellow; after imposing his iron grip on it for a while, he'd gradually lost interest. His hydroplanes allowed him to stay afloat, and he claimed to hang on to the business only out of philanthropic compassion. Besides, general opinion had it that Brigitte was turning things around.

Neither neon light nor enticement stood out as I approached. Fascination was all that drew me towards that impregnable den, that viper's nest braided from esophaguses and gullets, duodenums, jejunums, ileums and colons, urethras and ureters twisting in the dark like large galvanized worms rising like spellbound cobras that make men stand though they're only machines that swallow and defecate, that eliminate and discharge.

I knew Boisvert ruled invisibly over this wriggling mass of entrails.

I suddenly stopped moving, attentive to the silence. The door opened onto an obscure bustling. Several round holes riddled the wall near the casing. Bullet holes, I uttered.

A detail prompting me to try a grand entrance. I imagined a camera shooting me full face and affected a heroic bearing. I was the tenderfoot who had to fit in with a gang of blackguards versed in activities both shady and lucrative. My presence cracked like a whip over this small closed world. All heads pivoted, gazes fixing onto me as I stood stiff as a post. I moved forward, shrugging, staring at the great dizziness before me, walking like a hesitant bull before the espada. With a start, I leaned on the bar. Behind me, the silence could be cut with a knife. Right away, Brigitte joined in my game. Seeing me, she barely sniffed, to show slight surprise. Then kept a very professional distance between us. Her golden hair streamed beneath the oblique glare of a consumptive light. Nuggets palpitated between her fingers, and I felt an incredible thirst.

I made the first mouthful last. Brigitte was rather silent, awaiting the sequel. I sent out signals and she allayed suspicions. Then, suddenly, someone tossed out in a dull voice, "Don't you think it smells like rotten meat in here?"

"You mean it smells like the Outfitters!"

"Well! The young clerk! They let you out?"

Another belched out, more conciliating, "Come and sit down, you little comedian!"

I turned around, a beer glass pointing towards me. Everyone spoke, people congratulated me. Legris was there, sniggering and sycophantic, scratching his scabs as though they were lottery tickets, scratching the sores of others to earn a free beer. Moreau was also there. He flashed broken teeth amid a movable mouth his cheeks kneaded into a bad smile. A double-chinned trapper with a thick beard also stood with them. The visible part of his face had huge gentle eyes. But I learned the Indians were deathly afraid of the large hairless red dog he'd sic on anyone daring to venture too close to his home. A renowned poacher and builder of log houses — he'd put them up in a flash for outfitters throughout the region — he also seemed sound, honest, and likely a little stupid. Next to him stood an outfitter with an indifferent and cruel gaze. He was the prototype of all outfitters and had a setup near the reservoir, where he devoted himself to roguishness, having left it the time to get plastered here. The old

Muppet rounded off the gathering, fidgeting in his seat, shaken
by spasms he tried to pass off as fits of hilarity.

They let me slip into a gap between two slabs of muscle and
now crushed me with their turbulent shoulders. I didn't speak,
watching them from the corner of my eye. I first had to
consolidate my position. When I was implicitly and unanimously
rebuked for working at the Grande-Ourse Outfitters, I made sure I
relinquished any responsibility with an appropriate nod. But,
already, an arm thick as a chest landed on my shoulder. The trapper
said, after crowning me with his beard. "Your problem, at the
Outfitters, are the redskins! You haven't seen the end of it when
you start associating with them...."

"The redskins?"

"That's right, the Siwashes.... The Indians!" translated Legris.

I thanked him for the disinterested warning. The Muppet was
beaming and twitching artificially. Eyes half closed, Legris was
savouring the fragility of my situation. Like a fallen boy scout, he
was ready to do somebody one of those favours for which his
presence was tolerated. The outfitter told everyone what he thought
of the staff at the Grande-Ourse Outfitters. In fact, it was really
personal. I must've turned pale. The young clerk no longer thought
this was funny.

Moreau continued: "Seems your boss guarantees a bear in the
ads he puts out in the United States, ha ha ha!"

"There are no bears this year!" said the trapper, shaking his
head while his locks remained still, glued down by the feverish
activity of his sebaceous glands.

"That's right," Moreau confirmed. "There were no damned
blueberries last summer! Eh!"

"No blueberries!" exulted the Muppet before wondering
whether he should clap his hands.

"Did you see any bears this summer?" Moreau asked the
outfitter.

"What?"

"Bears?"

"Hmmm."

They began shoving me gently, sluggishly, as though
warming up their muscles for the impending distraction. I wanted

to drink faster to rise to their wavelength, but the beer, spilling from my glass as though it were an aspersorium, landed around my neighbours' knees. They didn't seem impressed with that result. The shoving intensified. Friendly at first, they soon acquired a stormy intensity, and I was now flying from side to side, sheltering my pride behind a forced smile. I began to get up, and someone seized me with an indistinct grip, nailing me back to my chair.

As the fun was about to degenerate completely, Big Ben appeared in the door frame with a sense of timing that gave credit to his nickname. That opulent and peaceful flesh, stamped with affected indifference, headed towards the bar where Brigitte's bust was silhouetted by the frosted light. From the cheerful tangle of limbs soaking on the swamped pedestal table, polite forearms emerged and saluted: "Hello, Big Ben."

"Hi, Big Ben, old buddy."

Like an enormous Dali clock, he dragged himself slowly just above the ground, heavy with benevolent neutrality. He declined the glass which, now on my feet, I anxiously offered. He completed his routine tour and, after staring at Brigitte and me with a swollen eye, crossed the threshold of the door that creaked on its hinges and rattled in the night like the very heart of Grande-Ourse.

Gilles furtively looks at Flamand, who looks straight ahead. Legris has gone with his two beers, one for himself, the other for, we know who. That Legris. His shiftiness. A Champion. Category: complete insignificance. That gift for getting beat up. He must like it. Self-sacrifice. Traitors are always a little messianic. He has a finger in two pies. A rogue here, a prophet across the street. Legris is used to it. Not Gilles. Gilles is torn. Plagued by his secret dilemma. He the weak son of the hotel-keeper, the one sent to make the beds. Mollycoddle. He's heard that word. In the schoolyard. Gilles chases the ball. When someone blocks the way, Gilles accidentally kicks him in the shin. He hits hard for a mollycoddle. That's what someone called him. Faggot. He wouldn't hurt a fly. Reads books. Listens to Beethoven on FM radio. Effeminate.

That kick. To rediscover the strength of that blow. To choose a side once and for all, confine himself to it, cling to it. The schoolyard. Racial wars. Rocks flying from one side to the other. A gang of Indians against the Whites. Naturally. On

the skating rink, the day Gilles was balancing himself along the boards. A stone, the
impact against his temple. Through a curtain of blood, he saw red, indeed.

Legris puts his bottles down near the brown palms, on the Plexiglas. An
offering. Gilles has observed Flamand's stony immobility, in front of him. His
cold readiness. Gilles envies him, envies his enemy, feels torn, rejected. In love,
jealous, full of hatred. He seeks a role. The schoolyard, that kick. The stone. He
washes the glasses. He'll see to it.

❧

The two tiny worlds could coexist with their own parallel laws
and no visible connection. People sized each other up, baring their
teeth, blindly making contact in the night, it was an accident. The
next day, they continued to hate each other, to hate that nearby
otherness. The abyss was a few dozen feet away. They had only
one thing in common, obliterating all distinctions: indifference on
both sides.

I joined the Indians at the other end of the hotel, where they'd
sat down on arriving. Cowboy, the Kid, and Donald Big-Arms were
there. Judith accompanied them, but preferred to mingle with the
noisy crowd Moreau dominated. A turncoat on either side, it was
perfect. The balance was maintained.

I bought beer for the Indians and Benoît's voice, like that of
my conscience, rang in my ear with the accompaniment of a cash
register. Don't make the Indians drink. Don't make them drink.
They'll fleece you.

Frozen in his cryptic fatalism, Cowboy was looking at his full-
moon face, its seas of shadows and acne craters, in the sheen of the
imitation wood. He could smile and become serious without
transition, occasionally at the same time. Those two functions of his
moods seemed linked, as though interdependent. He could easily be
mocking, but humour made him sad. The Kid had a disdainful and
casual expression, and Donald Big-Arms chuckled discreetly.

The Kid proudly described the body-building workouts he did
each morning in front of his father's cabin. Lying on his exercise
bench, lifting weights with heavy grunts, then jogging along the trail
lined with scrap metal that tied the crude dwelling to the road,
sweating, sweating again, shadow boxing with resolve. Once back at
the lake, he'd jump in and continue moving his long supple body.

He was in pretty good shape, he confided modestly, hitting the palm of his hand with a clenched fist. And, besides, he continually perfected his handling of the *nunchaku*, that Japanese flail made from two sticks bound by a small chain. Used to knock out or crush.

"Why do they call you Karate Kid?" I asked.

"Best film I ever saw!" he replied with vigour.

Like superheroes in two-cent American comic strips, these Indians seemed dedicated to a kind of specialization of abilities. Donald Big-Arms' unintelligent brute strength was matched by Karate Kid's technical refinement, and by Cowboy's status as a marksman. Among his friends, Cowboy had the reputation of never missing a shot. He owned an ancient 30-30, probably used to harass the English invader before it had been recommissioned to the great nutritional quest. When holding the instrument, a hard pride radiated from the regular orbit of his face. Cowboy was also the aquatic hero, the amphibious phenomenon. He could stay under water minutes at a time, awaiting the depletion of his oxygen supply. It was said he'd acquired a taste for such exploits very early on, following a failed dive that was at the root of a kind of trauma. He'd jumped from a cliff and his head had sunk into the thick mud carpeting the lake bottom. By the time he'd been fished out, he'd left a little of himself under there.

The Kid swore to God that, one day, Cowboy had burst out of the water at Lac Légaré, right in the middle of Boisvert's protected geese, and dragged one of the birds to the bottom by pulling its legs, then wrung its neck for the benefit of the family table. Their culture was one of strength. Their aim in life? Close combat, hand-to-hand. Among their priorities, plans for revenge came before future prospects.

Vulgar laughter rose from across the hall; it's to parties what tremolos are to opera. Judith was causing a sensation. Cowboy and the Kid hated fat Moreau and his crony the trapper very cordially. They'd suffered numerous thrashings at the hands of that pair, had been accompanied more than once to the edge of the forest by the large red dog guarding the bearded man's cabin. They knew that, sooner or later, they'd have to fight again; they weren't afraid, they lived for that moment.

"Another beer, guys?"

Cowboy made me promise to accompany them to the traditional Saint-Jean-Baptiste fire, the following night. One of the biggest parties of the year, with a free-for-all guaranteed. They recalled the previous year's solstitial blaze with emotion; it had degenerated into an unforgettable pancratium, a harvest of bruises unequalled since. Donald Big-Arms listened, silent and fervent.

"You're our friend, Gilles," confirmed the Kid.

Admiral Nelson himself appeared at the entrance, distraught and incoherent. He came towards us and stood near the table. He scanned the room's every nook and cranny, scouring the surrounding darkness as best he could.

"Something wrong, Admiral?"

His upper lip shook at the rhythm of his mumbling. We understood he was looking for Hérode the cat, having just lost him outside where he'd taken him in obvious defiance of the Old Man's orders. He absolutely had to find the runaway before the latter's return. He was fraught with noble despair and the others mocked him, except for Donald Big-Arms, who honestly seemed sorry. Admiral Nelson's life turned into a cruel tale that night. He disappeared, pursuing what little affection the world offered him.

When I approached the bar, a hostile silence covered the nearby group, where, the previous moment, Moreau's throaty warbling had risen, along with Legris' persuasive cooing and the Muppet's approving squawking. I granted them the alms of only one look, unable to ignore that fat Moreau was surrounding Judith with bountiful offensive attentions. The nearness of this powder keg had an exhilarating effect on me. Brigitte lined up the bottles, with gentle knocking, trying to hold me back for a moment.

Alerted by the sound of fetid chewing, Legris intervened. My hair stood on end. His speech slid into gear, got carried away, a mechanical fable, a jamming of signals. I was his friend, he'd like me forever; little Judith, over there, he knew her well, she was mine if I wanted, I only had to know how to go about it, only had to talk to her. He slipped me the details.

I grabbed the bottles, gave him one, leaving Brigitte a good tip and a salacious wink, before turning my back to them. I felt the burden of an unexpressed accusation weighing me down. I was definitely breaking the rules, the village's spoken law. Just who was I, the wretched hireling of the loathed owners, to chose my buddies like this?

From his spot, Moreau pounded me with abuse that was loaded with insanity while tapping Judith's thigh, who seemed to approve. The aggressiveness of my friends rose a notch. To create a diversion and put a famous aphorism to the test, I got up and walked towards the venerable jukebox which sat imposingly on the other side of the hall, near the pinball. The selection was usually a decade or two old, but a few more recent hits jostled amid the hackneyed melodies. Cowboy joined me and, saying nothing, pointed out the hit that was really popular among the Indians that summer: *Vivre dans la nuit*, by a group called Nuance, with Sandra Dorion. He then made a second choice, a more personal one: *La Isla Bonita*, by Madonna, his favourite song. I wasn't going to bend over backwards to impose my criteria for sound musical education.

When the first notes soared at the back of the smoky hotel, a powerfully thrown beer bottle smashed on the wall above us, blending its crash with the as-yet unsteady flow of the melody. We were splashed with a fine mixture of old malt dregs and cigarette butts while glass pieces stuck to the label disappeared behind the device at a snail's pace. Moreau then barraged us with heavy laughter. He likely preferred western music.

Everyone stood up. The Kid was already rallying our ranks with style; a grimacing Moreau pounced on him at once, Donald Big-Arms headed for the station to which he felt assigned, and the trapper grabbed a chair, whistling for his dog just in case. And that's when Benoît crossed the threshold.

There was something so incongruous about his presence here, that everyone's momentum was broken. Everyone hesitated, filled with surprise. Benoît stiffly made his way through the mob, plunked himself before me, standing very straight, saying with fervour, "I've just had a call from the Company's main camp. The Old Man broke through the Seven Mile Bridge with his truck."

He let the announcement sink in.

"Come on, Ti-Kid, we have work to do...."

He hesitated, made a few lapping sounds then, looking at the three Indians, as though he'd just discovered them. "You come along as well, if you're ready to work. We'll need some arms...."

I mused that this was Benoît's finest hour. He'd finally been able to show leadership. He turned around as though in the army, and we followed him speechlessly, no one daring to break the spell. Much beer had been absorbed, and enormous quantities of it were now spilling out over there, in a stream draped in the colours of daybreak. I felt a strange excitement, like a kid freed without warning in the middle of a field. Walking by Moreau, I good-naturedly tapped his elaborate stomach, merrily pinched Judith's distended butt, and kept my most expressive wink for Brigitte who observed the parade with a derisive half-smile. What a woman! She wasn't in the least disturbed by all the commotion, and seemed about to applaud.

Day was about to break. Moreau and his friends looked at us leave without reacting, as though stunned. The Indians gave them knowing looks. Legris and the Muppet didn't want to miss a thing and were getting ready to head to the site of the catastrophe.

❧

G.B. loves G.K. Gilles Boisvert and Gisèle Kikendache. It's carved everywhere, on the birch bark, like in the Vigneault tune, on boards and sheds. Monoloy shouted the monotonous wind. A monologue, their love. A drab adolescence, cooped up in his hang-ups. Condemned to the awkward age, oily skin lying fallow. Young. A condition. Weak. A convict.

And Gisèle, who shows up at the hotel, followed by that dark-skinned peacock, tensed over jutting muscles. The proud bearing of Flamand, his wide shoulders, his palfrey teeth, a stallion, from mane to heels.

Gilles is jealous, of course. The glass washer dreams. Virgin. Fleas jumping on the spot, ants in his pants. Walking in his father's footsteps, gone over to propose adultery to that woman who follows Saint Peter. Gilles intones the fifth symphony in his mind, that's enough for him. Those Americans. Their soul is like a fish-hook.

They're suddenly in a circle. Around the pin-ball machine, the wolves. Gilles doesn't measure up, dad is right. Nothing to offer but beer, still more beer, beer, everyone. Their passion, like fish in the water. Cut them some line. Drown all this. Six feet of beer.

People haven't yet drunk enough, or else too much. They don't feel good enough or else too good. It's in their blood. Don't bother with anything. Serve and think about nothing. Let out some line, some feeling. Legris, that scoundrel, the Indians are his ingredients. The idea that things may get hot. Go right to the end this time, like in a film. Flowing beer gathers foam. And Gilles feels that. Something tells him that something, somewhere.

❧

Daybreak revealed a truly fine mess. The truck was large, very large. It appeared immense to everyone in the bluish-green mist of dawn. Driving it on this road was already an exploit. Its majestically inclined white mass seemed to spring from the stream, like a pathetic Moby Dick lost in fresh water. And this completely white truck was filled with beer. The front had crossed without a problem. It was already at the top of the opposite bank when the imposing back end was over the pile of rotten boards villagers persisted in calling a bridge. It had gently collapsed, like cardboard, and the truck had obligingly backed into the creek.

Leaning on a nearby stump, Big Ben was examining the scene. The Old Man was brooding alone near his mired juggernaut, his dewlap quavering faintly, as though a dying echo ran through it. There was no question, for whoever knew him well, that he would feel the slightest remorse, the least guilt. But we could feel he was tight as a spring, completely stiffened while waiting.

Our adversaries had all rushed over, uttering abuse. The Outfitters had very few friends in this hour of tragedy. The Muppet was shaking, not knowing what to think about the fabulous quantity of cargo spilling into the landscape. Legris was coming and going, torn between his diverging impulses. Moreau and his swindlers joked among themselves, with a taunting air. Others showed up, barely out of bed. News of the inconvenience was spreading like wildfire. For whoever took the interest of the whole village to heart, the scene was of course very distressing. But an immodest and euphoric pleasure could be discerned beneath grave expressions befitting the circumstances. It could only be explained by the Old Man having fallen flat on his face. The wind being finally taken out of his sails! Many individuals (and their ranks swelled with passing seconds) had come only to see him in this unfortunate position, his verbosity run dry, despondent, doubled up as though his poor bones had collapsed with the bridge. His tongue dangled uselessly, like those of large cervids who sneer, for the edification of passers-by, on the hoods of cars in the fall. Yes, they'd come for this and the unavoidable confrontation no one would have missed: the one that would happen when Jacques Boisvert reached the premises.

"Damned beavers," the Old man repeated stubbornly. "And to think they're Canada's emblem!"

In a short time, a bulldozer sent from Grande-Ourse began digging up the ground creating embankments on both sides to support the foundations of a temporary bridge. Early fishermen were already queuing up around the creek. Shaken by the hard cavalcade, they pulled themselves from their vehicles very sleepily, rubbing their eyes and bones, intrigued at first, then fascinated by the truck's position and the remarkable agitation gripping the Lilliputians around it.

The Outfitters' staff was assigned to the most urgent task: transferring the consecrated cargo to another truck sent in as a backup. The lightened truck could then be pulled from the bridge's pulverized debris. And time was of the essence, since some felt that the current would topple the vehicle. The frustrated stream was already looking for the best way to circumvent the obstacle. Fortunately, the merchandise was relatively unscathed. Frothy stains appeared here and there on the piled cardboard cases. A fuzzy beer film covered the truck floor, spilling into the brown water.

Beneath a sun that was soon broiling, the transfer took place in disorder, thanks to a chain consisting of Cowboy, Karate Kid, Benoît, and me. A case of beer to anyone lending a hand, the Old Man had promised, puffing himself up, moved by his own munificence. Donald Big-Arms, who was more individualistic, must've been napping a little farther on. Benoît was taking things very seriously and the Old Man was coordinating the process, which is to say he was everywhere and nowhere at once, barking useless orders, telling stories with a local flavour in the same breath. Besides, Benoît and he hadn't had to change their state of mind to jump into the action. Chronic worries and daily strokes of bad luck were familiar parts of their universe. Adversity never caught them off guard. This new thorn in their side, by its magnitude, did have a few virtues: for the time being, it silenced the infinite variety of ordinary problems. Big Ben did his best to keep out of the way.

My friends and I felt this was actually a break. A change of routine was really unexpected, and the prospect of spending a day in the open air, doing invigorating activities, brought beaming smiles to our faces wrinkled by effort, which it was wise to hide from the employer's sensibilities.

The emergency bridge (two plain metal beams spanning the creek) was soon in place and the Old Man recouped all his enthusiasm. Between two death cries and two contradictory directives, he endeavoured to provide a detailed account of his mishap. The indefatigable insomniac had reached the euphoria produced when fatigue and excitement are pushed to the extreme limit. He'd shot his bolt, fidgeting around and bellyaching like a kid whose twisted plans don't go exactly as expected but who, ignoring his sores, bumps, and future problems, insists on convincing everyone he had a really good time. He'd come up from behind to trumpet an aside into our ears, pivoted, disappearing again, elusive, almost managing to spoil our hard-working serenity.

Admiral Nelson had been picked up along the road, and was in the water up to his waist, busily fishing out still-usable flotsam. Handing us board ends which we nailed, higher up, across certain holes able to swallow a heedless rescuer. Honoured to be serving under the Old Man, Nelson was very careful not to mention Hérode the cat, reportedly still missing. He nodded like a happy dog, zealously approving each time the Old Man, roughly shouting a kind word to him, pointed out salvageable beams from his perch. For the moment, it was extremely important for the improvised stanchions supporting the rear of the vehicle to be left in place.

As Admiral Nelson was removing a beam from an eddy, under a rear tire, I thought I felt the truck move slightly. A barely perceptible tremor ran through what remained of the bridge. I looked at the others. No one had noticed anything.

"Be careful, Nelson!" I shouted above the din.

He was carefully retreating and everything seemed to stabilize.

As we stood beside the vehicle collapsed on its back end, a blazing sun burned the sweat in our eyes. We were getting thirsty with all those beer cases driven through our hands, over the rolling conveyor we'd brought along in spare parts from the store and assembled here, between the truck and the other bank. All this loot paraded by under our noses like in a supermarket, but there was no question of our popping a single cap! Moreover, this human ballet was about to be echoed by an aerial and hallucinatory rendition. The water was now the colour of rich earth. An entire population of riverside and amphibious insects had been disturbed and taken to the air, flying over the scene of the collapse with humour. Prematurely hatched blackflies were looking for victims. A squadron of dragonflies then deployed to take advantage of this earthly manna, and the whole sky was now a truculent buzzing, a serial microscopic assassination, a dance of death amid the blinding zenith.

❧

The tension. He's a simple spectator. That's the problem. You don't measure up, young fellow. That weighs him down. Handling his money, that's okay. But as for measuring up. You don't make the law, young fellow.

He thinks about his father. He, at least, doesn't hesitate. Fleece the customer. Full glass, empty glass. He took sides long ago. His law. Protection of property. He'd gone fishing with that wealthy trollop dragging around her old husband. Quite a hassle getting him into the hydroplane. Get a move on, magnate! They must be screwing on the bottom of the rowboat, while the poor Scrooge forks out the cash, locked up in the cottage, lying on his bedstead. Maybe he's able to go down to the dock? He secures his wheels and observes them with binoculars, the pitching and rolling. Last tango in Grande-Ourse. Taken for a ride, the old pervert.

Tension is important. Mitchell, American. Daiwa, a Japanese import. Zebco. Reels. The fish, native most of the time. How many pounds? No need to measure up with a reel. The spool does all the work. You adjust the tension, reel out, reel in, you're in control. Confusing the issue. Full reel, empty reel. A reel that complains. The tension rises, you slacken. Gilles was never very good at that. His blunders. The large walleye brought right back to the edge of the rowboat, in the spring. Oops. He grabs the monofilament, a mistake, cleanly broken. Some Stren line. The DuPont Company, Shawinigan, closed now. No landing net. And that monstrous pike darting towards a small island of grasses. Twelve pounds at least, says the father. His impression. He saw that flash of scales, the swing of the tail before the sprint. But the unreeling of the line is way too easy. Tension. Tension. All the time. The song of the reel. Enough reeling out. Tighten the screw. It's well fitted, trigger the drag, add a little pressure. Drops of cool water spurting out, strung along the translucent filament, a streak of sunshine in the morning. The large tapering body turns around a stump, there are swamped trunks, ghosts of drowned trees piercing the surface. And it ruptures. His father teases him, again. Twelve pounds at least. Never measured up.

The large pike has bitten the hook, shaking his missile head wildly, somewhere near the bottom. A colourful red-and-white Dare Devil dangles from his jaw like a banderilla. Living with that? The scar. Dare Devil. Red and white. Those pike that attack empty beer cans on the surface. The one he'd brought back, one night. A whip, nearly cut in half in the middle. Still had the strength to bite, hadn't lost his appetite. He'd slipped into that kind of plastic vice that holds a six-pack. It was cutting into his flesh and he went around with it on his back. Things returning to the surface you'd prefer never to see.

❧

Driven flat out, a pickup emerged from the north, flying over a string of deep ruts, pulling up, almost without slowing down, near the parked vehicles. This hasty parking manoeuvre earned one a long straight scratch that pierced the laborious grousing of water and men. But when Jacques Boisvert tore out of his seat, heading towards the distressed truck, wearing a white engineer's hat, no one thought of complaining about such an insignificant blunder. Everyone waited. To the great satisfaction of a little world for which virility still rhymed with truth, two old bucks were going to lock horns.

Jacques Boisvert unquestionably held the best cards. Hands behind his back, he toured the site in long strides, carefully hesitating before saying loudly, "Yeah, this is a fine piece of work, gentlemen."

An anguished, gasping, silence breathed in those words; he repeated, one octave higher, "This is fucking nice work, gentlemen."

The only answer was the growling of the eddies, swirling through the muddy water. No one breathed.

Walking along the large carcass, hitting its metal with his hand, Boisvert seemed to be making a quick survey of the damage, then finally howled without further restraint, "This is the fucking Outfitters' doing, gentlemen!"

A dramatic leap placed him in front of his fellow citizens who, imperceptibly, had drawn nearer. He shouted at them, "Don't the lot of you feel this is fucking nice work?"

He punched the truck's side, and the ivory-coloured sheet-metal echoed gloomily.

Up to his thighs in the water, leaning under the vehicle's belly, he added again, "Those people do nice work! They work at cutting bridges! At cutting us off from the rest of the world! At getting everyone fed up enough to leave, to beat it the fuck out of here as fast as possible!"

The atmosphere was about to turn riotous. A growing murmur rose from the small group gathered on the bank. The beavers must've been wondering what we were doing here.

"Yeah," agreed Moreau, who'd climbed onto a mound created by the excavation.

He let out a burp, carefully muffling it with his fist, swaying like a sumo wrestler on his mound.

"Yeah, Boisvert is right...."

Arms stretched towards the truck, that truck which in the space of one night had become a symbol.

And then our very own Old Man bounced back, resumed being the one each of us from the bottom of our hearts, wanted to see rise up, because he provided the only guarantee that the promised clash of titans would occur. He shook himself and charged in head first, like a rhinoceros, shortsighted and hard-nosed. Jumped off the bridge, landing on his knees and elbows, got up gesticulating, rushed towards the petrified mass of his detractors, tripped on stones, fell flat into the muddy water, waded about, groaned, struggled, and finally, red and convulsed, reaching his sworn enemy. Boisvert waited for him very calmly, and eyed him scornfully.

The Old Man began shouting everything that went through his mind, everything people around here had always said, about the necessity of getting together, helping each other, stopping the ceaseless quarrelling, not stealing, and loving your neighbour. Moreover, this stretch of road was theoretically under the old Company's jurisdiction, at least, so it was surmised, and the Outfitters couldn't take care of everything after all, highway maintenance, rotten bridges everywhere. Anyhow, everyone was delighted to see the Old Man trip up and land in the creek because they're all rotten, all profiteers, all dogs, a bunch of ...!

He clammed up for a moment, out of breath. But seeing Boisvert's mocking, almost pitying expression, he lost whatever

patience he had left, and yelped, filled with defiance, "You're a fine
one to talk about cutting bridges! Yes, you, ah, you, Boisvert!"

His malicious finger then traced out the sequel in the heavy air
before him.

"You, Boisvert!" still managing to find the strength to gasp.
"Cutting bridges! Twelve years! Eleven shots! I put my fingers in the
holes! The truth, Boisvert, the truth, eh?"

He was almost delirious.

Boisvert didn't answer, but stayed there, having turned pale.
Then, suddenly flaring up, he stepped forward. He seemed as
though he'd level the old swaggerer with a blow, but instead turned
towards the truck and, arms raised, palms stuck to the smooth
surface, pushing on it angrily, strangely pushing on it, speaking to
himself, "The truth? The truth is right here! The truth is your
truck, damned fool! It's the road! It's the damned road! Look at
them! Damn it, look at them!"

Moving his head without turning around, he pointed to the
tourists who, standing in the background, witnessed the entire
scene, passive and diffident. They fully realized they weren't
welcome. A whiff of unreality hovered over the area.

"The truth is cash and cash is the road and the road is them!
Them! Business as usual! All the time! On and on! If not, get
away! Away!"

"Why don't you go and tell that to the Flamand family,
Jacques," said the Old Man in a softer voice.

"Shut up you old toad! Shut up, d'you hear me?"

Boisvert tightened his lips. After a few seconds, he turned
around in a short burst and moved away, fists in his pockets, jaw so
tense you could almost hear his teeth grind. He passed the two
Indians, Cowboy and the Kid, without seeing them, though their
eyes were rivetted to him. Everyone exchanged glances,
disconcerted. The Old Man had pulled a card from his sleeve.

"Go and tell that to your son, over there!" he howled again,
stamping his feet.

He still couldn't believe he had this sudden advantage, and was
looking for other ways to drive home the nail.

Having climbed back in his pickup, Jacques Boisvert was
getting ready to remove another strip of paint from the adjacent

vehicle, when the large white truck rented in town, as though
belatedly shaken, started to heel and crack. It tilted, tilted over
progressively, more and more quickly, and a wild scramble
followed, everyone moving away, asserting priority. The choice
panic hinted I should perform a back dive with a twist. I ended up
face down in the creek, surrounded by small waves and dirty foam.
Very close to me, at the point of finally collapsing, the truck halted
for a moment, like the Titanic before it disappeared, and its back
end sank all at once, crushing the small bridge beneath its
hindquarters, scattering its remains into the current. Then tipped
over conclusively.

Without knowing why, I was overcome by anxiety. Eyes wide
open, I was looking everywhere, spitting water. But the Old Man
came round first, he yelled, yelled, "Nelson? Admiral Nelson? Oh
my God! Oh my God!"

❧

*Friends call him Crazy Sam. He has that glimmer in his eyes. The dull edge of an
azure blade. Slightly quirky, at best. At worst, you might say he's a few bricks shy
of a load. War at twenty years of age. Now in his forties. Physically healthy.
Korea at twenty. On the good side, obviously. The flame of liberty, right to the
border of China. MacArthur, he was the guy. Diplomats in the way,
unfortunately. In 1945, too young for the Japs. He followed the news in the
movie theatres. The Pacific under Hollywood projectors, Pentagon propaganda. For
ordinary people, the war was about rubber and saucepans. Korea in his youth. The
yellow men. Then, in Vietnam, he was given a command. On the front lines, but
the lines were blurred. Guerilla war, dope. Action, acid. A sizzling of grey cells. A
war of madmen.*

*Crazy Sam. His eyes have seen action. In Cambodia, fire bombs,
phosphorous in the night. Might is on our side, guys. The Mekong, pals. Waving
their large patriotic pistols. Their brains a little rattled, surely. A guy from
Pennsylvania, hunting and fishing, an expert bear killer. He knew Paul
Provencher, appeared in a film with Serge Deyglun, hunted with Xavier César
and Joe Ottawa in La Vérendrye Park. The first two are now dead. He returns to
Quebec each spring. The bear hunter.*

*His gaze still lingers over there, somewhere in the Orient. In the past.
Sometimes, napalm still coats his pupils. Crazy Sam is an inspiration to his
friends. A genuine lunatic, when he puts his mind to it. His war dance on the pool*

table, saluting the flag, standing straight up, a troop of stars in his head, the red stripes, Stars and Stripes, S.S. The arch of his foot rolls over a ball and Crazy Sam falls flat on his back, to the delight of his pals. It's a party and it's his fault. Crazy Sam has no balance.

Here he is approaching Gisèle with his cowboy hat. Legris sniggers. Crazy Sam loves war. His slanted eyes recall Asian brothels. Yes, over there, where the gods laugh, and the flesh is illuminated. Flamand is still leaning on the bar, sees nothing. Full glass, empty glass. Full glass. Takes his time. Another beer, Flamand? He's getting quite drunk. Gilles is the one who's enthraled this time. On his arm, he owes him that, for sure. Crazy Sam, over there? Beer, of course. Thank you, sir. That fire. That blue. You know, like the eyes of walleyes. Noctilucent, they call it. Group predators, they hunt at night. Lucifugous. With what? Yellow jiggers, of course, or then Vibro-Tails. They look like things from a sex shop. White flesh covered with golden breadcrumbs, nothing better. Shake and bake fish. Shake it, babe. To prepare it, impale with the tip of a knife. No, make filets, two swipes, a filleting knife, slender. Rapala, yes sir. Yes, shoals of predators. Those eyes, blue as an abscess.

❧

Attempts were made to drive away gathering onlookers, to remove them under pretext they'd get in the way. Some wanted to scatter them to the four corners of the planet, no one would've complained, all patience having suddenly been lost.

Crammed with baggage, packed with accessories, they filed across the fateful waterway. Eyes narrowed, impressionable, they tried to align their wheels as best they could with the two iron beams lain a few inches above the current, flogged along by the waving of a local, who, appointed to direct the traffic as a matter of course, had seen worse and who, rankled by the leeriness and infinite sluggishness of supplicants, brayed invectives rather than salutations as they passed.

César Flamand hadn't climbed out of his pickup and, stationed higher up, scornfully observed this bustling of ants. Cowboy and the Kid, now unable to lend a hand, had gone to join him. A stony immobility now imprisoned everything on that side. Suddenly, a rufescent four-wheel drive Jeep Cherokee appeared over the road, swiftly coming out of a turn, without giving the least hint of slowing down, heading straight for us. For an endless moment, it seemed as though it would use the truck's slanted side as a springboard and fly to the other bank. Everyone stepped back amid an incipient panic and, for the second time, I somersaulted into the muddy water, getting bloody scrapes on my knees to boot. I was beginning to get fed up. Only Big Ben remained still, yawning in the middle of the road, enormous and pudgy, probably the only one who finally caught the driver's attention. At the last second, without ever slowing down, he managed to change the Cherokee's trajectory, which flew down the bank. With impeccable precision, the four wheels left the bank, swirling through the air, landing squarely on the rails. The traffic attendant got to put out his pipe in a watery environment.

The Cherokee, having reached the other side in the batting of an eye, maintained relative control over the situation despite its breakneck speed, being stopped dead in its tracks by a tree. Four khaki-clad individuals immediately sprang out, laughing. One of them was pointing a video camera and right away began shooting the accident scene. The others had defiant expressions, like scouts having smelled an ambush.

The Old Man was already trotting towards them, crudely blurting out, "There you are, my friends! There you are! My friends, the Americans!"

The sturdiest one in the group, sporting a short beard, stoically endured the animated gnome's accolade. He considered the scenery for a moment and murmured, "It's a heck of a setup you've put out for us, old man!"

The Old Man thoroughly agreed. "For you, just for you, my friends! Oh, you know, what just happened is very sad friends, we're wallowing in tragedy, but it doesn't matter, ah, the bears are waiting for you, my friends! Look, we've just built a brand new small bridge! But he was a good little fella, that one, what was his name again, Nelson, that's it, Nelson! Didn't drink like the others, but he was still young.... Yes, a nice little bridge, but for a moment, down there, I thought you were going to jump straight over my truck! Oh, my my!"

The bearded one nodded modestly, while his pal, eyepiece rivetted to his orbit, relentlessly filmed away. The Old Man turned towards him, blurting out, totally enraptured, "Hey, pal! Is this ABC News or what? You need an interview, just ask me any time!"

When the bearded fellow, knitting his eyebrow, asked if there'd be any bears this year, the Old Man started to hop in every direction. "Bears? Did you say bears? Bears everywhere, pal! Waiting for you! Bears all over the place! Piled to the tree tops, I swear. They even come into the kitchen, at the store, there's a huge one in the area, ask Big Ben, the guy you nearly ran over!"

The film-maker was trying to centre the Old Man, a difficult, practically impossible, task. The latter was already heading back towards us, trying various grimaces of delight on his small face dripping with sludge.

"Pennsylvania, New Jersey, fine chaps! Good customers!"

The Old Man was so happy, he opened a case of beer in front of us. "Go ahead guys! Serve yourselves! It's on the house, boys!"

Benoît declined, while I hesitated before concluding that, with the heat, Admiral Nelson would surely understand, especially where he rested for the moment. I glanced worriedly at the small knoll where Cowboy and the Kid had taken refuge. The Old Man offered a friendly can of beer to the Americans constricted in their camouflage outfits, then to all those who'd supported the communal effort. This became a sort of official break. The Old Man opted for a Coke. He pulled the tab and a stream of brownish foam crawled over the clear metal. He spotted a case of Mister Freezes lying on the conveyor, which had been part of the cargo, and his gaze clouded over; he turned towards the spot where the little Indian still awaited a procedure now totally bereft of urgency. The case was half-opened and the Mister Freezes had melted in the sun.

Only Boisvert wasn't giving up. He'd jumped onto the bulldozer, hitching it to the huge white sheet-metal grave, the engine's ferocious howl rising skywards amid swirls of blue smoke. Boisvert was working, swearing, damning the whole world and no one dared tell him the truck was still too heavy, that it had to be unloaded some more. The bulldozer's tracks were disappearing beneath the surface, and Boisvert's feet were in the water, but he charged towards the middle of the lake. When, rocked by its tremendous load, the truck painfully slipped into the creek bed, as though finally carried off by the current, and when that damned board was removed and tossed into the woods, someone opting for

common sense convinced the amateur film-maker he'd better be
somewhat discreet, otherwise, one of the people finally rushing
towards the old pickup would surely take care of his camera.

❧

*Rounds for everyone. Another round. Gisèle included. Flamand included.
Everyone knocks back drinks. Gilles, too. Drink like them, as much, more. Speak
the same language, acquire that courage of unconsciousness. Gisèle drinks, Crazy
Sam drinks, Legris staggers. Flamand is drunk. Crazy Sam has his hand over his
heart, and his heart in his pocket. He'd like to treat himself to a nice little whore
in this backwater. Slanted eyes, like Saigon. The same race, basically. Bering
Strait. Through the Kamchatka. The reds. Historical materialism. No class. When
you accept a drink, you consent necessarily. Makes sense. Concomitant trade. It's
six of one and half a dozen of the other Amerasians. Two or three babies he left
over there. Crazy Sam counts on his green bills. His pimp speaks English,
explains the nature of the transaction to the main person concerned. Legris
negotiates like a slave trader. Flamand dozes alone, leaning heavily on the bar. But
no. He just got up. He just. Gisèle no longer hears anything, she's switched off.
This game of supply and demand no longer amuses her. Auctions of the flesh.
Flamand opens one hand then closes it; contracts muscles and tendons. Everything
about that hand is nerve endings. Gilles touches wood and drinks. Swigs his beer.
Full glass, empty glass. Full glass.*

❧

"So? What are they doing?"

"Sleeping. They're dead tired. Gone to bed for the night, I
think."

The Old Man gave a small chuckle of delight.

"That accident must've made a strange impression on them.
Talk about a way to greet visitors!"

He was talking about the Indians. Sad as he'd appeared when
Admiral Nelson's already swollen beer-filled corpse had been
pulled from the stream, the Old Man was much too practical not
to see the benefits of the tragedy. A little embarrassed, speaking in
the tone a carefully-pondered thought is delivered, he stared into
the distance, saying, "Oh, you can't imagine how it's affected me,
fellas ... you can't imagine.... But...."

He looked at us sideways. "But when you get right down to it, from a business standpoint, I emphasize from a business standpoint, the incident was a real blessing...."

Benoît, whose ears were used to that kind of reasoning, couldn't help but lift his head.

"Well, yes," continued the Old Man, happy to have exposed that sensitive spot. "With mourning on their hands, do you think our Iroquois will be given to drinking tonight? Normally, with Saint-Jean-Baptiste, they'd have kept us on the war path all night...."

The Old Man feared nothing so much as festivities.

"Yeah, it's true," conceded Benoît who, however, didn't want to prolong the discussion.

"And, besides," the Old Man said triumphantly, "Boisvert crawled back into his hole, did you see? What happened is his fault."

No one said a thing.

I was worn out. Benoît and I had unloaded the beer cases alone, stacking them in the coolness of the store's basement. Cowboy, the Kid, and Big-Arms had vanished without paying attention to the Old Man who, magnanimous during the mourning period, repeated his grandiose mark of gratitude to them reluctantly, modifying it somewhat, "And what were we saying, guys? One beer for everyone? How about a good Pepsi? You didn't steal it...."

Benoît, with the help of timorous periphrases, reminded the Old Man that he'd recruited the three natives in due form the previous day. The Old Man then agreed to credit their accounts by a few dollars.

"At least they won't see the colour of it!" he said congratulating himself, shaking the grime and crusts of mud that covered him from head to foot.

I needed to sleep, but knew I'd be unable to. I'd returned from the creek perched on the last of the salvaged beer stock, muscles bruised and soul despondent. Diving ducks would sometimes take off suddenly from the grassy bay of a lakehead. We spotted broods of mergansers spreading shivers across the leaden water with small movements of their feet and stumps. A tiny rabbit crossed the road, a great-horned owl took off from the branch of a tragic-looking pine, and I stupidly tried to focus on my thoughts.

For a little boy who didn't like beer, you might say Admiral

Nelson had got his fill. Closing my eyes, I could see the truck's white mass slowly falling over him, as he continued working while his elders bickered. Then the huge splash, the truck resting on its side, litres and litres and hundreds of litres of beer spilling into the creek, irrigating the entire countryside. He was found near the back of the truck, pinned to the bottom by a worm-eaten plank across his chest. The golden cascade gurgled just above him; the little fellow had drowned in beer. Left this world lungs filled with 50, Blue, Molson, and Laurentide.

The day had made me thirsty. I had a pressing urge, the need to forget that incident by getting smashed to the hilt. My senses were calling for their bi-monthly panacea, my dose of annihilation prescribed from time immemorial. At the store, a state of siege had been imposed at dusk. Despite the gloom hanging over the celebration, beer sales were going well, at least among the Whites. We'd salvaged enough merchandise to satisfy immediate needs, and the Old Man was rubbing his hands.

When 11:00 p.m. struck, he rushed to the door. He didn't try to conceal his cheerfulness, heaving it like a javelin. "That's it! 11:00 o'clock! It's over! They'd better have topped up their supplies, because we're closed at eleven. Closed! Oh! The bastards!"

As he was about to lock up, I stepped forward.

"Wait. I'm going out."

Without giving them time to react, I walked into the cold room, returning with a two-four under my arm.

"By the way.... A case of beer, that was the deal, right?"

My question surprised him.

"Well, er, see here ...," stammered the Old Man. "You work here in any event...."

"All right."

I asked Benoît to deduct the cost of this minor purchase from the pile of wages they owed me. Then, good night all. The night caressed my face with its warm breath, filled with bland hops and fiery yearnings. In the rectangle of light the door compressed behind me, Benoît mumbled and the Old Man wailed, "I warn you, mark my word! If you're not back by midnight, I'll lock the door and you can stay outside! Past midnight, this place is closed, understood? Closed! Closed!"

The same could rarely be said of his mouth. He kept on whining on the inside as I moved away. Inside my jacket, I squeezed a bottle of red wine I'd swiped from the shelf. As I neared the railway, I briefly thought about Hérode the cat, whose dismal fate we'd learned from an eyewitness on our return. This morning, as Nelson was reaching the large white truck, Hérode had fallen into an ambush set by the trapper's large red dog, and a partner of vaguely canine lineage, a disturbing, completely white mongrel no one had ever seen in these parts. Between the rails, each pulling one end, they'd literally ripped the cat in two, heading off with their own half, scattering pieces along the way. The mutt headed north and disappeared, and the other had gone home, under his master's porch, near the village exit. The incident brought more grist to the Old Man's mill and we were treated to a fitting speech: I told you he shouldn't go out. See what happens.

But, however much he spoke, this place was still going to the dogs. As I left, I noticed that our guard dog had broken his chain and, going unnoticed in the general commotion, had also run away.

❧

The Americans have put away their pool cues and closed their ranks. Crazy Sam is still giggling, Legris isn't as certain he can pull it off. Flamand, whose hand opens and closes. Closed. Crazy Sam was showing off. Not the type you can impress. Vietnam. Still alive. Everything has a price. That's what he learned. Voluptuous lips, buxom. Flamand, fists open, closed. Fists that articulate like a mouth. They don't speak the same language. Gisèle, pitcher in hand, billiard ball in mind. Her free game.

Legris remains carefully out of the range of that talking fist. Open, closed. He tries to placate him. Tinder. They play with fire around here. Flamand shoves Legris aside and moves forward. In the middle. Enormous. Sam the crazy one doesn't back off. Legris is insistent and caught between them. The extras remain in the wings, waiting. If Gilles weren't so paralysed. Prevent them from looking at each other that way. The harsh blow everyone dreads. Drink more, fall down, one pitcher at a time. Open, closed. Closed. A collision of colours.

❧

The electricity spread its comforts to the edge of the lake, where the jukebox had been hauled. The fire was already crackling amid the small square flanked by a booth and two benches. The jukebox rested imposingly near the pyre, a metal minstrel. Unloading my burden, I headed for the water.

It was beautiful to see the fire swell up in the night, as I pierced through the lukewarm surface of the lake. The rumbling of humans around the pyre seemed from another world. Blue-circled flames lapped the bottom of stacked logs that were crowned with old tires. The wood crackled briskly. Waxen heads hovered through the halo, evoking a knightly vigil. I panted as I lost myself in a meticulous breast-stroke, slashing through the cool water. It offered me a border, all I needed was to go down a little to lose sight of them, them and their light. My strokes spread a complicated pattern amid the empty bottles clinking under the surge of small waves. All day, locked up in the action like a needle in a compass, I'd been heading towards this cardinal moment where the day tumbles into tranquillity.

I grabbed a bottle, lifting it to the moonlight. Its contents gushed out and I enjoyed a resonant shower over my temples. Farther on, the springboard rose out of the gloom like an enormous batrachian. An intense urge to drink gnawed at me.

Tearing myself out of the lake, I climbed onto the diving board. The sweep of its oscillations increased while, stooped and awkward like an insect startled by the light, I tried to balance myself. The water's cold caress was more comfortable. I dove with a quiet arch that was brutally interrupted by the liquid explosion, returning into the cover of the frothy ink, beneath the unfathomable silvery film.

I was swimming towards the bank, silently propelled by attentive bursts, when Cowboy surfaced in front of me. There was something magical about the fluidity of his movements, reminding me of the scene in *Apocalypse Now* where Martin Sheen, set in vivid and sensual slow motion, inches his way out of the muddy water with, as a backdrop, paroxysmal dancing surrounding the sacrifice of a bull.

"What are you doing here?"

"My brother Christophe will arrive by train, tonight."

He began to move like a cayman, swimming parallel to me and barely rippling the water's surface. His hair was pearled with moon gleams and faded into the glistening expanse. We both remained quiet. I swam away on my back, blowing carbon dioxide into the coldly luminous firmament. In a corner of my eye, the rising flames now caressed the tree tops. I felt an undulation along my side and Cowboy surfaced again. He shook himself like an otter, lowered his water line and took in a little water which he immediately spat out. Again he disappeared into the transparent shadows, and I counted the seconds, then the minutes. He burst through the surface.

"Hey, Cowboy! You diving for pearls or what?"

He shook his head and drops flew off. "No, there aren't any here. A treasure...."

"A treasure in Grande-Ourse?"

"A treasure."

"In a chest?"

"In a bottle."

"A bottle?"

"A bottle with a cap."

"Hmm. That's logical. How much?"

"Don't know."

"And what's that bottle doing there?"

I was now speaking to a pair of legs rising vertically in the gloom. Following an oblique scissors kick, the flat and dark water closed over him, almost without sound. I tilted my head and looked at the sky: Ursa Major's inclined saucepan, a milky vapour wafted over the boreal night.

Cowboy was porpoising farther on, and I caught up to him.

"How are things going over there?"

"Hasn't started yet," he panted. "They're waiting...."

"For the death to be certified, I imagine.... I wonder if there'll be an inquest...."

"What?"

"A coroner's inquest...."

"César Flamand says it's Boisvert's fault...."

I mused for a moment.

"Yes, but Boisvert will say it's the Old Man's fault.... It's impossible to tip over a truck with your bare hands."

"Fernande also says it's Boisvert's fault...."

I'd heard that the school administration was urging parents to take legal action for criminal negligence. After all, this incident would deprive them of a name to register on their list next fall. The thought of a complaint in due form terrorized the Old Man.

"You know, Cowboy, you shouldn't stay under water so long, it's bad for your brain."

He confided that he didn't want to live too long, flashed an equivocal smile, and dove again.

❧

Gilles now heads towards the crowd. Crazy Sam get's excited. The symptoms: his shiny forehead burns, his hat shakes at the top of his skull. He jumps on the spot, his Stetson waltzes furiously on his head: Say, what's your name, big boy? I'm Crazy Sam. What's your problem, man? Don't you speak English?

Flamand doesn't budge. Crazy Sam walks forward in rhythmic stride. March. One two, one two, halt. Just under his nose. The others laugh. Sam turns around, a robot out of control, a broken toy. He stops on the tips of his toes, an inch from the Indian's face, eyes fixed on his. His face twists, the rest of his body remains absolutely rigid. His friends can no longer stand it. That mischievous face, remodelled through incredible expressions, contrasts tremendously with Flamand's impassive mask. Crazy Sam goes into free-game mode, like a puppet hanging from electric wires. Flamand remains still and perplexed before all this. Preserving his thunder.

What's on the watch in everyone's veins. That Indian must weigh at least two hundred pounds. The laughter of friends becomes forced. Crazy Sam monkeys around, scratches himself all over, thinks he's back with his regiment. One two, one two. Gisèle plays. Flamand waits. The name of this pin-ball: Search and Destroy.

❧

The family of the deceased was holed up inside a cabin across the lake. For César Flamand and friends, the company of this still unregulated body would replace the expected festivities. But, while waiting for the wake, people needed to drag their sadness around somewhere. Indians drank on one side of the blaze, Whites on the other. I was with Cowboy, sitting on my seat of beer. Admiral Nelson's untimely departure had undeniably cast a pall over the scene. The atmosphere of celebrations mustn't have been very different from the one that reigned on the other side. Brigitte dared to cross the no man's land to broach the conversation. She informed me that Jacques Boisvert was in a dreadful mood, and that she'd preferred to let him mope on his own. She was desperately bored and persisted in sipping her beer. I gave her a summary of the circumstances surrounding Admiral Nelson's death. Boisvert had told her little, having taken refuge in his pride.

A small boat split the gloom, grazing the dark mass of the springboard swaying at the end of its fulcrum, then ran aground with harsh scraping. Donald Big-Arms and Karate Kid jumped out and, feet in the water, completed the landing. Judith, seated in the bow, jumped to the ground, followed by a large woman whose presence alone explained the dinghy's heavy draft. They climbed the hill towards the fire. With the approach of this crew, Brigitte pretended to take interest in a character who, joint in his mouth, blissfully contemplated the flames.

Judith introduced me to her mother, whom I'd never seen. The friendly matron, no longer very fresh, lived in a shack a couple of kilometres away along the road to the reservoir, with the unavoidable tribe in the process of being broken up. She already had a comfortable lead in the drinking department, and immediately undertook to make my conquest. I had to protect myself from very precise propositions, and flattery administered with conviction while this lady, to the great delight of Cowboy and the others, was already groping around for my fly. Judith spared no effort to help me preserve my reputation. She stared at me, mockingly, "Aren't you going to join your girlfriend, over there?"

"Shhhhhh.... You know very well she's not my girlfriend."

"She's Boisvert's girlfriend!" said the Kid reproachfully.

But the mother resumed the offensive; things weren't going any better with her daughter. Each had grabbed a large handful of the other's hair; they were skipping rope with each other's locks and beginning to draw attention. This likely set the tone for the distraction that followed. It wasn't very long. Everyone awaited only this and its unfolding was regulated like a community leisure activity.

First, I joined Cowboy who was standing in front of the jukebox, swigging a beer. I noticed everyone was busily doing the same. Cowboy asked me for a little change and selected two songs for the evening's program: *La Isla Bonita* and *Vivre dans la nuit*. I punched in his selections. Barely had the first note been played that a bottle whistled over our heads, like a flare bleeding through the sky at the beginning of an attack. It flew like a comet, with no wall to interrupt its trajectory this time, and fell into a thicket. This was the signal.

❦

Crazy Sam suddenly feels the place needs music. He's never been able to stand silence. Silence is intolerable. A sound echoing back to his nights in the Orient resonates inside him. The great ringing gong of a Vietcong shell. A wound that earned him a medal. The noise, especially at night. His ears are filled with the Orient. Very unpleasant. He only sleeps in jolts. He never could tolerate silence. And that Indian over there, quiet as a carp. Crazy Sam, in front of the jukebox, recites out loud. Selections. Canned refrains. Western. Pop. Country. Homeland. Hesitates. Rock. Swaying. Julie and the Duguay brothers. Marcel Martel. Deraiche family. Quebec country music?

The large bear paw lands on his shoulder. Crazy Sam is about to turn around. The record pivots, there's clicking inside the chrome entrails. His hat has slanted over his crew cut. Quebec country music. A hollow Quebec. He knows that once he turns around, he'll no longer be able to avoid that big devil of an Indian.

❦

Thrown across the narrow beach transformed into an arena, Moreau appeared in the wake of his projectile, arms stretched as though to maintain his already shaky balance. Perhaps he remembered there was a good inch of beer left at the bottom and wanted to get his bottle back. When Cowboy and I, inspired by a similar preoccupation, moved aside in unison, Moreau came crashing into the jukebox, which fell over on the sand. In a few seconds, skirmishes broke out nearly all over and the fight was raging.

I haphazardly rushed the tall trapper and, hitting him repeatedly, managed to attract his attention. With a kick, he sent the Indian that had straddled him flying, and grabbing my collar shook me at the end of his arms like a harmless animal. He walked a few steps without letting me go and then, filled with a thoughtfulness that didn't fool me, put me down in the beer vat, in this case a refrigerator whose door had been ripped off under mysterious circumstances. My ass landed on the ice, cooling my ardour, which convinced me to be a simple spectator for the follow-up. Brigitte came over to keep me company, pointing out that the cold was a definite feature of our relationship.

The fray was confused. Moreau was fighting against Judith and her mother at the same time and, when he managed to step back a little, noticed they could manage very well without him. The large red dog was barking but didn't dare snap, pensively slipping through all those unguarded calves. Mr. Muppet was strolling among the groups shouting encouragements. Holding his bottle by the neck, vaguely thinking of using it like a truncheon. For his part, Legris was walking stealthily through the joyful outburst, grumbling cautiously, chin on his chest, as though leafing through a psalm book. Cowboy, with Moreau on his back, seemed well on his way to being thrashed and Karate Kid split the air like a windmill, multiplying moves, spinning on the spot and digging into the sand like a crab. He rarely landed a blow.

❧

Crazy Sam isn't laughing any more. A large fist moves through space, heading for his face. A split second lies between it and a luminous impact.

❧

Donald Big-Arms had just pulled himself from a patch of vegetation suited to a refreshing nap. He came out in time to stand up to the large trapper who was seeking flesh that was still undamaged. Their collision shook the ground.

In the end, Karate Kid, whose dizzying display continued to slash through emptiness, approached Legris with uncertain movements, who was now looking elsewhere, totally concerned with dodging a blow. Alerted by an important displacement of air, he pivoted at a totally advisable 180° angle, opening his eyes wide. But the only result of that excusable reaction was to offer a better target to Karate Kid who, swept along by his dervish's gyration, was already on him. Legris got a karate blow right in the eye and, under the stars, performed a few dance steps that led him behind the Muppet who was thrashing about like the puppet he was. Legris grabbed the Muppet who, surprised by the unsolicited touch, recycled his bottle: he turned around in one single movement and broke it over the skull with a vague profile whose owner he then identified, after taking a good look. Legris collapsed with a kind of grateful smile.

❧

The Stetson makes a short gliding flight and lands on the jukebox. Willie Lamothe wails as though the full moon were on his tail.

❧

The rest of the story is more or less lost in the tangled meanders of my memory. Seated on my improvised trestle, I continued twisting caps and gulping cold beer. Then, infected as well by the wind of madness, violence, and revolution which had risen under the Baptist's leadership, I got into an argument with Brigitte. "These long-neck bottles," I began, "remind me of a technique used to torture paratroopers in Algeria: they sit a guy on a bottle, with nothing else to lean on, slowly letting him get impaled."

"That's disgusting!"

"Yes."

"Couldn't you talk about something else?"

"No."

I added one or two cruel and stupid remarks and, since she was leaving, cried out, filled with bitterness, "If you'd seen a little twelve-year-old boy caught under a beer truck, you wouldn't feel like laughing either!"

I started crying for no reason. She moved away in long strides.

Then, through the general anaesthesia, the following fragments came out like evil genies from the shattered bottles of the Saint-Jean:

A bellicose wind sweeps across the station's platform. The Indians are here to greet Cowboy's brother arriving on the 2:00 a.m. train from Tocqueville. Cowboy fiddles with his tumescent face, a result of the hiding he got earlier. The natural shape of his face allows him to carry this swelling with dignity. The train pulls into the station and Christophe, Cowboy's younger brother, is thrown out even before it comes to a dead stop. Short and stocky, he picks himself up with the liveliness of a hare and, furious, faces the cap wearer who, also angry, lashes him with a few of the most venomous epithets in his vocabulary. Each of his sentences is crowned with the following phrase: "You fucking little Siwash! You goddam fucking little Siwash!" Christophe's only reply was to grab a huge stone and hurl it at the individual who, suddenly discovering the limits of the protection normally offered by his uniform, beat a hasty retreat towards the safety of the passenger car. The others, Cowboy and the Kid in the lead, follow their expelled brother's example, howling out with anger, and a genuine stoning takes place; that night, the Via Rail coach is given an official pelting. An imposing rock crashes against the window of a door that's just been closed decisively, totally shattering it. Smaller stones, picked right from the ballast, fly towards the large panoramic windows behind which huddle terrified and dumbfounded passengers from Montreal and other points along the line. Welcome to Grande-Ourse, ladies and gentlemen! Feeling they're no match for this raging mob, and to cover judicious budget cuts (there's no stationmaster to enforce protocol), the attendants, after consultations, think an emergency departure from these unhealthy surroundings would be more compatible with the survival of their train. More than a train or stationmaster, it's a general the rail men would've needed on that memorable June 24. Under an increased barrage of every stone that could be hurled, the locomotives haul the short carriage and its passengers out of range.

The small group flocks around the store's entrance. A deathly music rises from the ghetto-blaster someone is holding under his arm. Having lost all composure, I howl for someone to let me in, and on the double, because I'm an employee of the Outfitters and, as such, am entitled to certain considerations, it seems, like a complimentary two-four. Then, through the timorously half-open door, amid a fissure of light slashing the night, the stunned heads of Benoît and the Old Man appeared. Dishevelled and sleepy, they believed the time had come to pay with their lives. But that much wasn't required; all we wanted was the merchandise they guarded, to drink a little more to be able to remain standing. Caught between this entrenched camp and the horde laying siege to it, I'm trying to hedge between the two positions, irreconcilable from the beginning. In the meantime, the one named Christophe, a marvellous little fellow, heavy set, with long straight hair, wearing jeans and leather, the look of a rocker and a warrior's soul, a bundle of nerves and hard as a rock, grabbed my collar, clenching to the point of choking me, repeating continually, jaws tensed, filled with a yen to do me in before getting an answer, "Who are you? Who are you?"

He smells strongly of alcohol and suspicion. Cowboy and Karate Kid strive to hold him back, intervene and keep telling him over and over, "He's our friend! He's our friend!"

But he listens to that terse defence, showing every sign of a deep scepticism, pauses very briefly, then continues, holding my collar tightly, hissing through his teeth, "Who are you? Who are you?"

I'm brutally grabbed by four skinny and efficient arms, torn from the compact mass's grasp and drawn into the store where a state of alert reigns. The door closes in a whirlwind over the angry night. Benoît and the Old Man are yawning widely, ashen-faced and shocked. They look daggers at me, find me guilty without trial, a traitor to my country, to my Outfitters, to my reprieved country, to my dearest bosses who are filled with good intentions and sound values. I plead in vain to get a case of beer on credit, but the judges' verdict excludes compassion. I then inform the gentlemen that I want to go out, into the vociferating turbulence which waves its fist and continues to knock at the door. This is too much for the Old Man. "They'll lynch him!" he howls, wringing his hands.

Then, realizing such a prospect didn't only have bad sides, he orders Benoît to take me to the basement. The manager gravely leads the way, taking me to a hidden service door that will take me to freedom. In the meantime, I still manage to swipe a wine bottle from a shelf in passing. I press it against my chest in the dark and, later, draw it from my jacket like a sabre: it's Cuvée des Patriotes. Wow!

The three Yankees have hurled themselves at Flamand. Legris wants to hold them back. A first blow, from the American side, twists his head. In turn, Flamand lets out a powerful jab, rattling his jaw. Legris now only has to turn around to faint more comfortably. Gisèle takes advantage of the situation, adding her personal touch from top to bottom, then Gilles, catching him in his arms, knees him in the groin, asserting himself as well, instructing him to keep still. Farther away, Crazy Sam gets back up, totally punch-drunk; he'll have trouble eating toast tomorrow morning. He stays there, leaning against the jukebox. Willie Lamothe wails as though someone were pinching one of his balls.

Combining efforts, the three Americans will manage to escort Flamand to the door, but none will emerge unscathed. When Gisèle tries to foil an attempt to expel her, Gilles surprises himself, grabbing her around the waist from behind, trying to drag her he doesn't quite know where. She stamps her feet, his hands are full, holding her by the breasts, he feels she's caused enough damage as it is. She still manages to escape his grasp, elbowing him high up, without looking, then runs away and disappears into the night.

Legris lies on the pool table, as though dead. But the Legris of this world are hard to kill.

Gilles stays there feeling his fat lip and loose tooth. Crazy Sam was fed up and went to bed.

❧

I accompany the Indians back to their camp on the outskirts of the village. Large white tents push the darkness back around the clearing. As we arrive, a violent argument breaks out between Cowboy and Christophe. They hurl insults I'm unable to understand. Howls of discord soar, their fists and feet cleave the air. And then, seizing his brother's 30-30, Christophe points it and blindly fires into the darkness. Two, three shots thunder like condemnations, the hammer blows of death. I land flat on my stomach, close to Judith, also lying in the tall grasses. We play hide and seek with stray bullets and fear makes her squeeze my arm very hard. In front of us, with astounding courage, Cowboy has stood up in the night, walking towards Christophe who hesitates, threatens, backs up, swears, shoots in the air, on the ground, at his feet, and again straight in front of him, blindly. Cowboy rushes ahead and chases him. The gunfight continues in every direction, erratic, with flashes allowing us to locate their position each time the runaway turns around and shoots. I lie flat on the ground, Judith as well. They've disappeared, swallowed by the darkness. Judith says it's a bad omen, two brothers squabbling like hungry dogs, carrying their wild feud under the leaves. The music of the powder soars like an excruciating prelude in the Grande-Ourse sky.

Judith and I take refuge in one of the large ghostly tents hovering in the summer night. The air inside was stifling. I spot a woman; only her shining face, lit from top to bottom by an oil lamp, emerges from the surrounding darkness, floating there like a hideous mask. In the shadows drowning her lap, a child cries. The woman is ageless and seems rather battered. On her yellow and drooping face, a look of ghastly bliss, a sort of diabolical satisfaction expressing itself through a smile that's also a sneer, a snub to an entire notion of beauty. Her disgraced flesh is fat with the misfortunes of the world. And it stinks in there. Miasmas crawl around under the canvas, a strong odour of fuel permeates the confined air. The girl waves a rag soaked with a volatile liquid under her nose. She's high, her mouth is veiled by the odorous cloth. Seems to be worshipping. I wonder what it is. Judith, covering the child's sobs, fills me in: that, my friend, is naphtha. She slides up against me. Cowboy came under the canvas as well, crawling up to us on his knees. He finally managed to get his rifle back. They settled the problem with kicks. He informs me that the fat girl got off the train as well. Her name is Gisèle, she's Salomé's mother. The social services gave her back custody of that little bawler crying his lungs out between her thighs. Face buried in the rag, she takes another deep breath. A few drops of fuel fall on the baby. The gallon of naphtha lies beside him. He wriggles. I try to get my brain to work, to jar my senses. I have to fight off an invasive torpor, a painful spell. Frozen in its morbid snigger, Judith's head drifts in the darkness, as though detached from its mooring. Mine aches and I murmur incomprehensible things to myself before finally passing out. Good night, friends.

3

INDEPENDENCE day

B ENOÎT WAS TORMENTED AND HIS UPPER body could be seen
behind a small desk, bent over another rebellious calculation.
The Old Man, an instinctive calculator, never touched the books.
He specialized in concrete little swindles, in greedily haggled minor
profits. He needed to feel paper bills.

The Saint-Jean-Baptiste weekend had brought a new
procession of fishermen to our doors, a majority of whom were
from La Belle Province, and therefore used to all manner of price
hikes. They had the advantage of including unconditional gasoline
buyers in their ranks. On the other hand, the occupancy rate in the
Outfitters' small houses had permanently settled in the
neighbourhood of zero. Arguing that these rather spacious
dwellings, with their rather modern furniture, their rather
functional appliances, and their relative comfort were still better
than the crude log cabins rented at high rates by other outfitters,
Mr. Administrator considered the prohibitive price charged for
these lodgings to be a privilege. As soon as we told prospective

customers about our prices, they took off screaming as though skinned alive. Our pseudo-comfort went against the grain of their genuine aspirations.

We also had regular customers, often solitary types, prowling through the north for professional reasons. They included representatives from Crown corporations and heavily subsidized companies, railway foremen on inspection tours, scalers working for large lumber companies, Hydro executives who, helicoptered in, always brought along fishing rods. All these respectable rogues had one thing in common: they didn't have to worry about expense claims, and made it a point of honour, with our smiling complicity, to push their extravagant expense accounts to the limit. Apparitions that were sometimes surprising would mingle with the predictable crowd: prospectors out of Abitibi, disoriented adventurers, French or German travellers walking through the back country. When crossing the threshold, they'd utter the magic formula we'd stopped believing, "Seems you have rooms to rent?"

Brigitte, going against her interests, sometimes phoned me to palm off a prospective sleeper not overly heartened by the hotel's atmosphere. One night, we had to billet a great hulking brute sporting a fine moustache: the Indian reserve's police chief. The next day, the fellow seemed a little frazzled and in a hurry to be off. We subsequently learned that he'd preferred to spend the night in his pickup, because we'd lodged him near the old dispensary. Long ago, in the days of epidemics, the place had a reputation as a death trap, so the chief got scared of ghosts, there, all alone in the dark.

The Americans with the Cherokee had reservations with us. Mr. Administrator had sugared the pill with his publicity, and they'd shelled out a great deal to come and tackle *Ursus Americanus*. Everything seems so beautiful and easy in the pictures of specialized magazines. The four guys had coughed up a thousand slugs each, cash, at first contact, before neglectfully inquiring about the arrangements and installations at their disposal. The logistical aspect of the whole affair visibly didn't worry them too much. They were very eager to see the black coat of their dreams stroll by on an animal they felt was merely its depository, its usurper almost. They had arrangements with a taxidermist and already imagined the hide luxuriously spread on the living room floor, in front of the TV. As for the killing part, well, they'd taken precautions. Half-measures wouldn't be part of the game.

The day following Saint-Jean, after sleeping about three turns of the clock, they had a surprise for us. The bearded one, named Jim, explained that, two days ago, in their haste to storm into the village, they'd run over a dog whose rather battered carcass now lay in a ditch farther on. The Old Man walked over to the spot and, recognizing our ex-dog in the pile of hair and scabs, immediately found the words to comfort our friends.

"It's all right! It's all right! We wanted to get rid of it anyhow! Damn good thing! Saves us the price of a bullet!"

Our guests then displayed luxurious leather cases from which they pulled their weapons. A handful of locals had cut short their traditional swilling that morning to make up an informal welcome committee. The artillery alone, equipped with scopes worthy of the Mount Palomar observatory, probably cost as much as the total of benefits mailed each month to the local population.

The Old Man sighed with delight. The technological advancement of those nimrods was excellent for the establishment's image. When he pocketed the four payments in the Outfitters' name, we might've feared for a moment he'd have a heart attack. Eyes rolled upwards, he didn't dare shove the wad of large bills into his pockets, transfixed with anguish at the prospect of taking his eyes off it. He remained there, as though kayoed, as though hit in the brain by a rock while the Americans smiled modestly at the superiority of their exchange rate. Benoît, prodding the Old Man towards the safe, said to me over his shoulder in a steady voice, "Go and show them the hunting sites. Take the pickup. Keys are on the counter."

I escorted the quartet. Two of them climbed into the Outfitters' official vehicle with me, the Cherokee followed. They were large, rather sympathetic fellows from New Jersey and Pennsylvania, who listened to Springsteen with patriotic fervour and voted for Reagan because he allowed every citizen to have a weapon in their bedroom. After witnessing their arrival, at the small Seven Mile Bridge, I felt a kind of moral obligation to impress them. I gulped, tore off like the devil, taking the first turn on hub caps, before disappearing in the dust behind the store. We drove through the ghost town and the guy holding the camera continued filming the scenery swiftly parading by on each side, sinister and inconsistent, somewhat like the cardboard facades used for making westerns. When Jim asked for explanations concerning this weird state of desertion, I took a deep breath, hinting it was a long story. He turned to me with a slight smile and said kindly, "Well. Try to make it short."

I'd completed a final baiting tour while our sharpshooters girded for battle. I'd put aside a couple of carrion boxes and, towards late afternoon, decided to take them over to Cowboy. I knew a bear had been seen around the encampment.

The gravel road at the end of Lac Légaré, before aligning itself more or less along the railway, was twisted by an S turn over 50 or so metres. I always approached that passage briskly and, each time, felt the tires lose hold and skid over the sand with a moderate drift. I raised my foot, and the vehicle began to sway and flirt with the ditch, but finally got back on course. A rut brought me back to my senses like a kick in the ass on coming out, and everything returned to normal.

Afterwards, the road disappeared into the forest. The Kikendache camp was near the village, at the edge of a small peatbog in the middle of which lay a circle of water smooth as a penny. The railway's embankment separated the camp from the peatbog. Suddenly, approaching the spot, I hit the brakes, coming to a stop against a jeep parked in the middle of the road. Standing near the vehicle, rifle in hand, Cowboy saluted me without losing his composure. I got out to join him.

Seated at the wheel of the jeep, Crazy Sam was speaking to Cowboy with animation and a good deal of confusion, tapping his wide-brimmed hat. He seemed quite drunk and, slumped over the steering wheel, could only turn his head with difficulty. Cowboy was holding a beer bottle, likely a gift from the American. He took a good swig, handing me the bottle and suggesting I do the same. I noticed a bandage around his wrist; a memento from the brawl. I drank in turn.

Cowboy explained he'd just examined bear tracks on the roadside. The animal had shown up in front of the camp the previous morning at dawn, and his brother Christophe had missed it. So Cowboy had taken things in hand at twilight. For the moment, he remained there, jaw tensed over a smile, feet slightly spread, clutching a rifle in his right hand and Crazy Sam's liquid offering in the other. The bear was nowhere in sight, that much was agreed on. Crazy Sam gently rubbed his cheek and mumbled, mouth dangling, "Well, son! When you bring that bastard down, remember me: I'll give you a good price for the hide!"

Painfully starting the engine, he drove the jeep off at a cautious speed. He hadn't yet disappeared when Cowboy turned around towards me, saying, "Look carefully."

Then, fluidly stringing movements together, he threw the half-filled beer bottle in the air, letting the 30-30 Winchester speak, its stock having reached his shoulder in the meantime. The target exploded at the peak of its trajectory, its fallout showering a grove of young larches at the edge of the road. Vitamins rained down on the tender stretch of forest for a few seconds; everything shone with surreal clarity and intensity beneath the rays of the setting sun which, farther on, blocked the road just over the horizon. A young larch is extraordinarily green when touched by the light of a summer evening, and that green discharged torrents of softness into the bitter air and over the tangle of people.

If, from a nearby thicket, the bear were observing the scene, he couldn't have been very reassured. Farther on, amid a bend in the road, Crazy Sam's jeep had slowed down, almost coming to a standstill.

❧

Cowboy didn't turn down the two cases of bait: they might always come in handy. But, glancing at the forest edge, where the half-light opened up, he still said this strategic element seemed superfluous.

"Ti-Kid bear will return tomorrow."

Then, "Are you hunting with the Americans?"

"Let's just say I'm laying the ground.... Don't have a choice."

His face tensed up violently. He was gritting his teeth, "The Americans won't kill a thing!"

The Indians had a weird habit of hazarding prophecies about nature. I asked why, and he only said they weren't his friends.

Each summer, the Kikendache family left the reserve, located north of the great reservoir, settling on the outskirts of Grande-Ourse. In principle, the migration was prompted by walleye fishing and blueberry picking; in practice, it rapidly turned into a gravitation around the Outfitters' store, from which the clan drew its basic subsistence. Cowboy was particularly fond of Tropicana Chicken, a frozen food, packaged in yellow cardboard, more evocative of congealed animal fats than the sunshine of the south seas. But the name, it must be said, was very exotic.

As we pulled into the camp, Alexis, the eldest, was fiddling around with a bicycle which, at first glance, seemed to have been ill-treated from time immemorial. He saluted us, distant, potbellied, and pocky. His wife, an enormous Cree, was attending to food farther on, flanked by two kids who were already corpulent and gelatinous. She gave me an indulgent smile. For his part, Christophe was either asleep or moping, we weren't sure. Things were going rather badly for him. After firing at his brother the day before Saint-Jean-Baptiste, he'd gone and missed the only trophy likely to enhance his status among the others this morning. The gunfight, besides, had set tongues wagging in the village. The Old Man, for one, saw it as a sign of a violence now out of control, that would ultimately play tricks on everyone, if care wasn't taken.

The family portrait was still graced by Dagobert, who dealt with a homosexuality felt to be cumbersome by making himself most discreet and as mysterious as possible. In private, he gave himself the airs of an Oriental empress or an androgynous bayadere. His parents still remained on the reserve, having agreed to join up with their offspring later in the summer, with the two little girls who completed the tribe. Big Alexandre, however, was missing from the portrait, since he was doing time farther south. His kinfolk didn't really appreciate having this rather disreputable element in their midst, though it was generally agreed he had courage. All he needed to become a hero to his kinsmen was Cowboy's subtle charisma. This Alexandre, as mentioned earlier, was Judith's rightful boyfriend, and that's why she had to be discreet before opening her arms to guys around Grande-Ourse.

Cowboy put down his rifle. Judith, who'd been resting, soon joined us in the main tent. Big-Arms and Karate Kid were at the wake on the other side of the lake. Dagobert, Judith, and Cowboy were to drop by later. Over by the peatbog, the love-sick stridulations of thousands of frogs soared into the approaching night. Inside the tents, the usual happy disorder reigned hopelessly. The fir carpet was strewn with empty containers, carnation milk cans, sticky baby bottles, flattened Pepsi cans, and Mister Freeze wrappers shining like glowworms in the muggy half-light. Water was boiling over a camp stove by the light of oil lamps. The place smelled of unchanged diapers. The children shat with no let-up.

The conversation gravitated to Gisèle's return who, for the moment, was snoring some distance away in the shelter of another tent. I felt like an impressionable greenhorn.

"Does she sniff naphtha very often?"

They didn't want to talk about it.

"So what's this story about a treasure?"

"A treasure," Cowboy agreed.

"Gisèle's the one who saw it," said Judith. "Boisvert's son hid money before leaving. But it's a curse."

This incomplete story sparked my imagination, taking over from my neglected books. The Indians' superstitious aversion to telling more piqued my curiosity. I thought *treasure* was a beautiful word, a gem in itself, at once trite and mysterious.

Christophe slipped through the opening and dropped down among us. He was barely beginning to tolerate my presence. Quarrelsome and scornful, he made up for his small size by throwing his shoulders far back and swinging his small fists with studied spirit.

"So? The Americans?"

"The Americans? Going hunting tomorrow."

"Won't kill a thing!"

"Obviously."

I suddenly felt as though I were a high school guidance counsellor.

"The Americans," I said, "are the ones with the real treasure: a thousand dollars a head for one week's hunting and a bear in their sights. You should become guides!"

"Christophe," Judith observed impassively, "needs a good scope...."

"Aaah!"

"Not something we want to do," Cowboy said, gently this time.

"Seems Via Rail wants to banish Indians from the Sans-Terre line," I mentioned in passing.

"We'll derail the train!"

Part of the night went on the same way, squandered with more or less coherent talk, words tossed to the wind. I had a heavy schedule planned for the next day, and wanted to take leave to get some shut-eye. But they insisted I do more camping that night and, when I got up, Judith followed quietly with her train of hopes.

❧

Already grappling with cookware, the Old Man was humming his morning refrain. This was the big morning. Camouflaged from feet (heavy boots) to head (solid helmets), the Americans had slipped tinted shades over their khaki hoods and the addition of a gorget completed the weatherproofing of their outfits. Not one inch of white flesh gave away the North American lurking in there! Bodies wrapped in cartridge belts with enough ammunition to feed a machine gun, limbs stiffened under layers of underwear defying any climatic accident (the Old Man had warned them about the possibility of cool mornings), they could barely move, walking haltingly like deep-sea divers. Leading the way at the wheel of the pickup, I took them to the blinds, promising to return a little later in the day.

But they deserted earlier than expected, returning to the store wailing like calves. Appetites whetted by all that good meat nourished on grilled steaks, blackflies had taken advantage of the weaknesses in the synthetic armour to get at the chubby flesh. Once inside the defence system, they were impossible to dislodge, biting away to their heart's delight, with blood flowing profusely. Wrists and ankles, particularly vulnerable, were now adorned with ruddy bracelets woven by points of impact.

The expedition's official film-maker, the frailest of the four, suddenly felt ill and was struck down by a fainting spell. The Old Man came to the rescue. Instead of proffering first aid, he lavished words on him that his refined English seemed to render more objective, "It's nothing, pal! Nothing at all! I'll fix you a nice meal right away! How about it? A hamburger? Pure beef! It's nothing, nothing at all!"

But his condition wasn't too reassuring. While Benoît and I sifted through emergency solutions (once the phone call to the dispensary had been excluded, due to the nurse's absence, an air lift wasn't to be ruled out), a fellow hunter gave the guy one of his nitro pills, restoring a few shades of colour to his cheeks.

Next day, at first light, as though circled by the invisible hoops of a skipping rope, the Old Man was going from one American to the other. He'd grabbed a roll of tape and was busily closing the gaps. In the end, he'd wrapped the hunters with an aesthetic concern that was a credit to him. Wrists, ankles, necks, right down to the tiniest opening had disappeared under elegant twists of Sparadrap. The Old Man was even about to apply his medicine to the airways, left uncovered by thin slits, but Benoît rightly emphasized that it was probably better to breathe blackflies than nothing at all. Regretfully, he concurred.

The American nostrils therefore remained free to sniff the pestilence of bulk carrion all morning. Besides, that's the only scent they caught, since no bear showed up. After their return, the guys started to grumble among themselves. Jim proclaimed himself group spokesman, and came over to me. "Where the hell are the fucking bastards, Gilles?"

Remembering the lesson I'd learned at the hotel, I affected the serene authority of a local. "Oh well, you know, there wasn't a single fucking blueberry last summer, so it's no wonder there isn't a single fucking bear around, you know!"

I was rather proud of my tirade. But, while he went away without griping to chat a little farther on, I had an unusual sensation, a tingling on the nape of my neck followed by a trickle of cold sweat. An alarm was ringing in my head.

❧

When you can at least boast having seen a clump of fur or the claw mark of a large paw, sniffed a drop of urine or a very fresh dropping, you stroke the trigger with your finger, rhyming off propitiatory curses. You live with hope and get angry inside. Grande-Ourse resembled that immobile hunter, dizzy with expectations. Life followed its sinewy course, when it wasn't clearly staggering. Every morning at dawn, the Muppet went fishing at the same spot, near a grass bed polluted by hydroplane fuel spills. He'd tirelessly cast and reel in his line and, regular as a metronome, would grab and pop a small frosty drawn from the considerable stash he'd sensibly brought along. When questioned, he'd swear to God there were some small and temperamental walleye at a stone's throw. Then why kill yourself miles from anywhere? But he spent most of his time snagged on the bottom, hooked on water lilies, leaning over the side of his rowboat trying to free his line. Then, with short and awkward strokes, he'd row back to shore, returning to his station near the cold room. If the weather was nice, he'd go out and take in the sun on the doorstep, placing his beer in the shadow of a lintel, within immediate reach of his right hand, which dangled in the air like a rag.

Legris joined him later on, his features showing signs of the night. Nearby, Big Ben was happily dragging his potbelly around. His inertia curtailed the timid entreaties to enthusiasm Benoît still felt he had to give him on occasion. The Métis still claimed to be trailing the mythical bear that, since the beginning of summer, had taken him on an exhausting tour of the cardinal points. And the Old Man, wagering on the existence of that bear like Pascal on that of God, hadn't been loath to encourage him. But when no one was in sight, Big Ben stretched out on the concrete steps with grunts of pleasure, wrapped in amniotic warmth.

To maintain good customer relations, the Old Man always kept walleye in the freezer. Each time an empty-handed fisherman came to list his grievances at the store (it happened increasingly), the Old Man, getting wind of the threat, drew from the deepest part of his wits to salve the injured pride. He first went over the range of explanations: the weather (he carefully listed each of its components); the water level that was either too high or too low (with the damned beavers providing material for one of his most spirited tirades); the legendary passivity of the aquatic fauna's largest members (the big one's don't bite); satellite manipulation by the Russians. But he'd keep his favourite denunciation for the end, uttering it with particular delight: the most decisively harmful crew in the entire region were the Indians and their nets.

At this point of his appeal, when anguish painted over the sportsman's features, the Old Man headed for the freezer. He grabbed two or three aluminum-clad walleyes, which he'd convinced the Indians to sell, through one of those about-turns of his conscience no longer requiring any effort. Softly, he said, "Here pal, here.... This is for you, no I insist, it's a gift. I've got lots more just like this, and bigger ones, and the biggest ones are still in the water...."

If money has no smell, neither do fish sometimes.

Admiral Nelson's funeral took place two days following Saint-Jean-Baptiste. The Old Man displayed sincere grief. He left for the chapel with a tear in his eye, and had the same tear when he returned. I remained on duty at the store while everyone converged towards the top of the hill, where Admiral Nelson would depart for the little spot awaiting him in the large sand patch, next to Roméo Flamand.

Some miscreants, naturally, did miss the ceremony. While I was taking advantage of the lighter crowds, reading a novel, Moreau burst into the store and, with a few uneven strides, came over to stand in front of me. He hadn't sobered up since the Saint-Jean-Baptiste fire. Legris rushed over in his tracks, wearing a fine bruise on his temple, unsuccessfully trying to reason with him. Moreau hit the counter with his fist and thunder echoed throughout the building. I answered politely, "Yes?"

"Yougoddamfuckingclerk!"

The following second, he jumped onto the counter and, to my surprise, I had the dismay of having him in front of me. Only the pasty thickness of his breath now lay between us. He asked whether I was ready to fight and I understood that, through a lack of imagination, he'd quite simply abstain from suggesting motives for that action. This time, that was it. I was done for. Legris no longer moved — once bitten, twice shy — accepting the course of things. I successively turned both cheeks, but it was to find an escape route on either side. Then Jacques Boisvert appeared, wearing a black suit and tie. Having instinctively ascertained what was happening, he'd cut short his mourning on the hill to come here and check things out. Like some great actors, this man was first of all a presence, i.e., it was impossible to think about or look at anything else but him when he walked into a room. Notwithstanding any assumption of physical strength, the real basis of his vigour was his brain. The other day, a whole band of Indians, having left the reserve, had stopped over to make trouble at an outfitter's on the reservoir. The guy, scared to death, had phoned the hotel and Boisvert travelled 50 kilometres over bad roads to see what was going on. Just seeing him enter, folks scattered and cleared off. So what was going on? Well, nothing of course. Everything was fine.

Before him, the pathetic bragging of an oaf like Moreau simply didn't cut it. It wasn't too long before he found himself outside, crouching on the ground, tasting the sad delights of nausea. We were then able to observe, as Legris tapped him on the back, that his last breakfast had been as copious as it had been swallowed quickly.

"You're like the cavalry in films," I said to Boisvert. "You always show up on time."

"Speaking of cavalry, your Americans haven't killed any bears yet?"

"Ha! Ha!"

He sniggered without joy.

"Poor fellas, brought here by heavy advertising. A bedside rug guaranteed or your money back! Ah! Ah, the old bastard! Marketing! Marketing worthy of a frog swamp!"

"The ad was Mr. Administrator's idea."

"Irresponsibility doesn't excuse a thing."

A prolonged silence followed.

He seemed uneasy in that churchgoer's costume for which he was so ill-suited. And, in turn, his discomfitures intimidated me.

"Are there a lot of people?"

"What?"

I moved my head slightly towards the chapel.

"Well, yes!" he said dryly. "Everyone's there!"

He'd grown sullen and came near me.

"Nothing like a dead person to bring people together around here! Same applies to bears. If your Americans ever kill any, you'll see them shaking hands, jumping in each other's arms, taking pictures! Above all, death is a show. It's the same with a human being, except they don't take pictures. They expose him."

I felt I had to protest.

"It's not the same.... The bear is killed by a different species. But when a man kills another man...."

He waited. He was challenging me.

"I've forgotten what I wanted to say...."

"Obviously, whoever kills a bear won't win a popularity contest among bears...."

"That's what I meant," I said unsteadily.

"Whoever kills, always belongs to a different species, Gilles...."

His voice was florid. But I didn't have time to ask what he meant. He was already leaving in a rush, without saluting me. The door closed over the vision of his black outfit.

❧

Benoît was stooping before my eyes. The more he worked himself into the ground, the more the magnitude of the task seemed to increase before him, like a cancer feeding off his vitality. A magnitude that, besides, was largely imaginary, since his use of time could've been uneventful, with a little planning. But the unwarranted stress, a succession of coffees after midnight, an obsession with figures, and the asexual nature of his insomnia largely made up for the lack of work, strictly speaking. The Outfitters' revenues were far inferior to our expenses and Benoît worried about those kinds of details. The Old Man speculated unscrupulously about his chances of making it through the summer. The greenish colour the manager brought back into the light each morning offered bystanders a sure sign of his decline. But to finish him off, a death-blow was still needed, the sledgehammer blow, the tenth plague without which the Pharaoh would've never given in. A cruel paradox for this young man, whose love life evoked the Gobi desert, that the final curse arose in the pernicious form of love.

Gisèle Kikendache had slept with nearly every railway employee in these parts. The Via Rail guys were masters at impregnating her on the sly, before tearing off down the tracks;

they specialized in the hit and run, were masters of postcard paternity, keeping their penises parallel to the rails, hearts cramped in their uniforms, and caresses kept to themselves.

Gisèle entered the store one beautiful June day, heading to the cold room with a rolling gait. The Muppet came out of it unexpectedly and saluted her. "Well, dear Gisèle, back in the neighbourhood?" He then sponged an effusion of saliva with a resonant lick, blinking at the same time.

Gisèle had nothing of the beauty queen. Moreover, she sported a fine bruise that afternoon. Beneath her sweatshirt, with holes in the elbows, a paunch more mobile than the rest of her body bounced as she dragged herself through the refrigerated room. She emerged after a few minutes, lugging a two-four whose clinking bottles seemed to protest mildly. As I informed her of the price, she stretched a grubby finger towards the tangle of bills, punctuating the gesture with a piano-shaped grin, articulating laboriously, "Cre ... dit."

Benoît then came out of the storage room, hammering out as he ran up to us, furious and categorical, "Nooo!!! No beer to Gisèle! No credit to Gisèle! Nothing to Gisèle!"

I stood facing the Indian woman. Her tone was becoming threatening, "Cre ... dit!"

Benoît came over to stand beside me, shoulder to shoulder. He was rocking back and forth like a boxer. Keeping his eyes on the fat girl, he apprized me of the situation such as a minimal degree of lucidity required I see it. One, Gisèle was an unredeemable boozer. Two, she already owed the Outfitters several thousand dollars (the exact amount still hadn't been calculated). Three, because of her seven offspring scattered along the railway between Tocqueville and Sans-Terre, produced from white or native semen indiscriminately, Gisèle received substantial benefits the first of each month. Four, the totality of that enticing allowance was usually spent on alcohol before the Outfitters could get a single cent. Five, giving Gisèle credit was to sink hopelessly into the slimy bog of financial, moral (or other) stagnation. Six, Gisèle Kikendache was a living affront to any notion of integrity, pride, human respect, and dignity, a case UN experts, were they to study it, would unhesitatingly classify as non-recyclable garbage.

Confident of his arguments, Benoît reduced gallant remarks to the strict minimum, showing the poor woman the door. But the Muppet drew near, attracted by the scene, innocently proposing to settle the contentious expense himself. His offer was accompanied by one condition: Gisèle had to accept to sip the contents of the case in his company.

The Muppet was unique in Grande-Ourse: he always paid cash. He was irreproachable in that regard. Benoît, therefore, had to agree, grudgingly, and the wily pensioner dragged off the fat Indian woman, carrying the object of their thirst and the remedy to his loneliness. But before leaving, Gisèle turned around one last time and, blowing a delightfully obscene kiss in the manager's direction, purred a perfectly audible, "Thank you, Benoît, my love." Benoît looked at me, aghast.

❧

As soon as he'd escaped gravity, Boisvert made a hedgehopping dive and disappeared over the horizon. An intimidation manoeuvre? I should've been thinking. Anyhow, the stunt didn't stop Brigitte from rushing over to our place. Benoît was nowhere in sight and the Old Man had gone off with Big Ben to prospect for bear tracks. We were treated to all the pleasures registered on the program imagined the previous night in our respective beds. In the heat of the action, we couldn't hear that the hydroplane had droned back in the Grande-Ourse sky. There was knocking at the door. I ignored it: the badgerer would ultimately get tired, like the others. But a square opening pierced into the cold room's outside wall, and covered with a sliding panel, allowed beer bottles to be brought in directly. Boisvert kicked in the panel, squatting through into the small refrigerated room where we were giving off as much steam as two locomotives. He straddled our joined bodies, while Brigitte sat up, saying, "Oh!"

Boisvert, with a sardonic look, had already left the cold room and gone into the store. We could hear him rummaging through a freezer. Brigitte slipped into her denims. Without giving her time to button them, he opened the waist of her jeans with a rude gesture, and slipped a good-sized ice block between it and her stomach. He then pulled up the zipper and, insensitive to the expression of shock blossoming over the features of his companion, tied the button. Happy as a lark, sharp as could be, Jacques Boisvert turned towards me as I finished dressing, huddled behind a fruit display whose contents were of dubious freshness, "And now, Gilles, pal, open the door so we can leave without having to perform more acrobatics! And while you're at it, put a dozen ice blocks in my truck. It's a shame, you see: I was heading to the lake! Moving along and then, wham! I remembered I forgot the ice! They can't get along without it over there...."

He interrupted himself. The Muppet slipped his ecstatic head through the wall.

"Come in, come in!" Boisvert guffawed. "Your beer's waiting."

And he gave a resounding slap to Brigitte's behind, who left the premises with the dignity of an emperor penguin.

As if that weren't enough, Gisèle appeared once again and, scorning the main entrance as well, she tried to slip through the opening and into the room that interested her. But nothing passed from her torso down, despite the Muppet's efforts, who was pressing against the interior, pulling on everything that stuck out.

As Boisvert got back into his truck, Brigitte started walking towards the lake. He didn't insist and, jumping down from his seat, helped Gisèle get up instead.

"Come on, fat girl. I'll drive you back to the camp. We'll let these two get over their emotions."

She compliantly gave him her arm, and sat beside him in the truck. The Muppet looked at them, moved.

"Well," he sniffed. "Let the truth be told: Jacques has always had Gisèle's respect!"

I no longer understood a thing.

"Still, it's strange.... Anyhow, I think he's suspected of...."

"Oh no!" said the Muppet, indignant. I'll swear to it before witnesses! Jacques Boisvert wasn't at the hotel when it happened! Hadn't yet returned.... I know, I was awake...."

"You were taking a bath...."

"I would've heard the hydroplane!"

"All the same.... The other Indians would like to kill him."

"Yes. Except for Gisèle...."

And the Muppet excused me with a nervous nod. I couldn't know everything.

One night, six or seven guys wanted to have her. They were holding her by the
arms and legs, having lain her on the pool table, skirt pulled up, undergarments
torn off. The young waitress didn't know what to do. They told her to mind her
business. She tried to reach Jacques Boisvert on the phone, but there was no
answer at his mobile home. She finally ran out and a glow caught her attention
on the lake. He was in his hydroplane, at 3:00 a.m., making a last-minute
repair. When Boisvert burst in, the guy shooting his load didn't even have time to
put on his pants. The guys were outside before being able to say a word or deal a
blow. No one had ever seen Boisvert in that state. His face smeared with grease,
he was scary to look at, no one really protested. They all left in a rush. Moreau
was there, Legris, the trapper, a couple of locals, Crazy Sam, and a railway man.
Boisvert offered Gisèle a room for the night, then for another, then every night
during that summer. The summer following the death of Roméo Flamand, the
summer when Boisvert's wife drowned. But that room became a real brothel one
day, in every sense of the word, and people were talking. One night, he finally
had to throw her out.

"Now, if I understand properly, Muppet, you were there observing
all this?"

He wriggled.

"Just like I'm standing here, son! I saw everything!"

"I suppose you were waiting for your turn as well?"

"I didn't have time! Boisvert threw us all out, angrier than the
devil! Oh, don't worry, I've made up for it since...."

"I'm not worried, Mr. Muppet."

Each night, I found an excuse to disappear into nature, under the
disapproving gazes of Benoît and the Old Man who, from the
height of their purity, resolutely condemned the flurry of base
lechery on the point of swallowing me up. I melted into the night,
discovering I had dark wings and hovered beneath the conical and
tapering canopy of evergreens. I climbed the railway's shoulder and,
in measured steps, scaled the long horizontal ladder that
disappeared before me, in the direction of adventure. The large

white tents daubed the darkness with patches of light. To the right, the peatbog echoed with the persistent tremolos of batrachians, and scattered bats fluttered at eye level. I slipped into the tent and lay beside Judith. Christophe was spicing up the atmosphere with impudent jokes and grabbed me as an invitation to wrestle. Cowboy was stretched over a sleeping bag, daydreaming, head tilted back, eyes locked in by this cloak of heavy opaque canvas. Dagobert was pondering the determining factors, the full details of his condition. Alexis, farther away, was living his very own family life, slightly on the fringes. His companion, most of the time, took care of Gisèle's youngest child along with her own pair of brats.

Karate Kid was coming down the rails, throwing kicks sideways, decapitating some grassy plant which, having resisted pesticides, crawled up the embankment. He felt cramped under his father's sheet-metal roof, holding his clan council here every night. At 6:00 a.m., tomorrow, he'd again be over there, lying under his barbells.

Christophe hollered at me to go into my imitation of the Old Man, with the others echoing his plea in unison. I stood up in the mass of warm air trapped by the canvas and gave my little rendition; it was a sweet revenge, a sacrilege they revelled in with irreverence.

In a way, I was silently courting Judith. She didn't express those kinds of things, and hardly encouraged me to do so. We never added anything to our gestures. Her feelings were known indirectly, revealing themselves in action, minimally and fleetingly. She was a stripper of the affections.

I didn't dare look her straight in the face; my eyes wandered in all directions, and even she preferred keeping hers to the ground. She remained astonishingly remote from love: her hairless pubis which I discovered in the tawny glow of the propane; her musky odour which I soaked up with the curiosity of the neophyte; details that, during conversations, titillated bachelors like Legris and the Muppet. Coition plunged Judith into a peaceful indifference which she nonetheless sought with resolve. I penetrated her with a circumspection that quickly led to boredom. Her earthly weight was there and I clung to it, satisfaction was guaranteed; the other thing eluded our power. She was a bridge beneath me, and you don't live on a bridge — you either cross or jump.

Most of what I knew about Judith I'd learned from the others. She also had a child, which a devoted aunt was raising, for the moment, on the reserve. At sixteen, she'd met a handsome young fellow with a pony tail in a Sans-Terre bar: a White guy who was planting trees in the region, undergoing a rest cure for advanced dehydration. Both had fallen madly in love and, in the autumn, Judith had landed, already pregnant, in a Mauricie farming community, where they'd moved in with the guy's family, for beginners. The parents, wary at first, were now happy: here was a girl who insisted on attending Sunday church. She'd be a good influence on the boy. Judith even thought about marriage, but kept quiet, more than ever she kept quiet. After a while, they rented an apartment in one of those bare and strange concrete blocks that sometimes sprout in the middle of abandoned fields, on the outskirts of large villages. But the guy never found a job to his liking. His mood deteriorated along with his taste for the exotic. Following the birth of the child — a charming one, incidentally — he became aloof and she gained weight. In the spring, he went off to plant trees and met a vegetarian girl. The relationship gradually ended that way, an exemplary little story, reproducible in millions of variations. Judith went back home with a new member of the Métis nation.

Judith stayed in Tocqueville regularly. She frequented, if you can imagine, the tanning salon. When I told her she didn't need it, she pretended not to understand what I meant.

She had a brother doing 25 years at the old Saint-Vincent-de-Paul Penitentiary. Whenever she went to Montreal, it was to see him. He'd drunk to excess one night, and had awakened much later in a Tocqueville room, in a pool of blood beside a body riddled with knife holes. Judith claimed he'd been the victim of an injustice, perhaps even framed. But the cops had gone by what they'd seen when they opened the door. They'd gone out to throw up, then filled the report.

In the end, our conversations were monologues. We spoke especially about others. The both of us were taboo subjects.

"Gisèle's in love," she informed me one night.

"For real?"

She shrugged.

"With Benoît."

"He'll have his arms full."

"My mother thinks it's a bad omen that Gisèle arrived the same day as the accident."

"It was the day after, at 2:00 a.m."

"It's still a bad sign."

"An omen?"

"A curse."

"Ah. Gisèle too?"

"Yes."

Waking up the next day, I had a fresh impression of a confused dream, where words, just words, had paraded endlessly before my eyes, indecipherable and defying any attempt at organization even if I could see them with absolute clarity, eluding the grasp of a definition. I confided this to Judith before leaving, but she had no opinion on the matter.

◗

Sweeping was one of Benoît's favourite rituals. It was useful, what with all the dust customers brought in at every visit. He'd first cover the floor with that sweeping powder we used when I was a kid to clean the basement's cement floor. Stretching out his arm, with supple hand, to spread the green crystals properly, he looked like a people's sower on a propaganda poster from the days of Stalin.

"Well, if you ask me, it's a sure bet they'll kill something!" Boisvert would exclaim whenever passing through. "If not a bear, then someone from your establishment who deserves it, far as I'm concerned!"

Indeed, the Americans had been there five days and all their efforts had remained distressingly sterile. One morning, having slept straight through in the tent, I returned to my station with comfortable tardiness, in clothes whose sloppiness was more than eloquent. The Old Man came towards me, astounded. Words were no longer coming out, he had to grab his neck with both hands to bring them to the surface.

"The guys are sleeping! No hunting this morning!"

"Oh?"

"Saying there aren't bears this year! Some idiot's gone and told them there were no blueberries last summer!"

"I can imagine the type."

"Let's forget about the fucking bears!" Jim suggested calmly.

But the Old Man managed to quell that wind of revolt. In his view, the guys only needed to get their minds off things. He offered them a little fishing trip. Would a dozen walleyes weighing ten pounds apiece be enough to console these lovers of Mother Nature? Eh?

The sportsmen jumped into baggy denims, and with adequately uttered satisfaction, put on loose flannel shirts whose collars they carefully avoided buttoning. They completed the jovial getup with a fitting cap made of canary yellow material and covered with crests bearing the colours of the various shopkeepers, retailers, specialists, wholesalers, and licensed grocers operating in the region. If need be, the fluorescent cap typical of northern inhabitants would do, its crest bearing the arms of a dealership, be it for tractors, outboard motors, or all-terrain vehicles.

"That wind over the lake will keep the flies off you," murmured the Old Man with infinite solicitude.

They gave him icy gazes, then followed me, carrying jangling fishing rods and a respectable quantity of beer.

"Send them to Lac du Fou," suggested Benoît. "That's where the fish are biting these days."

He then remembered a detail. "Fishing? But we don't even have a single rowboat that's ready! We lent the only one we had to Legris last week!"

He feverishly picked up the phone while the Old Man, letting himself go along the wall, held his head with a sort of humble and fragile tenderness.

"Now where has Big Ben run off to?" wondered Benoît.

The Old Man started into a small Vachon cake, whose crumbs flew out amid shreds of his speech.

"Personally, young fellas, I can't go on. This kind of business is not for a guy my age. When I'm old, my friends, I'll have my own business. A real one, you'll see. A pontoon platform fifty feet long, lawn chairs and coolers, room for 30 people trolling quietly while sun tanning. Serious customers, not self-employed shopkeepers.

Owners of small- and medium-sized businesses, who are poorer
than their staff. No sir, the real thing. Nothing to do with freezing
their asses on a bench, being rocked by the waves with both feet in
the water and no lawn chairs. A nice pontoon with a large motor.
And they'll pay top price guaranteed."

An awkward and palpable reality dissolved as he spoke; his
wonderful platforms packed with fat cats floated away, rippling the
water's surface, and time passed, wrinkling his skin.

The Americans wanted to know what was going on. Benoît
howled, beside himself, "No, Gisèle, you're not the one I want to
talk to!"

He finally hung up the phone and, sighing, announced very
calmly, "Legris is at the hotel, drunk as a skunk. The rowboat is at
Lac du Fou. Everything's running smoothly. No problems."

I signalled the Americans to follow me. The Old Man was no
longer listening, displaying a strange detachment. Nose stuck to the
window, he observed in a droning voice,

"Well, we've got a visitor ... Fat Gisèle! Uh, oh, looks like she's
fallen off the wagon! She's coming from the hotel."

"Everything's fine. No problems," Benoît mumbled
mechanically.

"You're a nice guy, Gilles ...," the one called Jim said later, as
though trying to convince himself.

Squeezed into the back, rocked by the swerves, the others had
nasty mugs. They regretted having to leave their vehicle at the
Outfitters because of mechanical problems. They were modern
Americans who'd come here to test their sophisticated toys, the
same way their compatriots with decorated chests had tested
Cruise missiles over the Athabasca tar sands. Each night, these big
kids would line up in front of the wall phone in the store, while I
had to grapple with international codes. They seemed to take my
mediation for granted, grabbing the receiver without saying thank
you, inquiring at length about news from the little lady back home
and the swimming pool, yes the swimming pool; in the midst of
our spectacular fresh-water reserves, these fellows would pine for
the latest about their pool's chlorine level. Let's be fair: they also
appreciated being able to breathe air that wasn't too polluted, that
was practically pure. Oh, they appreciated this all right, but they'd

be much happier when able to drive around with the carcass of a black bear spread over the Cherokee's hood.

"You see, Gilles, we have nothing against you, but we can't help thinking that the Old Man back there is playing us for fools...."

Three voices lined up recriminations in chorus. The quarters they'd been assigned were a rotten slum. To ensure their sustenance, they'd been given, through an agreement with Moreau, a series of tickets entitling them to meals at the apish host's establishment. But, the food there, as soon as it was eaten, gave them the runs, making them rush to the bathroom. To cap it all, they hadn't yet seen the slightest tip of a bear's tail (this is where I had to inform them that, strictly speaking, *Ursus Americanus* doesn't have a tail).

Jim took it upon himself to speak on behalf of troop moral, which was pretty low. However, a fishing trip worthy of Saint Peter's nets, followed by a meal of fish cooked over a beach fire, might compensate for the few inconveniences they'd had so far. I then realized they honestly thought I was a hunting and fishing guide. The Old Man had really landed me in a nice kettle of fish. For the moment, I felt it better not to mention that, since my arrival in Grande-Ourse, I hadn't found a single minute to go fishing.

The forest paraded by in rhythm with my thoughts. A porcupine, then two astounded moose, dressed up the scenic part of the journey. We then crossed the chemically burned no man's land stretching beneath Hydro's high-tension lines. The nearest pylon, a precariously balanced giant, earned admiration from my tourists, which the word "shit" summed up with all the desired concision. At that moment, one of the three guys crammed into the back seat tossed an empty Budweiser can out the window. But Jim wouldn't stand for it. He ordered me to hit the brakes, then to back up and, while the boor was massaging his head after hitting it against the seat, he lectured him harshly.

"Now, guys.... We're not going to spoil this magnificent land, are we?"

"Ah, come on," wailed the other one.

But Jim was inflexible. Head lowered, the guilty party cleared his way out of the vehicle while my neighbour looked at the frail and colossal chain of tall structures stretching out as far as the eye could see at the centre of the cleared strip.

Elbowing his way back to his seat, the fellow, his misdeed rectified, popped the tab of another Bud. Arms crossed, Jim now gave all the signs of fancying himself a benefactor of humanity. Distracted and self-important, he shouted an order to me, "Okay! Let's head out."

❧

JITTER BUG WILLIAM WOBBLER RAPALA BRECK'S AGLIA LONG SWIM WHIZZ MEMPHREMAGOG SMELT MUDDLER MINNOW PICK-A-BOOM REBEL FLAT FISH CRAZY CLOCK HULA POPPER BLACK FURY VIBRA-TAIL VIBRO-ALL TORONTO WOBBLER DAREDEVIL JIGGS YELLOW BLACK BLUE WHITE FISH KILLER KING FISHER MOOSELOCK

Crazy Sam's tackle box resembled Ali Baba's cave. Its owner had painstakingly lugged the heavy contraption with tiny and rapid steps, properly bending his knees before dropping it with visible relief at our feet, with the loud noise of ruffled hinges. The huge metal box was covered with green paint that was flaking off in scales, and equipped with an apparently intricate latch whose central feature was a massive lock. A drum roll and a clash of cymbals were the only things missing as Crazy Sam opened it, striving for effect. When, topping it all off, he mentioned the word *sonar*, Jim and his pals shook with anticipation. So good ol' Sam had the modern fisherman's crystal ball? "Let's go get 'em!" Jim hollered, arm outstretched, no longer able to contain himself.

My Americans had been delighted to see this clown with a cowboy hat come out of his trailer, waiving his arms. Back home, in New England, Crazy Sam was well-known as an outdoor enthusiast. The walls of his principal dwelling, in Pittsburgh, were apparently covered with the antlers of large male cervids, as well as big fish, moulded, varnished, and well silhouetted above the fireplace.

Relieved at having left our friends in the care of a champion, I headed back to the village, coming across the Old Man just before the lake, in the middle of a turn he was negotiating with the majestic slowness of a turtle from the Galapagos Islands. A flurry of gravel flew up as I hit the brakes. He needed a good thirty or so metres to stop his vehicle. Then, tangled up in his gearbox, he stalled his engine twice, before managing to shift into reverse while I drummed my fingers on the edge of the door. He carefully stopped beside me, inquiring about the turn of events.

"Everything's under control, boss. I left them with Crazy Sam. They're at Lac du Fou."

"Good! Well done, Ti-Kid Gilles!"

Then, remembering life isn't only a bed of roses, he changed his mood.

"Go back to the store, Ti-Kid! Benoît has his hands full with that fat bitch! Personally, I wouldn't go back there for a million dollars!"

I looked at him with a sympathetic smile. One million? Everyone knew that for two bucks the Old Man would gratefully kiss the ass of the most corrupt creature in Quebec.

As I was about to leave, a crazed vehicle appeared around the curve, dust cloud in tow, sounding its horn as though the whole world had been compelled, right then, to spread rose petals in its path while clapping. He seemed to be asking for the right of way, but too eager to wait for us to clear the path, the speeding vehicle rushed towards us at full tilt. I backed up as best I could, with the Old Man confusedly aping me, and I surmised the space between our two vehicles was roughly equal to the newcomer's width. The latter entered the new corridor precisely, without slowing down, while the Old Man dove out of sight, metal scraping metal and a grating that recalled the roar of a dinosaur. I saw Legris' infernal head drive by, framed by the door and close enough to touch. He saluted me with a careless gesture. He kept the malicious expression for grand days and mischievous deeds, a look nothing short of ambitious. His hair was almost totally grey, with a curved and pointed tuft rising over each temple. He definitely had panache.

In two seconds, spruces had swallowed the vision. The Old Man quickly regained his composure. He glanced only briefly at the endless scratch that would henceforth decorate the Dacia, and devoted the following moment to thinking out loud, the essence of which reached me: Legris, completely drunk, and Lac du Fou

equalled problems, problems, problems. The solution, to catch him
before it was too late.

Without paying further attention to me, he struggled to start
his vehicle, and I had the leisure to twiddle my thumbs a little
longer while he managed with great effort to wrest a hiccup from
his engine. Then, affecting to increase his speed on this grave
occasion, he drove off in the sun-drenched afternoon, in pursuit of
new complications.

●

Gisèle had managed to break into the cold room and barricade
herself inside, ready to withstand a siege. I found the store in deep
crisis, which is to say that things were worse than usual.

The problem with Gisèle was her inertia. Without being an
outright pachyderm like Lili, she knew how to use her respectable
weight. She could, out of strategy or lassitude, become totally
limp; trying to move her then was like stirring cold molasses.

Benoît was at the brink of collapse, hanging on to the door of
the cold room when I reached him. I think he no longer had any
illusions, but obstinately refused to pull back.

"Gisèle! Open up!"

Gisèle incarnated the earth's capacity for resistance in all its
splendour. I wedged my feet against the doorpost and, like Benoît,
pulled with all my strength. Soon the obstacle caught in the
doorway allowed us to see the fat girl's grimacing features. Between
swigs of beer, she'd giggle with a sound that would frighten ravens.
Firmly hanging on to the handle, desperately clutching her beer
bottle with the other hand. Benoît placed his body in the opening
that was already narrowing radically, negotiating from his new
position. But, squeezed in there at her mercy, he quickly became
distressed. At thirty years of age, this precociously fattened woman
had some twenty years of lovemaking and procreating under her
belt and, full of compassion and designs, considered this virgin
through a light veil. Between gulps, she blew him tender kisses and
I love you, I love yous, that were so tender they could really make
you lose your composure. The question didn't even cross Benoît's
mind: his sense of duty prevailed at any cost. Yet he appeared to be
wavering, weakening, ready to slide down the slope of least

resistance. Yes, give in to all this, roll on the ground with her, blessed abandon, yes. Too much was being asked of this brave lad.

Gisèle took advantage of his hesitation, abruptly drawing him inside and, with the same movement, closing the door behind him.

I brought my face closer to the impenetrable barrier and said politely, "Well, I guess I'll leave you?"

Panic restored Benoît's strength. He pushed off with hands and feet, nearly forcing passage in the opposite direction, then grabbed my arm, holding on with all the energy he had left, saying very quickly, "You, Ti-Kid, are coming with me! We're going to get her out of there, okay?"

Gisèle had changed tactic. She'd just collapsed with a groan, like a sack, and tried to draw Benoît into her grip. We were already swooping down on her and, each grabbing an arm and leg, we hoisted and carried her over a short distance, before dropping her, on the last part of the journey, in the dust and pieces of gum welded to the floor. Gisèle suffered this ordeal in quiet, eyelids closed languorously over the soured milk of her eyes, still finding strength to say: "Benoît, I love you!"

Holding on to her bottle, she unctuously slid down the cement steps. A vaguely chastening Big Ben had observed our goings-on without stirring a muscle. Benoît shut the door, white as a sheet and so tense I nearly suggested he have a good wank.

❧

I spotted the Old Man's stalled vehicle along the road, but no sign of its driver. A white plume of smoke soared from under its hood. I saluted with a blow of my horn, then swerved to avoid a porcupine which, stiffened, enormous and gruff beneath his cloak of quills, was going on his merry way, then continued on mine. Lac du Fou meandered to the left and spangled in the breeze. One of those long and narrow lakes cast in the line of great glaciations. A rounded trailer stood near a small arched bridge at the southern end of the waterway. At the edge, Crazy Sam's rowboat was being rocked by shivery white caps. It was out of commission, as its owner had pitifully realized. The group had had to settle on using the Outfitters' dented launch. Legris' pickup was there, parked a few feet from shore as though it had been tempted to dive in. I saw neither hide nor hair of its driver. On the horizon, a windy chaos stumbled over wooded hills, as though possessed of an obscure threat.

Awaiting the return of the frail barque and its cargo of potential drowners, I had nothing to do but sip the beer that my instinct, whetted by outdoor living, had goaded me to bring along. These were my favourite moments, when the popping of a tab or the soft hiss of a twisted cap ushered in a break. The rattling of a muffler at the limit of the quiet zone alerted my numbed senses. Flamand was heading my way at the wheel of his trusty pickup, accompanied by part of his clan. Time for the evening ride.

He slowed down and stopped beside the gravel pile I was sitting on. Salomé looked me over through the locks covering her eyes, then turned around. She was wearing her red outfit. In the waning sun, her shape imprinted itself on the retina, embedded itself into the hub of all desire, the crimson spot remaining before my eyes when they closed, superimposing itself over the procession of images when they reopened. I thought about the poet's words: *the pole is where your gaze lies.* Flamand got out and looked at her as well, while the children scattered. A shaky Fernande put her foot on the ground, sipping the froth from a beer. Reaching out, I grabbed a finicky little boy who was passing by, lifting him above me in the light.

The grumbling of humans welled up in the steep hills surrounding the lake. The strained speed of an engine focused our attention in the distance. Shouts, laughter, curses blended with the even drone. A boat soon appeared, very low above the unsteady mounds lifted by the wind, getting lower and lower as the safety of shore approached. The picture became clearer; they were obviously taking on water every time a lively swell struck. All seriously loaded, empty brown bottles faithfully marking their wake.

Flamand slowly shook his head, and I suddenly felt sympathy for him.

"I was minding the store during Nelson's funeral," I explained apologetically.

He nodded. He knew.

I looked around, as though trying to find a topic of conversation.

"How goes the scraping?"

He spat.

"Not very fast. And you?"

"Oh, I've stopped that. I have to take care of those big kids over there."

Dusk was about to fall. Flamand muffled a slight laugh, "The bastards are crazy."

"Yeah."

A mutiny had just broken out, the oars standing at obtuse and unexpected angles over the water. Resounding insults echoed against the sheer rocks bracing the first cedars.

"They've got problems," Flamand observed.

He was blinking, and pulling out his chin. I closely observed the countless wrinkles and crow's feet criss-crossing his face, weaving a variable pattern. His lips were cracked and moved constantly, as though to repel a drought, pulling the hardened skin in all directions. You got the impression nothing could ever stop this blinking of a hunted owl, or root out the dark sadness from his nervous soul. We both kept to words that are exchanged without affecting the balance, words which are the handrails of conversation. Turning my head, I wondered were my Little Red Riding Hood was.

Legris emerged from Crazy Sam's trailer, dancing crookedly.

"I didn't know you had free access at Crazy Sam's," I blurted out.

He didn't appreciate the suspicious tone at all.

"I was his guide when you were still in diapers, son!"

He was interrupted by a fizzy sound some distance away, accompanied by a tiny plume of bluish smoke behind the outboard. Legris laughed into his three-day-old beard.

"Hope the bastards can swim; no way I'm getting wet...."

Running his hand through his hair, he straightened out his horns and grumbled, scratching his throat, "Hi, Flamand.... Some ordeal we went through, just like that, eh...."

A heart-rending sob echoed from the pickup's running board, where a slumped Fernande was drowning her sorrow. Legris went over to her, contemplative and rather smashed. "Now there, old girl ... dearest ... Fernande! What can we say? The good Lord came to.... That little boy will be much better off this way...."

Flamand looked at him sideways. Legris forcefully argued his point with a profusion of emphatic gestures. "I personally tell you that little Nelson wasn't like the others!"

He looked at the two guardians in turn.

"Besides, it's all the Old Man's fault! What with his goddam beer truck!"

Spitting at the ground, he hit the tip of my foot. Then, having already forgotten the gloomy subject of his preamble, "You're working for them now, too, eh Flamand? The Old Man will bilk you, hook, line, and sinker!"

It suddenly became very clear in his mind that he was taking everyone to the hotel; it would be very ill-advised for anyone to try stopping him from buying rounds.

"Bring your old lady along, Flamand, it's on me...."

Then, following a cunning silence, he added, "With money from Pennsylvania, heh, heh!"

But Flamand was shaking his head and his tearful wife was sniffling loudly. The boat had stalled on the lake. Salomé drew near and, staring at me, kept a very clear distance away. Legris, graciously trying to spare family sensibilities, rummaged through his assortment of compliments for ladies."My, what a beautiful child...."

Salomé, however, feigning to console her adoptive mother, delicately grabbed her bottle, spiriting a few centilitres of bitterness from it. Flamand groused sluggishly. He finally rounded up his troop and, following an imperceptible salute, turned his back to us.

"What about you, young fella?"

Legris was champing at the bit, kicking the stones nestled in the sand like eggs with his boots.

"I'm waiting for customers."

A quarter mile away, posted at the bow, Crazy Sam was shaking the oar he used pathetically as a helm. Waving his hat in the wind like a flag, he'd assumed supreme command, shouting enthusiastically and barking orders. The others were fighting with the oars, struggling to start the engine, trying to extract a piece of grommet stuck in the rowlock cavity, bailing desperately in the meantime. The combined weight of the tackle box, beer cases, and water was driving up the water line. The Americans were cursing the Outfitters, and Crazy Sam was very amused that all this was taken so seriously. Legris burst out laughing and, in response, blaspheming fists were wielded above the waves.

"That old rowboat's had it!" he asserted.

"They're surely empty-handed...."

"Son, there isn't a single fish left in that lake. It's the Siwashes' fault...."

He grazed me with his sparkling gaze.

"Don't worry about your big babies! I'll personally show them the real Grande-Ourse!"

The engine finally started without warning and, following a few erratic manoeuvres, the small boat headed for shore, passengers jumbled together in water and beer. Its pilot, however, forgot to bring up the engine. Plunging into the muddy bottom, the propeller ploughed through the incline and, catapulted forward, Crazy Sam humbly kissed the granite.

❧

A large onslaught of mosquitoes followed the waves of attacking blackflies. The calm individual moved about through the sound of the maniacal and mechanical whirring of millions of tiny wings ventilating every cubic centimetre of breathable air. You'd swallow one or two now and then, getting used to the taste. Whenever you see folks speaking to themselves in the midst of the boreal forest, punishing themselves with heavy slaps, cruelly shaking their fists at the empty sky, it's generally because biting insects are in the air.

Legris cheerfully guffawed, swallowing an attacker gorged with blood, quickly and loudly spitting it out, shouting with boundless delight, "Hi, fellas! Hi!"

Our small troop advanced cautiously. The Americans walked as though in territory planted with land mines. I wondered what kind of greeting we'd get, following our triumphant entrance. Legris had pressed his horn as though possessed, while a clumsy delegation sprang out of the vehicles, jostling each other and guffawing, leaning on whatever they could.

The Indians filed out of their tents one at a time, casually walking towards us. Cowboy was swinging his old 30-30 at the end of his arm; Christophe had wrapped a bright red bandanna around his thick mop, making him look something like a Khmer Rouge from the good old days; Karate Kid's waist was tightly belted with a black obi, forming the crest of a scalene triangle topped off by two shoulders; finally, Donald Big-Arms joined up with them, looking apologetic for the slight delay. Dagobert, Judith, Alexis, and his wife, stayed in the background, observing.

The Americans halted in various positions, roughly lined up in ranks. Wedged between the two detachments, I felt I was about to witness official negotiations. In this thin-columned lowly temple, I'd be the unsung cleric, the sacred scribe conscious of his humble function as the needle of a seismograph. Legris took charge of things. First he addressed Donald Big-Arms, who was already drunk and, therefore, no longer disposed to listen to him. Legris could be very civil on occasion.

"You, pal, have placed a net or two in the area, I'm sure of it, eh, you rascal?"

He paused, coughed slightly, continued, "My friends here would like to buy a walleye or two, Donald, pal. They're ready to pay, of course...."

With conceit, he pointed to the four chaps who, behind him, displayed their nationality in their manner as much as in their getup.

Donald nodded his large square chin. The atmosphere was electric, flowing at ground level between us. Legris intervened like a referee between two teams; he and I were the anode and the cathode of a fully charged battery. Cowboy activated the lever of his rifle, click, seemingly distracted. Donald Big-Arms grumbled prosaically. The Kid was striking samurai poses and Christophe was gritting his teeth. The man with the camera turned towards me, already wielding his toy.

"Ask them if I can take a few shots!"

I turned to Cowboy. "He'd like to film you."

Cowboy shook his head very slightly and the rifle twitched in his inert hand. "No."

"I've got to take a few pictures of this," mumbled the man through the lens pointed in front of him.

"Tell him to stop, Gilles!" Cowboy hurled out.

The guy was barraging them with the hum of his camcorder. I had a pang of anguish.

Jim broke from the group, quickly reaching for his leather wallet. "Tell them we'll pay for this...."

I explained what they wanted, remaining composed, after swallowing a gulp of saliva. Christophe whistled softly. The Kid, stiff and angular, didn't reassure me. Cowboy tightened his jaw.

"No."

"They won't let you ...," I began.

Legris then burst out laughing, "Yeah, problem is they don't take MasterCard, here!"

At the same time, he stretched out an opportune arm and lowered the camera, uncovering its operator's busy face. He then scurried over to Donald Big-Arms, taking him by the elbow and dragging him further away. Behind him, he waved at the four Americans to follow.

"Come on, come on, come and show me your catch, pal! We talk and talk, and the fish is waiting, and when fish waits, it smells!"

He'd spoken with a twang, holding his nose, and his comical behaviour earned him everyone's indulgence. The ranks broke up and everyone breathed more easily.

"The Old Man was here earlier," Cowboy informed me. "Walking back to the store...."

The amateur film-maker was brooding, while Christophe, annoyed, gave him an impudent grin. The Kid, lively as a cat, stayed close on Jim's heals. Legris was very calm, indulging Cowboy with a light shove, saluting a touchy Alexis, who watched them go by, managing to deride the dark blue cotton pants that were Dagobert's pride, and caressing Judith with his eyes. She, in turn, glared at him, while he used the other side of his mouth to slip to his friend Jim, busy watching the Kid over his shoulder, "Tell your buddy I'll try to fix things, regarding his film.... And behave yourselves, god dammit, can't you see they have a rifle?"

❧

Crazy Sam had been in the area for some time, and was beginning to speak passable French. For the time being, his manic-depressive gaze hovered inoffensively over the road. A great horned owl gloomily took off from the shoulder in front of us, clutching the carcass of leveret in its talons.

"A great horned owl ...," Crazy Sam murmured.

The pickup was driving briskly along.

"How is Boisvert?" he asked.

"Oh, I dunno. Pretty well, I figure...."

"Boisvert is a very lonely man," he said point-blank.

He spat with style through the door window.

"Yes, Boisvert is very lonely...."

I shrugged.

"He mustn't be bored every day, with that little blonde...."

The remark wrested a faint smile from him.

"I'm not talking about that kind of solitude, you know...."

He seemed to ruminate for a moment, then, "You've surely heard what people say, right, Mr. Clerk? Those who claim that the father, not the son, should've gone to jail...."

I looked at the road. Another hare crossed it and, farther on, a brood of partridge took to the woods. The mother was craning her long neck, dragging her wings.

"Chickens," he continued. "No one's brave enough to say that to his face...."

He sighed, racked by a strange melancholy.

"The Boisverts were only trying to protect their business...."

He seemed to be angling for a confirmation from me. I merely shrugged.

"I don't think his son ever came back, eh?" he continued. He never mentions it, anyhow. It's, how do you say, a delicate matter, a subject that's, how do you call it?

"Taboo. A taboo subject."

"Taboo...."

Fancying that tone, he held it a little in his mouth.

"Taboo ... *Hibou*...."

Then, without transition, "He likes you a lot...."

"What?"

He stiffened, and repeated, "I think he likes you.... Likes you a lot...."

"I really can't see why you're saying that," I replied.

I'd have liked to change the subject, but he'd piqued my curiosity.

"Why do you say that? Do you know him well?"

"You know, I was there when it happened. Boisvert doesn't really have friends.... We barely speak now...."

I then had to swerve quickly. Legris was passing us, zigzagging crazily. An American, solidly hanging on to his hat, gave us a limp salute. From the box of the pickup, another hand was waving a pathetic, stiff, and shrivelled walleye. Donald Big-Arms, hoping not to worsen his case, hadn't dared cut two thin strips from it; it would've been fraudulent to call them fillets in any case. He must've felt lucky to be able to swap his catch for three lukewarm beers. Good old Donald! He couldn't have done any better, even with lessons from the Old Man. It was now his turn to learn about business, that socially acclaimed, fundamental betrayal that seduces you along right to the grave, the ultimate negotiable good.

Things had nearly gone awry over at the camp, when two of the visitors looked into a tent at the spectacle of a fat Cree woman stuffing food into the mouths of her children. They'd remained there, torsos engulfed by the canvas, thinking they were ethnologists and, when they called their reporter friend to the rescue, Judith charged out from a neighbouring tent, having to trigger a new diplomatic incident. Nothing worked, neither Uncle Jim's kind eyes, nor a sincere invitation to caress the Japanese-made trinket: the camera went flying, taking uninterrupted footage of the Grande-Ourse sky in passing. Looks had then been exchanged through the grating of molars and the chattering of canids. But Legris, again, pushing, shoving, and shouting exhortations at a run, had managed to gather his troops just in time. They'd finally cleared off, their only take being the spindly fish whose silver sequins reflected the day's fading light.

"Time to go boys! I'll show you the best place in town! There's a blonde girl there who smells a lot better than this fish!"

Crazy Sam, my guest, had remained in the Outfitters' pickup.

"Look who's coming!" he suddenly cried out.

There was no mistake: the Old Man was approaching along the railway, dragging his feet, visibly washed out. I hadn't managed to see him on my second trip to the lake because he'd walked off the road to get a little water to refresh his radiator. In vain. After abandoning his vehicle, he'd taken a three-or-four-kilometre constitutional under a sun high as a raptor. Then, following a break at the Indian camp, he'd taken a short cut over the rails, but was too old for this and walking with a crazed expression, stumbling on every crosstie. I braked gently, and when he'd drawn level with us, he hurtled down the embankment, staggering up to us, incoherent, with a deranged gaze. More than ever, he reeked of old ram sweat, the olfactory equivalent of his signature. He grabbed my sleeve, still able to utter a few orders streaked with bronchial wheezing: Son-Go-Lac-du-Fou-Amer-Friends-du-Fou-Ham-Americans-Lac-du-Fou-Ha-Legris. Then, as I helplessly pointed to the dust cloud which, over there, was already dissipating in front of the hotel, he grabbed the door handle and gently slipped to the ground before passing out.

❧

The freshly skinned hide was blood-soaked, dangling shapelessly from a crude wooden frame.

"I knew he'd be back," Cowboy recalled modestly.

"How many shots did you fire?"

"One."

Standing near him, I let the black hide's harsh reality filter through me. A primeval taste of blood pulsed in my mouth. The bear's skull, which I touched with a kind of disdainful sensual pleasure, had a small, perfectly round hole halfway between the eyes. I whistled admiringly.

"Christophe is jealous," explained my friend with satisfaction.

Around us, the camp rustled with a cheerful indolence. How could I describe the hot and thick atmosphere, heavy with casual resignation, that reigned over this Indian camp on the outskirts of Grande-Ourse? I can't imagine that now cursed place without feeling an atavistic chill of pleasure and pain going right to my marrow. That display of disorder in the conquering half-light, that sovereign idleness where a tacit solidarity was the only rule, filled me with a taste for adventure that ancient frontier writers wouldn't have disavowed. I was fantasizing beneath the stars. Inside the pallid tents, above the fragrant and gummy boughs blanketing the ground, the chemical winding of the protective spirals soared into the night like incense towards the mosquitoes. The poison filled our mucous membranes as we awaited the future's impure arrival.

While we took turns holding the blood-dripping trophy, Cowboy solemnly handed me two long and yellowed carnassials, the animal's teeth, their curving roots having remained whiter beneath the flesh.

"For you," he said simply.

I thanked him and pocketed them without further ceremony.

"Are you my friend, Gilles?" Cowboy asked.

I answered yes, even if Cowboy remained the incarnation of the stranger to me. He fascinated me more as an archetype, a product of his culture, than as an individual. Our friendship only made sense on a plural basis, it was a fundamental friendship, indifferent to the details which usually underlie affinities. It's the Indian I liked in Cowboy. I was perfectly aware of this positive discrimination. Acceptance of the inalienable opacity of the other seemed the only possible link between us.

With Judith, this innate distance became incongruous. Words usually circumscribe it, but they surged back in this case, again lost in a primary superfluousness. Though we strove body and soul, we only experienced a distant complicity, a blunt sympathy, managing to garner from the unattainable only the markers left by the daily ebb and flow, at the reach of everyone. This opening redeemed us for the duration of one night, but the conversation of bodies has its limits.

The night after Cowboy killed the bear, I was making love to Judith with the clearheaded fury of a trapped animal. I strove to lock myself inside her, with no possibility of escaping, to remain present, the prisoner of her arms. I was no longer oblivious to her passivity, wanting to tear the veil off that chaste composure. I'd placed the assorted preparatory stimulations, the wet arsenal of lingual prologues and gingival ruminations, in cold storage. I took her in one fell swoop, bearing down on her flesh, my waist creating a wave over the rolling stillness of her body, my loins moving beneath her opaque skin that was already folded near the stomach. I wanted something to happen, anything but the predictable rejection and the awkwardness of the anonymous puppets we always become whenever we bustle around too long for nothing. My mind was elsewhere and I had the deep-rooted impression of constantly being carried off to another place.

Everything that existed before that night belonged to the past. The only certainty about the future is that the men who make laws and destroy lives will come around. What is certain is the present moment, in this bed, like gritting your teeth on the edge of a blade. Wide-open eyes will never really close completely. During each of those irreparable seconds, Gilles is sentenced, alone with his flaccid pecker, alone with his unflagging body. Gritting your teeth. With his thumb and forefinger, he grabs the one that's loose under his tongue. Yes, the forefinger that. He thinks about something else, yanks it firmly and it's there, in the palm of his hand. A hole in his mouth, and blood. A souvenir of Gisèle. Those dreams where he loses his teeth, dreams of death. Quite a nudge of the elbow. He doesn't know where to put that tooth, remembers fairy tales, a long-gone childhood, places it under his pillow. What's the belief? Tomorrow, a silver coin. Where from? Tomorrow. Time like a sentence. The entrance, the Indian moving away, face against the horizon at his feet, eyes full of earth. Gilles grabs his penis and his forefinger is cold. He tries to recall his favourite mix: Gisèle is a calendar girl. Gisèle's face hair eyes and the girl the white cowboy hat and the big tits spreading the denim jacket. The impulse happened on its own, filling his hand. His whole body stiffened, concentrated into a red point of heat about to explode, stiffened so much his legs hurt as though he'd walked a long time, all day, turns around, looking at the pillow, looking for a hole where, in the soft spot, move forward, pumping; then on his back again and it squirts over his stomach, drops fall on his lips like rain what it tastes like his member throbs, his asshole palpitates and everything contracts and relaxes and the white liqueur at the edge of his mouth and the blood. That taste of guilt.

One night, waiving her usual restraint, she invented a groan to prove she didn't dislike the action too much. Then, to that still timid whimper, another answered in the night, a cynical echo prolonging itself like the call of a wounded animal. Then, a sardonic cackle rose, like a cascade of bursts or a long and sharp snap, near the camp. My blood froze. Judith was panting and opened her mouth; not a sound emerged. I slipped on my jeans and immediately went outside. A presence stirred in the shadows. It took shape rather quickly: Christophe. Wound up tight as a spring, he kept his arm raised towards the railway.

"It came from over there!"

Without deliberating further, we scaled the embankment, aligning our long strides above the sleepers, between the two smooth metal lines shining in the moonlight. A dark shape gradually materialized before us.

The brown and rugged profile swayed heavily between the rails, struggling to maintain its direction. Hoarse singing glided towards us, blown along by the cool breeze that rummaged through the bushes. Frogs and tree-toads echoed it from the far end of the peatbog. We stopped, disappointed. Donald Big-Arms waddled and skipped towards us, betraying the precariousness of his balance with each step. His unshaven beard, puffed up with froth, came to life as he saw us.

"Hey, Ti-Kid ... Ti ... Kid Gilles, hic, Ti-Kihic Gilles, with Ti-hic Chris ... Chric, Kid Christophe ...!"

Christophe cut short the emotional outpourings. "What are you doing here?"

I struggled to stay calm. "Were you the one who cackled, earlier?"

"Me?"

Donald Big-Arms cast his wild gaze around, nearly falling across the rails. Wide twirls of his arms allowed him to restore his upright position, and his distraught eyes lingered over the forest, the wild curtain facing us with all subtleties dispelled. He shook his head several times, mumbling in a flat voice those words I wouldn't forget, because of everything that would happen afterwards. "It's a curse! Fellas! A curse!"

Christophe listened, serious as a camerlengo, nudging me with his elbow before turning back, closing our investigation, for the moment.

I was preparing my defence as warblers pierced the clear morning with their trills. This time, however, my entrance as an unworthy employee went almost unnoticed. The Old Man was pacing, hair standing on end, all grimaces and sweeping threats. The Americans had spent the last forty hours drinking with Legris, and had just sent the Old Man packing in no uncertain terms. Jacques Boisvert was just leaving the premises. He'd offered to tow the broken-down

Dacia to the front of the store, looking as though he were having fun while the Old Man's pride was trampled.

"I decided to take it out of there," he tossed out as he came in, "because it wasn't too attractive, tourist relations and all that. Our friend Legris was taking a few pieces. I told him he was wasting his time if he thought he could sell a single one of those bolts, because it was made in Romania, eh? He settled for syphoning the gas."

Benoît and the Old Man were wondering who could've told the Americans the story about a shortage of blueberries. When they questioned me, my mind flew off in search of the ideal scapegoat and I got no satisfaction from thinking of a head crowned with two mottled spikes.

"Must be Legris," I said.

"The bastard!" choked the Old Man.

However, Benoît had just spotted the twist of paper under my arm.

"What's that?"

The Old Man drew near, sticking his nose to the package that was sticky with ink and blood, and couldn't help but step back.

"Yuck!"

"What?" Benoît asked.

I opened the package, showing them pieces that had dried in the open air and blazing sun the entire previous day. We could already see piles of fly eggs jumbled in propitious folds.

"Bear meat," I explained, full of pride. "A gift from Cowboy."

This was too much for the Old Man. He slumped into a chair and, while Benoît sniffed carefully, the air from his lungs came out in small breaths as he struggled to prevent words from stumbling. "You mean, Ti-Kid Gilles, that.... Now let's go over this again: yesterday, you take my American friends fishing, and all they can bring back is a pathetic little walleye coming directly from Indian nets — they told me that one often enough. And today.... Today, they sleep in because some genius told them there wasn't a damned bear in the woods this year, and you, Ti-Kid Gilles, bring us bear meat, again saying it's from your damned Indians, who killed a bear as they came out of a tent in the morning, just like that?"

Feeling this summary to be sufficiently accurate, I hinted a gesture of agreement.

"It was only a small one...."
Both looked at me.
"Really, I swear, it was only yeah big...."

They sighed in perfect harmony. But we weren't dealing with sentimental types: the Old Man leapt up and resumed control of the operations. Sure, things had vacillated for a moment, the abyss never being far from the strongest raptures, but there you have it, order now came galloping back. With a haughty gesture, he pointed to the landscape's vast stretches and, his old paw resting on my shoulder like a small buzzard, spoke decisively.

"Go on, son. Go and check the bait. Stir it all up for me properly, put a little life in there! Tomorrow, our friends will think something visited the area.... An old trick.... That'll teach them to sleep in.... Hop to it, go on!"

And, lowering a sparkling eye on the bear meat I still held, "Go and shake up that carrion, pronto!"

He turned around and, observing that I was standing there mulling his advice, prodded me in the ribs, cawing like a crow in the cornfield, "Go on, Ti-Kid! Go on!"

I immediately scurried off to attend to the bait.

☙

The local economy seemed to recover partially at month's end, when a harvest of welfare cheques filled post office boxes. Benoît's great challenge would then be to obtain at least a first instalment from his debtors, all of whom suddenly seemed anxious to head straight from the post office to the hotel's taps. If credit was king, it ruled like a despot. As for occasional customers, they'd escape the yellow card system, but were issued a temporary line of credit in the name of the uncertain solidarity necessitated by remoteness. The risk had to be run, and credibility was wagered on like you bet on a horse. The agreed amount was noted on an active invoice which, along with the matching carbon paper, was then slipped onto a nail driven into the wall. With the passing of days, the bundle acquired a thickness proportional to the magnitude of the apprehended deficit.

Along with his family and friends, Cowboy enjoyed the recognition conferred by the allocation of the official card despite their status as irregular vacationers. But when the time came, Benoît knew how to crack down hard on them with moralizing hints. A massive exodus of all the Indians occurred at the end of each month with the regularity of a natural phenomenon. To get the benefits provided by federal authorities, many had to return to their permanent address, in Sans-Terre or Tocqueville, towns in whose taverns they'd immediately test the Bank of Canada's solvency.

I'd promised Cowboy I'd store his bear hide, with the greatest of secrecy, at the back of a small cellar under the shed used as a second cold room. We usually stored boxes of white bread that had been shipped by train in that tiny cellar, building up unassailable stockpiles. The whole-grain adventures of avant-garde bakeries were hardly appreciated in Grande-Ourse. People consumed great quantities of that sacred white bread of our fathers. Malleable as putty, it would've been difficult to distinguish it, in a blind taste test, from the cardboard tabernacle it came in every week, fresh or not.

I took advantage of the bread duty, that day, to carry out the concealment. I hung the skin from a meat hook dangling in the frigid air like an animal tusk, and then placed a small container beneath it, because the blasted fur kept dripping blood one drop at a time. I left the whole lot just like that, communing with the underground world.

Skirting around the corner of the store, I spotted Gisèle along the railway in the distance. Approaching with her jerky and sleepwalking gait, tugging along a kid I'd already seen in the tent. He was hanging on as best he could, scraping the ballast and bouncing on each crosstie with staggering docility.

The alert had been given inside the store. The Old Man was going from one window to the next to keep track of the danger's progression. He proffered good words over his shoulder.

"We have to be patient, she's taking the train tonight, with the others, the whole bunch of dogs! We'll have some peace, Ti-Kid, some peace.... The train guys are the ones who'll have problems.... You can't imagine how much I pity them!"

Tongue hanging out, he savoured that idea, the comfortable misfortune of others. Night was falling, beautiful and soothing. I decided to go over to the train station to whiff the scent of boiling oil which overran the platform when the locomotive arrived, and that noisy vapour gushing from the brakes when the nervous train gratingly glided to a halt.

I first had a weak coffee at the restaurant. Salomé was at the counter with her girl friends. Moreau's wife, sickly and pimply, gave me very unpleasant looks. No longer being on familiar ground undermined my confidence. Salomé was twirling on her stool, fidgeting and snubbing me with exemplary diligence. I was looking for something to say to her. Inquire about her age, perhaps? She might've been thirteen years old, let's say between twelve and fourteen. In Quebec city, Champlain had had a twelve-year-old concubine, a native girl of course. And princess Pocahontas, who betrayed her people to save the hide of Captain John Smith in Virginia, was twelve years old as well.

A door slammed violently, distracting me from my musings. If she wanted my attention, she'd succeeded: Salomé had left without a word, or the least sidelong glance for me to remember. There was probably little she didn't know about my sleeping patterns at the camp. Nothing, nothing in the world can compare with the rancour of a girl that age. All I knew was how to desire her at the brink of the extreme ledge, above that inviolable territory and haven of purity to which passion, paradoxically, brings us closer with each step.

Moreau came out of the kitchen, soaked in sweat and the smell of rancid oil, still holding the spatula used to peel overcooked meat patties off the grill. I pretended to read a copy of the *Journal de Montréal* that was at least a week old. He leaned over me, his rotten teeth gritting. "Anyhow, that one's too young for you!"

"I didn't ask your opinion."

I polished off the dregs of my coffee and, offended, left without hurry.

The area around the train station was soon overrun. They were all there: Flamand, the father, with Fernande. Their crappy brood of various origin. Cowboy and his band, Judith and her mother. An abundance of children everywhere. Salomé had returned to join the tribe, and they were gorging themselves with sweets, rounded lips pumping Mister Freezes of every colour of forbidden fruit. Judith casually came over, strutting around a little in the vicinity, but I was distracted by the show.

A delicate euphoria filled the air that the setting sun shaded vermilion and saffron. The entire clan was a rebellious circle. Cowboy grimaced cheerfully, Judith's mother made music with her laughter and everyone, Christophe, the Kid, Big-Arms, Dagobert, Alexis with his fat Cree woman and her dirty-faced kids, all of them, the rotten eggs of the surprise picnic basket prepared over generations, gave off a dizzying sulphurous reek. I remember a frail child with jet-black hair dutifully sucking a grape-flavoured Mister Freeze that was bruise purple. That beautiful and bloated child ended up in my arms and I pressed him against me despite the large drops of juice raining down on me. Grandma Fernande, puffy, easy-going, and slumped in the pickup, undressed me with a charming and idiotic gaze, and forced me to back up a few steps when, after tossing her empty bottle far away, her wrinkled hand showed a marked interest for my parts. Salomé's disgusted intervention was needed to beat back the good matriarch. I was having a whale of a time, savouring the contagious extravagance like an elixir, the invincible carelessness of these people whose subsistence was forever guaranteed by the reigning democracy, while being deprived of what's needed to survive spiritually.

The train's arrival was an event in all the tiny communities scattered along the railway. The station's platform was a meeting place for everyone in Grande-Ourse, its right-thinking folk, dimwits, boozers, failed louts, as well as its apprentice patronesses. During those moments, the gap between the White village and that of the Indians was sharp and astounding. The two groups couldn't mix, rubbing shoulders without making contact, without recognizing each other. In that region, the social contract made no provisions for anything of this kind.

All heads turned then turned away when fat Gisèle appeared, lustful pout and beer froth on her lips, walking down, tumbling down the embankment without releasing her last-born's tiny hand as he picked mud from the ditch. She was returning from the store, where she'd pestered the manager with questions about love and credit. The disgraceful display she offered never failed to put scandalized expressions on the animated jaws of Grande-Ourse's good ladies. Something had to be done, she should be denounced, the social services would take away the custody of that one as well, and it was shocking to see.

Malicious gossip hugged the walls behind the Indian woman's large and stooped back.

When the train pulled into the station, a worried murmur ran through Indian ranks. Everyone was now watching for the crew's reaction. Ever since the events of the Saint-Jean, natives were supposed to be forbidden on the train.

"You think they'll let you on?" I asked Cowboy.

He seemed relatively confident. He was right. They boarded without a hitch. Judith explained, "They know we're going to get our cheques. It's easy to settle, where they're concerned...."

"But on the way back, you'll have nothing left...." I noted shrewdly.

I was decidedly starting to lose some of my innocence. Judith suddenly took her leave, in the native style. By way of farewell, she gave me a carefree and approving smile before heaving herself up behind the others. Gisèle had to be helped up the step, and her brat, who was already disappearing beneath the wheels, had to be brought back.

"Take care," I called out to Cowboy as he jumped onto the moving train.

An attendant greeted him coldly amid gushes of steam.

When all the Aboriginals had left the platform, I felt that the company I kept was beginning to weigh me down. People moved aside as I walked by, looking elsewhere as I approached. You obviously can't please everyone. I then got a sudden urge for fraternal solitude and headed to the hotel.

❦

There wasn't a soul at this hour, save for a blind-drunk Jacques Boisvert. Brigitte, leaning on the bar in front of him, listened with concern and smiled at him. She looked at me, then again at him. Wrapped in his supreme contempt, Boisvert was drinking hard. Keeping the bottle of Saint-Léger within reach, preferring to serve himself. He hadn't spoken to me since the cold room incident and

I no longer frequented Brigitte. Following a seemingly endless moment, he gently moved his head, saw me and, suppressed a tender smile.

"Ah! Gilles! Gilles! The clerk, the Company clerk!"

"The Outfitters," I corrected willingly.

He approved with a grunt, curiously happy.

"Happy to see you, old pal," he said with calculated slowness. "I'm really happy to see you again, Gilles."

He emphasized the G of my first name with feigned solemnity. He invited me to take the stool next to his.

"What'll you have? Scotch?"

Before I could answer, he grabbed the twenty-six ouncer that was casting a shadow on his face and, in a glass Brigitte had promptly placed before me, poured a superb drink of the amber liquid.

"It's on the house, son. The house...."

His eyes wavered at the edge of a daydream and he placed his chin in his hand. Brigitte gave me a wink as large as the hotel.

"Yeah! Really happy to see you again...."

He sighed.

"You, Gilles, aren't like the others. Like them! The braggarts and the big mouths! You don't go for empty, meaningless talk...."

He sat up and looked at me. He batted his eyelids, glazed by the strong sun, and leaned over me.

"To protect what you love, Gilles, you don't need words full of air...."

He spit on the floor, then returned to his glass.

"Air is for silence and geese.... The geese, Gilles...."

"Silence?" Brigitte gently scoffed. "We can't even hear ourselves talk in your Beaver...."

He got angry, pounding with his fist. "Silence! Silence isn't only a question of noise, good God! No! Silence is.... It's a question of...."

He scratched his head.

"Space," I proposed modestly.

He rewarded me with a stiff slap in the back.

"I was sure you'd understand," he concluded, looking composed.

Encouraged by the throat-clearing noises I made at regular intervals, he lifted his glass and chanted, in a sudden burst of enthusiasm, "To Confederation!"

Seeing my lack of reaction, he got angry.

"You didn't know tomorrow was Canada Day?"

"I didn't."

"Well, young fella, holidays are important in a frog pond like ours! Around here, old pal, we live for holidays, do you understand? Holidays!"

He again pounded the bar, triumphant and furious.

"A holiday means the tourist who comes back, like a fish in the current, money coming in, money to buy the booze to celebrate the damned holiday, and that's the cyclical pattern of life in these parts, pal...."

I glanced at Brigitte, who shrugged passively. Boisvert continued, in a more measured tone, "But you need more than American quarters to become an American...."

He again pounded the bar, the flying glasses catching his attention. He'd filled the conversation to the brim. He then seemed extremely weary. Brigitte turned towards me, caressing the nape of her neck. Boisvert emptied his glass in one gulp and, furious, "Around here, we're always caught between the ass of Indian women and the pocket of Americans!"

He was silent for a moment, and poured himself another scotch. Then he shook his head and looked at the door. It opened onto the night. No one was there.

"You do your own thing, Gilles. You hang around with who you want, but you should understand ... how things are done around here...."

His eyes swept across the theatre of glasses, with its backdrop of bottles of every size. A bitter pout stretched his bony face, ravaged by immense solitude.

But since he really wanted to broach the question, I decided not to miss the chance to get information.

"What exactly is that story of a curse the Indians talk about?"

Boisvert turned to me, "You've heard about that?"

"They claim that...."

"What?"

"That you managed to topple the truck, just by pushing it with your bare hands."

He didn't answer, but closed his eyes. His light-flooded face was strangely transfigured. His beard was several days old and I realized he'd been drinking for some time. He opened his eyes, seeming to climb out of an eternity.

"I never listen to stories.... Their superstitions make me laugh."

He finally shook off his torpor.

"My hotel keeper is lovely, isn't she? Yes, I know, you had her as well. But if you want my opinion, the ice is far from the best place...."

Brigitte couldn't prevent a laugh from pursing her lips, and I lowered my head like a kid caught red-handed. Adding to my ordeal, my host slipped an arm around my shoulder and trumpeted, protective and petulant, "That's just what she wants, Gilles.... Tonight, she's yours. A little young flesh, that's just what she wants!"

"You're talking nonsense, old man!" said Brigitte without getting flustered.

"Hey, be polite at least! Sleep with him if you like! With my blessing!"

He was exerting himself amid our bashful silence.

"Here, have another scotch, Gilles! Brigitte? Beer? Rounds for everyone!" He trumpeted this all round, but the place was empty. "Truth is," he resumed in a low voice, "some nights the old man has trouble providing essential services. Demand exceeds supply, you might say...."

Brigitte was quietly having a good laugh.

Two light-haired striplings clad in green and wearing fine boots came in with measured steps. I'd already seen them in the area. They sat down in a far corner.

"Hi Jacques. Hi Brigitte."

"Good evening, Messrs. Game Wardens."

Boisvert, who'd turned around to follow them with his eyes, nodded and, behaving generously, "Logically, my offer of rounds for everyone should still apply.... Brigitte! Why don't you ask those elegant young men what they'd like in their glasses. Even if they belong to a race that doesn't inspire much confidence in me, they have a right to quench their thirst as well."

I was looking at the two guys from the ministry. They were very fashionably dolled up.

"It's about time," blazoned Boisvert with ironic certainty, "that we had a little elegance in our Quebec forests!"

"Well, speaking of elegance...."

Looking like a swindler on the run, Legris had just crossed the doorstep, nodding in every direction like a frightened grouse. He spotted Brigitte dashing about, her tray lifted high, and expressed the opinion that a humanitarian action was in progress.

"You're just in time, as well," Boisvert acknowledged spitefully.

Soon as he had his bottle, Legris courageously approached the conservation agents, taking a seat two tables away and, slumped against the back of a chair, began pouring his heart out, "You're a bunch of dogs! To me, game wardens are just dogs and will always be dogs. Everyone around here agrees, but no one's brave enough to say it! You're two fucking dogs and dogs have no business here. Dogs stay outside on the porch or lick the floor."

The elder of the two, in his early thirties, with the physique of a cavalry lieutenant, swept aside this stream of abuse with a casual gesture. He wanted to focus on less pitiful preoccupations. But Legris persisted, the only one who could be heard. The second game warden had a flabbergasted expression. No one deserves to be treated that way, and people felt bad at having to witness it. The two guys only wanted to relax a little after an exhausting day, and this louse wouldn't leave them alone.

When, as Legris continued to blather, the cavalry lieutenant slowly stood up, adjusting his belt, Boisvert pivoted and his furious voice cleaved the rarefied atmosphere,

"Legris, you've said enough."

The other rolled his eyes like an innocent victim.

"But Jacques, you know it as well, they're just dogs and...."

"Shut up, I tell you! Didn't you hear?"

"But Jacques, they're...."

"Shut up!"

"Jacques...."

Legris was whimpering, ready to beat his chest. He literally crawled out of the establishment, just barely finding the strength to tell us in passing, "At least the Americans are...."

He didn't finish his sentence. Boisvert had just put his foot on the floor and Legris scrammed. But, as he was about to disappear, he slipped his nasty head through the door, "The Americans are beginning to be rather fed up with the bears in Grande-Ourse!"

The night swallowed him along with his sniggering. I inhaled a puff of the cigarette Boisvert had offered. He let out a long stream of yellow smoke while a shiver ran through his shoulders. This incident had sobered him up. "Legris, you see, is the worst Grande-Ourse has produced and, in a way, what's most pure: an accommodating spirit under the guise of independence.... The genius of compromise.... And a big mouth, obviously.... You don't understand how they are, Gilles...."

An idea flashed through him. He drowned a coughing fit with a lavish swig of Saint-Léger, then hollered into my ear, while Brigitte was sponging the spatters, "I've got it! I know what we'll do, Gilles! So you can understand!"

"What?" I said with my most naive expression.

He was squeezing my arm hard enough to hurt me.

"Tomorrow, you'll take the day off!"

"The day off? Why?"

"To see, Jesus Christ! See how it is! How insignificant they are!"

Brigitte was looking at him, intrigued as well.

Boisvert was now saying, as though already thinking of something else, "Say, carrion's fine and dandy, but your Americans haven't tried molasses yet, eh? Our parents' good old molasses. Oh, you really don't know anything...."

❧

"If you think I feel I have to sleep with you just because your Indian woman has gone into town and that Boisvert thinks he's a pimp...."

"That's not what I think, Brigitte."

"That reassures me. Now get undressed. I want to see you naked. Try to get a bit of a hard-on, if you can...."

I very humbly admit she took me completely by surprise. I followed her instructions and she placed me on the bed herself, playing with my legs, studying my relaxing gnarled body. The bitch even allowed herself to graze, with sublime distraction, the tip of my glans which, freed from its bluish sheath, seemed to have been dipped in a quart of iodine. I was tense as a bow string, and she was massaging the interior of my left thigh, thinking about something else.

"Brigitte...."

"Shhh."

She finally got up, went to a chest of drawers, and pulled out a pad of unlined paper. She sat near the bed, mentally measuring the distance before selecting a pencil.

"Hey! I'm going to fall asleep, if I go on like this!"

"That's not allowed. Don't move a hair, and do as I say."

I observed the austere hotel room surrounding us.

"So this is where you come to draw...."

"That's why we're here, pal."

Part of the night went on that way. I had to control my breathing, but wasn't able to control my erection. This room was both Brigitte's studio and the portion of intimacy she could steal from her man when she wanted to.

"Our best lovemaking is when he gets off his hydroplane. He says it's the vibrations...."

"What does the sexologist think?"

"I know what he feels, up there.... Love is all about power and, up there, he's all powerful."

"Perhaps this isn't a good time to talk about him, Brigitte."

"Not at all. You pose, and I'll do the talking."

"Just one question...."

She waited.

"Are you going to spend your whole life here?"

"Your thing is softening, Gilles Deschênes."

"Shit. Lack of stimulation. Do you like naked men?"

"It all gets a little ugly past a certain age, but...."

"But?"

"Masturbate a little."

"Hmmm."

"When Jacques described all of this to me, the first time, I cracked. I said: okay, I'm packing my bag. I didn't have tons of valuables to carry anyhow."

"And then?"

"It's not so bad, after all. You get a taste for it."

"Brigitte?"
"Mmmm."
"What do you know about his son?"
She gave a start.
"Nothing, except that he has the same first name you do. He never talks about him. Jacques Boisvert is a man of great silences."
"I find him rather talkative."
"With you, he's different."
"Hmmm."

She looked like an industrious schoolgirl, the tip of her tongue showing through pursed lips. I was beginning to sink into sleep. This bruised mattress, veteran of a thousand quickies, was sucking me into its womb, spongy as peat moss. Brigitte's last words were all twisted when they reached me, like a duckling quacking for its mother at dusk. She was working hard on her drawing, my phallus had softened, and I again dreamed about all those words streaming disorderly behind my eyelids, like all the words in the dictionary forever pursued by their definitions, an oscillating association of free words, gradually written inside me, in a strange and intimate language.

❧

My flying experience was limited to those large transatlantic carriers that make you feel as though you're in a theatre, with filet mignon instead of popcorn. But aboard a Beaver, the feeling of being wrenched from the ground is much more distinct. Your immediate reaction is to hang on to the vibrating bulkheads, like being in an outhouse during an earthquake. The Beaver restores the feeling of effort, clearly reminding you that humans always escape their nutritive substratum by cheating in a way.

Heart in my throat, shaken by the craft's sustained vibration, I saw the general store dwindle, and the station shrink as though it were awaiting an electric train. The chapel dropped to the ground like a beaten dog, Moreau's house seemed made of Lego blocks, and the hotel appeared elongated and flattened like a snake skin. I saw the white house that had belonged to the bosses of the old Company, with a minuscule César Flamand scraping away at its side. I saw Grande-Ourse become a toy in my imagination, a model on the hazy sketch of a life that was losing its horizons. And I understood Jacques Boisvert's calm arrogance: every day he took the only valid shortcut to rival the giants. Each new flight allowed him to subject the village, to integrate it a little more into his experience of men and women. He was in the habit of rising above the fray and disengaging. The pusillanimous and vulgar bustling of that wretched village must've seemed very relative from the height of his cockpit.

"What do you think?" he blurted out, making the old crate do a quarter turn to the left, then to the right, as though saluting the docile landscape whose complete scope extended beneath our feet.

He'd continued drinking scotch late into the night and early hours of the morning. He was still holding the beer he'd grabbed to rinse his mouth. As the Beaver banked to head north, three large whitish flowers blossomed. Boisvert stared at the sky ahead and didn't hint at noticing I was focused on that precise spot. One of the camp's occupants (I recognized Christophe by his jacket) came out of his shelter and, reduced to the size of a plastic soldier, stopped to look upwards. I saluted him automatically, certain he couldn't recognize me at such a distance. I then jumped when I noticed he was waving his fist.

Boisvert let out a brief chuckle that was quickly drowned by the engine's roar. We had to yell to be understood.

"They know my plane really well. They've even shot at me. Gives them a target to practice on."

He hollered the information in an even tone, in a good mood.

"I always make sure I get a lot of altitude before I pass over their flea nest. A 30-30 has a rather limited range. In the case of moose, for instance, a 30-30 isn't worth a rabbit fart. For bear, that's another story. But when they get rich enough to buy a .300 magnum, I'll take a detour, don't fret."

There was a silent spell, then, "They hold a grudge against me, what can I say?"

"Oh yeah?"

He gave me a strange look, then leaned his head out the window, heavily jerking the joystick. The hydroplane tipped on its side, plunged into the void, like Second World War planes nose diving in newsreels. I saw Christophe's image expand in fast motion, his incredulous face filling the space before he hit the dirt as we flew just above the spruces at the sound of Boisvert's hysteric laugh. He turned to me to see whether I was holding on tightly with both hands to whatever was in reach, and his triumphant laughter intensified as he straightened the hydroplane's crazy course.

"Why hasn't that one gone to get his cheque?"

"Christophe? He's sulking. Waiting for the next train."

Grande-Ourse soon tumbled into the mixing of air, fading into nothing while the Indian camp faded into less than nothing. All of the green country engulfed the space beneath our wings and I glimpsed the glorious expanse isolating Grande-Ourse; it was both its misfortune and the source of its charm. All that remained was that green, stretching out as far as you could see, on all sides. Variations of green applied to an infinite palette, with a glimmer either subtle or intense, interrupted only by the blue of the countless irregular and multiform lakes. The eye jumped from one botanical sequence to another, caressing the changing textures, more tender over old clear cuts and the scarred bite of fires, harsher atop stands of grey pine. All the hazy variations paraded beneath us, all the gradations, from the celadon green of alder groves to the spinach green of mature leaves, to the bottle green of balsam firs to the absinth green of marshes covered in water lilies, all of this gradually fading into approaching peatbogs, whose shades of yellow, thrush grey, and white along the confused outline of the lakes grappled for dominance among the pistachio-green or apple-coloured brush strokes of isolated larches. And, above everything else, flooding the boreal forest right to the edge of the taiga, the bluish green of the ruling spruces, contemplated in broad daylight, overwhelmed creation with its unified mass.

Boisvert was quiet now, rushing along the surface of this rolling landscape like a brook on a mountainside, fully belonging to the movement that carries it.

The country then turned into water. Under the hydroplane's belly, a shimmering encircled the earth, surrounding it all over, taking possession of the expanse: water everywhere. We glided above an inland sea the colour of steel, its peaceful unfolding only occasionally interrupted by the sudden looming of an island silhouetted like a pillbox amid the waves. The sun multiplied sorties, bombarding the surface of molten platinum.

"The reservoir!" Boisvert proclaimed simply.

He drew a picture in the air, in the direction of a vaguely bordered horizon. He explained, still hollering, "The reserve is somewhere in that direction. They had to move the whole band when they built the dam! Engineers figured water would flood everything, so the government resettled them. Their actions weren't very brilliant. Bureaucrats dragged their compasses over a map, then shoved them in the worst hole imaginable, right in the middle of a swamp, with mosquitoes and the whole kit! They began dying in there, yes sir, they weren't happy, and had fevers; it seems they were catching everything that went around, dropping like flies. So they up and resettled them again, a real tribe of Israel, pal! Put them where they are today, on the north shore of the reservoir, on a jutting point, a kind of peninsula. It's a nice reservation, they're in seventh heaven; they even have subsidized new houses! Hey, buddy, we're not laughing! Residential construction! You wouldn't see that in Grande-Ourse!"

"Except for Moreau...."

"Well, we won't see a roof on that despicable camp very soon!"

Heated up, he seemed to speak to the invisible propeller in front of him, to get carried away with his engine. The frequent turbulence rocked the Beaver like the needle of an electrocardiogram and, each time, I had to stabilize my insides with an unsteady hand.

Boisvert guffawed, "The Old Man must've told you that going up with me was dangerous?"

"Well...."

The plane veered suddenly and lost altitude while, leaning towards the door, he observed something the cabin hid from me. He then dove towards a chain of islands, where a cluster of rectangular and greyish buildings that looked like barracks immediately stood out. My word, he really did take himself for a Stuka pilot. We flew just above the dismal shacks while I brought up my knees to cushion the eventual fatal crash.

"A summer camp!" shouted my guide at the top of his voice. "It was a summer camp! Closed now! And for good! Do you know the story?"

I said no, slowly regaining my composure while the Beaver
climbed higher. Boisvert told the tale.

A young black boy had been sent to a rather special summer
camp where children were initiated, the hard way, to the joys of
living in the wild. He'd stolen a canoe under cover of darkness
and ran away, crossing half the reservoir in waves twice his
height. He ended up in a luxury outfitters, where a French chef
greets you with caviar and champagne before serving you a purée
of this and a quenelle of that. And then the boy told his story:
he'd been mistreated at the summer camp; beaten, locked up, tied
to a post, tortured; in short, it was a real Nazi camp over there.
An inquiry followed, but the other children didn't talk, no one
ever proved a thing. Well the boy's father was an influential
senator from the northern United States and the place had to
shut down. Camp supervisors said the young black boy had lied
to get even with those in charge of the establishment where he'd
been sent against his will.

Boisvert caught his breath.

"All that because of *stories*...."

He was obviously waiting for my invitation to go on. I gave
him satisfaction, "Then what?"

He turned towards me.

"There's no place here, Gilles, for expert wailers and
professional complainers. The only law around here is work.
Brawn. The gun. A rifle beside your bed, all night, all night."

"And then?"

"Those who can't face the music, who are scared of their
shadow and bears, and who need the law from down below, they
do what the black boy did: they run away however they can and
tell stories."

An hour later, he landed the Beaver on Lac Dérangé, a vast and
secluded expanse. Boisvert employed three very quiet natives to
build his fishing camps. Once we'd jumped off the floater onto the
dry land, the silence up there was dizzying. Boisvert and those
young people didn't speak much. They had me taste a delicious
northern-style *cerviche*: chunks of walleye marinated in brine with
garlic and lemon. They were indeed very quiet, with photos of
pinups above their bunks. Pine boards echoed all day with the

sound of their hammers. Up there as well, the cycle would soon begin: cottages and fishermen, areas isolated at first, then linked by bumpy roads, then vacationers, the cottagers, a closed circle, a vice around the water. And these Indians, hammer in hand, pushed back a little farther up.

"I didn't know you hired Indians," I said cautiously on the way back.

Boisvert grumbled.

"When they use axes to build rather than smash, we get along. They aren't allowed a single drop of alcohol up there; it helps...."

Following a long pause, he shouted in a rasping voice, "Look over there!"

All I could see through the blurred circumference stirred by the propeller were the azure-marbled green carpet and lakes turning to indigo.

"Over there!" he insisted, darting his forefinger at twelve o'clock. "Look carefully!"

I then spotted the village fading into the sun's reflection in the distance, not believing my eyes at how small and touching it was. Submerged in the mass of vegetation, a slight quiver betrayed it near the horizon, barely scratching the smooth woolly surface.

"Grande-Ourse!" Boisvert said without taking his eyes off his village.

With a sweeping gesture, he took in the scenery unfolding on either side of the plane, adding with emphasis, "And all the rest is Canada! Oh!"

He seemed to immerse himself in his thoughts for a moment.

"They huddle like sheep, flies on carrion, and call it a community! A bunch of lame ducks in a wading pond, feeding on crumbs! Quack quack! With rounded backs in their corner, beaks in the water, turned in on themselves, unable to manage without the tribe but unable to get along either. That's the reflex killing Grande-Ourse, Gilles. Not the Company's departure, nor the arrival of the Outfitters. Grande-Ourse is quite simply too small, and the rest too big."

He allowed his gaze to drift with our navigation. Forestry roads, down below, etched grooves that weren't always visible, and quickly erased by the changing light produced by large cumuli pouring out their radiance. Boisvert again said, slightly adjusting our course, "Problem with Grande-Ourse is there are too many chiefs and not enough Indians."

He again pointed to the village lost in space. "Do you understand why they have big mouths now? Because silence would swamp them if they didn't."

He looked at me sideways.

"Do you still spend nights reading books?"

"Not really."

"Did you know there's a library at the community centre?"

"Yeah," I answered without much enthusiasm.

I'd found two novels by Hubert Aquin in it, and Yves Thériault's *Agaguk*, but a more extensive inventory had revealed the meagreness of its collection.

"What are you reading now?"

"*Ulysses*, by James Joyce."

"Oh. An Irishman."

"You know him?"

"No. I'm Irish from my mother's side."

"I should've guessed."

He no longer listened, already absorbed by landing manoeuvres. Grande-Ourse was expanding, but so little, in the extinguishing satiny distance. For a few more minutes, we flew above that impossible to cover blotting-paper landscape, the flat and profound silence that was impossible to bury, flanked by speechless and directionless snow serfs with their numbers and cries of agony.

❧

Prosperity is a full dump. The line fitters stay at the edge of the village. A feast for everyone. A feast for the bear. Night and day. They saw a big one, hanging around there, has his habits. He stuffs himself with Bourassa's manna as well. He likes to signal his presence in the area, lacerates the signposts. His signature.

At the edge of the day, the forest stands on end, creating a barbed wall. They set out in the cold air, it's still dark. The father whistles. Not a word is exchanged. The inaugural ray that coppers the rounded hill is like the sound of a bugle. Song of the hunting horn and goose bumps. A brief and inevitable shiver runs across Gilles' skin.

Death will soon look you in the eye. Death advances, taking its time. Where the whole village vomits its trash in the stench rising into the air, like the fumes of the world's putrescible nature, the father drives his truck. Before really getting under way, the day waits, like everything else, the burning of the powder. Gilles desperately tries to seize the moment, to hold it back. Simple things grab him by the throat: the sun rises out of the night, hanging by a brass thread, victory of the reappearing day, like a ball of fire, from the black soul of emptiness and the universe. This sunrise of blood stirring its vapours. The dull shimmer of a brass cartridge case in the hand. Arriving near the dump, they have to get out and walk the rest. Get closer. Gilles carries his Lee Enfield .303, British, old-fashioned, military and imperial. And then, two eyes. He's there, standing out against the daylight. Blacker than anything.

❧

The Old Man looked at me with distraught eyes. He seemed far away, beside himself. Benoît explained what had happened. The Old Man had wanted to get back to taking care of the Americans. If there were no bears, he'd show them what real good fishing was in this part of Quebec. He took them out to fish for speckled trout, a noble yet unpretentious breed, in a secret creek he knew. They'd fill their baskets without a hitch there, and be back in time for supper.

But the Old Man, whose memory had a tendency of failing, had got lost trying to find his famous creek. The five men had spent a hellish day cutting a path through thick brush and blackflies. Completely disoriented, half crazed with fatigue, they'd finally got back to the road at nightfall without having dipped the tiniest barb of a fishing hook in the promised proliferation. It was simply a miracle the Old Man wasn't hanged high on the way back; perhaps it was the small size of trees along the road.

And now, he looked at me without understanding.

"The what?"

"Confederation."

Benoît, keeping an eye on the pumps, was on the lookout as he sucked his gums, impassive as a soldier from the Twenty-second Regiment in front of his sentry box.

"Might help business pick up a little, yup."

"Well, yes," I said to the Old Man. "I took a little holiday today...."

The Old Man was tired. He opened a dazed mouth the colour of clay. I could see the embolism approach in that empty gaze he lowered over his shoes and alternately raised towards me, as though to confront two related impressions. The congestion, the blockage, the violent coronary that would stop this chatterbox so that the grim Reaper riding his high horse could lay him in his grave.

"In the plane with Boisvert?"

He was clearly putting me with the desperate cases.

Big Ben made his entrance, thump, thump, thumpffft, brimming with effortless joy. Benoît and the Old Man approached, arms outstretched, but a sententious nod arrested them in mid-course.

"Ooooh the big bear! Ooooh Ooooh the big bear!"

He was still running.

The Old Man slapped himself on the forehead. The gears finally started grinding. The possibility of a scheme could be deciphered beneath the purplish, grotesquely distended and drooping eyelid.

"Sit down, Ti-Kid Gilles. I have to talk to you."

His tone was proper, very professional. He almost got straight to the point.

"Today, because of your ... um, holiday, I had to go down into the cold room under the shed to get a case of bread."

He paused. I waited for him to continue.

"I found the bear skin."

I finally let out the sigh I'd prepared. The Old Man cleared his throat.

"I have a ... deal for you, Ti-Kid Gilles."

Revived, the merchant's instinct once again brightened his sly face. I looked at him without saying a thing.

"If my American friends could leave this place with a bear skin, a single small bear skin, doesn't matter who shot it, perhaps they'd be less inclined, when they get back home, to sic half the United States on us? Eh? What do you say?"

I invited him to continue.

"Gilles, old buddy," he noted shrewdly, "you seem to get along with the Indians rather well."

"Oh yeah."

He leaned towards me with a conniving expression. "You can be sure the Americans will pay handsomely! They're ready to do anything to save their trip! Money matters don't bother them any more than fly bites. You'd have to convince your friend Cowboy."

"Still, fly bites seem to bother them a little."

"A figure of speech, Ti-Kid Gilles, a figure of speech!"

"Yeah."

"I'm leaving the whole business in your hands! Still, I hope the guys won't offer them a fortune, after all. Besides, we're too kind, ah, that's our only problem, we're too kind with that gang of dogs, I mean that gang of...."

Benoît jerked his forearm forward, throwing him a coin, like a peanut to a monkey.

"Another one for your collection!" he explained.

The Old Man's eyes widened. When I closed the door behind me, he was rolling an American quarter in his feverish fingers and, pursuing his soliloquy, kissed it without false modesty.

The Americans had been scheduled to leave on July 5, since the bear hunting season ended on the fourth. The day before the deadline, the Old Man, having gotten over being snubbed, had headed south at the wheel of the now empty transport truck he had to return to its owners. To be perfectly honest, his departure might've been partly due to an odd habit the Americans had had over the last few days: they repeated everywhere that, before returning to their suburbs at the centre of the universe, they fully intended to make themselves useful by wringing the old scoundrel's neck once and for all. The Old Man therefore slipped away the morning of July 4, as discreetly as the size of his truck allowed. He disappeared beyond a horizon of sickly trees, promising to return soon and that he'd resume control of the situation, he'd show everyone.

When night had fallen, the Americans, lead by Legris, stormed into the store. More or less peaceful and very boisterous, they multiplied unexpected nudges, at the risk of bruising poor Benoît's ribs.

"Want to phone home?" he proposed, hoping to calm them.

But no, the guys were no longer thinking about pools, flowerbeds, or patios. They were thinking about national independence and whisky. Jim reflected their state of mind perfectly, saying, "We have nothing against you, manager. You're okay too, Gilles. Now that the Old Man's gone, we'd like both of you to come and celebrate with us."

Lending weight to his invitation, he displayed a bottle he said contained all the demons in hell along with their friends and little brothers. The liquid was sold under a remarkable brand name which I immediately thought I'd already heard of: Christian Brothers. Brandy, and damned good. Perhaps Benoît, so puritan by nature, was impressed by the product label. Maybe fatigue and weariness had finally got the best of him. He accepted.

A jubilant Legris immediately proclaimed himself chief architect of the great reconciliation. The guys even pushed courtesy as far as inviting César Flamand, who could still be seen on his stepladder, stuck to the large white house every day. Ill at ease, he politely declined. We then very quickly lost our heads. One heck of a bonfire flowed from the flask, ladies and gentlemen, fireworks and a wild beach fire, a transfusion of sulphur with absolutely devastating corrosiveness! The tangible universe clouded over, thunder struck lips, tongues and palates, and the canons of propriety spat out orders in vain. Soon, the change having been imperceptible, we were all gathered around the hotel pool table, and our friends sang out a vibrant *God Bless America* to all those scoundrel American black bears right to the Russian border, with Legris, good old Benoît, and myself singing along, hands on our hearts.

❧

Prudence. Precautions. Walking stealthily on the soft sand. The bear vanished like a shadow. It went back into the thickets which are no longer quivering. Boisvert shakes his head. No need to worry. He looks for a hide-out. Did you see how big he was? He was treating himself to a good piece. Gilles and his father are inside the body of an old car stripped of its seats. A little fluff is scattered on the ground.

All the trees are filled with shadows. Stretching out with anticipation. The man and his son who's old enough to carry weapons. An ambush. Crouching inside the rust-eaten body of a large sixties car, likely stolen in the city. Its last kilometres. At the end of the washboard, with a clean conscience. The shattered windshield opens up before them. As though a trip were ending in this spot. In a shell that's Gilles' age.

The anonymity of the grouse you can take down with a well-placed stone, and a little luck. A hare you pick up in the winter, its neck slipped through the snare, ears stiffened, legs crooked and convulsed. Squirrels, chipmunks, sparrows beheaded with a precise shot, with a pang of anguish, from the first BB gun. Vanished innocence. But this time, this game. Different. Comings and goings, an individual. His own mystery. Bear. The way old-timers pronounce the word, like a sign of respect. Uncle Denis, once. Didn't hear a thing, because of the falls. Face to face with the family; large, medium, small. The bears follow each other and don't look alike. A dash on both sides. And the bear cub seen coming out of the woods, right in the afternoon. Where's the mother?

Condemned like all the others, nonetheless. By the range and power of the rifle. But a smell of danger. Sometimes, the accident. A camper is eaten, the sleeping bag becomes a wrapper. When they shake their fleas in the spring, in a bad mood and a little hungry. The miserable craving that brings them here, to this rotten place, littered with trash. The entrails of society. A rustling of leaves. The rifle raised. A .303 Lee Enfield, a British make. They exterminated human beings with that. The ancient and tenacious slaughter. The backdrop opens up, allowing the day's star attraction to move through. Stays there, at the edge of the wood, a hesitant blotch, sniffing the hominid with irritation.

❦

As far as anyone in Grande-Ourse could remember, no one had ever seen such a thing. Benoît leaning on his pool cue, like a bishop on his crozier, going so far as cursing the name of the Outfitters. He was mimicking the Old Man as well; it was decidedly becoming a habit, "Well, boys, it's over! Over! I've about had it up to here with this crazy job! It's over! Over!"

He piled it on, giving us quite a show: the sagging features, vengeful old age. Murder of the father in the highest degree, a crime of *lese-senility*.

"They're all dogs! Dogs! My American friends! My American friends!"

And the manager talked, talked as though it were the first time. He was speaking on his own account for the first time. He spoke, overcome with sincerity and love for everyone, but was crushed, each second, each season, each century, by the misfortune of his existence. He rebelled and shook his fist, defied fate, noisily encouraged by the small assembly that judged and condemned along with him. Benoît on the rostrum, finally, and someone to listen, finally, and words that no longer suffocated under the hood of shame he felt about himself. He shouted, liberated, and it was beautiful; he shouted, and, crucified by life, revived by whisky, he finally had the right to make a show of his suffering. It was his hour of truth and heresy, his very own primal cry.

"One of these days, god dammit, I'll open the door, just open the store's door wide, then I'll wave at everyone to go ahead, I'll tell them: take all you want, go on, don't be shy, the pleasure's all mine. Then I'll tell the Indians: why don't you take all the beer you can, okay? And the hell with you, I don't care anymore, god dammit!"

"Then you'll say to fat Gisèle: I'm gonna fuck you tonight, bitch!" suggested Legris with empathy.

Benoît nodded sadly. The bottle, passing by in that area, detoured into his fingers. He stood up, stuck out his chest and, heart heavy as a battleship, lashed out with another tirade.

"And the first one who treats me like his servant again, who gives me orders, the first bastard who asks me for a pack of *Craven A* without saying please first, or thanks after, well guys, I'll answer him very calmly: get your own pack of *Craven A*, mister farmer, and then shove it up your asshole to the filter.... Afterwards, sir, I'll be polite and give you a light, if you wish!"

Legris and I had just fallen into each other's arms. I was awfully moved. And though the Americans didn't really understand a thing about Benoît's tirade, they still applauded and joined in this healthy cathartic process. Fat Moreau, making his entrance, almost fell flat on his back. He went straight to Benoît.

"That means you've left the store ... unattended?"

The restaurant owner's voice had broken at the end of the phrase. Benoît's laughter made him choke; he then let out a howl.

"No one! There's no longer anyone there! Even worse, Moreau, damn Moreau, you fat bastard! Even worse: I didn't even bolt the door!"

He laughed hysterically and, with his pool cue, demonstrated the nightly bolting. Then hit his forehead, interrupting the laughter for a moment, managing to groan, before being again overcome by the uncontrollable contraction of his pharynx.

"I'm not even sure I still have my keys!"

Then, waving a beer bottle, he sang out in a bitter voice, "Haaaave ... a little swig of beer, my kitten!"

Contrary to his natural inclination, Moreau didn't even think of handing out slaps indiscriminately all round. Something grave was taking place, no mistake about it. An odour of treason permeated this highly charged atmosphere. When the dust settled, no one doubted it, nothing would ever be the same again at the Grande-Ourse Outfitters.

But Moreau didn't have to think very long, something his normal abilities prevented anyhow. The night train had, indeed, just pulled into the station. We could hear it whistle as it departed. The locomotive must've been near the Indian camp. I turned to Brigitte, who was glancing at the door. I followed her movement, seeing the Indians harmoniously jamming through the door frame in pairs. Cowboy and Karate Kid led the way, followed by Christophe and Donald Big-Arms, with Judith and Gisèle closing the ranks.

I realized things were going to get complicated.

❧

Judith had blood on her t-shirt and jeans. Gisèle was still standing in the door frame, her girth pressed snugly against it. Cowboy saluted me and I signalled the others to wait for me. I ordered beer for everyone as I walked in front of the bar. Benoît hollered that he'd foot the bill.

"Hi, Cowboy, hi, everyone!" I said in an overly loud voice.

Damned brandy was going to our heads.

There had been considerable havoc in Sans-Terre and our friends displayed a nice medley of bruises, bumps, lacerations, and gashes of all kinds. Cowboy still managed to smile despite a heavily swollen upper lip. Christophe, however, wasn't smiling, a skilfully handled chair having added to the depth of his fixed gaze. Karate Kid was sporting makeshift bandages around both hands with some pride, and something like a ringing of bells could be detected behind his round eyes marred by an admirable wound right in the middle of his forehead. Donald Big-Arms' nose had been transformed into a bloody cascade, limply resting against the overhang of his mouth. Big-Arms, through the remaining hilarity that grabbed him by the shoulders, assured us he'd fixed the opposing party in far more memorable fashion. Judith was busy closing some gap in her apparel while Gisèle, blue a little everywhere, bled mostly on the inside.

Brigitte brought our drinks, taking on a distressed expression. I slipped her a tip, reminding her that Benoît had volunteered to foot the bill.

"Yeah, what exactly has gotten into him?"

"There are limits to what a guy can take in life."

"Your friends seem to think otherwise...."

"Hurrah for America!" I said, lifting my glass.

Shouts and crystalline clinking answered in the distance. Brigitte returned to her station. Gisèle, after hesitating on the threshold, dropped among our twelve knees, rolling to the floor a little farther on. Once back up, she spotted a much better place to collapse and crossed the entire hotel before wrapping her arms around a not really surprised Benoît, who was too drunk to give rise to that kind of reaction and, besides, didn't have time to protest: an enormous mouth lubricated just right submerged his face. He tumbled, Gisèle fell over him, and we lost sight of them.

"So, guys? How was Sans-Terre?"

"We got into a fight," Cowboy resumed.

"Oh yeah. With who?"

"Some White guys."

They drank ceremoniously. Judith slipped next to me and her kneecap pushed in the fatty part of my thigh.

"What about the cheques?"

"All spent," she observed with an ounce of regret.

Speaking to Cowboy, I immediately got to my slight problem. "Would you like to make a little money?"

"Depends."

"The Americans. Ready to blow their wads for your bear skin, old pal. Name your price...."

I naively thought he'd recognize the wisdom of my proposal in all good faith. But, wanting to be a rogue, he sprang up, threw his chair far behind, shouting for the entire house to hear, "A thousand bucks!"

"What?"

I did a half turn. Lord Jim from New Jersey stood there, his friend the cameraman as well, ready to record whatever came next. I grabbed my beer and had a swig. It was now time to give myself that unflappable air that suited my complexion so well. Striving to be as impartial as possible, I told Jim, "He wants a thousand bucks for the hide."

The American shouted, very loudly, as though calling on a higher authority, "You mean that, having paid a thousand bucks just to get here, and staying a whole week without seeing a single fucking bear, we're asked to give another thousand to this asshole here for a rotten hide he probably stole from his fucking grandfather?"

Shaking with rage, he looked around and asked with a kind of humiliated sincerity, "Now guys, is there some motherfucker playing fool with us around here?"

"What's he mean?" Cowboy asked, vaguely interested.

"He thinks it's a little expensive," I explained.

❦

The movement of his muscles beneath the heavy fur. He stretches like an ink blot, moving along the slope towards the hood of the old car, a Pontiac, towards those two hunters thinking frantically while the bear slips out of the thicket on his large paws, treading over crushed cans, the skeletons of manufactured objects, products picked to the bone. An animal fed on civilization and the past. On decaying matter and detritus. Sometimes it takes a little stroll through the village. Through carelessness. Shows up between two houses. It's hard to go by unnoticed. Sometimes, as well, lingers a little on the tracks. Then the train. Again last week. A mother and two cubs scattered in every direction. The train blows its whistle, too late. A deaf bear? Its monstrous ancestors harassed the grimacing clown, the humanoid who got no rest in palaeolithic caves. He comes out in front of the old Pontiac, blocking the road, an opaque point of impact.

Go ahead, shoot. Earth's gift to men. From hide to gall bladder, from claws to teeth. The meat of life. Gilles obeys. No can't. Raises the gun. Can't. Everything trembles suddenly, the earth, the flesh, the rifle. The heart jumps like a hare felled in the snow. The target, a moving drop of silver, over there, between the icy lips of the sights. At the very tip of the barrel like the end of a tunnel. A bout of fever. Even the old timers know it. A classic. Spared so many heads, animals destined to be butchered. Wounds. The infernal beat of the pulse, the heart taking up all the space inside the chest, inside the shell of the venerable Pontiac. On the cooled forehead, a salty dew seeps from the skin. The shape becomes blurred. A pile of charcoal. A conical head haughtily turned towards that old car. The temptation to drop everything. A precursory distaste. Go back to bed. Too bad. But the father isn't worked up. The father's oppressive presence. Too bad. Anywhere. Through guesswork. Haphazardly. Eyes closed. Eyes finally closed over this sad circus where the targeted wary omnivore plays half-heartedly with an old bike frame. In the approximate direction of that shadow gathered up into fleeting movements. The entire night has fled, condensing into a point that's precise, precise, precise. Whizz. The bullet reels through the air and the bear has disappeared. A dull cracking, accompanied by a muffled groan. The bear made an oomph. A brief moan then soars and dies out. Missed, says Gilles. But Boisvert doesn't agree. You hit him, son. Mustn't have gone very far. And they both know what that means. The job has to be finished, and properly. Properly. Climb out of the dead Pontiac and cross this dump.

❧

Cowboy was very clearly enjoying his position. Legris, who'd followed the start of the conversation, naturally tried to suggest a little compromise he'd devised to the parties in attendance. But Moreau, watching over the meeting's progress, wasn't going to tolerate anyone spoiling such a promising initial round. His misplaced involvement resulted in the old bachelor being laid flat on his back.

Cowboy looked at me, then at the Americans; the Americans looked at Cowboy, then at me. Judith slipped right up to my ear, "It's not for sale. Not to them."

"What did she say?" Jim asked.

At the same moment, bothered by the camera movements, Donald Big-Arms, moved his upper left arm, the only one still usable, in a circular arch, sending the device spiralling to the floor, again displaying the contraption's astonishing resistance. His fortuitous tracking had pointed it straight at the entrance, no doubt allowing it to frame the spectacular arrival of Crazy Sam's boots, who stopped and riveted an avid gaze at his feet. Oooh, Crazy Sam's eyes, filled with a folly so calm and restrained, always on the point of blowing up! Dizzy, he threw back his shoulders and clicked his heals in the purest military style, aye aye sir!, before sending the camera flying out of sight with a solid kick. The owner of the said object opened his mouth, but nothing came out.

Already drunk, but without staggering, Crazy Sam went up to the small gathering. Noticing his compatriots, he exclaimed in a soft yet grumpy voice, "Gentlemen, it would be a great honour for me to offer everyone a beer."

"Crazy Sam!" the Yankees murmured, delighted, save the one who'd gone after his last year's Christmas present.

The newcomer was rapidly apprised of the disagreement between the two groups. He slowly screwed up his eyes, staring at Cowboy's swollen face with dreamy intensity.

"A thousand bucks, eh?"

He stood there waddling, shifting his weight from one foot to the other. Then, without warning, he pounced at the Indian. His friends managed to retain him and Cowboy moved back, elbows spread out, looking for room to manoeuvre. Crazy Sam's animosity took everyone by surprise. He continued to struggle, spewing insults.

That's when old Flamand slipped into the room and came to stand before us. Everyone quieted down. He moved nothing but his eyelids, holding gazes, skinny as a rake, furrowed as a canyon, bringing a new dignity into this place. He hadn't set foot here in twelve years. Even Benoît, who'd disappeared beneath tons of Gisèle, had the presence of mind to lift his head and register the historic event. Flamand moved like a cat and took position beside the Indians. The two troops were now facing off on either side of an imaginary divide.

Crazy Sam, always unpredictable, suddenly regained his good mood. "Mister Flamand!" he said, opening his arms. "Be my guest, won't you?"

The Indian batted his eyelids, moved his eyebrows, swept the air with his mane, breathed through his nose hairs, and generally maintained the continuous agitation of his other phanera. That was his answer. Some turned to Flamand, some to Crazy Sam, anticipating the next volley. The two men meticulously studied each other.

"Won't you celebrate our National Day with us, Mr. Flamand?"

He immediately raised an arm, "Waitress! One beer for me, and one for this man here who's thirsty as hell! What brand do you drink, mister?"

Silence.

"Bring two Molson Exes, please, lady."

Brigitte made her way through the groups. She seemed to find the tension bearable, for the moment, but I felt it wouldn't take much more to kindle her anxiety. Flamand gazed at the two bottles with shining eyes, shaking his head. But, as though irresistibly attracted despite everything, he grabbed the offering and placed it in front of Cowboy, who watched his every move.

"You won't share a toast with us, eh?" asked Crazy Sam softly. "You refuse to drink to our country?"

He turned to the others.

"Should we consider this an offense, gentlemen?"

"Drink it!" a voice bellowed harshly.

"Drink it you stinking old skunk!" said someone from the same direction.

Flamand stretched a hesitating hand. Cowboy beat him to it, wrapping his fingers around the bottle, emptying it in two resonant gulps. Crazy Sam let out an indignant oooh. Jim whistled angrily and stepped forward. I was beginning to wonder whether I shouldn't take my hands out of my pockets.

⁓

Lying in the grass, he no doubt awaits the death blow very quietly a little farther on. But the black blood. Bad sign. The viscera. A slow, conscious death. Dirty business. Happens. Gilles advances, weapon on his hip, his father follows with bare hands, but. The enormous bear stands before them, front paws folded over, in an expectant posture. Those late-afternoon TV documentaries. Kodiak. Nice images. Blood-streaked salmon. This one seems large as a grizzly. His father courageously whistles admiration. But this isn't the time for contemplation. Thirty paces away, groping along, the animal explores the verge of its death. Go ahead, son, he's yours. Father says in a clear voice. The bear puts his paws back on the ground. Moves very slowly. It walks towards them now. God, he doesn't seem in a hurry. Gilles thinks as he raises the rifle weighing more, weighing too much, a ton more than anything.

That black shimmering mass wading in blood. The effusion is completely visible in
the tangle of matted fur. One paw after the other, all sticky, as though. Gathers his
strength for one last showdown. Shoot. His father speaks, not too loudly, and very
distinctly. Finish the job properly, a sacred principle. The ritual of execution. The
ebony beast rolls like a rock, a train moving at the back of a tunnel. The top of the
rifle, a very straight rail. The sights scan over the crimson lather blotting the black
coat. One more step. Another. He's so close. How to do it, father doesn't panic.
Gilles is brave, rifle squeezed the trigger between the eyes exactly between aim for
the head father advises can't miss him dad you son the failure when he notices with
amazement that the safety latch hasn't been taken off, the lock shoot, the lock, the
breech is like ice in his hand and no time to, nothing else but.

☙

Flamand, veins of his neck protruding, looked at the other bottle
Crazy Sam now offered with kind insistence. I felt the tourists were
taking the joke a little too far.

"He doesn't drink!" intervened Karate Kid nervously.

"Please drink ...," Crazy Sam warbled. "Just for me! Please ... to
the United States of America."

"Try this one," Jim proposed.

He handed him the bottle of Christian Brothers. The liquid
spat out tawny reflections under the lamp that was too low.
Flamand opened his fingers and examined the palm of his hand.

"Okay, that's enough!" warned Brigitte, observing the scene
from a distance. "Are you quite through with your childishness?"

"Everything's all right, sweetheart!" sniggered Legris. "He's
just trying to get you more customers.... Your boss is the one who'll
be really happy!"

"The past is over and done with," Crazy Sam said, strangely
solemn, glaring at Flamand. "You have to let it go, man, you're so
sad all the time...."

The Kid split the air and stopped. He'd just been grabbed
around the waist from behind. Donald-Lard-Ass tried to get up
but, finding the soles of his feet a little too round for his liking,
immediately fell back. Moreau, coming out of his torpor, lunged
forward, hurling insults, "Don't move, you bastards! We're gonna
kill you bastards, kill all of you!"

To make up for the philosophical weakness of that endeavour, he was clapping his hands, looking thoughtful. Judith rewarded him with an elbow to the solar plexus, and he eased off.

"Young ladies don't have the manners they used to," Brigitte pointed out, having drawn closer.

Legris agreed.

Overburdened by weariness, Cowboy was getting ready to pounce.

Flamand half-opened his mouth as though to speak, his tense fingers skimming over the table. A cry of pain rang out. Karate Kid had bit the hand of his American, and tossed him over his shoulder, headfirst into an ashtray. Meanwhile, the bottle of brandy had vanished and Flamand's hand clasped emptiness. Jacques Boisvert stood there, very erect. He looked around at everyone, notably giving me a friendly smile. Then, clutching the bottle with a long calloused hand decked with a frayed bandage, he brought it to his lips. A good third of the poison was left in it.

"Ah, I was really thirsty!" he explained afterwards.

He had another swig, downing the bottle, to everybody's amazement.

"Cheers, everyone."

Then looked at Flamand severely, scolding him like a child caught red-handed, "You're not going to start touching that stuff again, César? You know it isn't good for you...."

They crossed gazes, of tempered steel and ancient fire. And I was seeing everything through a blur, having ceased to exist as anything but an indifferent receptacle for a stream of beer and brandy. I felt, how can I say?

❧

To turn around, clear off without a murmur, to clear off and snag your feet in a root jutting from the ground, set there like a snare, and while he falls head over heels in the black and dank humus suffused with odours from the dump, thunder peals behind him, above him, terrifying and powerful, loud enough to rupture his eardrums. He tries to get up, stumbles again, manages to pivot and falls on his back, the stranglehold of the earth on his shoulder blades. The Colt .45 thunders again, and again, and again, his father holds it with two hands like a cop who's in training and the bear's almost close enough to touch, so close he can no longer be missed. The bear rows with his large paws covered in bristling fur, rows and drags himself moaning at the feet of Boisvert who shoots, again shoots point-blank with the pistol he drew like an expert at the last moment, dealing the death blow of powder at the back of the beast's neck, in the end howling in triumph, the end of the suspense when he feels with the tip of his boot the inert snout frothing with blood. He turns around and the weight of his silence bares down on Gilles lying down with shame, frozen in his failure. The enormous black bear hugs the dump ground, four legs fully spread, tongue dead, chops covered in a puke of red currants.

Boisvert burped heartily and went to stand in front of Crazy Sam. With exaggerated polite gestures, he straightened out a wrinkle in his collar, his counterpart not batting an eyelid. Their gazes crossed; Boisvert wasn't batting an eyelid either. He finally moved back a step, giving a heavy slap on the American's back. "You old loon! Looking for someone to drink with, you old loggerhead? A round of drinks on the house for every damned American in Grande-Ourse! Well, while we're at it, for every damned Indian as well! Hey, Brigitte! Honey!"

Brigitte slipped among us as though she'd awaited only the signal. None of this astonished her and she clearly preferred amicable outcomes. Once everyone had been served, Boisvert took the Americans aside and, speaking to Jim who, incidentally, had ashes coming out his nose, tapped his sternum with an inflexible forefinger, "Hey smart aleck! Listen carefully! Bear hunting ended at sundown, but don't worry, we can take care of that."

The other fellow, flabbergasted, was watching him. Boisvert mimed his account with wide gestures, as though speaking to a deaf-mute.

"Now listen, you bastard! You take a piece of ... a piece of lard, a piece of," he lowered his gaze over his counterpart, lingering below the thorax, "... fat! You take a piece of fat, you see, and stick it over a fire!"

Jim was scratching his ear lobe. This unfathomable Boisvert was beginning to interest him.

"But then, if you want to make sure they smell your setup from hell...."

He disappeared down the hall, heading towards the kitchens. His strides were those of a giant. He returned almost at once, mischievous, waving a pint of molasses bearing the label of a grandmother wearing a head scarf and flopped in her rocking chair.

"Molasses! Molasses!" Boisvert repeated, elbowing poor Jim in the ribs.

Everyone laughed with relief. The atmosphere had suddenly relaxed, as though Boisvert had shouldered all the pressure himself. Ready to tear each other's guts out ten seconds earlier, the rivals now only wanted to make peace and take advantage of the free drinks. Boisvert raised his glass in one hand and his pint of molasses in the other. "To the United States of America, and to bears, god dammit!"

Only Crazy Sam, gloomy, and César Flamand, perennially dour, didn't take part in the jubilation.

❧

He picked up Gilles with a firm hand. Come on, stop trembling. That cold, residual fear in his stomach, like having to go. Father and fear penetrate him to the bone, with the plunging gaze of a predator, of an eagle forever at peace with his strength. Dusts off the .303 covered in black earth. Boisvert nods. Safety latch. A classic. The dead bear lies at their feet, gnarled shoulders sagging, having become his own burden, the final weariness. Boisvert says nothing. But when he tells the story maybe he won't relate it. But consoling this boy, impossible. He hushes up. The tension. Gilles sobs, at that very moment. Not for himself, but for the bear. That crazy idea came to him at the sight of the contorted animal, its large back, those invisible holes in his skin. The really pitiful idea of asking its forgiveness, forgiveness for having shot first, forgiveness for having participated in this, forgiveness, forgiveness for having killed it as well.

❧

I was struggling, caught in a snare, and awakened with a start. Brigitte was lying in my bed, so attractive, so slender, so naked. She moved slightly, opened the corner of an eyelid, sighed.

A sweet creature.

"How are you?" she asked with the tip of her fingers.

I had a splitting headache. Suddenly, I started for the second time.

"Shit! Where are we now?"

She'd shown a lot of patience that night.

"In the store, dummy. More precisely, in your room."

"The store? But ... the Indians.... Did they break in?"

She caught me by the neck, forcing me to lie down again.

"Big Ben was there. He was found sleeping in front of the entrance, his back to the door. It was impossible to pass through there, pal.... You'd have more luck trying to stop a train by standing on the rails."

"Oh, I see. Big Ben. Oh, my head."

She kissed me on the cheek, then the forehead, and I was already starting to feel much better. I moved back and admired her as though seeing her for the first time.

"What exactly are you doing here?"

She was softly taunting me. Very softly.

"You're really quite a number, Gilles. Jacques went to make coffee for the Americans. I think they'll go hunting. They don't give a damn about what I might do."

We heard noises in the next room: the groan of a very happy woman alternating with the squealing of a rodent.

"What's that ...?"

She signalled me to lower my voice.

"Gisèle. With Benoît."

"Oh no.... No!"

We both laughed. The unthinkable had happened. I lent an ear: Benoît was snoozing, snorting, and moaning, in the good care of a needy Gisèle.

"She practically carried him on the way back," Brigitte said, still laughing.

A question came to my lips, she guessed it.

"If you're thinking about your Indian woman, she left with fat Moreau. Really, you don't remember a thing?"

"Judith? Not really. Very glad for her."

"Still, you seemed to really appreciate her little language lesson."

"Language?"

"She showed you how to say *no* in hers...."

"I remember. Something like *maha* ... Blowing on the H as though it were boiling mush."

"Speaking of mush.... If I hadn't been there when you

wanted to play music on the jukebox, Moreau would've turned you into mincemeat."

"Again? Thanks. Music doesn't soothe manners around here...."

I then rhymed off the few lines of Verlaine my faulty mnemonics allowed me to recall. And also: *Mon auberge était à la Grande-Ourse/Mes étoiles au ciel avaient un doux frou-frou.* And then the film of my elusive dream returned to brush against my encephalon, those words, always, and their incoherent cavalcade.

"What are you thinking about?"

"My favourite recurring dream."

"What is it?"

"I still don't know."

I let myself fall way back, into the thickness of the pillow. Renewed strength rushed between my legs.

"Brigitte, I lo ..."

"Shhh, I have a boyfriend."

"... ve you."

"Hmmm."

"Did you bring your drawing pad?"

"No, we'll have to get down to business."

"Hurrah!"

A rumbling passed over the store and surrounded the room. The window rattled on its dwarf wall. Brigitte lifted her head like someone sniffing the wind.

"That's the Twin Otter," she declared.

"What does that mean?"

"Two things: first, he has several passengers; second, we have lots of time."

A grunt of surrender came through the wall. Benoît was snoring, and Gisèle moaned in the night, "Precious! Oh! Precious! My precious!"

4

CHRISTMAS
in July

MR. ADMINISTRATOR HAD BEEN GIVEN A very clear mandate to shake up the place thoroughly. Shareholders wanted results. The situation had stagnated for too long. Firing the Old Man was still their first priority. In the absence of the main party concerned, Mr. Administrator took comfort in his resolution.

The day following the fourth of July, we'd seen his pickup rushing down the hill, approaching at great speed. I was able to evict Gisèle without causing too much damage, with help from Brigitte, who then disappeared through the secret door in the basement. My head was like a football, but I was able to stand up. Benoît was still laid out. Effusions with the boss were kept to the strict minimum. He'd just bumped into the Americans at the village entrance as they were finally heading home. The bear, freshly felled by bullets and sprawled on the hood of the Cherokee, was sure to go down in the region's hunting records.

Mr. Administrator requested an interview with me and I immediately understood I was about to receive a sizeable blow. My

obscure and comfortable position as a subordinate drudge had
reached its term. I was now being asked to climb to the front lines.
The boss placed his hand on my shoulder, a gesture I hate more
than anything.

"While I draw up the financial sheet, you, Gilles, take care of
the rest. In a word, you're the new manager. I'll be there to help you."

I clicked my heels against a rotten board and trotted off to
that new adventure. Recommendations, warnings, advice, war
measures, etc., already rang out behind me, "We'll have to be
tougher! No alternative! No more credit! We've been too lenient!
Too lenient!"

Benoît had started to lose his grip over the last while. Mr.
Administrator conceded that a holiday would be very good for
him. The next day, the manager hurriedly hopped on the train, as
though carrying off a shameful secret. This strategic withdrawal by
a serious young man caused some astonishment among the
population. The knowing shrugs of those who'd taken part in the
Independence night helped feed local gossip.

As soon as news of the furlough got out, the Indians decided
to test my resolve. This change seemed to herald all kinds of
benefits whose extent remained to be verified. They were extremely
amused by my promotion and I somewhat apprehended the way
they'd treat me now. Absorbed in the still uncertain exercise of my
brand new authority, I could see them coming with their minor
blackmails. Without consulting Mr. Administrator too much, I
continued giving them credit for basic foods and commodities.
One single rule had to stand at any cost: not one drop of beer
unless it was paid for in cash. I remained firm on that point,
earning endless sulks.

This was the beginning of July, and the playground
beautification project was in serious trouble; calls to order by those
in charge had been futile. The Indians spent all their time in front
of the store, on the cement steps where the sun blazed and the flies
droned. They landed there shortly after waking up, around mid-
morning, and their fierce poses made them look like a popular
militia committed to my protection. Tourists were a little
intimidated and would be scared stiff when crossing this peculiar
honour guard, but, deep down, they savoured the exoticism of

these hard-featured savages whose eyes were narrow slits. When no customers were in sight, I went out into the heat to stretch my limbs among them, to chat while swatting mosquitoes and those terrible deer flies. Judith no longer accompanied them. She preferred flaunting herself in Moreau's company, and people were saying that the latter's relations with his domestic harpy were hardly rosy. The sky perspired and my scorching thoughts disappeared into the distance blurred by the furnace's moving air. Often, through sheer idleness, we'd let silence burrow between us.

"The Americans," said Cowboy, "have killed a bear."

He was wincing, as though extremely sceptical in this excruciating light.

"Yeah. With Boisvert's help.... Boisvert, his molasses, and his rind of lard."

"Boisvert."

"A mother and three cubs," the Kid noted, looking at the ground.

"Three? Are you sure?"

"Three," answered Cowboy.

"What'll they do without their mother?"

Pensive nods shook their heads.

"Die," said Cowboy.

But the Muppet was coming towards us. Riding sidesaddle on the motorized tricycle, tenderly given over to the motion, Gisèle let herself be tossed by the bumps Moreau used as an excuse to rough her around. She'd been drinking and her body, deprived of her scarce faculties, undulated without defence. Way before the vehicle had stopped completely, she'd fallen flat on the dry sand; it seemingly wanted to engulf her, so that she, an insult to common sense, would no longer be seen. She rolled to the ground, crawled, flattening the sharp grasses and managed to stand up while the Muppet parked his vehicle, his neck compulsively twisted by a knowing laugh. This minor role as chauffeur and servant suited him marvellously, along with its easily imaginable benefits.

It was usually difficult to read any emotion on Gisèle's face, which the inclemency of nights in the open air had chiselled into an obscure system of bulges and dark zones. But the day she fell head over heals off the Muppet's tricycle, the disarray imprinted on her features could've been spotted by anyone. She planted herself in front of me, hardly recognizing me. She smelled of naphtha, and her clothes were permeated with it.

"Beh ... Beh ... Benoît?"

"He's gone, sweetheart!"

She tensed up and grabbed my collar, "Beeer!"

"No! Not today ...," I said with sympathy.

The Muppet then foisted the grotesque projection of his skull on us.

"Beer?" he creaked like an old hinge, "No problem Gisèle, dear! How many do you want? We'll drink it quietly over at my place...."

I knew the Indians were looking at us. I leaned over the counter, grabbed the Muppet by the scruff, and drew his face closer to mine. My voice hissed like an old radio, "You've already made her drink all night and screwed her once or twice, which at your age ought to be enough for a while, right? Why don't you go and suck on your beer so we can get a little break from seeing your rag face!"

I released my grip. He was massaging the top of his head, taken aback, trying to figure out what had befallen him. The silence was so thick you could cut it with an axe.

The Muppet finally shook himself, shivered like a freshly croaked nag, thinking he'd regained his composure with a whining laugh that fooled no one. He wasn't used to seeing his little business displayed in public like this. He turned around and moved away, slowly, tending to his wound. Right up to the door he toyed with the hope of being called back, reassured that all this had been only a joke, that no one really thought he, an honourable pensioner, could behave in such a questionable manner. But his retreat got no such consolation.

Meanwhile, Gisèle had moved on to the next part of her great offensive.

"Wannh, wanna talk to Behnoît!"

"I'm in charge while he's away," I politely informed her.

She brought her face closer, taken aback.

"I'm replacing him, Gisèle. In his official duties, of course, and surely not those that are private," I added, scornfully eyeing the ravaged plumpness that invaded my field of vision.

"Who decided that?" she shouted, extremely excited.

"Mr. Administrator," Cowboy whispered in a cunning tone, mixed with ironic respect. "He's in the office, over there, and mustn't be disturbed...."

With a tread heavy as a day without wine, dense as unleavened bread, Gisèle headed for the back of the store.

●

Mr. Administrator was a professional accountant. After successfully completing his corporation's exam, he'd blossomed in the bitterly flowered universe of numbers. During his career, he'd learned to size up loan applicants at first glance, and bank accounts no longer held any secrets for him. Alternately a financial investigator, branch manager, and international cash mercenary, he'd been asked to unravel incredible imbroglios, to disclose ingenious swindles, and preside over the recovery of desperate situations. However, nothing had prepared him to deal with what he found, in this midsummer, when he decided to tackle the Grande-Ourse Outfitters' accounting.

He first had to confront the filing cabinet filled with yellow cards. Its amoral mass, near the cash register, was the most visible lair of the establishment's debtors. He then had to venture to the other side of the counter to get the dozens of unpaid bills slipped onto a nail, which had finally stuck together, forming a kind of compact and difficult to digest mash. He then mercilessly tracked down, through drawers, on high cluttered shelves, in the least corners, even under furniture legs, ancient and secret debt acknowledgements, written in a hasty, often illegible hand. Finally, as a last recourse, he was forced to rely on the memory of the walls, whose slats were profoundly grooved with pencil marks, in some places bearing vestiges of crude inscriptions signalling purchases that were never paid, recalling the passage of other unknown debtors, at one time verbose, and now on the run.

He'd crawled out of that jumble like a botanist at the heart of the selva, retiring with his precious supply of enigmas to the back of the store, inside the windowed storage room he'd occupied for the last three days, surrounded by a worrisome silence, head streaked by profound vertical creases. He could be seen, knotted with effort, behind the desk covered with notebooks and documents, in the feeble halo of a penitent lamp.

I was informing Brigitte of the latest developments. She'd just arrived and sweat was furrowing her t-shirt between her breasts.

"So, you're the boss now?"

The tone was sceptical.

"Well, I haven't made it quite to the top yet, you see.... My immediate superior is having fun with his calculator over there.... No, I manage the commercial section...."

She approved with a distracted nod.

"In fact," I continued, "the big boss is at the point of undergoing the decisive test...."

"Mi ... Mi ... Mister?"

Without looking up, Mr. Administrator signalled her to continue. Totally concentrated, he hadn't seen her coming and Gisèle was already upon him. A heavy rustling lifted the piles of bills and the hoary locks of hair on the brave man's dishevelled temples. He let himself fall forward, face buried in the scattering of papers.

When she came back towards us, Gisèle flashed a lopsided smile.

"Beeer!"

Mr. Administrator was trotting behind her.

"And I suppose you have money to pay with, hmm?"

"Creeedit."

"Oh no."

"Benouah, he slept with...."

He wanted to place a hand on that voluptuous mouth and looked around, distraught.

"Yes, yes, I understand," he coughed slightly, completely pitiful.

As Gisèle was about to flesh out her confession, the accountant stoically walked to the cold room, face stiff as a sugar-loaf. "So what were we saying? A two-four? .... Is that right?"

I looked at Brigitte who was sighing, sincerely saddened.

"Poor Gisèle!"

The other Indians were paying close attention to the scene. The boss returned clumsily lugging the case of beer. He declared, somewhat shyly, but nonetheless categorically, "We'll let her have this on credit and then she'll leave! Okay?"

"Okay, boss."

"She promised she'd leave, after ...," he insisted, already absorbed.

In the light of noon, Cowboy was walking towards us, rocking his shoulders with his usual carefree attitude. He hesitated when he reached us, flashing his all-purpose smile. Mr. Administrator muttered a flustered salutation.

Like Daladier and Chamberlain in Munich, he'd negotiated relief on the cheap and pretended to ignore what awaited him.

✿

When the Old Man returned, a dense traffic of beer cases and Indians cluttered the store front. Not understanding a thing, he rushed inside: Mr. Administrator, leaning against the wall and slightly overwhelmed by the events, was puffing a little.

"It's so hot!" he murmured to convince himself. "We almost can't refuse them a little cold beer...."

"For humanitarian motives!" I confirmed before the Old Man's accusing look.

Cowboy, holding his fuel supply as he was leaving, gave me a slight salute. The Old Man, head in hands, watched him leave. When Gisèle had stepped through the doorway, squeezing the case of beer against her like a nursling, followed by the big boss giving her slight tepid slaps on the back, Cowboy and his pals had understood they'd now have to redirect their strategy: they'd no longer kill themselves arguing endlessly with a mere underling; dealing with subordinates wasn't worth it; the head is what had to be struck. Gisèle had created a dangerous precedent and I was worried. I thought I'd set the record straight and helped establish my reputation by dealing with the Muppet expeditiously. But Mr. Administrator had just short-circuited me, and it would doubtless be very difficult to restore a semblance of order to this mess.

The Old Man, meanwhile, was melancholically banging his head against the walls. "Too late! It's over! Over! We're caught in the system! Over...."

In the days that followed, while Mr. Administrator

disappeared beneath slovenly layers of paperwork, the Old Man did his best to clear out the riff-raff camped at our doors. Sometimes, returning from one of those strolls for which he'd become a master at dressing up with some excuse, he'd find the listless brood submerging the porch. He'd then rush at them and, twirling in the searing wind like a scarecrow in a field of oats, scattering all of them with wide gestures, "Don't you damned laggards have anything to do? Go on, get to work, you bunch of good-for-nothings!"

Laughter that was already dissipated slipped through his fingers, he cupped his poor dried-out hands around his mouth and ran after them, shouting abuse, always intent on their moral elevation, always seeking their greater edification. "You're gonna lose your wonderful government subsidies, if you go on, you race of sluggards! Around here, we produce, make profit and pay taxes, we aren't in the business of fattening you up while you remain idle, you lousy heaps of dried-out dog meat!"

The Indians didn't always know the exact meaning of the Old Man's words but, running no risk, they smiled complacently whenever he showed up, taking their own good time to get out of the way. The Old Man would lay it on, feeling their biceps, furiously deliberating.

"It's a shame to see this, all the work that's being wasted here! A real waste! I'll personally find you a job!"

"You're going to wreck another bridge?"

"The bridge? The bridge? Ah! Ah! The bridge was rotten! Just like the bunch of you! Rotten! No good!"

He was sweating profusely.

When Gisèle asked about Benoît, he avenged himself with delight, with ecstasy really, twisting the knife in the wound. "He's gone! Gone! He's fed up at seeing you and your friends! You disgusted him, are you happy? He's gone to see real people and get himself a little girlfriend in town!"

Ever since the Americans had left, the Old Man had regained his form. He was in his element everywhere, more than ever Grande-Ourse's great games coordinator. As soon as he could lay his hands on a recent newspaper, he'd rush to the billboard, once again having become the depository of all destinies. Waving the page with the winning numbers like a miserable shredded wing, he'd stop in front of the pinned combinations, already comparing frantically, hesitating, double checking, body stiffened, hand crooked, like a pointing Irish setter.

One day, when arithmetic proved an unrewarding science, Mr. Administrator tore himself from his confinement, approaching along the aisle and leaning over the Old Man's shoulder, asking, humble and grave, "Did we win?"

❧

The Old Man would always bounce back. Without fail, he'd show up with a new trick up his sleeve, a new string to his bow. He'd engaged in a commercial operation of his own invention on his last stay in the city. We helped him unload large cardboard boxes that were strangely light.

"Bread?" I asked sceptically.

"No, but it'll put some on the table!"

With the manners of a travelling salesman, he spread out the product of his latest illumination before us: caps, t-shirts, and sweatshirts, all bearing the colours and grand-sounding name of the Grande-Ourse Outfitters.

"Nice rags, eh?" beamed the Old Man.

He buzzed around us, excited as a child.

"To keep our customers, we have to tattoo our name on their chest! They'll become our best publicity!"

"On condition we start having customers," I cautiously pointed out.

Mr. Administrator was moved, wringing his hands, approvingly pinching the fabric exhaling the nauseous scent of brand new items.

"But.... The price?" he inquired before unbridling his enthusiasm.

"Not expensive, not expensive ...," the Old Man asserted.

"Nice rags!" Mr. Administrator admitted.

What followed happened very quickly.

César Flamand's pickup pulled up in front of the store, filled with festive Indians who immediately poured out of the vehicle, storming the establishment. They were all there, Cowboy,

Christophe, the Kid, Judith and Salomé, Donald Big-Arms, Fernande and even Gisèle, slumped at the back of the vehicle, foot jutting out, all very cheerful and brimming with sunshine and good brew, all of them grinning with the exception, naturally, of Flamand Senior who was waiting for them, leaning on the steering wheel.

A free-for-all broke out. Merchandise snatched from the boxes passed from hand to hand, delighted exclamations rang out, people slipped on sweatshirts with cheerful groans, t-shirts were stretched out in every direction, people were adjusting caps onto their very tipsy heads. And this super fitting session unfolded before the Old Man's disgusted eyes as he struggled to retrieve his material from the impious group.

"Whoa there, don't touch! You'll tear everything! Don't dirty anything, careful! Hey, bring that cap over here, it's too big for you, pinhead!"

He literally didn't know which way to turn. Meanwhile, I'd returned to my station behind the cash register, and looked on the scene lovingly, with a sympathetic eye and a light heart. Soon, a lineup bearing the arms of the Outfitters paraded by the counter as though for an inspection. Each had found a shirt and cap in their size. In an ultimate offensive to turn things around, the Old Man came between the profaners and me. "That stuff isn't yours, you mangy bunch of dogs! What are you moochers going to do with all that!"

He turned to Mr. Administrator in despair who, still tangled in his recent contradictions, refused to compromise himself and requested my opinion with a brief chin gesture. I was the manager after all. So I shrugged and calmly declared, avoiding to look at the Old Man, "Clothes are included in basic needs! We have no right to deny them this!"

The cash register began to ring, and invisible money went on to increase the sums piled onto the credit notes. Salomé was beautiful enough to eat in her bright red sweatshirt. It bore the print of a moose with powerful antlers, against the backdrop of a silhouetted bear, rubbing shoulders with an Indian nymph and a fish jumping out of the water along a perfect curve. I thought she looked so comical beneath the prolonged bill of her cap that I was

unable to suppress a burst of timid laughter which she immediately
returned. And when Salomé laughed, a hint of union and
allegiance filled the air.

*

Cowboy was soaked. He'd spent the whole morning in the lake.

"What good thing are you up to, Cowboy?"

"Nothing."

"What bad thing are you up to?"

"Nothing."

"Is there anything I can do for you?"

"Come in for a swim."

"You know very well I'm working."

"The Old Man can replace you."

"No."

He looked at me grudgingly, and I felt there was something
strange and aggressive about him.

"I'll go afterwards."

"You're my friend, Gilles?"

"Of course."

"You're the one Salomé loves."

"Hmmm...."

He'd drunk quite a bit, but there was something else.

Cowboy never talked to me about love. He once told me he'd
asked Fernande for permission to date Salomé. But the old lady
had asked him to wait. That was about one or two years ago and, at
the time, saying that Salomé was a child wasn't a figure of speech.
That account had stuck with me, since I felt his request to be
rather comical. Otherwise, Cowboy didn't mention girls or sex, and
wasn't known to have any other associations.

The Kid, for his part, had gotten a girlfriend on his last stay
in Sans-Terre. He remained very discreet about the whole affair
but, since his father didn't have a phone in his shack, the Kid now
came over to call on my good offices every night. It had become a
ritual, no doubt as valuable as his morning workout, a
complement to it all in all: I'd dial his number, he'd grab the
receiver and hang out there, eyes sparkling, only opening his
mouth exceptionally, transmitting sighs mostly, while the same

probably took place at the other end of the line. They'd spend a quarter of an hour listening to each other breathe, drawing a little confidence from the process.

"She's going to come and visit pretty soon," he'd say following the session.

Cowboy pointed out an orange metallic container that was half-hidden under a shelf, "That's what I want."

I stared at him without a word.

"I need it! For the lanterns, at the camp."

"Do you swear to it?"

He swore and closed the deal with a not very persuasive smile. I didn't have a degree in conscience guiding and could do no more. I let him have it on credit, like everything else, and he left with the precious fuel lapping against the sides of the can, picking up, as he walked by, a beer bottle that had warmed while awaiting him on the windowsill.

I turned around, finding myself face to face with Mr. Administrator and the Old Man, who'd already been watching me for a while. Both had their arms crossed with an air of wonderful certainty. A tiny electric pencil scurried beneath their scalps and they were hurriedly taking notes.

"How are you?" I asked in a voice that was too clear.

They nodded in perfect unison. The boss stepped forward and, with a perfectly senatorial economy of gestures, dropped a heavy file folder onto the counter; papers covered in studious scribbling fell out from either side. His hand hovered over the exhibit as he spoke.

"To be honest, strictly nothing can be understood from the company's numbers. Save one thing."

He breathed deeply. Besides, he was the only one to do so.

"Except for this, Gilles: credit is killing us! We're in the dark red, pal, in the crimson!"

He made a spiteful gesture towards the door which had just closed behind my friend.

"The Indians!"

"Yes?"

Leaning over, he looked me straight in the eyes, while the Old Man feverishly agreed. There was no way to escape them, they ruled over facts. "Do you know how much Gisèle owes us?"

He wasn't moving. The Old Man held himself back with both hands.

"No idea," I answered.

"Seven thousand bucks!" he hammered out with a kind of masochistic satisfaction.

The Old Man turned away, crying with rage and despair.

"And that's a conservative estimate," insisted Mr. Administrator. "We'll probably never know the exact amount. The bookkeeping has been a disaster."

I felt compelled to take Benoît's defence.

"It isn't only the Indians, you know! Take Moreau...."

He interrupted me with an imperious gesture.

"I'll deal with Moreau! He, at least, has a business. That means we can talk."

He walked towards the window where the lures were displayed, drew open the sliding panel, and lifted a pair of miniature snowshoes trimmed with a red and green ribbon. With his other hand, he hooked a pair of miniature moose-hide moccasins, which had a decorative function as well, and were bound with a leather lace.

"But this? Is this commerce?"

"Benoît's doing," I explained, filled with good intentions. "He buys a few crafts from them, to encourage them, and sells them for a lot more than he paid. Did you see the price?"

"That's not the issue!" concluded the boss, shaking the cheap rubbish as though it were a cluster of small bells. "The issue, first of all, is that these thingamajigs don't sell! And secondly, after squandering their cheques in town, those people are only too happy to come back here and place themselves under our protection, because...."

"We're too kind," I concluded despite myself.

"Too kind!" echoed the Old Man.

"We're not missionaries!" the boss shot out rebelliously.

Unable to continue pretending to be doing nothing, the Old Man walked over to the door and fiddled around with the bar. Through the window, we saw Cowboy lugging his gallon of naphtha, sprightly walking along the railway, a bottle dancing in his other hand. Mr. Administrator stood between that vision and me. "They're hoodwinking you, Gilles!"

"They're going to fleece you!" said the echo.

He pounded the counter's metallic edge then, grimacing with pain, stated the store's new policy, "From now on, for the Indians, it's cash or nothing! Cash, do you understand? For beer, clothes, food, naphtha, everything! Cash! We're not here to do charity, we're here to do business! Those who aren't happy can always go elsewhere to see if they get better service!"

"Cash!" said the Old Man, looking at the sky.

And he got the idea of clapping two or three times.

"We're through with being too kind," resumed Mr. Administrator.

"Kind, kind...."

They'd almost managed to disturb my composure.

❧

Brigitte came over to shop in late afternoon. The heat was scorching, and she'd slipped on the skimpiest garments on the market. She swayed her tail in the shady mugginess of the aisle, making waves deep in my stomach. But there was no way I'd treat myself to a little philandering during regular hours. I settled for melting on the spot when she came up to the cash register. Her slightly protruding teeth sparkled when she said, "It's hot as an oven, in here!"

"That's because of the refrigerators, they act like thermal pumps, you see...."

"Poor you, stuck here.... We'd have to go swimming...."

"Oh yes! Naked! Any time! At midnight!"

"I have something else to tell you, listen: we're organizing a Christmas in July, at the hotel. There'll be a gift exchange. Are you in?"

At my request, she briefed me about a local custom. I learned that, on camp grounds and holiday pastures where people quickly became neighbours, it was really felt to be too bad they couldn't see each other at the Nativity. So it became a custom to organize a somewhat parallel and off-season Christmas celebration. First of all, it consoled those in the habit of heading to the tropics to get skin cancer when the North wind picked up; secondly, in small villages subsisting mostly from tourism and activities practised in the warm season, citizen shopkeepers were allowed to get a share of the economic manna that unavoidably follows December fir trees.

"In any event," I observed encouragingly, "we have lots of fir trees."

"Come over tonight. I'll get them to draw your name."

"My name?"

"You know: that of the happy mortal who'll get the privilege of receiving a present from you."

"How well said."

"Jacques has gone away," she added after hesitating a moment. "He had to fix one of the camps...."

"I'm a very busy man, Brigitte, but I'll try to get away. On condition you use something more exciting than a hat...."

"Come over, you'll see...."

As she was about to leave, she added, "Your friends are beside the lake, over there.... It's a big party, they're all on their backs."

She saluted me and left. Then, popping her head through the door, grimacing, "Come and fill me up, you big lug."

I followed her, then turned on the pump, unscrewed the cap and, with the nozzle held at waist level, filled Jacques Boisvert's pickup with gasoline. Brigitte sponged the sweat running down the indentation of her neck. Her upper lip was shining and humid. She studied me with a mocking gaze.

"Made any headway with the very young girl?"

"What are you talking about?"

"Nothing. I'll need to have your name on a piece of paper."

"With my phone number, and anything you want...."

"When will you come?"

I gave in to temptation, placing a fluttering hand on the launching pad of her hip. The gauge displayed an amount, the trigger blocked, and drops of gasoline squirted from the mouth of the tank.

❧

They were all there, seated in a circle, Indian-style in the darkness. It looked like a gathering of old sages, but they were desperately young. I sniffed the odour, before dropping down among them, heals under my thighs. They made the usual jokes. But the cascade of each phrase dissipated into babbling and distant laughter. There was no fire at the centre of the circle. The fire was in their heads. The naphtha can sat prominently amid the shadows, a large congealed flame, the nerve centre of a daydreaming attention. Cowboy placed a dirty rag against the container's neck, flipping it in one fell swoop, holding the dampened cloth against his nose, as though to blow it. He pressed it against his nostrils, inhaling deeply. I got a distinct whiff of the heavy and noxious aroma. Cowboy returned my gaze without seeing me. He gestured simply with his hands and breathed deeply. The silence was penetrating and disquieting. Cowboy slipped the rag to Christophe who sniffed it in turn, deeply, noisily. Not showing the least emotion, he was saturating himself right to the core. Judith, slumped a little further away, was flying so high that we were no longer there.

Cowboy handed me the rag that Christophe had dampened a second time. It now stank of gasoline ten feet away. He offered it amiably, "Want some?"

"No thanks," I replied very wearily.

Trying to shake the helplessness rivetting me there, I said, like a first-class spoilsport, "Do you know what that stuff does to your brain cells?"

He nodded, with a fixed gaze, "We don't want to live old."

Karate Kid then grabbed the pallid thing, sniffing it voluptuously. I didn't feel good. I felt compelled to break up this slow circulation of euphoria, and it pissed me off. I lowered my head, overwhelmed.

The Kid was caught in a pang of uncontrollable laughter. And I secretly envied that laughter which meant: I want to die young and hot-blooded.

Because survival had become a bore to them.

I was about to get up and leave when a shiver ran down my spine. Salomé had just crumpled the oily rag in her composed fingers, raising it to her immobile face. That was too much for me. "You're not touching that stuff!"

She let out a distressed and mocking giggle, but I was going to put a stop to it.

"Listen...."

I became the target of their sniggering and surprised Cowboy looking at me, his expression furrowed by pity and conceit. They remained there, in a world apart, beyond the reach of my good intentions. My words were sullied by too much morality, and good dope was too rare and expensive. Buying time, I yanked the rag out of Salomé's hands and brought it to my mouth, sniffing it warily while my conscience tried on another half-belt of good and evil. Wasn't the consideration of Salomé and her circle worth a pointless whiff of gasoline vapours?

"Okay, that's enough!" I murmured, tossing the rag into the middle of the circle.

I grabbed Salomé's hand, forcing her to get up and follow me. She protested feebly. Cowboy got up, filled with rancour, "What are you doing?"

"I have to talk to her.... So long, Cowboy. I'll buy you a beer later, whenever you want, old pal...."

She followed close behind and Cowboy fell back into apathy with the others. At that point, I didn't care what they thought or even if they still could think. Salomé was unscathed and asked me naively, "Will you buy me a beer?"

This little girl really wanted to go astray.

❧

We found Gisèle, rather drunk and treated with naphtha as well, at the hotel where she was doing her best to catch the attention of two fishermen who were busy relating their latest adventures to a Legris who was all ears. I bought Salomé the promised beer, then one for me, another for the mother. Legris was paying close attention to the show. Before going to savour our refreshments on the doorstep, I reminded Brigitte of the purpose of my visit. She held the hat while I fished out a piece of paper from the pile.

"I'm not allowed to sell alcohol to a minor," she warned bitterly.

"You're selling it to me, Brigitte. Listen: it was either that or naphtha, so...."

"Social work fits you rather well.... Seriously, don't you think she's a little young?"

I walked a few steps then turned around. "Don't you think Boisvert is a little old?"

"I'm thirty years old, Gilles Deschênes, I...."

I was no longer listening to her. Bringing the piece of paper closer to my eyes, I confusedly spelled out the name I'd just drawn. Then, never short of noble gestures, I fell in Gisèle's arms and, pushing her, rolling her, pulling her, I got her to step through the door. The three men seated at the table found this fat girl irresistibly amusing.

"It's too much for one guy on his own!" Legris observed with his usual tact.

"What is it?" Salomé asked.

She certainly meant the small piece of paper I held in my fingers, and not the gelatinous mass I was towing.

"This? Oh nothing. Unless you still believe in Santa Claus...."

Salomé didn't want to go back home. There'd been a fight between Flamand and his old lady, about a bottle, and that's why she'd joined the merry little group, with the firm intention of spending a sleepless night.

Walking from the hotel, we ran into Christophe and the Kid, who were hanging around. I gave them my beer to share. Somewhere above us, we heard the howling of a young wolf. It was Cowboy. Perched atop the radio tower, belting out tremolos, yodelling roulades, and filling the night with an incorporeal howl. It gave me goose flesh.

"He's angry with you," mumbled the Kid sadly.

"He's gonna jump," added Christophe with that tiny stubbornness which made him so engaging.

"Okay, I'm going."

Salomé didn't say a thing. The beer was affecting her. Gisèle, farther on, was sniggering distractedly.

The structure rose to a respectable height. I immediately understood I shouldn't look down. The tower was crowned by a kind of crow's-nest where two people could stand by squeezing a little. Cowboy stopped his modulations, and I slipped next to him.

"Hi, big fella. Weren't you high enough already?"

He smiled quietly, cheeks shining like apple melba.

We overlooked the shivering forest that faded into the shadows. Scant lights pierced the confusion beneath our feet. The circular handrail surrounding us — a thin halo striped in red and white — seemed very flimsy.

"I'm going to jump," Cowboy said.

"Not on your life, pal!"

"Gilles...." he began sharply.

"Yes...."

"When I dove into the lake today, Nelson caught my foot...."

"Oh...."

"He wanted to hold me back."

"That would surprise me."

"It's a curse, Gilles."

"I've heard that."

"Are you going to sleep with Salomé?"

"Cowboy, if everyone continues to mention it to me, I'll do it just to be left alone!"

He remained lost in his thoughts. We could hear Gisèle on the ground singing softly. He touched my elbow. "Is the store open, Gilles?"

"Afraid not, Cowboy."

There was something strange about that intimacy on the narrow platform. I was eager to get out of there.

"Will you open the store for me?"

"If you want beer, the hotel is still open. Besides, I owe you one."

But he slowly shook his head.

"That's not what I want."

"What is it that you want?"

"I want some chicken."

"Tropicana Chicken?"

"Otherwise, I'm jumping," he explained, bringing his face closer to mine.

I had to recognize his gift for simplifying situations. Eyes dull, he repeated, emphasizing each syllable with difficulty, "Tropicana Chicken."

"You know, Cowboy, I still haven't eaten the bear meat ..."

He didn't seem surprised at all.

"Okay, let's go. We're going back down!" I said finally.

I sank into the darkness and he followed. I had the impression of returning from far away, of coming straight down from the sky. Cowboy was faster and more agile and the soles of his shoes were level with my eyes. Slipping on a rung, I grabbed his heel and he stopped moving for a few seconds. I'd later remember his words as a premonition.

❧

Gilles finally gets up. The sun rises as well. The whole village knows, now. At the store, in the cottages, that's all people are talking about. People watch the hotel entrance from their kitchen windows. And watching the sky. He dresses ceremoniously. This village has always been a prison. His fellow escapees, recruited elsewhere. Beethoven, CBC radio. Chopin, Balzac, paperback. Jules Verne. The land of furs. The Reader's Digest. *George's lung. Our condensed book of the month. Real-life adventure. George's spleen. Flamand's back.*

Go on. Playtime is over. Leave. Face the facts. Like a rat.

His father is in the kitchen, swallowing. What happened is now between them. He looks up from his plate, stops chewing. His son holds back tears. The first ones, since yesterday. Boisvert gets up and walks. His long collected strides. Relying on his judgement. Crazy Sam? His word. He's okay. The Indian woman? It was dark. Nobody. Only the two of us. The cops? A guilty party. All those bullets in the body, the back filled with them. Self-defence, no. But Gilles is still a minor. Won't have any problems, says the father. Gilles holds his breath. Has he heard right? Plead for leniency, a reduced sentence. The right to defend his property. A drunken Indian. To say that. You. Fired. Do you understand? You bet. Twelve years later. That debt. Time. He breathes very softly, now. Would like to refrain from living. The best solution. His father returns to sit in front of his plate, eggs shining, bacon he likes crisp where grease pearls. That breakfast he finally swallows, business as usual, before getting up and retching in the sink.

❧

The Old Man had slipped the bar back, obviously. But we could count on the legendary keenness of his ear. Soon as I began methodically shaking the door, he was there, our very own grouch, in his underwear, amid his carousel of odours.

"Four o'clock in the morning!" he muttered mechanically.

I didn't feel too drunk. Walking to the kitchen, I stopped in front of the perforated panel where the key chains were hanging. While the Old Man had his back to me, I slipped a set into my pocket, trying to muffle its metallic jingling. Then returned towards him, at once destroying the wonderful satisfaction he'd got from tightly closing the entrance.

"I have to go back out," I asserted simply.

He managed to convert his indignation into a foul mood, again playing doorman. I returned into the night, looking in the dark for Salomé who'd brought her mother to wait for me a little farther on. I flushed out the two Indian women in a thicket along the railroad. We detoured to avoid the large white house where, worn out from his daily battle, Mr. Administrator rested.

The key quarter-turned and the door opened quietly. The interior was clean, almost quaint. I'd chosen the house at random, but it was in good shape. Salomé shielded her eyes from the harsh light.

"This is your palace, princess."

Gisèle opened and closed the cupboards with crashing and banging, already looking for her provision.

"Any beer?"

"I've got what you need!" I said, pulling two bottles from my vest. "Here's your baby bottle, old girl."

Salomé looked at me sideways. I expected she'd feel that supplying a few liquid ounces to help her mother sleep was a charitable gesture. Perhaps she wouldn't think me very different from all those fishermen passing through, all those Legris and Muppets who made her mother drink to keep her quiet and very agreeable.

After a few energetic swigs, Gisèle had a moist lip and told me I was to sleep between her daughter and her. Salomé pretended not to have heard and stole a sip from the unattended bottle. I tried to remain serious.

"Shh.... Shh.... Quiet, Gisèle."

"Between my daughter and me!" she chuckled heavily.

I walked into a bedroom. The layout was perfect for our happy trio: three single beds filling a cramped space saturated with a sweet musty odour. Two of the beds were parallel, the third perpendicular. On the wall was a 1967 calendar with a tattered and faded photo; the only decoration in this harsh room. A cheerful hunter posed beside a deer which, showing posthumous scorn, stuck his tongue out at him. Gisèle dropped her head onto a pillow. She quickly snored away.

I stood in front of Salomé and felt responsible for everything. It was as though, with this key to an abandoned house, I held the destiny of Grande-Ourse, that of Salomé and her family and friends. I touched her hair and she smiled at me. She'd grabbed the bottle abandoned by Gisèle and was gaining confidence. A thought crossed my mind: in ten years, in five years, even way before, she'd jump men as well. I kissed her cheek and showed her the bed where she'd sleep. I immediately hid under the sheets of the other bed without undressing. Scarcely had I turned around when she was tickling the soles of my feet with her toes.

"Hey, is there no way to get some sleep around here?"

I was happily very tired and played dead. She put an end to her boldness and went back to bed. She soon fell asleep and I mused about the reward my exemplary conduct would earn at Last Judgement.

I didn't sleep a wink. At one point, Gisèle mumbled for a beer, without waking up. I sent her to the devil, raising my voice the least possible and she stopped groaning. A timid glow filtered through grimy windows at the edge of dawn, and I squirmed out of the sheets to draw the curtains. My shadow then crossed the cold floor, stretching towards Salomé's warm proximity, swearing to disturb not a thing. Her response was to squeeze beside me; I bided the remaining time staring at atoms of dirt on the ceiling.

I thought about Salomé's life. Born fatherless, from a mother widowed by gunshots, brought up in a group and a little lost ever since. Placed in the custody of a quiet and melancholy grandfather who, however, did like children. Her stepmother, a friendly and habitual boozer. Her natural brothers and sisters scattered left and right along the railway. Grade school with the nuns, like the Quebec of old. And now what? I didn't even dare turn around, for fear of awaking her. I would love to meet her in her dreams.

Rolling over, Gisèle pulled her sheets in gruesome bursts. She asked for another drink, and disappeared in a trance of some kind. Her deep voice gave me shivers.

"Gilles! Gilles! The lake.... The bottle.... The cap!"

"What are you talking about, Gisèle?"

"The treasure...."

"What treasure?"

"A treasure in a bottle...."

An indefinable anxiety seized that hollow voice. She was more than usually delirious.

"The cap isn't on the bottle...."

"A bottle of what, Gisèle?"

"Don't remember.... The brand...."

Salomé's breath brushed against my neck. She wanted to know what was going on. I questioned her about the treasure story. She'd always heard that a sum of money lay at the bottom of Lac Légaré, in a spot known to Gisèle alone. She'd once disclosed her secret to many, but no one ventured there because of a curse. Gisèle no longer talked about it, save in her nightmares. Salomé herself didn't seem overly troubled by the story, taught to her in childhood no doubt, like a fairy tale or a myth. She immediately went back to sleep. Her barely audible snore was the echo of an angel's whisper. Each of her tiny movements was a source of sharp and matchless delight for me. Minutes passed, marked by the mingling accompaniment of our breathing, and I strove to extract the gist from each nanosecond. Moving my head slightly, I could see Gisèle stirring in the chaos of her bed. She resembled real life.

❧

Construction industry vacationers filed in around mid-July. The low wage earner indulging himself in a grand fishing trip with his brother-in-law (they'd talked about it so much while watching hockey games) couldn't always afford a four-wheel-drive. He'd drive the Grande-Ourse road in his overloaded large used car, taking it through the grinder. Each newcomer had a little story to tell us about a breakdown, with an accusing look. By an astonishing coincidence, Mr. Méthot, a very resourceful man, the closest thing to a mechanic in Grande-Ourse, had had the idea of vacationing at the same time as everyone, in the two last weeks of July. And the low wage earner and his brother-in-law would repeat, in a state of shock, "No mechanic? In the whole village?"

It was then my duty to inform them tactfully that Grande-Ourse wasn't, technically speaking, a village.

"Parts department!" the Old Man shouted to make them feel more comfortable.

He talked to them about specifications and performance, seeing each snag as a renewed source of elation. The parts hunters would follow him into an incredible maze of chrome and copper where, in his muddled enthusiasm, he soon managed to get them lost.

Moreau's restaurant had some good days. Cars would line up disorderly on the property from 5:00 a.m. Drawn-looking fishermen would lean under their machinery scowling. Moreau couldn't have been awakened by an artillery division, and missed excellent business opportunities due to a hangover that had become chronic. His wife could barely stand him even at night, when he wasn't out the whole time. She held the fort as best she could in his absence. An exemplary early riser, Mr. Administrator hadn't missed any of this affluence. After a few days, he decided the large restaurant's pockets must've been swollen as a priest's prostate and that it was time to ask for his due.

"Next time he shows up, send him over. I have a few words for him...."

The boss was going to show us how to deal with recalcitrants.

In mid-afternoon, Moreau charged into the door, opening it without slowing down. The majestic roll of his shoulders drove away all the Indians that had been hanging around. Giving me a conniving sign, he headed to the corner where the large-format goods for his business were piled. Effortlessly, he grabbed the two metal barrels filled with mustard and ketchup, ogling the huge pot of relish and its cousin with the pickles, which meant he had to make a second trip, and left at a brisk pace. Without turning around, he tossed out the formula he used as a salutation, and I said with maximum discretion, "The boss wants a word with you."

He briefly seemed to juggle the two enormous containers, then put them down with ease and marched on the accounting stronghold. Raised voices coming from it betrayed a certain tension. When Moreau returned, swinging his fists beside his body, Mr. Administrator scurried behind him, howling in a high-pitched voice, "What kind of language will it take to make you understand?"

Moreau grumbled, huffed like a bull harassed by a wasp and, turning around at a clip, grabbed the gentleman by the collar, lifting him effortlessly to the highest shelf. He didn't need to say a thing: his counterpart made a slight gurgling sound; perhaps it was a sign of unconditional agreement with any objection that might've been raised. Moreau dropped him, grabbed his barrels of ketchup and mustard, and left. The Indians kept a genuine security perimeter around him.

Mr. Administrator dusted himself, coughing slightly. Distractedly, as though expressing an afterthought, he said without looking at me, "There's a little dust on the shelves, Gilles. You might go over them with a dust cloth."

"Okay, boss."

"Dust cloth," he repeated, walking away.

❧

One fine morning, after over two months in Grande-Ourse, I saw my first White policeman, when a Cessna dropped him off at the end of a pebbly runway at the village entrance. The previous day, Gisèle had taken a key from the pocket of a Legris under temporary anaesthesia, driving off in his pickup, remembering only later that she didn't know how to drive. She nevertheless sped northwards to the great reservoir, nearly taking out a group of tourists driving towards her. The misadventure ended past Two-Miles in a very thick mass of alders covering a beaver-flooded area. She afterwards admitted she'd first thought of driving all the way to Montreal to pick up Benoît's trail, but had gone in the wrong direction. She got out with a good-sized scratch but, this time, the lid had blown off and Legris filed a complaint. To get some peace and quiet, the authorities agreed to dispatch a constable. The latter wouldn't have travelled here for so little, but three or four files had been lingering on his desk from time immemorial, and he wanted to take advantage of his visit to confront a few witnesses. He notably questioned Boisvert and the Old Man about the beer truck, but no official blame was laid. This paternalistic cop had a clear preference for private admonitions.

Sporting a moustache and greying, he looked at us with an indelible smile and a solid equanimity. No doubt a result of having served in wild regions. He and the Old Man were thick as thieves, the latter, moreover, serving as his principal contact and, might as well say it, his informer. The policeman knew everyone in

this nest of vipers. He enforced the law here with detached
cordiality and avuncular patience. He shook my hand, thinking of
something else and, to get away from Legris' bawling, asked to see
the accident scene.

With the doddering crackle of the Dacia, he and the Old Man
set out for Two-Miles, following the Muppet who, God knows
how, had managed to get himself certified as a witness. He was
carrying the victim on his tricycle: old Legris, who was completely
drunk, open-handed, singing his head off, and baptizing with his
beer the requisitioned vehicle that followed.

The next day, when twilight was tinged with purple, Crazy
Sam came to the store. I first thought he was completely plastered.
He walked towards me like a robot, muttering jerky and
incoherent words.

"Anything I can do for you, Crazy Sam?"

He gave me a stunned look.

"Would you please.... Call the police?"

"The police?"

"Yes, please.... Oh, please, call the police, please...."

Sam was extremely shaken and had trouble speaking. I was
forced to let him down horribly. "You should've come over
yesterday! He was making his annual visit!"

Nodding a sunburnt face, wild-eyes smouldering, he was the
picture of disarray.

"No police.... No police, eh? Let's call them, all right? Please
ask them to come, I'll pay."

He, the war hero, was asking for the help of an obscure
provincial police corps? I was anxious to tell this to the Old Man.
He grabbed my arm and reiterated, with the nasty confidence of
those who bank on the sovereign virtue of dough, "Call them.... I'll
reward you...."

"They don't usually come out for trifles, you know...."

He tried to grab my shirt collar.

"I want to report a crime!"

I looked him straight in the eye, "What kind of crime?"

He lowered his head and, in a hollow voice, "My fishing box....
They've stolen my fishing box!"

His despair was sincere and I very seriously gave him my

opinion. "You probably forgot it somewhere, Crazy Sam. Think about it! Do you think they'll send a helicopter at taxpayer expense? For a fishing box, even as well equipped as yours? You should look around your trailer."

He energetically argued his point. His fishing box was worth hundreds, even thousands of dollars. I grabbed him by the shoulder and obligingly accompanied him to the door. I was fed up at playing telephone operator.

"Look carefully, Crazy Sam.... It must be lying around at the edge of some lake...."

He left, stretching his empty hands before him, like a lost man.

🐞

Business as usual. Father's instructions. Await the outcome. Over there, in the cold room, cold meat. This morning still. Gilles has to tidy up the rooms. People around here take him for a girl. He's being demeaned through that chore, it's deliberate.

Crazy Sam is in the hall. He's going away. Returning without waiting. The police? Nothing to say. An American tourist. If the police want him, they can come and see him in his country. Pennsylvania. He has a lovely black eye, this morning. The Indian has one hell of a punch. Gilles clenches his teeth, heart in his throat, lips set, looks for the missing canine with the tip of his tongue. Crazy Sam returns to his country. Empty handed, with his friends. He prefers not to be questioned. Trouble, no thanks. He heard gunshots, doesn't know a thing. Crazy Sam, an American. He didn't sleep well. Bloodshot eyes, wrinkles. Everyone aged last night. Crazy Sam says don't worry. You'll be all right. All right Crazy Sam. He opens his mouth as he's about to leave. To say something. That Gilles was in a state of. Legitimate high. The door. The back. Flamand. There's one who won't grow any older. He was the only one who really slept that night. All that remains for him to do. His whole future is behind him.

The bedroom. Cans lie among scattered towels speckled with yellow spots. Ashtrays are full. Cooled ashes spoil the furniture varnish. Filthy American. Having breakfast over there, at the restaurant? Uselessly teasing the sweat-drenched waitress facing her grill? Or else he vanished straightaway, without lingering. What an immense weariness. Clean up the place. Dirty sheets tossed in the garbage. He throws away his childhood permanently.

A cardboard rectangle draws his attention, on the bedside table. Crazy Sam's fishing notebook, forgotten there in his haste. A register of his catches, with temperature, date, various details, weight, type of lure, etc. Pages and pages. The

accounting for a whole month's fishing, to the nearest fish. Back in his country:
the articles. Prestigious magazines. Field and Stream. Outdoor Life. *A*
columnist. Payed to practise his favourite sport. Culled anecdotes, the bones of
adventures. At home: fabulous tales, an epic, sensational exploits. The small
walleye will grow big. With words, the miracle of prose. The pike that got away,
grown gigantic, returns to haunt thousands of enthusiasts, the fervent and
fanatical. Fishing stories born here in this matrix. The filter of reality, a
magnifying glass. But something suddenly interrupts his daydream. Under the
full ashtray: a note. Not a word. A note from. He lifts the ashtray. A cigarette
butt in its grave. The bank. The head of which president? He grabs it delicately,
holds it between the light and his gaping eyes, as though to check the watermark.
He murmurs: but it isn't true!

⋅

Stars rain down in thousands and the long ether mane sprinkles its flakes of light in the deep night of Grande-Ourse. The aurora borealis glow from a stationary core, layering painters' palettes of colour, creating enormous mottled cones, in constant rearrangement, spreading the tentacles of evanescent squid, the large genitalia of disincarnated women, caressing the horizon's jagged palisade with their opalescent suction cups. The spruces huddle, cones swelling with the heat they've gathered. The lake is barely rippled, stretching out at the foot of the mountains, smoothing its waters to greet the next influx of images. Near its shore, inside an unhealthy cabin, César Flamand has dropped his expression of perpetual sadness, having to sleep now and again. But he turns in his sleep, nearly awakens and worries instinctively, feet plunged into the wasted stomach of his coarser half, Fernande, dreaming she's a fern in the undergrowth. Near them, children sleep indistinctly. The Kid faces the wall, farther away, arms hugging an absent chair. He'll get up soon, grab a barbell, run along the trail, perhaps wank in the middle of a mossy clearing, awaiting the evening and his French kiss over the phone. Donald Big-Arms snores with abandon and thrashes about inside an imaginary net. Some distance away, the trapper's large red dog barks and his master swears, head immersed in the pillow, without breathing apparatus. In the enclosed patch nearby, under the sand, Admiral Nelson drinks beer forever more. He no longer looks at hydroplanes, traps marten, or thinks about university. Across the lake, near the small peatbog where water and soil mingle intimately, beneath a large surveyor's tent, Cowboy and the others have sniffed a little more naphtha before going back to dreaming what few dreams they have left. Christophe, the youngest one, Dagobert the queer, Alexis and his Cree wife. Bears and blows. What dreams they have left. At the hotel, Moreau threatens to smash everything if he isn't served a last one and Legris cringes. Nearby, in his mobile home, Jacques Boisvert, numbed by the toil of another day, sleeps restlessly. At times, he stirs abruptly. He always awakens too early, way before dawn, then can't go back to sleep, or find his daily peace of mind. He needs to find a target for his elliptical musings. He looks forward to the morning he'll be able to elude thoughts, the past aroused by inaction. That young clerk hired by the Outfitters. Reminds me of mine, well, he's the same. Brigitte fancies him. Brigitte's warmth. To remember it, Boisvert stretches his body, curls up, listens to the cracking of his bones, racked every day by a healthy fatigue. That young girl should close the taps and come back to warm my skin. The Muppet takes a hot bath to fight off the revulsion for sleeping alone which just gripped him. Fat Lili is dozing, slumped on her chair, the television crackling like a fire since the film ended. Lili never dozes more than ten minutes at a time. She just dreamed that a man inserted his muscular foot between her legs, making love to her that way, foot pushed into the soft flesh up to the ankle. It was one of those dreams you think you can control, with the guy wearing about a size twelve. Big Ben fell asleep soon as his head hit the pillow. He snores so loudly that his trailer gently vibrates and the nocturnal fauna is perturbed all round. Tomorrow, Big Ben will take his time, if no one bothers him. The Old Man, on his sofa, nods gently, still ready to get up, rifle in hand. Mr. Administrator shuts his eyes over his book, a biography, alone in a bed that's too large and too white, inside the house which Flamand hasn't finished scraping with his steel brush. Flamand is being conned and everyone knows it. Though it's not his fault, Mr. Administrator sees numbers parade by all night behind his eyelids. In the dark cold cellar under the shed, Cowboy's bear skin hangs from a hook, dripping blood that slowly

turns rancid. Over at Lac Du Fou, Crazy Sam sits with his back to
a stump, pondering a moon crumbling over the water. He can't
sleep with that noise in his ears. If his missus were still alive she'd
warn him, haemorrhoids, seated on the humus, which stores the
cold. The contact of the earth, through the fabric, feels icy as a
corpse clasping its last handful. No police, here. Naturally. That
was long ago. And somewhere else, we never know where, inside
an unhealthy cabin or trailer, inside a surveyor's tent or under a
hotel table, in the Muppet's bed or the shelter of the spruces,
beside a barely rippled lake or even — who knows?—inside a
house in the overly large and overly white bed of an accountant
fallen asleep over his book, anywhere, but anywhere except the
couch with the broken springs where the Old Man champs at the
bit at the back of the store, Gisèle sleeps as well, Gisèle is drunk
and Benoît has gone.

In sleep or insomnia, Grande-Ourse crosses the night like a
canoe that the first shoal can rip open. The dogs bark and,
tomorrow, distinct Grande-Ourses will again rub shoulders along
their implied borders. At the hotel, Brigitte closes up, goes through
the final motions, finally going to bed to tickle her insomniac so
that he remains hard. His sagging buttocks when he gets up in the
morning. But he has balls. And Gilles Déschenes is a fucking idiot.
On the upper level, surrounded by naked walls, criss-crossing
beams, and boards piled in the darkness, Moreau grabs Judith and
shoves her against a makeshift partition, feeling everything he can
get his hands on. It smells of treated wood and sawdust. He'll take
her standing up, without any tricks, only Moreau can lift Judith
that way and they'll make love with sullen violence inside that
never-completed castle. Moreau will say me and you Judith here.
One day. In that unfinished house. Legris eavesdrops from a
window without panes. He's so afraid of being alone.

As for me, oh, me, in a ghostly house in the abandoned part of
Grande-Ourse, I'm caressing the daughter of that Gisèle who's
drunk, dreaming, sleeping, who'll no doubt be a grandmother
before she's thirty-five. I'll forever know that the true wealth of the
earth is now rolling through my fingers; it isn't gold and I forgive
simoniacal humanity. The appetite of the world palpitates like a
gigantic octopus over the simple things in life. I hold the reins, I

hold the train of a queen. My eyes drift along her stomach which is hard and fragrant as softwood. A day without her is as long as a day without hands.

●

Because of this general holiday, the world suddenly seemed to remember Grande-Ourse. Over two consecutive days, we were visited by the bishop and the member of Parliament. People were suddenly taking care of us.

Leaning against the cash register, I dreamt I was sleeping when a voice sounding like a church organ drew me out of my drowsiness.

"Hello, young man!"

The bishop's handshake nearly pulled me over the counter. Mr. Administrator was already rushing over, impatient to vaunt his establishment.

"So, this is where heaven's pastures are protected against the secular onslaughts of the forest!" intoned the dignitary, striking a pose.

"Hello, father ...," began Mr. Administrator timidly.

"People call me monsignor," the bishop coldly reminded him, smiling nonetheless.

The boss, whose devotion couldn't be doubted, was deeply embarrassed. Our visitor, ignoring him completely, observed me from beneath the pediment created by his endless frown. He pointed to the opulent bags that underlined my gaze and declared, jovial and preoccupied, "Either this young man works too much, or...."

"A little of both," I said politely.

He gave me a knowing wink and, definitively turning his back to the boss who was greatly vexed, cooed, "Oh oh, we know what goes on, eh, inside those large white tents at the edge of the forest, oh oh, those young people!"

He suddenly had a tender expression. A little more and he'd shed a tear for some ancient virginity. He then abruptly turned away and shook Mr. Administrator in every direction with a handshake whose secret he'd likely learned from Knights of Columbus high on amphetamines.

"You're the boss? This is the first time I've seen you," he was speaking in a reproachful tone, "I've just spoken to members of the committee for the survival of the village, do you have two minutes?"

He dragged him off, already pounding him with rebukes.

As he was about to leave, the bishop leaned an imaginary mitre over me, whispering in a confidential tone, "Be careful about masturbation, young fella! For a growing young man, such a waste of substance is tragic!"

I thought he was about to give me statistics.

"Don't worry, monsignor," I answered tit for tat.

He went off reassured, with the lofty head carriage that distinguished him, as though he'd insisted on scraping the top of his cranium against the door frame.

If the bishop's handshake was brutally strong, that of Mr. Member of Parliament, in all honesty, beat my personal endurance record. His sticky paw oozed an unpleasant aroma of habituation, and he'd ceaselessly stroke your palm, annoying you with cosy enthusiasm. Square-shouldered and ruddy beneath his clownish impudence, he'd never look his counterpart in the eye, preferring to probe just a little to the side, using his standard speech which was adaptable to any circumstance. He was, in short, very proud to see that the village of Grande-Ourse, the jewel of his riding, was still driven by that unfailing vitality he'd already observed in — when was it? — before the last elections anyhow, and moreover, dear friend, your business is spearheading the entire region's economic recovery, because, between you and me, that idea of privatizing a whole village is brilliant, eh, with the municipalities causing the government so much anxiety, who knows whether global rural privatization wouldn't be, in a final analysis, the ideal solution, it's still better than downright closing the books, right, as was still done in the recent past. Moreover, if you recall correctly, but with the party in power at that time, it wasn't surprising you'll say, I know, but now, here, yes, in Grande-Ourse, you're showing us the path to follow, the way to go, the new philosophy, the direction to take at all costs: rationalization, drastic restructuring, and draconian austerity measures, belt tightening and balancing the budget, technology and performance and especially, especially, especially, competiti ... competiti....

"Competitiveness."

"Thank you, you're showing us how the population itself can take charge of its heritage, and the private sector, heh, heh. We are here in a land that's nearly virgin, after all, brimming with promise, the planet is becoming a jungle, we might create a kind of experimental enclave in your quaint little village, you see, a genuine haven of individualism, the paradise of wilderness investment, the private domain of world entrepreneurship."

His secretary, who accompanied him everywhere and piloted the governmental Cessna, obviously knew the spiel by heart. What's more, she was vigorous, attractive, and profoundly bored despite her distinguished gaze. I eventually lifted an arm, waving it to get the attention of our brave elected representative. "I'm all for it, dear sir, but you might start by mentioning it to the boss...."

He abruptly stopped mid-sentence and, in eyes that finally turned towards my person, I immediately recovered my status as a little nobody. He nonetheless tried to maintain his stride, saying distractedly, "It did occur to me, you seemed a little young...."

But, enticed from a distance by that long-winded speech, Mr. Administrator was already rushing towards the illustrious guest, salivating. He held out a hand large as a plate, and the MP flung his buttery right paw into it. They walked off without releasing hands, both of them, like lovers, speaking the same language, sharing the same lies, leaving me defenceless in the pleasant company of the bush pilot-secretary. In two sentences, they'd pronounced the word *subsidy* at least four times. I again heard the people's representative say mellifluously, "We can really feel how much the population loves you.... Your Outfitters, sir, is the soul of this village."

After being forced to discuss eminently temporal questions with the big boss of the diocese, the previous day, Mr. Administrator was now being lectured on the soul by the riding's master of patronage. It goes to show you can no longer trust anyone.

❧

My double life was starting to leave marks on me that had nothing to do with trade. I had to reduce the frequency of my nightly outings. In the day, I remained the friendly manager. On the outside, I implemented the shareholders' directive, and appearances were maintained: all credit to the Indians had been cut off. At night, after eleven o'clock, I agreed to certain arrangements. But there was friction between Cowboy and me. He openly accused me of treachery. Torn between demands of the job and impulses of the heart, I was in a bad position to answer to those charges. I often slipped canned mushrooms or shrimp to the Kid on the sly, sometimes even a can of Tropicana Chicken, to console him for the gallon of naphtha I'd just refused him. But Cowboy no longer lowered himself to such methods.

One night, Salomé came to see me. Fernande needed condensed milk for the children. I remembered the Old Man's warnings, "They'll try to soften you up, you'll see! It's a tactic! They'll ask you to give them milk for the children!"

I hopped in the truck with her. I really enjoyed sweeping past the hotel in a whirlwind, driving at full tilt down the narrow road, guided only by the halo of the headlights. Salomé gave me news about Cowboy. He swam almost continually and had told her the same story he'd related to me: diving from a cliff, once, he'd felt an icy hand grab his ankle and try to drag him to the bottom.

"Dagobert," I confided, "told me of a strange belief: when five people walk around a cemetery at night, the fifth disappears."

The road leading to the cabin was strewn with scrap iron and heaps of rust, evoking the desert landscapes of the southwestern part of the continent with their square, blood-coloured hills. Three or four noisy mongrels greeted us in the yard, where automobile shells scattered their pieces. The cabin's interior was tiny, rustic, dirty, and inviting. Flamand nodded approvingly when he saw the can of condensed milk. He was cooking rice over a gas stove. Hydro-Quebec's power didn't reach these parts. Fernande was wearing her red scarf and sky-blue dress. Opening the can, she proposed to cut out a pair of moccasins for me from a moose hide whose smoky aroma wafted through the room. The Kid was there as well. He inquired about my business in two words, then, "Are you gonna sleep here?"

"Well...."

"You look tired," Flamand observed.

"He works too much," explained Salomé.

"How goes the scraping?" I asked the father.

"Not done yet...."

"Doesn't pay when it takes so much time ...," the Kid added with a hint of humiliation.

I only approved sympathetically. I didn't want to tell César how much he was being exploited. He mightn't even have believed me. I'd learned that the Old Man had no intention of paying him in cash. When that contract, whose end no one could see, was fulfilled, the employer would merely deduct the amount from the sizeable account the Indian already had with the store. Which all boiled down to the same, naturally. But, while awaiting the next government cheque, with a revoked credit margin and wages in invisible currency, Flamand was not only falling behind on his estimates, he was falling behind on emptiness.

Salomé dragged me outside and introduced me to the tribe's newest resident: a tiny leveret César had flushed out from a pile of boards that morning, and which, curled up in a pitiful ball, was now assessing his new status as a domesticated animal. A great-horned owl screeched in the distance and he pricked up his ears.

The moon traced a large column of exploded mercury over the lake as we stood quietly before the display. I was dead tired and felt good. I needed nothing else and felt ridiculous. Things were in their place. The Kid, not a very good chaperon, clumsily came out with his weights, making as much noise as possible before asking me to join him. I immediately accepted, pleased by the diversion.

Back inside, they showed me pictures. They adored this. The family album was always lying around within reach and portraits could be seen everywhere. The Direct Film store in Tocqueville owed them a good part of its prosperity. On a wall, a print of Admiral Nelson looking out with small naive eyes over his distorted mouth. Flamand's eyes hovered between Salomé and me. He was no doubt conjecturing about my relations with the jewel of his guardianship. Nonetheless he offered me the pot of steaming rice. "Want any?"

I realized I'd again forgotten to have dinner and gladly accepted, only a little embarrassed by the extreme simplicity with which César Flamand served me a meal, though I'd cut off his supplies a week earlier, in the name of my kind. The Kid slipped me a plate and I did justice to their hospitality, to that scanty, universal bowl of rice. And later, when I had to return here, I first

made a point of placing a loaf of bread, butter, cheese, and other
basic staples in a cardboard box, along with one or two treats and
some condensed milk for the children.

●

*In short, it would be a tip. A kind of bonus. A form of compensation. An
encouragement to crime, after the fact. The wages of the sacrificial victim. Gilles
did the work for him, in short. Leave it in full view, for the first person who'll
enter. Besides, someone took pains to write an almost ironic* take care. *It's the
same writing as in the fishing notebook. He tries to think, heart pounding. His
tongue probes the cavity that tastes like blood, in his mouth, and he then remembers
the tooth under his pillow. That money. His good fairy? What to do? Finish the
clean-up first of all, business. Leave this miserable room. This life. But, especially,
his father mustn't know. He'd worked enough. Every man for himself, now.*

*First thing he came across was that empty twenty-six oncer. The brand:
Christian Brothers. He ponders, wipes his chin with the back of his hand. Soft skin
and nascent whiskers. Talk about a tip. He spots a bottle cap, forgotten there as
well, after rolling onto the floor. Crazy Sam uses it for still fishing, for angling as
they say. A struggling twelve-inch carp as bait, with the hook run through its body.
The large pike makes a gurgling sound and the bottle cap sinks. Angling. That
crumpled note in his hand. Gives him an idea.*

●

Early next day, Donald Big-Arms took me on a canoe ride. Wanted
to show me a beaver lodge at the other end of Lac Légaré. I scaled
the huge pile of branches and, through a ventilation shaft, we
could hear this year's litter gently moaning. I thought about Grey
Owl and Commander Cousteau. Donald Big-Arms was moved as
well. On the way back, I honed in on a small object floating near
the shore amid a cluster of water lilies. A red and white bobber. I
wanted to swerve towards it, but Big-Arms seemed in a sudden
hurry and rather reluctant to deviate from his path. His powerful
and pigheaded strokes, in the back seat, forced me to paddle all the
harder to rectify the trajectory.

Later, at the store, the phone rang. It was Cowboy. He was
calling from an outfitters at the edge of the large reservoir. A party
that had left the reserve had just pulled up there and Cowboy,
who'd gone out to meet them, was looking for a bush taxi.

"Will you pick us up, Gilles?"

I was alone at the store. My superior was spending the day at the reservoir, in fact, with the Old Man. The Outfitters had acquired a somewhat grassy lot strewn with round stones, where Mr. Administrator saw grand things arising. It was oppressively hot. In principle, even for a fee, the kind of operation I was being asked to perform had been prohibited by the recently decreed austerity. The Old Man's tiny cerebral calculator excelled at evaluating each trip according to the price of gas.

"I'll be right there," I answered simply.

I grabbed two cold beers and shoved them into a satchel then, after locking the door, climbed into the pickup. No one would die if the store closed for less than a half hour. To stiffen my resolve, I repeated to myself: in the forest, helping out is the first duty.

The time for idleness was over. I'd again worked very hard the previous day and was fed up at seeing a cavalcade of privileged beneficiaries of annual vacations, free weekends, and generally decent and democratic leisure activities, while I'd had no respite in weeks, slogging from morning till night. Fatigue was seriously beginning to dull my reflexes.

The first beer did me a lot of good. I took the curve at the end of the lake, performing a typical controlled skid, cheerfully darting along beneath the low forest gently set ablaze by a ferocious drought. The second beer followed quickly.

Cowboy couldn't hold a grudge very long and seemed happy to see me again. Agreeing to pick him up was seen as a sign of goodwill. The whole band was cheerful. Christophe, arms freed by a tank top, forehead wrapped by a headband, was talking about the rapidly approaching powwow. Cowboy informed me that his parents would arrive soon. A tolerant and bearded old man had piloted the long motorboat between the rocky islands and headlands bristling with dead trees. They'd leave the boat here, on the shore, ready to set off again. Among those who disembarked: an aggressively sociable little old lady, a fat cousin and her brat, other children and grandchildren, all of them forever nomadic. They loaded their gear, including the outboard, into the pickup's box. Christophe and Cowboy sat in the front. The others piled into the back as best they could, and I began the journey in the opposite direction with a genuine cluster of people hanging on to the pickup.

"Will you come to the powwow, Gilles?"

"What's a powwow?"

"A big party," Christophe answered. "Lasts a week, full of girls, competitions, canoe races...."

"Lots of girls," Cowboy confirmed.

I pondered, looking at the road.

"I'd have to ask for holidays...."

Beer ran freely in the back. We drove past Crazy Sam's den, I honked and jeers rang out while the American, standing in front of his trailer, shook a whimsical head. Cowboy and his brother laughed. They traded jokes in their language. The wind swaddled the windshield, spilling over into the open windows. The old woman gave a heavy punch onto the sheet metal above us and handed me a beer through the window. I was so hot that I guzzled it in no time. After a few minutes, another bottle materialized in the rear-view mirror, immediately suffering the same fate. It was already my fourth and I was beginning to feel good, very good, everything was running like clockwork. Cowboy looked happy. Christophe was impatiently stirring about on the seat. I pressed the accelerator, euphoric, the pickup swayed and gravel flew beneath the tires. I looked back now and again to make sure no one had fallen off. It was a wonderful party, improvised and moving. The speed ruffled the hair, the bills of caps split the air like spoilers, the wind puffed clothing like sails and chests were thrown out, decked in the colours of my beloved employer.

I'd agreed with Cowboy that we'd drive the others to Flamand's, on the other side of the village, before returning to the camp. He wanted to stop at the store to replenish our beer supply. I was forced to resume my official attitude, reminding him it would be impossible for me to give them credit. He said nothing, then I saw the lake approaching. Cowboy stretched his hand out to me, two curves appeared in rapid succession and we were on them. I managed to negotiate the first one, but a curtain of alders immediately stood in place of the second and, following the noisy contact of vegetation, water was rising over us. The truck hit a large rock and continued moving over the water before slightly nose-diving. I saw Indians flying overboard. We were already drenched from head to toe when a panicked Christophe grabbed my arm.

I surfaced after slipping through the door. Christophe was still hanging on to me, terrified. He was scared stiff of the water. We regained our footing and I had the strange reaction of drinking from the bottle I'd hanged on to. It tasted like an old 50. The heads of laughing Indians surfaced around us like corks. I relaxed, seeing them have a good laugh. I started into a hiccuping chuckle as well, while Christophe spat out green liquid. The party went on. I thought about the face the boss would make, about the Old Man's wailing, how he'd surely reprove me for not drowning the whole band while I was at it, and all I could do was repeat stupidly: that's a good one. That's a good one.

Fortunately, the two grandparents had landed in shallow water. With a few toothless yaps, the old lady was right into the general mirth, and the boatman was amazed at how quickly he'd got back in the water. Everything was happening as though we'd all dove together for the sole beauty of the thing. And suddenly, a detail hit me. I began counting heads, seeking a certain round mug whose disappearance couldn't fail but create a void; everything sank into confusion and agitation. A shout: "Cowboy!"

Wading, splashing everyone, I dove down to look for him, fully resolved to let my lungs be filled rather than give up. All we could see now was the pickup's roof awash with the ripples. Water was all I found inside. I surfaced, desperate, ready to dive again. Christophe, taking refuge on the shore, shouted something to me which I didn't understand and then the alleged drowner, no doubt feeling the suspense had lasted long enough, emerged with a splash, proud of his stunt. He looked like an overgrown frog.

"Cowboy! I've been looking for you at least five minutes!"

He caught his breath, before saying with all composure in the world, "Almost."

Nearby, keeping us company in the lake, bawling, spluttering, and crowned by a very decorative water lily, the Muppet, whom we'd surprised fishing in front of his favourite grass bed, was struggling to pull himself from the mud beside his rowboat, which was swinging so strongly.

❧

"Where'd you find that, Cowboy?"

I examined the bill without understanding.

"I found it!"

"You don't mean.... The treasure?"

He nodded gravely.

"Yes, but ...," I hesitated.

The tensing of his jaw was visible. "If an American gives you this, you'll take it?"

"Yes...."

His eyes sparkled. "Don't forget to calculate the exchange rate, eh!"

After all, it was none of my business if some morons had been robbed. And what did I care about a new Coffin Affair? I nonetheless ventured these cautious recommendations, "It'll look suspicious if you spend too much all at once, Cowboy.... I mean: while waiting to find out if the cash is really yours, you understand?"

I gave him change in hundred dollar bills and he went off with his loot, a two-four and a can of Tropicana Chicken. The door had barely closed behind him when Mr. Administrator was standing in front of me.

"You're selling beer to the Indians, now?"

"He paid cash."

That's all I had to say.

"Oh yeah?"

"Yeah...."

I looked him straight in the eye. "With American money...."

With those words, the Old man sprang from his hideout, "*American* money? But that's good, that's plenty good! My buddy Crazy Sam must've hired him as a guide for a day or two...."

"Crazy Sam had his fishing box stolen."

"His jewelry box? Oh my God! He must really be depressed!"

"So the money doesn't come from Crazy Sam," Mr. Administrator resumed.

"Maybe he bought a bear skin or moccasins from them?" the Old Man insisted, somehow excited by the conversation. "If the Indians have American money let them spit it out!"

"I totally agree!" I approved, peering at the boss defiantly.

Subdued by numbers, he admitted defeat. But didn't like it. Lili then appeared, immediately followed by Legris, who didn't want to miss a thing. Lili was telling everyone that Mr. Administrator had promised her a job over the phone. Confused and cautious, he refused to commit himself further or make a retraction. Ever since the business to do with the pickup, two days earlier, Lili increased the frequency of her visits, following the situation carefully.

My two mentors had made quite a face when they spotted us fraternizing in the water, on their return from the reservoir! This time, it was clear: I was in a state of total disgrace. They'd tolerate my presence till Benoît returned. The latter was now reaping the harvest of his absence, and his standing had soared in the boss's eyes. But Lili never missed an opportunity to remind him she'd once done the job, as well, and that she'd maintained order with efficiency, if not elegance.

She'd just seen Cowboy walk away with his lunch.

"God dammit! If I were in charge, those deadbeats wouldn't hang around very long!"

The Old Man looked at her with a loving expression that was fearful, nostalgic, and admiring, and Legris joined in the concert, "Without us, hides would still cover their asses!"

"But that's not all! The best is yet to come!" pledged fat Lili.

All heads turned towards her.

"Big Alexandre recently escaped from his halfway house.... More sleepless nights in store for Grande-Ourse!"

"The police chief again told me!" the Old Man ranted, while his limbs went off in all directions: "Let them in, then shoot! We'll come and pick up the pieces!"

He slumped into a chair, his poor heart asking for mercy. Legris, no doubt thinking a finishing touch was needed, allowed himself to add, "If we don't stop them, this place will revert to Indian territory. Your nice houses, Mr. Administrator, will fall into their hands! Besides, it's already begun!"

He gave me a satisfied look then wiped the corner of his lip. I tried to control myself. But right then, I'd have willingly smacked that forever-half-open big mouth, and flattened the large warty nose he always shoved in everyone's business. While Mr. Administrator and the Old Man were assessing his insinuation, Lili, scenting the sizeable revelation, grabbed Legris by the shoulder, then the clavicle, then finally and directly by the scruff.

"Over here, handsome! I'll buy you a coffee at the restaurant! It's been a long time since we've had a private conversation!"

Whenever his feelings were appealed to, Legris couldn't resist.

That night, Grande-Ourse celebrated Christmas. Christmas in July. The day had been sweltering, with the refrigerators ferociously pumping heat into the store. Outside, no breeze sponged humidity from the heavy air. The ground was flaking, the sand blowing away. Even the peatbogs seemed to have run dry. Any frayed mosses clinging to bare rocks would crack like matches under every step.

But Grande-Ourse was celebrating Christmas. Christmas among Whites.

So much the better for them, but it mattered little to me. They'd exchange gifts among themselves.

I met up with the Indians on the beach, where they'd made a little fire. They were contemplating it, seated in a circle.

"Where's Cowboy?"

Chuckles rose from the orange-coloured shadows.

"At the camp, with Gisèle. They mustn't be disturbed...."

"Oh yeah?"

"Did you bring any beer?" Christophe asked in his jerky delivery, almost puffing each word.

I had a couple in a bag and popped them open without being coaxed. With two bottles for five people, the role of generous older brother was becoming rather thankless.

"Did you steal them?" the Kid inquired, eyes sparkling over the fire.

"Oh, I don't know anymore, with their system.... I'll surely end up paying for all this...."

"Haven't they fired you yet?"

"That'll come!" I answered.

Donald Big-Arms put his large clumsy paw on my shoulder. "You'll come and stay at our house.... You won't have to work...."

"Hey, Gilles, isn't it true that Christophe got scared, eh?"

"Christophe? My God! He was thrashing about like a baby over baptismal fonts!"

"Huh?"

Christophe gave a kick into empty space. The embers blazed and a brand hopped like an incandescent beetle.

I looked at Salomé as she lowered her eyes over the flame, seated with her legs pulled up, pensive. She pulled away from the circle and walked a few steps.

"Judith has told everyone that Alexandre is going to kick your head in," Christophe whispered to me.

"One more thing, eh.... Is he dangerous?"

"He's crazy."

They nodded in silence. The Kid leaped to his feet, cutting a dangling spruce branch with the edge of his hand.

Laughter reached us from the hotel and a slight crash of breaking glass glided towards us across the lake. Brigitte must've really wondered where I'd run to. Our two beers were empty.

"Tonight, we're breaking into the store!" Christophe announced.

I shook my head without bothering to contradict him. He read my thoughts and said in a low voice, "Cowboy has beer."

"Okay. Let's go."

Everyone was standing. Salomé had vanished. I detoured through the woods, inhaling the heavy redolence of bark pearled with resin. I thought I'd stumble on her unexpectedly, but she jumped on my back and dragged me to the ground, in the tepid mud asleep beneath the dry leaves. I managed to get up and elude her feints.

"Let's go have a drink with Cowboy!"

She shook her head, standing before me as though to block my way. I took her by the waist and tried to knock her off balance, but she slipped through my fingers like a grass snake. She finally moaned, panting, "Stop!"

I'd just immobilized her.

"You're going to tell me something now, Salomé: where did Cowboy get all that money?"

"He found the treasure."

"The treasure of Boisvert's son, right?"

"Yes."

"Just one more question: does Gisèle know who shot your father?"

She hesitated.

"Boisvert...."

She struggled and I tightened my grip.

"But which Boisvert, good God?"

She didn't know. Didn't want to know. Resigned, I released her and she followed me. The small band was moving towards the railway. Christophe and the Kid were squabbling, with Donald Big-Arms alternately serving as their sandbag and referee.

"We have to hurry, if we want any of it to be left!"

"Well, Cowboy's rich."

"Yeah, Cowboy's rich."

I should've known something was shaky about this artificial enthusiasm that I believed was essential. Cowboy had a rather cool reception in store for us. Not only had he not touched his beer supply, but Gisèle, who dragged herself out of the tent after him, and whose tousled hair betrayed a very recent commotion, also displayed an exemplary sobriety. She remained there, confused and timid, avoiding our gazes. Even the odour of naphtha had disappeared. Whenever Gisèle sobered up, the shame of her existence came back to her all at once.

Cowboy looked at Salomé, then Gisèle, then me. The four of us made a strange rectangle. He smiled sheepishly, remaining quiet before the barrage of brazen questions put to him by his brother and friends. Salomé walked away from us to join her mother. They snuggled up to each other. Salomé was tiny inside Gisèle's oafish arms, who was whispering words of affection to her, genuine ones. I had a lump in my throat when Cowboy approached. The Kid solemnly declared, "We've come over to get you, pal. To party."

"To party?" Cowboy repeated.

Fatality permeated his voice and his gaze was vacant. Christophe had already disappeared, heading towards the creek we heard babbling in the dark. He returned with a case of beer.

"Let's go," concluded Cowboy.

Perched on that rock, the same one a young Indian boy dove from not long ago, and nearly didn't resurface, Gilles turns around and contemplates the lake. He paddled vigorously, filled with savage energy. He sees the hotel in the distance. An entire stretch of reality remains on the other side. In a few hours, it'll be behind him. He sees the geese streaming past along the water, majestic and peaceful. His father gives them grain each morning, in makeshift troughs at the edge of the lake. He remembers the poacher who placed Victor # 1 traps at the bottom of a trough immersed in shallow water. Birds would catch their heads in them, drowning with their asses in the air. To see them fly. Their perpetual migratory returns. Their nobility and haughty serenity. Their celestial and seasonal bellowing. That elegant arrogance of great ladies. The order of things.

He takes his gear out of the bag and slides his hand into his pocket. Only one note. He rolls it up and puts it in the bottle. Fills it with sand to ballast the whole thing. Then pushes in the cork, where he's solidly anchored the fish-hook. He ties the line to the tiny loop at the end of it and unwinds the monofilament, cutting it off at the desired length. A bite. Slides the plastic bobber onto the other end of the line. Red and white. A knot he tightens meticulously. He looks over his system. Tied to the bottle, the bobber rolls, moves around, bounces on the rock, making slight hollow sounds. The red half, alternating with the white half, at times appears on top, at times on the bottom. Christian Brothers and a thousand dollars US. He feels a presence behind him, at the edge of the forest, and jumps like a stag on the look-out. He stumbles as he pants, an animal at bay. Gisèle is there, observing him strangely.

It was past 3:00 a.m. and the Christmas party was winding down. While I hesitated on the doorstep, the Indians waited for me inside the rectangle of light projected by the open door. Grabbing my courage with both hands, I entered the hotel's malevolent smog where a glacial silence greeted me. Brigitte displayed her annoyance.

"I hope you brought your gift at least?"

"As a matter of fact, no, Brigitte."

I told her about the purpose of my visit and she grimaced.

"I'll be closing shortly. Wait for me at the entrance, I'll fix you up.... But I think it's lousy, your way of...."

"Why don't you organize a New Year's in August, Brigitte? That'll give me the chance to make amends!"

I joined the others outside: Cowboy, Christophe, Karate Kid and
Donald Big-Arms. My foursome of followers. Our idleness was like
a challenge to the entire world. Salomé and Gisèle hadn't followed.
They were no doubt ripe for a little talk about family relations.

"Gilles! Mimic the Old Man for us!" suggested Christophe.

I was somewhat tipsy and already making a few cheerful
strides when Boisvert's voice pierced through my backbone.

"Gilles! Wait!"

He caught up to me.

"You didn't come over to the party?"

"No."

"You didn't miss very much," he conceded. "But in small
villages, you can't afford to miss too many opportunities to have a
good time...."

His attitude was friendly, his delivery slightly inebriated. He
controlled the slightest shifts of his expression with the same
definitive authority as usual. I would've liked to ask him very
simply not to stick around. The Indians circled us imperceptibly.
Their wheezing created a feeling of oppression.

"I see you're celebrating with your gang," Boisvert observed.

He stared at me pensively. I had nothing to say to him. I'd
resolved to let things happen, soaking in this atmosphere of
confrontation with a kind of unavowable enthusiasm. A shiver ran
through the Kid, and Cowboy broke the spell, "You, Boisvert...."

"Yes. Me, Boisvert...."

Feeling things had heated up, he abruptly stepped back, elbows
high, placing his hand on the hunting knife hanging from his belt.
No one moved.

"You, Boisvert...."

"You guys never forget, eh?"

Cowboy pointed to the ground at our feet.

"He fell here."

"Any time, guys, I'm ready!"

Some people came out of the hotel, and the tension subsided
somewhat. A chap inquired whether everything was alright and
Boisvert walked off with him to have a discussion. Then, after the
last customer had left, Brigitte showed up with beer. Cowboy
reached for his money, but she stopped him with a gesture.

"It's a gift. I'm coming with you."

She concealed her vexation poorly when Boisvert came back towards us.

"You're going out?"

"Yes."

"Where are you going?"

"That's my business!"

I felt that Boisvert couldn't allow himself to appear weak in our presence. Brigitte took my arm.

"Are we going?"

Boisvert now held my other arm. We were tugging at each other somewhat, and he remained very polite, "Brigitte, if you go off with him, we're through...."

"Oh yeah?"

"Listen," I said laboriously, "we're only going...."

But suddenly, he pushed me away with his hand, an Indian grabbed him by the shoulder, sluggishly delivering a blow to his ribs. He lowered his head like an old buffalo who'd been challenged. Someone burst out laughing while he backed away and rallied his pride.

"If that's how it is...."

He gestured in Brigitte's direction. "You've chosen...."

Then, to me, "Be careful about who you hang around with, Gilles. You'll never change the colour of your skin. I wish you luck when you have a hundred of them against you."

And he turned his back to us, disgusted. But Brigitte wasn't going to allow him to get away just like that, with a moral victory. She rushed forward and, forcing him to turn round, plunked herself in front of him. A spat followed the likes of which the stars of Grande-Ourse had never seen, with a vicious Brigitte laying out a few plain truths to the old man and, take that, and he for his part answered back holding his own with all his customary and usually triumphant bad faith and defending this fragile conquest that piece of youth offered to him by fate against the facile incursions of a young dunce who thinks he knows everything about life in the north, in the north that he, Jacques Boisvert having grown up here had in his gut; and that's what she, Brigitte, didn't understand, that she refused to see, that this country she loved, that she discovered with him, he who embodied it right down to its contradictions, yes, in its always rebellious and untamed harshness and at the same time his infinite need to communicate which made them all reach out to each other and to the stranger, naturally. But she replied that she'd had it with offering her body to him every night at the very least every week and sometimes even in the morning when vigour returned Boisvert's still stiff, and offering her labour all day every night; and hell, she was only in her thirties and already wearing her body away her capabilities working for him, and why couldn't he give her a little compensation, why not a little compromise like couples do from time to time, eh? why not, you old mule of a pigheaded, mean, old simple-minded sexist macho? I've endured you because of affection but you are lamentably uncompromising and always alone in your corner with everyone against you, and I understand you, yes, but try to meet me halfway instead of always wanting to dominate the entire world, you who are so much more superior, Jacques Boisvert.

In the end, she came back towards us, and Boisvert went in alone.

Before going through the hotel doorway, however, he turned around one last time.

"Oh, by the way!"

He again stood before us.

"I was going to forget your gift...."

And, pulling his hand out of his jacket's huge pocket, displaying all of his restored confidence, he offered me an Indian doll, one of those miserable things like the ones found in store windows along Montreal's Saint-Catherine Street, with black braids, long eyelashes and batting eyelids, deerskin fringes, and a glass-bead tiara: Princess Pocahontas herself in the form of cheap junk.

He looked at Cowboy and company, laughing in their faces without a sound.

"One last thing, Gilles," he added gently. "I'm rather fond of you, yes, rather fond, but mark my words: if anyone harms Brigitte, tonight, you'll have me to deal with tomorrow, pal. You'll have me to deal with."

He turned towards her and bid us good night.

Though I was pushing with my shoulder, the door wouldn't open. The bar, of course.

Must've been around 4:00 a.m. The train was rather late and the Indians were resolved to await its arrival.

"We only have to knock!" suggested Donald Big-Arms.

"Go ahead, pal...,"

I stood aside, and his muffled blows shook the entire building, reminding me in a shiver of my first nights in Grande-Ourse and the wonderful anxiety of those sleepless hours. This time, I'd really gone over to the other side.

The Old Man showed up on the double. I ordered the others to hide and let me take care of him. At the sound of my voice, he opened, appearing in his shabby underwear.

"It's you?"

He quickly apprised me of the most recent developments: thanks to Legris, Mr. Administrator was now aware I used his houses for purposes other than tourism. He'd parleyed with Lili during the day and it seemed my fate was settled. Anarchic administration, irresponsible behaviour, repeated antics, corruption, and the appearance of a conflict of interest: my number was up. Beneath his apparent satisfaction, there was a trace of consideration in the Old Man's tone which touched me. He left me to ponder this and headed for his dear sofa, scratching his butt.

"Business is business, my boy," he yawned before retiring.

A moment passed. I opened the door, making the least possible noise and the pack entered the hencoop. The way to the cold room was clear. Their faces lit up with delight. A criminal spirit overcame us. We exchanged comical expressions filled with wonder. A childish hilarity escaped from mouths that were immediately stifled. Wallops landed haphazardly in the dark. I was urging the troop to plunder, as I tripped, caught myself, as I chucked wilted vegetables at their heads, bunches of shallots, and heads of celery. "Serve yourselves! It's our turn to celebrate Christmas! Tonight, it's the Great Free For All!"

Brigitte was enjoying herself madly. She bit into a long carrot and whipped us like beasts of burden with the bundle of stalks she'd grabbed. A dam had just burst, and what good citizenship was left in everyone was dying out.

Cowboy took a last two-four and Donald Big-Arms was walking out the exit carrying a genuine cardboard tower, while I grabbed another bottle of bad wine and Brigitte, Christophe, and the Kid, overcome by a raging hunger, helped themselves to armloads of filling and unhealthy foods, when the entire scene was suddenly flooded with light. The Old Man was there, grimacing, finger still hooked on the switch. Before he even began to think, he disappeared and returned, armed with his rifle, to the front of the store where we remained frozen, tangled in the furious bright light. When he realized what was happening, the Old Man took on the appearance of a poet in a trance, a fanatic of Allah before the desecration of the Great Mosque. He lifted his arms skyward and howled in his shrillest voice, "Well! There they are! The bastards! There they are! Well, I knew it! The dogs are here! Where do you think you're going, eh? Eh, you dogs? Hey you, there! You! Let go of that or else...."

He seemed to have jumped out of a comic book and I had to suppress my laughter. He pointed his rifle straight at us.

❧

She isn't aware, wants to know what he's doing. Yet she should be crying, over there, with her family. What's that? He explains. A bottle. Money inside. The plastic cap, so he can find it again one day, if he ever returns. Do you understand?

To return. Money. Gilles then realizes she doesn't know. Not yet. She erred on her side, all night, or what remained of it, while he tried to forget everything, satisfying his urges with his hand. Gisèle hasn't seen her family. She knows nothing. She's been looking for Roméo, ever since, her Roméo in the night. Oh, Flamand, whose blood already reddens the annals!

She steps forward, stretching her arms out to keep her balance on the green moss filling the cracks in the rock. Gilles asks her to stop, to not move forward, to stay there. She opens her mouth. Looks at the bottle. The money. The American who wanted to sleep with her. Who bought himself a murder. She doesn't realize it. She's so beautiful. She smiles mysteriously and moves her hand forward. Gilles squeezes the bottle and turns towards the lake. She approaches, presses against him, curious. She shakes her head, daydreaming and seemingly indifferent. She should be told, he wishes he could tell her. That it's unjust. That it's not just him. In the shadows,

there was also. But a roar is heard and a helicopter soon lacerates the sky, its rotor
clearing a path like a scythe reeling through the clouds.

The Old Man pointed his weapon at Cowboy and motioned him
to put down his load. The latter moved to be in a better position
to face him, but his fingers didn't release their hold. He slowly
raised his other hand to his neck, pulled out the machete placed
along his back and waved it provocatively. There, the Old Man
finally had his little victory. He'd waited for this moment, had
desired it in every possible way, this confrontation whose stakes
were very clear. He had him in his sights, now, that enemy
drawing his strength from the night, and when I saw him raise
the rifle, leaning as best he could against the upright of a shelf,
resting on the complete assurance of his rights, I closed my eyes,
paralysed and ashamed. But nothing happened and when I
opened them, Brigitte had stepped forward and placed her chest
in the line of fire.

The Old Man lowered his weapon, very pale, then let his arm
drop along his body and, without blinking in the harsh light,
looked at the ceiling. He called the universe as his witness: no one
could say he hadn't tried. He turned around, disgusted, and went
back to bed. The party could go on.

The helicopter blades cleave the air, and it swoops down from the south like a large
scarecrow, driven by the gears of a logic that will carry Gilles away. So long,
Gisèle. The copter shades the sun for a moment, loses altitude, and lands pronto.
The air it blows creates a metallic sparkle on the lake. That's how he'll leave. This
spinning guillotine will cut him off from his past. What happens to him. My name
is Gilles Boisvert and I killed a man, but that's not all.

Donald Big-Arms got depressed after a few drinks and had
something to tell me.

"I'm the one who stole the guy's fishing box."

"I should've known. Someone strong was needed to carry off
such a piece of furniture."

I told him he'd saved hundreds of fish from a certain death. He was in the mood for pouring his heart out. "Y'know, Gilles, girls and me...."

"Still, with muscles like yours...."

It wasn't a laughing matter.

"Girls are crazy!" he then proclaimed.

Cowboy, seated a little farther away, was digging in the can of Tropicana Chicken. He was smearing grease all over himself, licking his chops. Big-Arms got up, also hoping to get some consolation from the cold chicken.

Judith had joined us and was religiously listening to Brigitte giving her a kind of sermon I didn't care for at all. Christophe and the Kid joined them. Cowboy had left the chicken to Donald Big-Arms and, pacing the surrounding area, cursed under his breath, trying to pick a quarrel with inanimate things. I remained aloof, open and opaque, available and absent, plunged into a state of prostration and wavering of the ego which becomes so natural to me past a certain level of intoxication. Everything glided over me. I sometimes envy those whom alcohol renders aggressive, tearful, violent or merely a hundred times more stupid than usual. Profound drunkenness brings me into the world of silence and I attain a level of undifferentiated existence which is like the ultimate comfort on earth.

But, in the midst of my practical little annihilation, my relationship to Cowboy suddenly began to radiate a pressing necessity. Our link was a mooring cable or a tow rope, simple and solid. At that moment, however, I felt that what dangled at the end would forever elude me if I continued sinking into my indifference, unable to react. I felt the need to go up to him and say, "Cowboy, tomorrow I'm gonna eat bear!"

He only nodded, half-convinced.

"Where's the skin?" he asked.

"In the shed's basement.... With the daily bread."

He listened to a sound in the distance. The train was about to pull into the station.

When the potbellied couple set foot on the ground, their luggage had to be carted off to the encampment, an exercise all the more difficult since sobriety was sorely lacking in everyone. The operation took place in wonderful disarray. The father and mother, whose pilgrimage had been drowned in especially intense boozing, were more or less able to stand and, for a moment, we were afraid we'd have to carry them. They were two fine American Indian specimens, ladies and gentlemen, as corpulent as they were ravaged by various skin diseases: eczema, shingles, sores, scruff, psoriasis, scrofula, smallpox, and what else? Every form of skin rash imaginable seemed to have found a meeting place on those few square feet of red skin. The father resembled Louis Cyr, though less stocky and more imposing, with a slim torso and everything else massive, monumental. The wife, besides the all-too familiar and typical premature ageing, dragged around a humpbacked and poorly distributed obesity. They wavered terribly on the tracks, two immense and tragicomic penguins, surrounded by their merrily chirping progeny, looking for the right direction between swigs. We finally managed to take them to the camp. I thought I saw embarrassment in the look Cowboy snuck me, eyes rivetted to the rails, but we were all floundering way too much to concern ourselves with moral problems.

When his parents were settled inside the tent (as far as they were concerned, they could've slept on the ballast), I returned to the station with Cowboy to get the bottle of Cuvée des Patriotes I'd stashed before leaving. We drank without letting the bottle touch our lips, in long swigs bitter as this landscape of peatbogs and dozing water-holes, tripping on the spikes of the railway we followed back to the tents. We rivalled to see who had better balance, invented endurance tests, walking parallel on our own rails, sometimes leaning on each other when we were about to fall, and passing the bottle without letting up. His arm wrapped around my shoulder, Cowboy ceaselessly repeated in the same piercing tone, "You're my friend, eh, Gilles? My friend, eh?"

"We're the greatest friends in the world, Cowboy."

"I'm your friend, Gilles."

"Yes. Yes."

We then promised each other all kinds of things. I encouraged him to flirt with Brigitte who found him rather attractive, yes yes, she'd told me, he implored me to sleep with Judith again, he'd set it up for me, yes yes, it would be easy. I talked about Salomé, of that gentle and sacred love, a genuine infatuation reminding me of the pangs of my youth except that this time, there was a redoubtable sexual impasse, and he assured me that when you really get down to it, love is the same everywhere and that to unburden his moods, on the whole, he preferred really fat girls like Gisèle whose swaying loins, and that volcanic lake between her legs, he praised in enigmatic and chosen terms.

We stood facing each other, leaning over the rails glimmering towards the dawn whose pink lips already kissed the tops of spruces and larches. Suddenly, in that round and candid face, overcome by fatigue and grimacing with merriment, behind that face and in front of him, I saw his father's features emerge — the features of the fat Indian Cowboy would one day become — as though they'd busily been sculpted and extricated from unadulterated material, revealed and exalted line by line, wrinkle by wrinkle, ravage by ravage, superimposed at this moment, inexorably sagging and swollen. He was already transported into the future to be catalogued a failure as well. That vision quickly dissipated, but fascination with it lingered, leaving a bitter taste in my mouth. Both of us wavered on the iron ribbon dividing the forest and the country; Cowboy tilted his head and howled like a wolf, howled like the entire night. I touched his arm.

"We gonna get some sleep, pal?"

"What for?"

"Don't know. What'll you do tomorrow?"

"Nothing."

I glimpsed the emptiness of a future that would engulf me as well and realized he was right. To sleep no more. To stay under water and hold your breath, for good.

"Gilles! I found the treasure!"

"I know, Cowboy."

"Gilles! Nelson's dead!"

"I've heard you don't feel a thing when you drown...."

At the camp, Salomé looked at Brigitte's blond hair with loving admiration. Christophe seemed extremely intimidated and the Kid was more or less cuddling up to Judith. The three women of my summer were there, together for the first time. Seeing them filled me with happy despair and tremendous desire, like an avowal of weakness, to love the entire world.

"Come on, Cowboy. Let's go and see the girls."

"You'll come to the powwow, eh, Gilles?"

"Yes sir."

❧

He turns his back to him and holds the bottle up to the sun. One last glance. The light kindles its transparence. He lets the line slide between his fingers. Pulls on it. The cork is firmly pushed in. He smiles wearily. Gisèle says he looks like a witch with his missing tooth. Her fault. As he's about to move, arm pulled back like a soldier throwing a grenade, Gisèle tells him, you know Gilles, perhaps if you and I went out together. She doesn't realize. As if this were the moment. Now that it's coming out. But oh those words! Their echo! Those words that the memory of the water will preserve. If we went out together. One day earlier, only.... Went out together. Together. We. If. Witch. Went out. Go out. Quiet.

❧

Night had flown by, sprinkled with lots of noise. In the morning, we had to get back on our feet despite this, despite our pounding heads, distraught hearts, and the reminder of vanished pleasures on the membrane of every last cell. I learned afterwards that Cowboy had had a violent argument with his father, about the squabble that had degenerated into a gunfight during Saint-Jean-Baptiste celebrations. The father had blamed Cowboy because, despite his twenty years of age, he was recognized as having an authority his legitimately older brother was unable to assume. The father stood firm: the weapon which had caused the panic belonged to Cowboy; it didn't matter who fired it. Their quarrel echoed to the four corners of the camp, with the mother's prolonged sobs accompanying the duo. It had caused quite a racket.

Someone later told me of another circumstance that had escalated the drama. The father had got wind of his son's sensational discovery and had immediately requested the pile of money, a scheme Cowboy opposed with all his might, given the troubled state of his old man's judgement.

On coming out of the tent, I saw my friend standing in the middle of the place.

"How are you Cowboy, pal?"

"Fine."

"What's up?"
"Nothing."

That was the last time I heard him render that minor and implacable verdict about his daily lot. I felt it better to leave him on his own and returned to the store, ready to face a court martial. But, meanwhile, Mr. Administrator had been visited by fellow shareholders, whom he'd provided with as complete a view as possible of the smooth running of his apostolate. He didn't want to risk spoiling the stay of these honest backers with an awkward settling of accounts. My sentence was therefore deferred until their departure. For his part, Cowboy dropped out of sight. I refrained from asking about him for three days.

When the time came, while the dust settled and salutations were exchanged among the perplexed businessmen, Mr. Administrator only had enough time to broach the preliminaries. Salomé was already bursting into the store, rolling the eyes of a frightened gazelle. Through her tears, we couldn't really understand what she wanted, but a shattered Kid and Donald-Nasty-Look followed her and informed us that Cowboy had just been found.

❧

The bottle flies through the air, the line whistles. The red and white bobber takes off behind the glittering mass and the whole kit lands right in the middle of a marshy grass bed no one will think of exploring, making a muffled splash, deadened by the large aquatic leaves. The thousand-dollar bottle, weighed down with sand, settles on the bottom, raising a nauseating mud cloud. The translucent line rises diagonally to the surface where the two-coloured bobber blends into the vegetation between large yellow and white water lilies.

❧

Drowned in the peatbog near the encampment. Three days earlier, just after we'd parted in the morning, he made a kind of snare with one of those unbreakable metal leaders used to protect fishing lines from pike bites. He slipped it around his neck and fastened the leader to a twenty-pound monofilament tied to Crazy Sam's huge fishing box, he the famous American sportsman. He carried the large object to the farthest edge of the peatbog, where the thick moss carpet abruptly gives way to a deep black water hole. He threw the box into the hole beyond the tiny impassive mouths of the carnivorous plants proliferating there, then followed it.

No one had worried at first. Running off into the forest, even for a prolonged period, wasn't unusual for this taciturn and solitary son of nature, especially following an argument. But after three days, the hideously swollen body had surfaced. The mother, whose piercing cries had alerted the others, had been the first to spot the soles of his running shoes at the surface of the water. The body was hanging from the bottom and now floated almost vertically, feet pointing towards the sky and resting on the delicate film separating the two worlds. It was as though he'd merely wanted to go for a little stroll beneath the panorama, on the flip-side of the reflections, that fresh-water cowboy strangled completely upside down.

5

THE
powwow

WATER FAR AS THE EYE COULD SEE. Land floating only here and there in jagged shreds, in drifting fragments of forest. Going through a narrow pass, we came out on the main part of the reservoir. The open water caressed the heavily sunken sides of the boat; somewhere above us, stuffed into an official hydroplane, Cowboy was finally returning to his element.

He'd awaited events in the cold room, beside his bear skin. This conservation measure had been needed because of the continuing heat. A government aircraft had finally taken the body away so that a duly appointed specialist might examine it and authenticate the suicide. The Indians, gathered around the warehouse, escorted him with dignity. Calamity had befallen them for the second time in less than a month and they stood very erect. I was unable to cry.

Mr. Administrator hadn't mentioned my being fired for some time. The Old Man came and went at the front of the store, unable to conceal his good mood, "A real blessing!" he liked to repeat to no one in particular. "The whole damn gang will return to the reserve for at least a weak! And Big Alexandre will go there directly, without coming through here! A real blessing, I tell you!"

Looked at sideways, the Old Man lowered his voice and added, contrite, "But he was a good little fella, that one.... Remember, he helped us unload the truck, when the bridge collapsed. Ready to work for nothing! Better than the others, the whole gang of dogs...."

The Old Man had made hamburgers at noon, the day following the morbid discovery. When I told him I'd pass this time, he was completely disposed to excuse my lack of appetite. His face changed when I grabbed the dark and smoky meat off the counter, still wrapped in newspaper.

"What's that?"

"Bear," I grumbled in a barely audible voice.

Clusters of fly eggs could still be seen in the creases of the crumpled flesh, like an unknown seasoning.

"You're gonna eat that?"

A deathly hush hovered over the kitchen. I fried the meat up crudely and swallowed it all, while the Old Man sank his disgusted pout into the grease of ground beef.

❧

A brilliant white cloud undulated at the surface of the water. César Flamand, hunched up at the tiller, gave me a sad smile and redirected the boat, taking us closer to the curiosity. The thick cloud soon swelled up, erupted and scattered, revealing its true composition. A flock of gulls whose immaculate blanket covered a tiny rocky island. The birds now livened up in every direction, spiralling upwards, squawking in protest. *La Isla Bonita* was on my lips.

I'd hoped to keep my job long enough to still be there when he came over. Two days after the corpse had resurfaced, Crazy Sam showed up at the store. He had his shopping list, but was especially looking for news. A little earlier, he'd gone over to the camp to pick up his fishing box. The lock had been broken and two or three baubles were missing, but he wasn't going to complain.

He placed his purchases in front of me and put a ten dollar bill on a can of food. And then, with serenity, as though all my spring training, all that drumming of dollars had been fated exclusively to secretly prepare this incomprehensible operation, I gave him his change, adding a first hundred dollar bill, then another, followed by a third, and yet another. Until I'd reached nine. Then, one, two, three twenty dollar bills appeared, quickly joined by a ten and a few green dollars. To top it all off, small coins jingled onto the counter. In American currency. I'd never been so precise with my calculations. Crazy Sam's eyes widened. He stepped back.

"There you are," I said gravely.

He let out a bogus sounding chuckle and informed me that I'd made a mistake. A very important mistake, he specified. I replied that I hadn't, that all this money had been found in his fishing box, at the bottom of the peatbog. Salomé had brought me the cash, saying no one at the encampment would touch it. I added that there were one thousand American dollars here, less the cost of a two-four and a can of Tropicana Chicken. And since he stood there, looking at me stupidly, never opening his mouth, I took a small piece of paper out of my pocket which I unfolded and showed him. His name was gracefully handwritten on it.

"You can also take it as a gift...."

He took the paper and examined it, then pocketed the money and disappeared, leaving his purchases behind. To remain in the mood, I cried out to him, while he turned his back to me, "Merry Christmas, Crazy Sam!"

❦

A great roaring gust flew over, nearly tossing us all into the waves. I looked up in time to see the grey shape of a jet fighter moving away at dizzying speed, skimming over the water. Low-level flights were frequent in the region. As the thunder swept towards the horizon, our pilot mumbled an unintelligible curse. I turned to Salomé, who was snuggling against me under the waterproof canvas. The boat was hammering the waves, and we had to scream to be heard above the din, "Cowboy's plane?"

"Surely not!"

She raised her eyes towards the crazed movements of the gulls which the supersonic passage had transformed into a snowstorm.

When we'd taken the body of his twenty-year-old son out of that dark and humid cellar, the father, an enormous mass of pain, had approached to lift the sheet and quickly dropped it. The family had to await the medical examiner's report to take possession of it.

"Look at them!" the Old Man said, tugging my sleeve. "They're genuinely sad! They'll moan for days and nights when the body is exposed! Well, folks, I think I'll go over there to represent you with dignity!"

Mr. Administrator was pacing up and down inside the store, worried and stiff, slightly touched by a shiver of bereavement. He was unable to remain insensitive on such momentous occasions. But the Old Man and Mr. Administrator didn't try to conceal their eagerness to see this solemn gathering break up. Rummaging through the back of the counter, the Old Man pulled out a yellow card. "Anyhow, far as credit is concerned, it's a dead loss, folks! You think his family will pay off his debts? No way! A dead loss, I tell you! We won't get a penny back!"

It was becoming almost admirable in him, that faith in his narrow finality, the dull-witted fierceness of his certainty. Mr. Administrator gave him fleeting approval and withdrew to contemplate the teachings of misfortune in all modesty. I followed him and remained standing in front of him.

"You know, Gilles...."

"I'm taking a week's vacation!"

He glowered at me.

"I'm going to the powwow," I continued. "Cowboy had invited me, I'm going to his funeral...."

He crossed his fingers and considered me with somewhat sceptical interest.

"Problem is the Old Man is talking about going as well. With Benoît absent, we can't afford to lose two men at the same time, you understand?"

"Boss?"

"Yes, Gilles...."

"I deserve to go over there. More than the Old Man."

He thought for a moment.

"You were ... rather close, that Indian and you, eh?"

I felt a hard object in my pocket.

"I'll go and get my things."

I stopped in the doorway and, turning halfway, "It would've been stupid to come all the way up here and never go over there."

❦

Over a dozen of us were slumped and piled into the bottom of the motorboat. The Kid was pondering, seated in the bow. The froth lifted by the boat lashed his face and he spat forcefully into the broken waves. The youngest passengers were fooling around, threatening to compromise the boat's stability at any moment. Old Fernande then waved an emergency oar, laughing while she tried to deliver heavy blows on the adventurous heads. She scolded the recalcitrants, for the sake of form, and for the pleasure, providing us in passing with novel glimpses of her dental panorama. Old man Flamand, seated very quietly in the back, elbow bent over the motor's handle, was cleaving swells at an angle. Sometimes, when I turned around, I'd catch his shifty gaze focusing on the nape of my neck, and he'd only slowly turn it away, as though with regret. He seemed to have serious problems with my going to the reserve. From the start of the crossing, already sensing the importance of that stay, I was concerned about the reception I'd get. A point of land larger than the others loomed from the confusion of the shores, dissipating the liquid infinity. Houses appeared in bright spots behind the trees.

❦

A beaver splitting the surface of the small lake with its flat head swims towards them. Boisvert says nothing. He smiles on the inside and when the muscular tail slaps the water, his wife's start rekindles his nasty laughter. She looks around, bewildered, he signals to her that it was only a diving beaver. They can no longer see him. He doesn't resurface. The rowboat glides imperceptibly and only the hum of the motor can be heard in the morning. The woman doesn't talk either. At times, she opens her mouth, she's getting ready to, but something in her husband's eyes stops her, holds her back at the edge of, she doesn't know how to broach the subject, but thinks of the departed son and would like to speak. To know what really happened. They face each other, have been on bad terms since her return, on bad terms since nearly forever, in fact. Boisvert watches the two lines, the top pieces of the rods and her, she examines the point where the lines disappear into the invisible,

*on either side of the slight wake grazing the depths. They face each other and don't
speak, people don't speak when they fish. They embody the spoken word and it's Zen
as anything. The chasm between them becomes more tangible than ever, in that silent
encounter where the dreary task diverts them from the dialogue that won't happen,
while they await the fish that still doesn't bite. The woman opens her mouth again
in the end, but it's to let out a brief scream of surprise and sudden chill in the icy
water, because Jacques Boisvert, absorbed in his thoughts, forgot to initiate the
manoeuvre to avoid the half bottle of bleach which serves as a marker and slides
along the hull while the net the Indians set winds around the propeller, until the
rowboat rears up sharply, quickly tipping into the dark and final cold.*

⁂

Night was falling on the boreal forest when I followed the others
into a plain wooden shack transformed into a chapel of rest. The
wake was already under way. Piercing hymns, derived from Catholic
missals and translated into Algonquin, soared into the muggy air,
gently came back down, and were soon repeated in chorus by the
assembly. The ancestor's mournful voice was so poignant that I
immediately got a lump in my throat. It was skilfully hoarse, rose
and spread out in hypnotic swirls and lulling twists before falling
again, fading and fraying, only a tight and brittle link between
hearts, floating in the air like an ethereal hand.

The coffin's lid had been closed over the face of the corpse.
Cowboy hadn't received the attention of a sophisticated embalmer.
Above the bier, beside the scrawny flowers and their bleak array,
coniferous branches had been arranged as though to recreate a
stretch of forest. Their layout reminded me of the dry branches
trappers place strategically on either side of a trap or snare to
ensure the animal will pass through the proper spot. Amid the
charming religious trinkets sprinkled here and there in that funeral
bush (a devout image of the Sacred-Heart-of-Jesus, a figurine of
the Virgin Mary, a rosary with large yellowish beads, a picture of
the pope) were a few misty photographs chronicling episodes in
the life of the deceased. Cowboy the trapper, smiling with his first
beaver (the Old Man would've been proud of him); around five
years of age, menacingly waving one of those cap pistols; wearing
a red shirt, standing meditatively near another casket, that of
Admiral Nelson, in Grande-Ourse; in a church, or chapel, little,

for his first communion; later (for confirmation, or his profession of faith, perhaps), squeezed into a navy blazer with a bow tie resembling a blood stain strangling the budding Adam's apple. And that inherent sadness forever on his shoulders, his back, his face, like a deposit, a misty veil before his eyes, a mineral vein showing on the surface, confident of itself beneath that skin with fleeting colours.

Night shrouded the wake and the chorus sank into it, on the heals of its sacrificed child. Drowsiness swooped down on me in muffled gusts of inattention. I struggled against them as best I could, pampered by piercing responses and sinking into treacherous trances. This recital in an unknown language wove a kind of huge mantra around the room which tended to tear me away, despite myself, from the innocent and precious display of that exotic grief, of that poorly disguised pain shared without motive. My head began to nod, and I tried to focus on the coffin, unable to resist running after stray thoughts and doubts. Was my friend really there, beneath that final metamorphosis of salutary wood? Had he not been snatched, the ultimate despoilment, by the invisible justice which had had the final word?

All the weariness of this already squandered summer filled me and I cut loose, carried along by the songs, savouring their caress and that taste for tears free from clerical pomp. I mysteriously felt myself belonging to that display of mourning, as though an entire chapter of my past, having always taken cover on the opposite side of the mountain, had finally accepted to come to me.

I lost my footing, the scenery went flying in the batting of an eyelid, and all that remained were words filing past my closed eyes, words without continuity, like always, detached from their logical sequence, an infinite string of language seeming to follow the decree of a higher knowledge along the axis of restless sleeping. For the first time I knew I was on their level. I was conscious of being there, seated amid fraternal jostling, and words wandered through that room, along the walls and in my head, blending together, in Algonquin, in French, it no longer made any difference. I didn't understand them more than before, but now realized that Cowboy was talking to me through them. Hey, pal! Dip your 30-30 into the cutting steel of your gaze, draw your tin pistol and

knock some of those terms down for me, like pipes at the fair,
while they dash insolently towards oblivion. Have mercy. Allow me
to peg their empty grimace onto my pupil.

And all this time, it flew away, and life flew by in the opposite
direction, and I dreamed and remained able to think, to think that
the key was there, in that endless dream resembling abstruse texts,
in that studious delirium that seemed to create an enchantment.

❧

Streaming over his face, blood flowed into fine rivulets that skirted
mounds formed by coagulation. This quite obviously left him
indifferent. Seated with eyes half-closed, he dozed in the pool of
slack sunshine splashing the porch. He resembled a fat sleeping cat,
with only his pride unscathed. The picture's immobility was broken
only by the chair's rocking.

"It's Alexandre," Christophe pointed out, apparently
indifferent, as though merely to inform me.

The fellow seemed of uncertain age, though rather young. A
network of more ancient scars appeared, like a foundation, in
certain spots of his poor blood-soaked mug. He looked exactly like
a veteran just back from the front. Wrapped around his right hand,
a half-undone reddened bandage held together his bloated fingers.
He had knuckle-dusters in his left hand.

"He's been in a fight," Christophe explained, shrugging.

"Oh really!"

He told me to wait for him, nimbly springing onto the
stairless porch. I was practically sleepwalking. I'd learned that for
Indians, the expression *wake* isn't a colourful concession to
tradition. There was no way they'd falter, or prematurely sneak
away from the body. In my case, the family had been indulgent,
allowing me to sleep two or three hours all the same, in a shabby
basement summarily converted into a guest room.

I shifted my attention back to Big Alexandre, or what took his
place. I couldn't decide whether that sluggish fellow was well and
truly comatose or only pretending. I examined the vicinity. The
house was on a hill, in the middle of the peninsula, overlooking the
entire reserve. The hub of the settlement consisted of small houses
— cabins, more precisely — having neither power nor running

water. But the periphery of the original town, thanks to a program of construction subsidies, had recently expanded to include several tidy and comfortable bungalows, exact replicas of the reproducible model which bestows a glaze of normality on the universal suburb. The principal difference was in the landscape design: the Indians neither sowed nor planted. They preferred exposed earth.

While I watched for Christophe's return, scenes from the previous day stormed me in a swirl. However much we strive to hold time back, the course of funerals always and infallibly speeds up in the end. People turn to the grave and would like to linger, grab a handful of earth and mix it in their fingers, try to remember the tiny spot each will occupy in turn, on the lower level. But the sand runs dryly in the clenching hand.

Cowboy had been carried on a pickup reminding me of the one belonging to the Outfitters, except that it was brand new. The casket had been perched on two beams placed across the vehicle's uncovered box, and taken to the cemetery on this carriage with everyone walking behind. I don't remember any religious service taking place.

The tiny cemetery was enclosed by a wire fence. The service got under way amid profound sorrow. The father took control of the operation. Stooped and devastated, he passed the hammer to each of his sons, who took turns driving nails into the coffin. When only two nails remained, he handed me the hammer and, in a state of shock, I made the metal echo against the wood as well.

The hole had to be dug. The father handed out two iron shovels which began to come and go between the ground and the low sky. When he deemed the contribution sufficient, he grabbed the shovel and passed it to the next digger. When my turn came, I performed the task very solemnly, overcome and grateful, aware of all the strange and friendly gazes which either accepted or judged me. Cowboy made us sweat that day. We tried to lower the burden a first time: wouldn't pass. The opening had to be widened by cutting into the grave's ochre edge. The coffin finally got back on course and was lowered into the ground in the simplest manner, hemp ropes uniting our shoulders beneath the heavy box. Then, after the next of kin had thrown the first fistfuls, opening hands made for shaking other hands above the grave, after girls from the

band had lain isolated florets on top of the casket, the shovel
resumed its cycle and the box was gradually covered. As I was
about to start on the pile, I remembered something and took the
bear tooth out of my pocket; it bounced off the pine, raising the
echo of a destiny that no longer meant anything. I added my
shovelfuls to the others and, soon, all this belonged to the past,
like the rest.

⁕

Big Alexandre's slitty eyes suddenly darted bolts of erubescence,
and I realized he'd observed me the whole time from behind his
thick and hairless eyelids, without for a moment thinking of
sponging the slow bleeding which plastered that grotesque sticky
mask onto his face. I observed him secretly, without moving. His
chair had continued to rock and I was beginning to be eager for
Chrisophe's return.

He finally came out and hurriedly dragged me along.

"Never come here alone!" he advised bluntly.

In fact, my vigilance was running a strong risk of flagging. I'd
recently got into the strange habit of no longer being able to sleep
whenever my body was in a horizontal position. The powwow
began almost without transition soon after the burial, the Indians
having all fallen into morbid celebration and raving madness. A
type of organization governed these outpourings, of course:
canoeing and skeet-shooting competitions, and other tests of
strength and agility were on the program, including the colossal
bingo that would plunge the entire village into a quasi-mystic
fervour at twilight. But the powwow, as I was about to learn, was
especially the ideal occasion, the one awaited and dreamed about,
for wreaking havoc.

Worn out by insomnia, my sense of danger was losing its edge.
And, a rumour reported by Karate Kid had it that Big Alexandre
had a very clear idea about how I was to be treated on Indian
territory. As soon as I'd arrived, I'd been placed in the protection of
the Kikendache family. Christophe, without appearing to do so,
followed close on my heels as a body guard, his only salary being
the ability to display familiarity with the stranger. Under the
Kikendache's modest roof, I indulged in a relative feeling of

security. I knew that Christophe would call anyone who showed me
ill will to account, and that Karate Kid wouldn't hesitate to pull
out his *nunchaku*.

Cowboy's parents welcomed me with discreet consideration as
I walked into their cabin with a muffled tread. They offered me
Kraft macaroni and a profusion of lukewarm tea swamped with
sugar and milk. The Kid pointed his girlfriend out to me, from a
distance: a young tigress about sixteen years old, hair coloured red,
whose tail wriggled like a pair of springs. Salomé came around
towards evening, and we sat on the porch, without saying a word,
watching the others walk by. Night was falling, no one slept, and
the next day I was tired, tired. My life seemed stretched to the
breaking point and an increasing dizziness was sapping my balance.

In the days following the funeral, I dragged myself around the
reserve, disoriented and dazed, suffering through contagion from
the chronic limpness that befell each morning of the powwow
following the night's excesses. I'd become a topic of discussion, a
phenomenon creating perplexity. The Indians I came across would
stop me right in the middle of the grassy paths they used as roads,
hailing me from their porches, astonished. All asked the same
question, "Who are you? Who are you?"

"Who are you? Who are you?"

Shit. They'd end up getting me to doubt myself.

Apart from the manager of the Hudson's Bay store, pale faces
like mine could be counted on the fingers of one hand in this area.

With all notion of time dispelled, I went around in circles,
exhausted, while everyone replenished their strength, trying to
acquit myself morally of Cowboy's existence once and for all. At
times, I'd go and lie down, eyes wide-open in cabins filled with
oppressive odours, on one of those beds where Indians sleeping
any old way rubbed shoulders in mid-afternoon.

Besides his shack in Grande-Ourse, César Flamand owned a
cabin on the reserve. I once made a stop there and found Salomé
and Karate Kid in a state of alert. The former came over to me,
while the latter took the time to crack his knuckles before saluting
me. Her great agitation, and his abnormal anxiety, betrayed an
atmosphere of crisis.

"My father is getting smashed," Salomé resumed.

"Like everyone else, I guess...."

"Yes, but...."

She didn't dare go on.

"He'd stopped for twelve years," the Kid completed.

Fernande had taken refuge with relatives. A TV sputtered a volley of images in the afternoon darkness. The three of us remained quiet and watched TV, attentive and squeezed onto an antique ottoman having a dubious capacity, especially considering we soon had to contend with a creature as big-bottomed as possible, Gisèle, sticky as honey and gently disgusting.

Salomé had slid between the Kid and me, with Gisèle occupying all the other side. Her dream was coming true, after all. I was squeezed between mother and daughter. I don't recall what we watched. We took whatever came on. My attention was entirely focused on the slight pressure I felt on my outer thigh. We rubbed feet, knees, hips. Our approaches meandered like a mountain road. I got up to leave and Salomé followed, saying she was going for a constitutional in the moonlight. We didn't want to provoke Gisèle, who was always quick to resume her grieving, whining, and the habit of peeing in her sweat pants. She'd had another hard day.

❧

In days of old, to pick up aboriginal males, girls would sit at the entrance of their animal hide dwellings, engrossed in observing boys walking by. If one of them slowed down, then sat beside the chosen one, she could show her attraction by immediately going inside, a gesture the suitor was invited to interpret as an appeal for the immediate consummation of the mutual interest. If, on the contrary, the young girl refused to uncross her legs, the guy could rightly consider the affair to have gotten off on the wrong foot.

Traces of this interesting custom persisted on the reserve. When the street came alive at night, young people reproduced, no doubt unconsciously, the fertile ritual of their ancestors and, spread out in small scattered groups, went around the village on the look-out, seeking those postural preliminaries. They referred to this practice with a fabulous euphemism: *going for a stroll*. Whenever I asked Christophe to explain what he intended to do on his walk, he'd answer: *going for a stroll*. Moreover, this caged-wildcat routine seemed a logical activity in an area whose boundaries had long been set by the infamous Indian Act. Luscious girls no longer adorned the front of some rustic hut, they now lorded over the loose-planked porches of houses needing paint, looking with studied indifference at clusters of indecisive boys parading by who, after all, only needed a large convertible to be in step with the broad mass of North Americans. And girls also formed their own bands, wandering about on the heels of the opposite sex, bombarding the fronts of houses with anxious gazes.

During the powwow, the community centre provided a temporary station for all this roaming. I've rarely seen anything stranger than the Indian party I attended one night during that week. Everyone stood along the walls, in the large recreation hall, as though petrified before the dance floor whose empty space seemed, through some strange magnetism, to have pushed back and flattened everyone on the periphery. I had the impression of rubbing shoulders with a kind of magic circle whose core had been devastated by an explosion. The only ones enjoying themselves were the children playing on the floor. Music vaguely resembling disco swept it with ground swells, marvellously uncurling the hair in everyone's ears. People stood there, backs to the wall, just staring at each other, with amazing modesty and reserve. The sale of alcohol was prohibited inside the building, as it was throughout the reserve, but beer could easily be obtained at the entrance from dealers charging forty dollars a case, arguing that the valuable merchandise had travelled two hundred kilometres over bad roads to come and wet your whistle. Returning from one of those expeditions, more than one vehicle had plunged, with cargo and passengers, into the troubled waters, seasoned with chemical pulp, of the large river hugging the road.

Finally, a guest band climbed the stage in the corner of the hall. Everyone adjusted their lascivious movements to the sound system's rough tremolos. These young fellows were very popular among Indians, having put together a rather diverse repertoire, cheerfully blending country, Latin-flavoured rhythms, international beat and their own brand of folk. And, what's more, authentic aboriginal lyrics crowned this vigorous fusion of influences. They toured reservations throughout the province during the summer, participating in various powwows. Which goes to show how robust was their health.

Back on the streets' crushed stone and the social desert of the governmental prefab, heavy metal is what the ghetto blaster bawled into the heart of the night. Following the show, we went for a *stroll*. Christophe was trading smutty stories with the Kid who was staying close to his girlfriend, perched on her stiletto heals. Dagobert and Judith accompanied us. Salomé was sitting Judith's baby that night, and the general opinion was that Donald-Big-Arms had gone off to get drunk. Delighted, Christophe ceaselessly repeated, "This place is full of girls, eh? Full of them, eh?"

He'd had an extremely plump young girl as a lover for a few days, but had quickly grown tired of going around with her. In fact, there was an overabundance of females and the powwow, at first blush, appeared as the promised sexual paradise. All the Indians with whom I spoke said they were convinced I was here for the girls. However much I talked about Cowboy, about Cowboy's death, they'd only half-submit, clinging to a compromise: I'd covered all that distance to bid my friend farewell and to meet scads of girls.

The bad influence of this talk is no doubt what made me commit an undeniable gaffe in that regard, one that would cause me problems. After sharing the contents of a case of beer with the five above-mentioned idlers (and blown the rest of my savings), my wariness let up and I allowed an imposing four-foot matron to wrap her arms around my exhausted body, decimated as I was by the emotions of the previous days. With the help of alcohol, I broke down completely and realized only too late I was dealing with a local version of Gisèle. My friends vainly tried to rescue me. "You leave our friend alone!"

"Do you want us to get her out of here?"

"She always does this!"

"Hey, Gilles, you'll get AIDS!"

Judith was disgusted and said nothing.

But I'd crossed the Rubicon, and her arms had the pressure of a bear trap. Afterwards, in a more or less animated state, I was a slave to that energetic wild creature who held me captive in a borrowed bungalow until morning. I walked away from that catastrophe, soul in tatters. News travelled quickly on the reserve, and the scandal became impossible to suppress. Next morning, Salomé promptly bolted as I approached and a radical deterioration of our relations followed. All I could ask myself was what I was doing here with my sterile thoughts and my stabbing despair.

Time became blurred. Only one reference point remained valid amid that tedious succession: the night. Everyone wandered in it with souls at half-mast, bruising, damning, and avenging themselves in it, pining for someone and moping with hatred in it. And during the day, everything collapsed again and a deathly silence reigned over the filthy cabins. I was the only one left to walk aimlessly, arms dangling, head lowered under the intense light, too guilty of every crime ever to sink into contentment.

Gisèle sometimes crossed my path. Having relapsed into her favourite pastime, she'd go crashing against the porches of wood houses, expressing herself with difficulty between bursts of her tragic laughter. She always managed to ask whether I had a place to spend the night, never failing to renew her offer of welcoming me in her bed.

"Between my daughter and me!" she'd specify through her toothless smile.

"Hang in there, Gisèle!"

And I'd let her stagger across the street, too tired to feel sympathy.

"The bottle! The bottle," she'd cry out, finally collapsing.

Her vision nonetheless haunted me. Other times, my circumambulation would be interrupted by the reserve's only police officer (and therefore chief), the fat fellow with a moustache who'd been afraid of ghosts in Grande-Ourse. And this reminder brought a furtive smile to my lips which didn't offend the friendly lawman. Without getting out of his car, he waved at me to come over and wormed his way up to me over the window of his powerful vehicle. He told me straight out, "There's a gang that wants to smash your face in, but I'm watching them. You should still be careful. So long."

I was now under police protection. That was just great. I bitterly bemoaned my lot one afternoon, prostrated in a guest room at one of the houses in the development. And the next day, after honouring my host's hospitality with vague words, I headed for César Flamand's house, near the water, fully resolved to remind him of his promise to take me back to Grande-Ourse.

A penetrating odour of raw meat and urine would strike anyone walking into the reserve's oldest dwellings. I stepped over a large white fish lying on its side on the floor, staring at the ceiling with a protruding eye. Dearest Fernande was completely sober and very attentive and I behaved like a son. She sat me down in front of a rough table and insisted on serving me moose steak. That would be a change from Kraft macaroni. As for the rest, the poor woman had plenty to worry about. She told me about her family troubles while I devoted all my attention to the succulent odours being born under her fingers: her old man had gone off to get really drunk and Salomé was prowling around a little too much, and bad company was threatening to carry her off. I was already smelling the wild meat avidly, and asked her what kind of company she thought I kept.

Fernande still hadn't heard about my problems with the four-foot harpy. That simplified things. Anyhow, I absolutely didn't feel like sharing my worries. My appetite was calling me, and for a few minutes I gave up on asking any more from life.

Leaning over me, the old lady parted her hair and showed me, on the right side of her head, a reddened bare patch the size of a dollar coin. The previous day, she'd had a resounding argument with one of her rather tipsy daughters, who wasn't very used to normal doses of the beloved poison. The two women had literally gone for each other's hair, with Fernande finally opting for the decisive blow. Hadn't seen her daughter since, she explained, sniffling. And now, Salomé was going to turn out badly as well. The moose was delicious.

I tried to feel concerned, but a tired man has no feelings. Besides, most problems find a solution when people get totally fed up. All I wanted was to get out of this quagmire. I really liked Salomé, but wasn't her father after all. And, what's more, the end of summer was approaching. I'd leave, subjected to the predictable whims of the seasons. The great catalogue of crushes would include another summer passion, that's all. I'm not the one who invented life.

"Where's your husband?" I inquired while eating.

She didn't know. She'd heard him howl in the distance late at night. It was said that damning Jacques Boisvert had become his sole occupation. Drinking had plunged him deep into the past and, over the last few days, he'd gone around waving his fist, shouting his defiance everywhere. Alcohol had wakened the wounded beast in his paternal heart, and his now-generalized rancour was boiling over. I wished the lady good luck, thanked her for the excellent game, and went off to look for the man who'd promised to take me back home.

❧

On the dock, onlookers waited for swift canoes to show up, encouraging crews with their hails. The event included a portage and the paddlers had to touch ground without losing their rhythm, quickly lifting the streaming craft with great difficulty. They disappeared down the trail, breathing hard, pectorals palpitating, exuding magnificent pride. Paddles cut sideways through the water and, in short light strokes, gently propelled the canoe in double time; this mingling of eight arms with the element was like the harmonious gyration of pistons. I'd have liked to entrust my return to Grande-Ourse to those valorous paddlers. Gunshots in the distance suddenly made me jump. I looked around, and it took me a little while to realize I had nothing to fear. The trapshooting contest was in full swing farther on.

❧

César Flamand painfully stood up, taking time to study my feet before hanging his dead gaze higher up. Then pulled himself out of the mud puddle he'd just fallen flat into. Flowing dirt filled the least fissure of his wrinkled face and his eyes reminded me of oily rags. He had a few wounds and bruises, but the muffled quivering of his voice betrayed more considerable damage. A bitterness had arisen inside him and he persisted in looking at me with a cutting gaze filled with hatred, hatred of my insolent equilibrium, perhaps, hatred of what was happening to him as well. That hatred welled up in his mouth like an ancient heave repressed for too long.

He steadied himself as well as could be expected, and his bandit's beard was full of crust and other instructive remainders of the three-day bacchanalia which had ended his vow of abstinence. He grabbed my collar, wanting to drag me towards him, but I backed up, struggling to move my face away from his. He spat lumps as he talked to me, and took his turn asking the established question, "Who are you? Who are you?"

I felt he really wanted to look right through me, from the limbo where he waded, a minute quantity of vital substance and mineral salts already half dissolved.

"Who are you? Who are you?"

"You know me, Mr. Flamand.... The clerk from the Outfitters in Grande-Ourse."

But he was on another planet and, over there, I was far from being an ally. He shook his head with fierce stubbornness, almost lost his balance, and grabbed my throat with a kind of feverish despair, wailing, "You're a Boisvert, eh? You're a Boisvert?"

Jumping back, I tore myself from his grasp, disgusted and furious. "Are you crazy?"

He was standing up, panting. I think he'd really gone completely mad. I told him about my intentions, "Mr. Flamand, I want to leave. I want to return to Grande-Ourse...."

He craned his neck. With a fatalist gesture punctuated by a clicking of his tongue, he pointed to the grey sky where low clouds were gathering. Only then did the stupidity of my request hit me, this poor wretch could barely stand and here I was, in this rainy weather and howling wind, asking him to take on a huge body of water whose wrath was notorious.

I abandoned him to his unsteadiness. Had to think about my transportation problem. César Flamand again shouted, behind me, "Boisvert! Boisvert!"

I knew from experience you have to be wary of characters somewhat given to fits of anger, emotional outbursts, and impulses of all kinds. They always have ringside seats at the mischievous lynchings that fill the phantasmagorias of history.

❧

The mystery exuded by that excessive and intense living was an intoxicating venom to me. Swimming in this elementary tropism and collective race towards decrepitude made me dizzy. I'd lost sight of Salomé, and the other girls were both very simple and dreadfully complicated. My reputation had been poorly established from the start, since the nag had illegally confined me.

One night during that week, I went over to the recreation hall, and allowed myself to be carted off by Judith, who didn't take very good care of herself and now looked twice as old as her eighteen years. She cooed and went for my heartstrings while I reeled off sweet words in a jumble, and she convinced me to be her babysitter. The previous sitter had already left when I arrived, ready to get to work, in a house at the top of the hill. I didn't sleep and patiently awaited the progenitor, hoping to find some early morning comfort from her. I went through incredible efforts trying to tame that hazel-eyed munchkin sprawled in the crib. He was barely a year old, digging into his intransigence like a young squirrel or a terrorist. The curiosity and wariness of that tiny ball still don't belong to reality. The only thing beyond language is brute animal motivation and the perfect dullness of experience.

I changed my first diaper, as proud as if I'd been his father, and the best thing that happened to me during that long party with blurred contours, which coiled up over itself, was to dip my hands in the gently concrete shit of an infant, and to pray for him in one way or another.

Next day, his mother returned to the fold, fists buried in the creases of her blood-speckled sweater. She was cursing the whole world. Her jeans had been drenched with ketchup as well. For a split-second, I thought I spotted the true face of misfortune, the meaning of that word when you get used to what kills you. Through an unfortunate coincidence, the baby was wailing at the top of his lungs when his mother arrived, crying as well, and howling inanities in the language of her ancestors.

"Calm down, Judith, I'll take care of...."

"Shut up! Go away!"

"What's gotten into...."

"Go away! Shut up!"

She threw me out with a final volley of abuse, adding by way of a supreme argument that Big Alexandre might show up for breakfast. I then sprouted wings, going off like a good pilgrim with my bundle of novelties and inexpressible feelings. There were

still some people on the street. The light was harsh and my head
was bursting all round.

☙

The entire day, I tried to find a watercraft to pull me out of this
mire. The possibility of using the road seemed remote. I'd run
into fuzzy promises and breezy assurances. Try as I might to shake
my counterparts like apple trees, all I got most of the time was
the silence of an opium addict, which did nothing to remedy my
persecution complex. Few people could be found standing up
during daylight hours. The reserve bandaged its wounds in the
morning, and the powwow's languid magic cut us off from the
rest of the world. I felt like a prisoner there, condemned to
wander while awaiting the fateful moment when something would
finally happen.

At the end of the afternoon, I came across the venerable
grandfather who'd sung psalms with a nasal twang at the wake,
clinging to him like a saviour. He was holding a child by the hand;
with all his wits visibly about him, he promptly saluted me. He
looked at me with naive and dreamy amazement. I inquired
whether he owned a boat. But he didn't speak French and the little
girl, who stared at me with large black eyes, translated my
question. He soberly answered no. I wanted to prolong that
discussion at all cost.

"Tell him I liked his traditional songs, at the funeral...."

He listened to my message, nodding his handsome snow-white
head, then spoke, as though humming, with a gentle quaver.

"What's he saying?" I asked when he'd finished.

The little girl looked at me with insolence.

"He said you won't leave this place. Not before *they* let you go."

"I see. Thanks for the information."

I went off, like a tourist, and immediately spotted the on-duty
cop driving in slow-motion nearby. As promised, he was keeping a
vigilant eye. Car traffic on the reserve prevented his going
unnoticed. What was seen most often were children speeding by on
their all-terrain vehicles. The chief gave me the latest news: Big
Alexandre was telling whoever would listen that he'd soon turn my
skin, bones, and everything in between into dog meat. Someone

told him I'd been at Judith's place that morning and his aggression had climbed a notch.

"He can do what he wants, I don't care...."

I'd had it with those stories. I already knew I wouldn't leave this place on tiptoes. Christophe was busy with some sentimental dip and making himself scarce. And I was slowly getting used to the idea this unpleasant encounter would soon happen through mere probability. I came across Karate Kid on a trail leading to the water's edge. Riding a lime-coloured mountain bike that was made in Japan.

"Will you sleep at our place tonight?"

"Will Salomé be there?"

"Probably. My mother will cook some walleye."

This finally decided me. He went off to meet his girlfriend, swaying like a dancer to bite into the ruts of a steep hill, after assuring me he was getting ready for a fight.

☙

I'd gone for a swim. Once I got used to the garbage scattered on the bank, the water was delightful. On the way back, I was refreshed, dawdling along somewhat, slightly disoriented, and came up to that bloody house where Big Alexandre had his quarters. He was rocking on his chair like a cobra, and signalled me to approach. It was time to opt for clarity. Freeing my hands by putting my bag down in the box of a parked pickup, I walked towards him and, hopping onto the porch, placed myself at his mercy. His most recent wounds had begun to scar and, with a little effort, he could've smiled a little. Scattered hairs sprouted between the scratches. He plunked himself in front of me, and looked me over. Nothing else happened. I warned him I'd have to leave, because I'd unexpectedly just discovered a need to shave, but he promised he could help me out and dragged me inside. He offered me an electric razor in the bathroom, which reassured me about the purity of his intentions: you can't cut a jugular with that. He left me alone and, nose stuck to a bad mirror, finding myself in the deepest part of the lion's jaws, I scraped that three-day-old beard before proffering hasty thanks and taking to my heels, giving up on trying to understand what had just happened. Meanwhile, the pickup had disappeared. With my bag, my things, and my papers. I had to settle for still being in one piece. Closely shaven.

❧

All the available space was filled with loud sleepers and dreamers. I dropped in the middle of the bunch. My eyes got used to the darkness and I recognized Karate Kid, Christophe, and Donald Big-Arms, who'd wrapped the other two close to his chest and was snoring with ease. Moreover, Salomé was there snuggled up to a pillow, wide awake, a small curled-up ocelot scanning the darkness. She sent me off to have something to eat, impressed by the resonance of my stomach rumblings. My stomach knew how to manage when it was a question of being pitiful.

A greasy barrel collected waste water beneath the kitchen sink. It had to be emptied regularly. I ate some white buttered bread and went back to lie down aroused and tense as a spring. She gave me some space.

"Only one thing brought me here, Salomé: Cowboy. He's now buried and I'm acting like a...."

My dismay got the best of me and tears came streaming out, without warning: everything I'd held back since Cowboy's death. Salomé wrapped me with her arms that were too short.

"It'll be alright. It'll be alright."

"I have to get out of here."

She shrugged, but I complained all the more.

"Your father thinks I'm a Boisvert, now, can you imagine?"

"My father is sick," she said in a tone meaning something else.

"I've heard you're doing crazy things...."

"I stroll around."

"Salomé, why did Cowboy do it?"

"People at the camp say there was a curse. They heard laughter...."

"I know. I was there."

She touched my cheek. I went on, "It was my idea to get the case of beer. The next day, I met Cowboy, just before...."

"The curse," mumbled Donald Big-Arms in his rest.

"You couldn't have known," said Salomé.

"With him, no one could've known...."

The Kid groaned and opened his eyes, "He said he'd do it!"

Christophe was killing a bear and killing him again in his sleep and Donald Big-Arms was still groaning, "If I hadn't stolen that damned fishing box, as well.... The damned box...."

It should henceforth be compulsory for anyone committing suicide to write a note clearly explaining their motives. That would help avoid the kind of ridiculous situation where everyone feels compelled to shoulder part of the burden and where guilt becomes a kind of collectively administered possession. Cowboy carried his secrets into the cold seals of his coffin, in the ultimate intimacy of his choice. I observed that no one mentioned the famous bank note which, tossed into the waves twelve years earlier, had successively become a message in a bottle and the treasure inside a box. The main witnesses hadn't yet been called to testify, and I couldn't help thinking that circumstances had brought me to the reserve only to fulfil an extraordinarily important duty of expiation. Cowboy had only been an instrument of this process, the victim designated by a decree whose instigator and real signatory remained quiet.

❧

"Thanks for accepting the charges."

"Don't mention it."

"What are you doing?"

"Oh, not much."

The operator's distant and totally callous voice had just faded, while Brigitte's wove its way into the receiver through heavy crackling.

"So, I hear it's a wild orgy up there?"

"For your information, dearest Brigitte, I'm not having any fun. Besides, my vacation seemingly wants to prolong itself.... How will I get out of here?"

"Well, pal, we don't have time to feel sorry for you. There's a fire up here! The Outfitters shed! The whole village is at the site! They're waiting for a Canadair plane to spray all of it. The brush is dry and they're afraid the village will go up."

"What about the truck? Big Ben?"

"He never made it up the first hill. The truck went off in reverse, Big Ben was crying like a child."

"And you're staying there?"

"Oh, I've got a pretty nice view from here. Besides, I didn't come to the woods to hang around crowds...."

"It might still be smouldering when you get back.... If the flames reach the fuel barrels stored there, all of Grande-Ourse will be blown to bits."

"Just my luck to miss the show of the summer...."

There was a moment of silence. I was strangely moved, and had a knot in my throat when I started speaking again.

"Brigitte...."

"In any case, pal, your vacation has a lot of tongues wagging around here...."

"Brigitte, I miss you so much."

"Well, we barely know each other.... Maybe some day.... Did you know that Crazy Sam hasn't stopped asking questions about you?"

"Oh yeah."

"I'll let you know. And I hope you'll fill me in as well...."

"Hmmm. Sure, okay. Tell Jacques I send my best regards, straight from the reserve, and that they're about to scalp me up here. So long!"

I hung up and called the store. Lili's deep hoarse voice lowed a greeting loud enough to burst my eardrum. She immediately sent the operator packing.

"Gilles who? No way!"

I dialled I and called her directly. Her roar went straight through my brain and I asked timidly.

"Is the Old Man there? Or Benoît, maybe?"

"Grande-Ourse Outfitters" she interrupted impetuously. "May I help you? You'll have to make it quick, we don't have much time to waste here!"

"Any news about the fire?"

I think she recognized my voice, but preferred to stand behind the high wall of her contempt. Lili had conquered, Lili was triumphant, and I was providing her the unexpected opportunity of turning the knife in the wound. "The village will go up in flames," she said with assurance. "Do you want to know anything else, boy?"

"How did it start?"

"A young savage, as might've been expected. A pup from

Gisèle's litter! His mother went off to get drunk on the reserve and
he was playing with matches!"

She quieted down, then, "Well! Is that all you wanted to
know? I have work to do while everyone else plays fireman!"

"Okay, okay," I grumbled, putting down the receiver.

I thanked the mistress of the house, offered to pay for the cost
of the second call, but she refused. I bid her goodbye and went out
into the darkness. The reserve's streets had suddenly emptied. A
religious silence hovered over the tiny houses and plywood shacks.
As I walked in front of the community radio station, a vehicle
pulled out of the street in front of me. The chap made an
emergency stop, jumped out, and rushed inside.

"Bingo!" I heard him gasp.

I detoured by the Kickendache house. All of the tiny band had
gathered for the great bingo game on the radio. The crackling and
monotonous voice read out pairs of numbers through the speaker.
Cowboy's mother offered me macaroni, but I'd eaten at Flamand's
place, so I settled for a cup of weak tea. I really hated that terrible
habit of pouring an avalanche of cream and sugar into it! The
father was pensive, eyeing me sadly. My tensed and hollow face was
beginning to intrigue them.

"Where's Salomé, guys?"

They didn't know. Worriedly bent over their chequered cards,
as though on the lookout for a sacred mystery, they barely heard
me. The organizers had promised very interesting prizes.

I decided to head over to Flamand's place. The prospect of
having to walk the empty streets alone hardly reassured me, but
bothering Christophe or the Kid was out of the question at that
moment. I imagined Big Alexandre and his gang were bingophiles as
well, since no misfortune befell me. The cabin's surroundings were
swathed in silence, but a flickering light came through a window. A
raised voice pierced that wall of shadows and I drew near.

❧

*For the first time in his life, Gilles fully grasps the death of a man. The furious
man just hit the door with heavy axe blows, cutting into the wood fibre, and the
call of blood wells up in his veins. To point a rifle towards that door, aim through
it, someone. The beginning of the end. Gilles has held that rifle for all eternity. He*

moves forward, heading to where the gap with the long teeth covered in sap is widening. An attack against property: formal law has always dictated the appropriate response to men. Heart pounding, he approaches the door's wooden core; that's when that disconcerting thing happens. This damned Indian has put an end to his antics, passing his head through the slanting and gaping hole with the shredded periphery. An Indian head looking at Gilles, puffing and trying to speak to him. Gilles moves back instinctively, walks to the bar and grabs a bottle, a last one, oh the last one, this time it's really the last one. He goes back to the door, to the hole, through the hole he hands the bottle to the Indian who snatches it and pushes insolence to the point of saying thank you before turning around, staggering away, axe on his shoulder, drinking straight from the bottle. Slowly walking away, a lictor with an illicit solemnity, as though he had all the time in the world, as though the event had been defused too quickly. He takes his time, never-ending, that Indian's back, that Indian seen from the back. Gilles opens the door hanging on its hinges, and slips outside beneath a shower of stars. He squeezes the icy rifle with both hands and then before him in the axe's outlaw glimmer.

❧

It took my breath away. Through a gap in the curtains, in front of the bed and in the room's clutter, I saw César Flamand holding Salomé by the shoulders, forcing her to remain seated on the bed, leaning towards him. His fly was undone and he was rocking on the spot, extremely drunk after so many days.

Stunned at first, I realized that trying to think was useless, and ran around the corner of the cabin. I burst into the kitchen, where a complete calm reigned, glanced over at the living room where a forlorn television was exorcising the darkness, then tore into the bedroom, knocking the door open before brutally shoving the old man who went crashing into a corner, tangled in his pants. I grabbed Salomé by the hand, she didn't ask any questions.

❧

She said nothing and smelled of beer. She shivered, wrapping herself in her arms. I was exploding.

"My God! I knew Indians loved their children, but this!"

She started crying. I was still in shock.

"Why did you let him do that? Why didn't you defend yourself?"

"But Gilles! ... He's my father! My father!"

She repeated this enormity as though it could've been the final word on the matter.

"First of all, that's not true! Your real father was shot down!"

Her tears poured out. I would've liked to console her, but was unable to control myself. Smitten by heavy revulsion, I was moving around like a sleepwalker, with a stiffened neck. I was fed up with the filthy warmth of their overcrowded shacks. More than ever felt I was from elsewhere, from nowhere, a poor ambassador drawing all his prestige from the absence of tracks behind him, from the frivolity of his past. The hull of a car rested near the reservoir's still waters.

"I don't feel like going back to see the others," I sighed after a moment.

"We can sleep here," she said between sniffs.

I glanced at the seats. The stuffing was nearly intact. I hugged her in the back seat. We were an amorous couple of adolescents, one precocious, the other backwards, American teenagers following the Second World War, after the prom or a Saturday night movie. We embraced in that America which unfolds on the screen, strained to the breaking point, the innocence of the free world, the stumbling block of major religions, the starting line of fashionable wars. We were at the beginning of nowhere and we were in the north. I looked through the shattered windshield, beyond which no road began. All we could see was the same dark water everywhere, a dark water that swallows you and your friends head-first at the end of every adventure.

I no longer felt any desire and love seemed a complicated formality. I felt I had just enough ability to cuddle Salomé against my hairless chest, but she gently pushed me away, asking, "Where will you go when you leave?"

"Don't know. I'll disappear."

"Like a ghost," she said with a sharpish voice.

"Yeah. A ghost. I glide over things and my name is Deschênes. You folks believe in them, eh? ... In ghosts, I mean."

I looked into her eyes, with a comical intensity, not fully convinced about having to take myself seriously. I was humming half-heartedly, but couldn't recall the melody, only the lyrics.

Sometimes I live in the country
Sometimes I live in the town
Sometimes I get a great notion
To jump in the river ... an' drown

"What's that?"

"Ken Kesey. An old American song, used as an epigraph to his second novel. It's called *Goodbye Irene*, the song, I mean. I've forgotten the author's name. But I'll bet it's like that of a football player. It's nothing, really."

"What's nothing like?"

"Like when you stand too far away."

She frowned.

"Nothing is when movement attains the perfection of rhythm which is found in the disappearance of any impression of that movement...."

She frowned everything she had left to frown, then kissed my neck. The only spontaneous show of affection she ever gave me. I felt very comfortable being so close to this little girl.

"I have to leave tomorrow," I decided abruptly.

"Alexandre and his gang want to beat you up."

I burst out with forced laughter.

"I was shaking so much in the bathroom that I managed to cut myself with an electric razor!"

"You have to leave," she agreed.

"Still, I can't swim out of here!"

"Cowboy could have...."

"Obviously."

"I love you."

"I thought Indian women never said that...."

She bit her lip, already regretting it.

"Do you want me to teach you words in our language?" she added.

"No."

"No?"

"No."

"Maha."

"Maha?"

"Yes."

"There are other words I'd like you to teach me...."

"In Indian?"

"No. Words that come to me early in the morning when I'm half asleep. I can see and read them, but not combine them in the right sequence ... Lomax. The singer's name. I just remembered."

She was looking at me.

"Salomé?"

"Yes?"

"I forgot to tell you: your little brother set fire to the village of Grande-Ourse today. Good night now."

❧

Aani Koni. He remembers that old song from the time he had a fling with his cousin in the forest cabins, the fir-bough shelters where the first thankless emotions, those of in-breeding. He was terrified of what was hidden there, in the angle of the woman during his vacation on the farm, at the ends of the earth, in the Joliette region, an area far more pleasant than these damned grey pines standing on burn-offs to ensure the needle blanket's sinister continuity. Here, in grey-pine country, there's Gisèle, whom an exogamous Gilles always contemplates from afar because he's a child of distance, and Whites, here, and Indians, here, are peoples of distance. And then Gisèle grows up and gets a boyfriend. He mounts her yes they were seen in the woods she Gisèle mounted by he who now yes he who Flamand who in front of him, that large Indian back walking away, taking his good time and Gilles watches him leave and the gun in his hands, but he won't do anything because thou shalt not kill but he's suddenly there to his right Jacques Boisvert in the flesh his father an apparition he's come back without a sound from his lewd devotions to that high society woman who lets herself be screwed on some deserted tiny island with only moss for comfort while the husband in a wheelchair, wheels locked on the dock, oh Boisvert is there, now, it seems he knows everything, that he's seen and heard everything, analyzed, grasped, learned in a photographic flash and he raises that high calibre whose phallic barrel gradually becomes parallel to the ground and Gilles, this time, this time, Gilles, Bang! a first shot pierces the night, when you stand right next to it, such a shot wants to knock you down, Bang! the father who shoots and gives the example, the exemplary father, Gilles also raises the impetus the position is contagious and the thunder propagates the visceral violence Bang! Gilles has fired in turn that makes it a duo in the back of the Indian who's disappeared Bang! they nonetheless shoot in the general direction shoot into the darkness, shoot as though to kill the entire night everything it's always hidden, protected, exacerbated, the gunfight echoes throughout the entire village everyone hears it Boisvert fired first, Gilles fired afterwards perhaps they fired at the same time after all those eight shots and then three more to be quite sure and no one will be the same afterwards from the next day on, to leave, even if it's hard to explain, to expiate, tomorrow they'll find the axe its head driven deep into the earth, near the pool of blood.

❧

I was awakened by my own cry of anguish. Panting and drenched in my own sweat. I sat up briskly trying to regain my bearings. It didn't come back to me at all, that car hull lost in the dreary dawn. It took me two or three seconds just to remember where I was, and first of all *who* I was. Salomé's sleepy voice tried to calm me, "What's the matter?"

"I had a dream...."

"Your word dream again?"

"Well, it did have words, girl, it did have words.... But I understood what they meant...."

She yawned. You never could have imagined such a tiny mouth could hold so much air.

"In my dream," I said, "I was shooting at an Indian!"

I swallowed my saliva while she waited, bored. Her frustrated sleep was drawing her downwards.

"That's not all," I continued. "In my dream, Jacques Boisvert was my father!"

She looked at me inquisitively.

"And the Indian...."

She turned her head slightly and spotted something behind me. "Oh oh ...," she said immediately.

Heavy blows on the windshield made me jump. I turned around crookedly to face the war party which had formed spontaneously in the early morning. I slipped on my boots, spaced-out, and managed to kiss Salomé on the cheek before opening the door and stepping out. These people hadn't slept all night; their faces were shrivelled and their attitudes fared no better. I knew this was the worst moment of the powwow, when anything could happen. Big Alexandre had a fresh cut on his cheek, which seemed to smile nastily in the half-light. Knuckle-

dusters wrapped his fist and he punched his palm, cheerfully
oblivious. He looked like a small beast on a leash. Behind him, the
guys from his gang spread out around the car, as though it
could've lurched forward and escaped.

César Flamand struggled just to keep his balance. He moved
his body like an owl, keeping his head still and staring at me with
glazed eyes. What I managed to read in them gave me little
pleasure. Gisèle was facing me, her twisted and multicolored head
split by an approving grin. Judith kept somewhat to the side. I
awaited the outcome, tensed as a set trap.

Big Alexandre had approached the car, carefully scratching it by
dragging his wrist along the fender. He pulled Salomé out of the
seat, grabbed her around the waist, then pushed her aside bluntly.
He just stood there sniggering, waiting for the scenario to unfold.

"Are you sleeping with my daughter?" asked a groggy Gisèle.

"You offered her to me yourself, remember, old girl?"

Flamand grumbled. Still speaking to Gisèle, I turned towards
him.

"Supposing I did.... I wouldn't be the only one, apparently...."

He staggered two steps forward, pointing his yellowed
forefinger at me: "Boisvert!"

I tried to smile, to create a distraction, but was still troubled
by the brand new nightmare of which this grotesque confrontation
was no doubt the logical extension. I turned towards the others
with a distressed expression.

"He's been repeating that since he began to get drunk...."

"Boisvert!" hollered a rapturous Gisèle.

The Indians traded hesitant gazes. Salomé, standing apart
from the group, was timidly observing what was happening. She
hurled insults at Gisèle who didn't seem overly annoyed. Alexandre,
with a threatening look, hinted an order for her to be quiet. Gisèle
walked towards me, bombastic and ridiculous.

"You're a Boisvert!"

I spread my arms to show my helplessness. An unpleasant
signal crackled behind my ear. Big Alexandre was going around the
car. I motioned him not to move, but all this was becoming
laughable, and the others were already closing the circle. Salomé
then performed a dance step over the hood and came to join me. I

would surely appreciate the beauty of the gesture when my flesh burst into the greyness.

A hum made heads turn: the police chief was parking his vehicle nearby. He had a little difficulty standing, but nonetheless walked over to the suspicious gathering he looked at inquiringly.

"I didn't do anything to them," I confided in an aside.

He gently nodded, studying the expressions of the protagonists.

"He's a Boisvert!" belched Flamand, twisting his fingers.

"He's been saying that since I've been on the reserve," I explained to the policeman.

Knitting his brow, he then requested, very politely, "May I see your ... identification?"

He stretched out his hand. I reached into my pocket, feeling for the absent wallet and immediately realized what an abominable trap fate had drawn me into: stripping me of my things, they'd stolen my identity. Deprived of my social definition and of any immediate recourse, I was at the mercy of this unstable mob. For lack of any proof to the contrary, I'd conform to their law. After a moment, I nodded and answered in a flat voice, "I don't have any papers, chief.... They stole them...."

I pointed to Big Alexandre and his gang, disillusioned. The cop diligently scratched his head.

"Liar!" shouted one of the pals who was eager to go into action.

"Yeah," mused the chief.

He moved back two steps, which I interpreted as the signal he could do no more to help me. Flamand grabbed my T-shirt, again spitting out in a monotonous and diabolical voice, "Boisvert!"

"Yes, yes, you're right.... The dream...."

The point was simple: I was going to pay for everything, for everyone, since forever.

But not without a fight. I shoved the old man harshly, Salomé kicked him in the shins and he fell backwards with a pathetic squeal. Big Alexandre adjusted his knuckle-dusters. Salomé started to move to place herself between him and me, but Gisèle intercepted her with a cluck, burying her in her bosom. All I could see was the leather band studded with steel points. I tried to imagine its impact on my forehead, which would split open, allowing all memory to flee. I made a frantic survey, seeing only the police chief leaning against the trunk of his car and, farther on, surrounding the peninsula, the water, all the water. As the armed fist hovered at the level of its owner's swollen face, right before it hit, a distant humming was heard. There was a hissing and, striking like thunder, the *nunchaku* rolled around Big Alexandre's arm, forcefully holding it, both ends of it solidly gripped by a Karate Kid more mischievous and Japanese-like than ever. Christophe stood beside him, as foolishly threatening as a bulldog, having just drawn Cowboy's machete, which he'd slipped from behind his back as had its previous owner. Alexandre was moaning with pain but, immediately afterwards, an engine's drone again filled the entire space.

❧

One question still arises: since his father was travelling in a hydroplane that night, why didn't Gilles hear him return? Why didn't he have any knowledge of the aerial manoeuvre needed for his father to turn up that way, standing beside him, holding a rifle? The answer is rather simple: tensed with his entire being towards the adulterous act, Jacques Boisvert had been distracted when the time for departing formalities came. As a result, he ran out of gas during the flight back. It was already dark. Then, not at all taken aback, with very confident instinct, he managed to keep his plane in the air and glide to the safety of Lac Légaré. After knocking the heads off the few last spruces barring his access to it, he performed a perfect, smooth, and quiet landing, returning a barely scratched aircraft to the fold.

That's what he told Gilles the following day, before his son, to pretend that life goes on, walked into Crazy Sam's room, to make the American's bed. But then a second and last question arises logically: how do I know all this? The answer is again rather simple: Because, in some way, I am Gilles Boisvert.

❧

Everyone looked at the sky, towards the reservoir. Growling swelled in the distance. At first, all we saw was a bald eagle soaring very high above the reserve, seeming to observe the scene from beneath its judge's wig. Dove-white gulls were maliciously harassing him. And then, lower down, going in the opposite direction, a lonely goose flew over the shore, honking and banking to avoid the people standing still in the morning. Finally, a loon cried in the distance.

As the engine's roar became clearer, everyone spotted the rapidly approaching Beaver weaving its way beneath the leaden clouds the sun would likely soon break through. Big Alexandre winced and, despite the chronic swelling of his eyebrow, managed to read out loud the inscription on the fuselage: "Boisvert Air Service."

A petrified silence greeted those three words. The hydroplane lost altitude and, having spotted the only beings still able to stand within a radius of several kilometres, it flew over us at the height of the spruces. Everyone ducked and César Flamand, who'd managed to regain his balance in the meantime, dove once again. I glimpsed Jacques Boisvert's angular profile. Firmly in the saddle in his cabin, he leaned over to give me a look I figured was malicious. Someone was seated beside him.

The airplane flew over the reserve, performed a tight turn, going around the peninsula, then over the water. Its pilot seemed to hesitate over the procedure to follow. Flamand had painstakingly got up and, waving a scrawny fist, hollered for the whole world to hear, "Damned Boisvert!.... Damned!"

The craft, however, was once again heading towards us. And suddenly, the engine hiccuped and misfired, making the seconds stand still. Everyone held their breath.

"There's lots of water, he can land anywhere," the Kid observed.

In fact, the huge body of water suggested an easy landing. But the dying plane, choking amid grating sighs and bluish emissions, pointed straight to the Indian reserve. It approached rapidly, too rapidly and, while the propeller, shaken by slight jolts, was definitely growing lifeless, it once again hedge hopped over our small dazed group. This time, everyone hit the dirt....

Except me. I merely ducked and, lifting my head, caught a last glimpse of Jacques Boisvert, bush pilot and toughest of the tough guys in Grande-Ourse: facing me, and so close I could clearly see the whites of his eyes, he gave me an incredible salute.

The hydroplane dove towards the hill towering above the peninsula and, as though it were an ultimate provocation, crashed right in the middle of the wire-fenced cemetery where at least one plot was freshly turned over. When I reached the summit, exhausted, everything was consumed by flames and a series of explosions thoroughly shook the cabin. The aircraft's underbelly had ploughed the ground, toppled gravestones and crosses before engulfing the site with purifying flames. From neighbouring houses, sleepy occupants converged towards their desecrated cemetery, stunned and wild-eyed, opening hung over mouths wide as the boreal land.

The remains of Jacques Boisvert and Crazy Sam — who'd insisted on accompanying his Quebec friend — were later removed from the Beaver's charred debris. From the murky waters where his spirit now wanders, I'm sure that the Indian whom his friends called Cowboy was able to appreciate the bonfire lit for the last day of the powwow.

❧

Time has come to extinguish the spiral born in the spinning slipstream of bullets projected from two convergent barrels that famous night which, still today, resounds with the echoes of their crime. During my entire stay, right to that apotheosis in the form of an ordeal, I felt that Gilles Boisvert had followed me in spirit, as though to defy that harsh law of exile which the eleven fateful shots sanctioned the summer he was seventeen, which the years still chant in the secret of his memory. That night, a father disowned a son; afterwards, everything happened as though that disowned son had delegated me to Grande-Ourse to force the father to expiate his part of the blame. I became the redeemer of a murderous trinity.

I now understand that the chap who was drinking brandy at the Café Central, on Pentecost Sunday, was fatally that Gilles Boisvert dreaming of returning to his native land, in the high country. That Gilles Boisvert, whom the real world had failed, and who'd stealthily returned to the scene of the crime thanks to a bottle of spirits, was able to confront his father through me. That day in the bar, he spoke of the murderer in the third person; seems evident to me now he was that third person. I remembered what he'd said about the complement who took the rap. Jacques Boisvert, he, and I formed a complete sentence. As well, I suddenly realized the words that followed me in my sleep, that haunted me since we met, basically told nothing but his story. That story which, though I still didn't understand it, obscurely inspired me and which, written in all languages of the world, was universal and recognizable by me alone. He forced me to enter the non-existent book he mentioned. I no longer know who wrote what in all this. Nor whether Gilles Boisvert preceded me over there, or if he proceeds from me instead. One way or another, he will have had me.

Crazy Sam's presence aboard that hydroplane proved my reckoning to be right. I'd guessed accurately about the equation when I'd repaid the American, through the workings of the Holy Spirit, essentially, the sizeable tip he'd given the hotel keeper the day following his offence. I was the middleman in an old settling of accounts. And when I see that chap again before his bottle of brandy at the Café Central, I'll be able to tell him while toasting that it's finally time to close the books.

❧

I haven't heard much from the Indians since returning to Montreal. At first, Salomé would call me. She recently had been placed in the care of another foster home, and had deserted to join her half-brother, Karate Kid, in a Tocqueville apartment. She frequently returns to Grande-Ourse in the summer. We saw each other again once or twice in Montreal. She has a sister or cousin who lives in the area and dances naked in a club. But things are no longer quite the same, and phone calls have become less frequent.

When I returned to Grande-Ourse from the reserve to pick up my things and head south down the highway, I managed to see that the Canadair had rapidly snuffed the flames. The fuel barrels hadn't exploded and Grande-Ourse was still standing. The village still exists, it seems, but the population has dwindled by half. You might imagine they've been granted a reprieve, but those people become ferocious when their survival is at stake.

More considerable damage was inflicted on fat Moreau's unfinished house. A firebrand carried by the wind fell onto the future castle and razed it. The Canadair couldn't do everything. Mr. Administrator's tourist village was spared, however. Snowmobilers stop there in winter and people are banking on the new international snow craze. Most shareholders have since sold their shares. I believe Mr. Administrator still goes back and forth between northern Montreal and the north country.

The store is running smoothly under Lili's direction. In the early fall after my departure, the Old Man had a heart attack, and a Cessna carried him to the hospital. Some people said he'd got his hands on a winning lottery ticket and couldn't take the shock. Likely a legend since no one ever found such a ticket. Salomé was there when the Old Man came back. Mr. Administrator hadn't wanted to take advantage of that slight ailment to give more permanence to his leave. The Old Man is half-paralysed now, and barely talks. But, he belongs to a breed that doesn't know how to die, and don't be surprised if, one day on the large reservoir, you spot a really long pontoon covered with American fishermen.

The Muppet still enjoys retirement. One morning, while fishing near his favourite grass bed, he hooked a northern pike which dragged his rowboat to the other end of Lac Légaré, and he had great difficulty returning to his starting point. His fish had been stricken by the tail, weighing nearly forty-five pounds, a shade under the world record for the species. Now there's a fishing story that will last him at least a thousand beers.

Big Ben quit as a volunteer fireman. His honour didn't outlast the truck's breakdown. I'm absolutely sure his name still figures prominently at the bottom of the Outfitters' pay schedule. For his part, Legris travelled all the way to Pennsylvania to attend Crazy Sam's funeral. As far as I know, he was never again seen in the area.

The trapper's large red dog isn't dead and still guards the northern highway.

Salomé informed me that hardly any Indians are left in the area. Relations between the two communities were hardly improving and some went back north. No one camps at the village gate any more. But Jacques Boisvert's tragic end made a strong impression on the reserve, and the famous Affair can rightly be considered dead and buried. César Flamand has stopped drinking for the second time in his life. As for Fernande, she starts up again at the first opportunity.

Salomé called me, one morning last February. Even in the city, we froze just by setting foot outside. Gisèle had fallen off a moving snowmobile the previous day, while it was crossing a railway. The driver of the high-powered machine, who'd been drinking heavily, never noticed he'd dropped his cargo and Gisèle slept there, between the rails, at minus thirty Celsius. The passenger train then passed, and the Via Rail brakeman wondered whether he'd hit a moose. Pieces were picked up on either side of the tracks. Salomé was reasonably sad. It's the kind of thing she more or less expected. She swore to me that Gisèle had had time to put a curse on the railway company and, as though by coincidence, their profits registered an unprecedented drop since then along the Tocqueville-

Sans-Terre section. They're even thinking about reducing the number of weekly train runs.

Brigitte returned to Montreal as well. She paints and lives in a huge space inside an old industrial building, near the Lachine Canal. She uses her apartment as a studio and vice-versa. She inherited the hotel and hydroplanes, selling the lot to Benoît for not very much. Business is going well. Benoît is living with a woman about whom all that's known is that she landed in Grande-Ourse one day and never left. Brigitte has registered in visual arts at university. I see her pretty often. Once the initial pain had dissipated, she said she was rather proud of *her man*. In her opinion, he came to an end that was perfectly in keeping with his character. And her plump belly is starting to betray the earthly works of that devil of an aviator. I try to imagine a genetic compromise between those two. Unless....

Brigitte acquired a shack in the Grande-Ourse region and expects to return every summer with the child. She kindly allowed me to pat the slight bulge. I take good care of the folk doll Boisvert gave me for laughs. Its long batting eyelids, eyes opened or closed depending on the inclination of its body. At this moment, they're opened.

Before leaving Grande-Ourse, I went for a last stroll at the camp. The large white tents had disappeared. According to Salomé, the spot will be cursed for generations. They'd planted a small birch cross right beside the peatbog, and I meditated for a moment beside this modest monument driving its only root into the layers of acid moss. An empty bottle of spirits lay near a blackened circle on the ground, but I recognized the brand: Christian Brothers.

And then, as I was about to leave, I couldn't resist. I retraced my steps, took off all my clothes, and dove into the black hole that opened beneath the layers of peat moss. But I didn't stay very long. My pilgrimage ended later, in front of the bread cellar which had remained inviolate, beneath the still-smouldering ruins of the shed. Like the American hunters, I now have a bear skin in my living room.

Last I'd heard, Salomé was dating Christophe, who wants to become a lawyer. I can imagine him questioning witnesses, "Who are you? Who are you?"

What's become of Cowboy's friends? Donald Big-Arms went back to the reserve. He goes away once in a while, sets traps he visits when he doesn't forget them, grumbles whenever he thinks about girls, drinks, and fights. He may not be unhappy, he survives. The last time Salomé saw Judith in Grande-Ourse, she reeked of naphtha. And now, the smell is rather like that of old fried food. She officially broke up with Big Alexandre and has moved into the restaurant; she has custody of his brat. Moreau is going through a divorce and has plans: a huge truck loaded with bricks was seen precariously balanced at the top of the hill. The new bridge, apparently, had held up. As for Karate Kid, he tried to do himself in, as well, on the clothes-rail of his Tocqueville apartment. He was taken down after five minutes. Salomé says he spent two days in a coma and that he still has some serious catching up to do. But the logotherapists noted a progressive improvement, and his case is felt to be promising. He remains slow and stumbles on words, but he was never really talkative anyhow. He doesn't have any elocution problems when speaking about his friend Cowboy. And he's recovering. He's recovering.

¹Translator's note: the English equivalent of "Hérode" in this context would be "rascal."